VOLUME
THREE

IMAGE COMICS, INC.

Robert Kirkman
CHIEF OPERATING OFFICER

Erik Larsen
CHIEF FINANCIAL OFFICER

Todd McFarlane
PRESIDENT

Marc Silvestri
CHIEF EXECUTIVE OFFICER

Jim Valentino
VICE-PRESIDENT

Eric Stephenson
PUBLISHER

Ron Richards
DIRECTOR OF BUSINESS DEVELOPMENT

Jennifer de Guzman
DIRECTOR OF TRADE BOOK SALES

Kat Salazar
PR & MARKETING DIRECTOR

Jeremy Sullivan
DIRECTOR OF DIGITAL SALES

Emilio Bautista
SALES ASSISTANT

Branwyn Bigglestone
SENIOR ACCOUNTS MANAGER

Emily Miller
ACCOUNTS MANAGER

Jessica Ambriz
ADMINISTRATIVE ASSISTANT

Tyler Shainline
EVENTS COORDINATOR

David Brothers
CONTENT MANAGER

Jonathan Chan
PRODUCTION MANAGER

Drew Gill
ART DIRECTOR

Meredith Wallace
PRINT MANAGER

Monica Garcia
SENIOR PRODUCTION ARTIST

Jenna Savage
Addison Duke
PRODUCTION ARTISTS

www.imagecomics.com

ISBN 978-1-60706-931-7

ga™

BRIAN K. VAUGHAN
WRITER

FIONA STAPLES
ARTIST

FONOGRAFIKS
LETTERING + DESIGN

ERIC STEPHENSON
COORDINATOR

CHAPTER
THIRTEEN

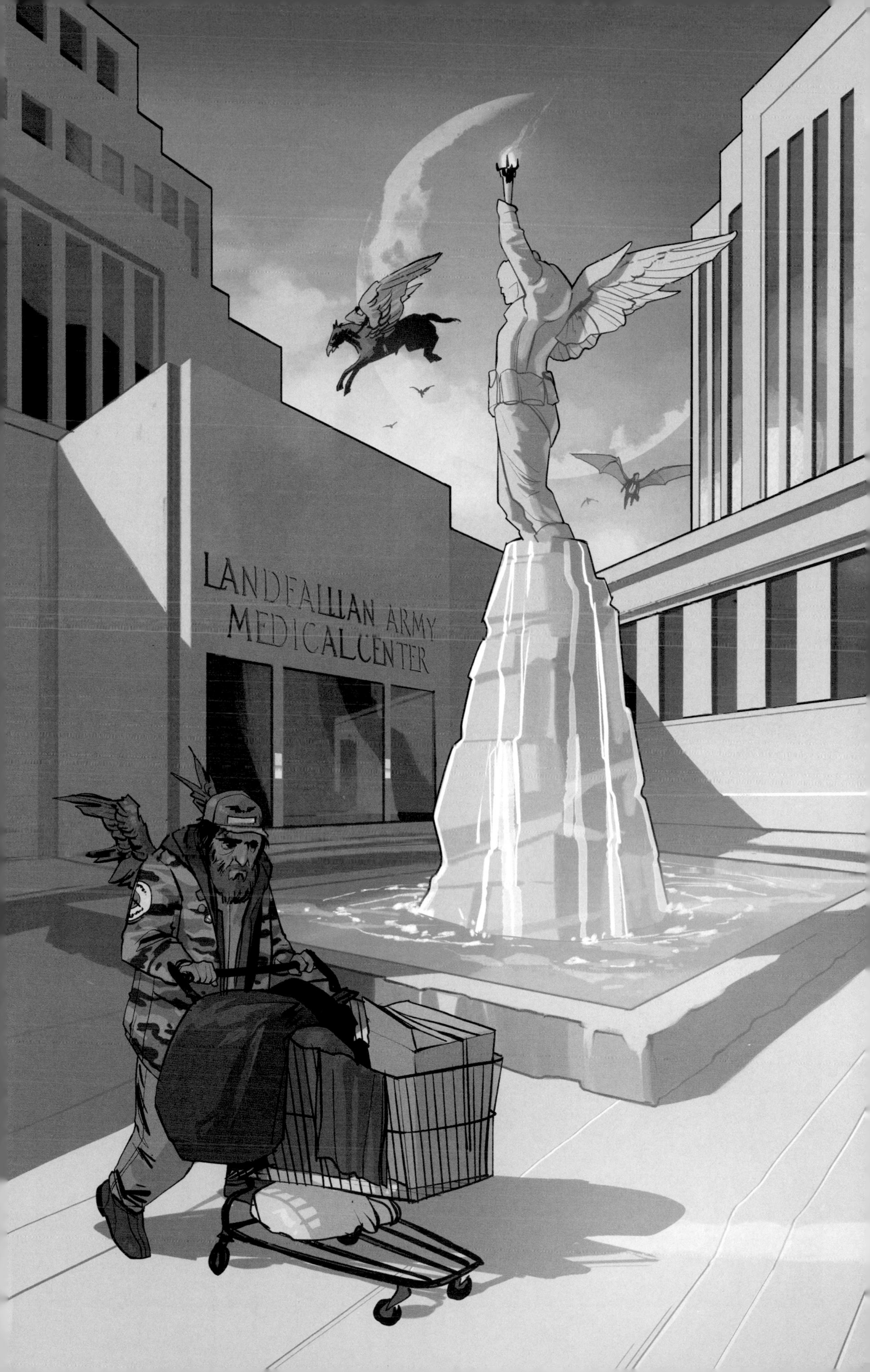
LANDFALLIAN ARMY
MEDICAL CENTER

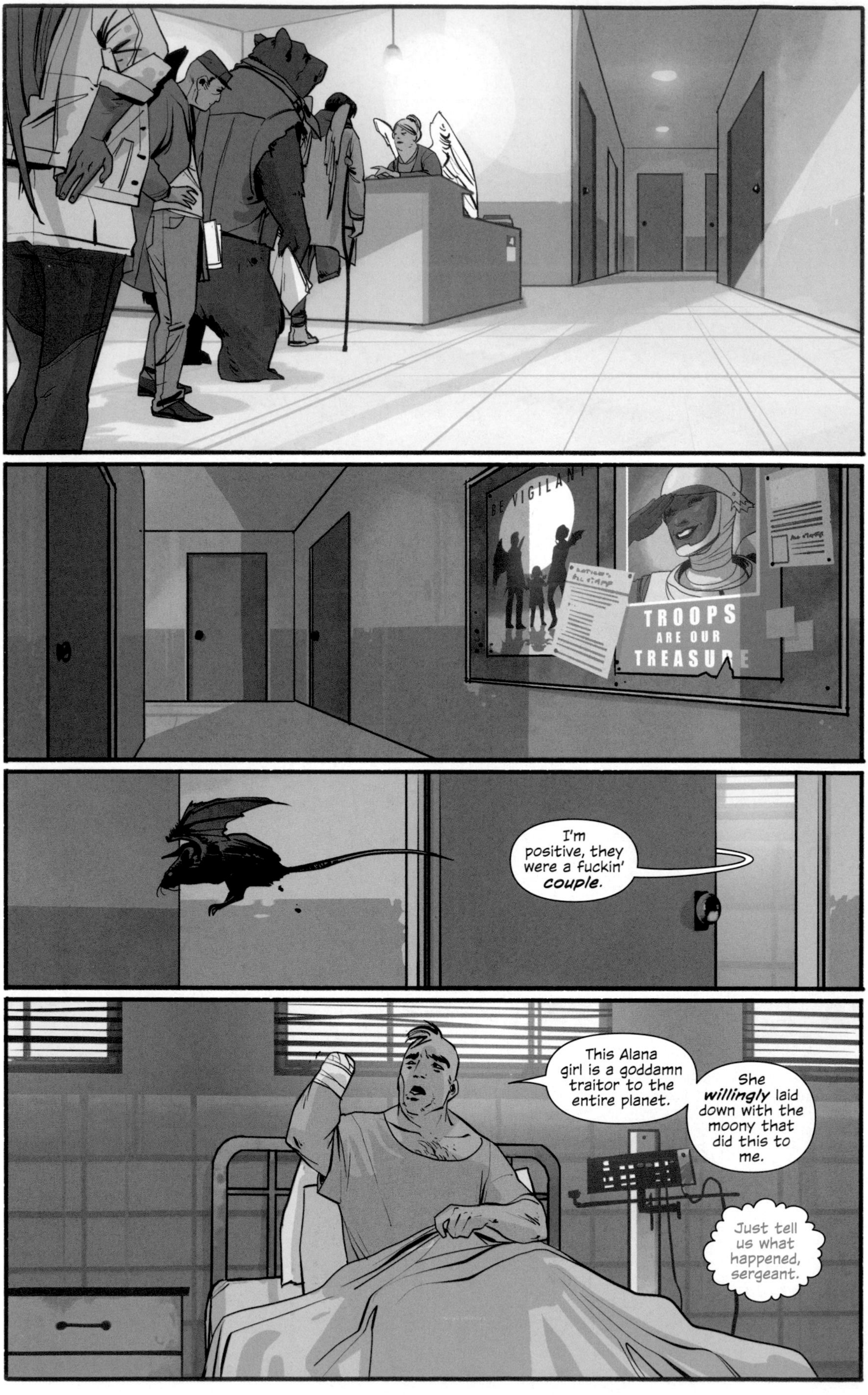
BE VIGILANT
TROOPS ARE OUR TREASURE
I'm positive, they were a fuckin' *couple*.
This Alana girl is a goddamn traitor to the entire planet.
She *willingly* laid down with the moony that did this to me.
Just tell us what happened, sergeant.

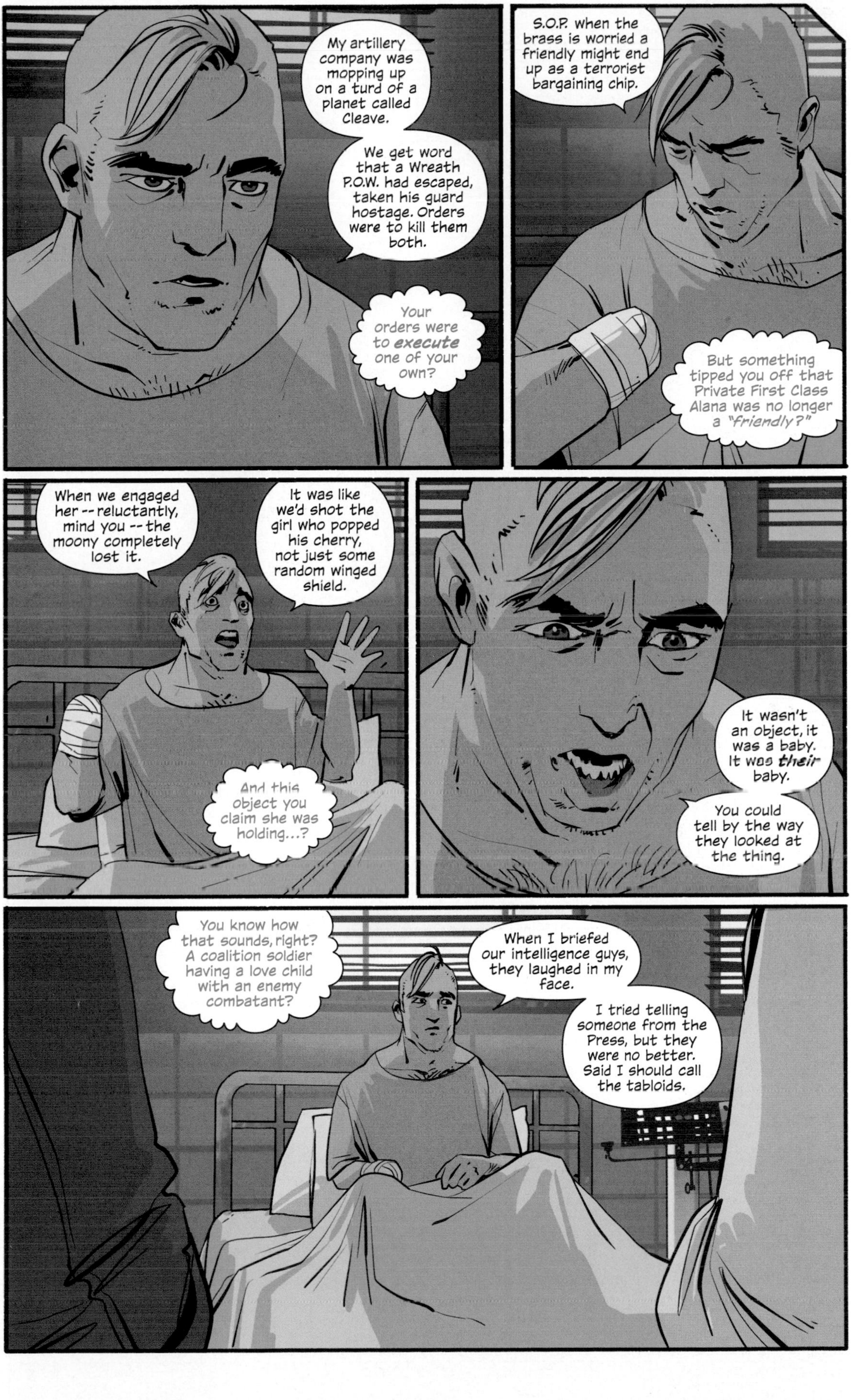
My artillery company was mopping up on a turd of a planet called Cleave.
We get word that a Wreath P.O.W. had escaped, taken his guard hostage. Orders were to kill them both.
Your orders were to *execute* one of your own?
S.O.P. when the brass is worried a friendly might end up as a terrorist bargaining chip.
But something tipped you off that Private First Class Alana was no longer a *"friendly?"*
When we engaged her--reluctantly, mind you--the moony completely lost it.
It was like we'd shot the girl who popped his cherry, not just some random winged shield.
And this object you claim she was holding...?
It wasn't an object, it was a baby. It was *their* baby.
You could tell by the way they looked at the thing.
You know how that sounds, right? A coalition soldier having a love child with an enemy combatant?
When I briefed our intelligence guys, they laughed in my face.
I tried telling someone from the Press, but they were no better. Said I should call the tabloids.

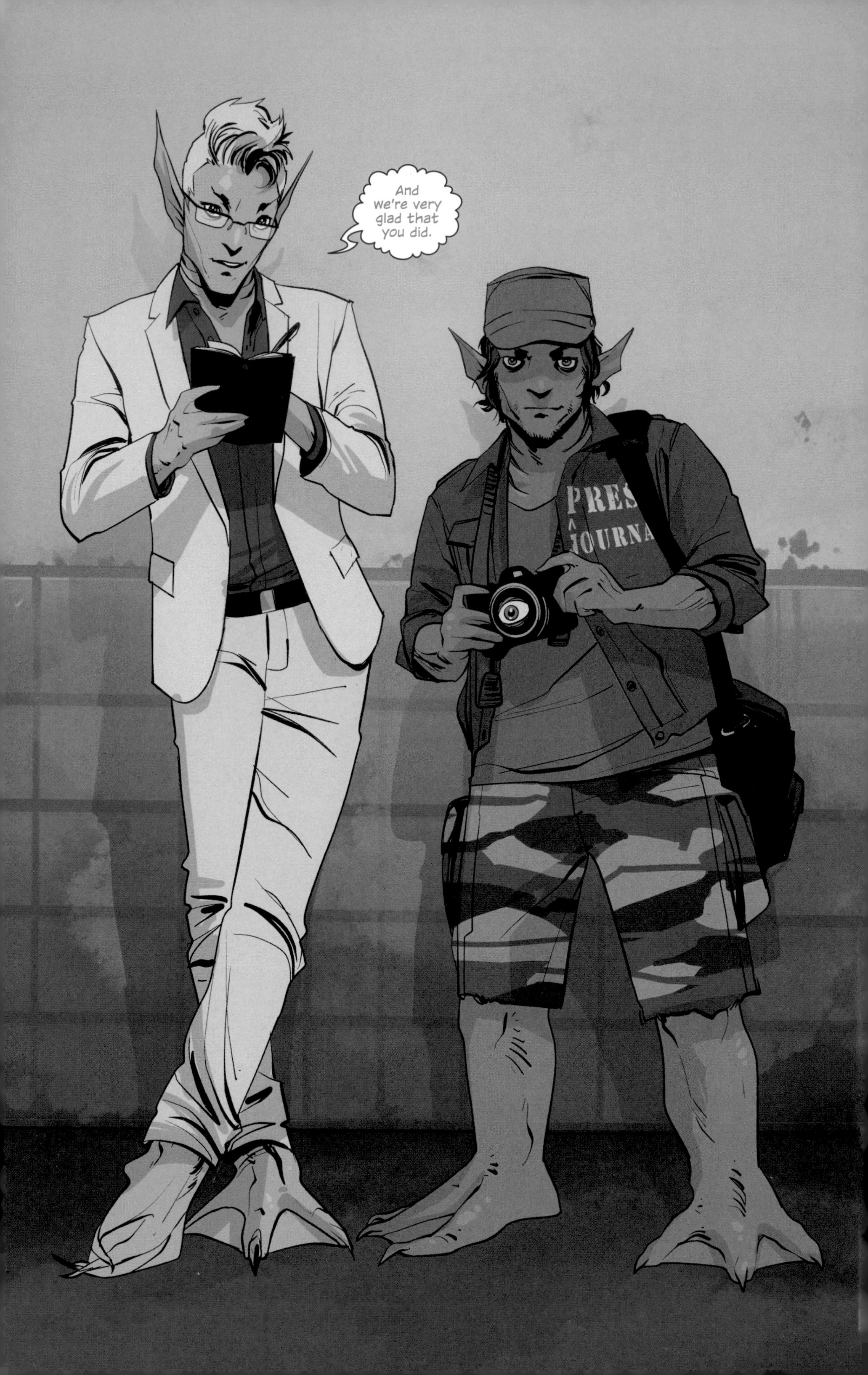
And we're very glad that you did.
PRES
JOURNA

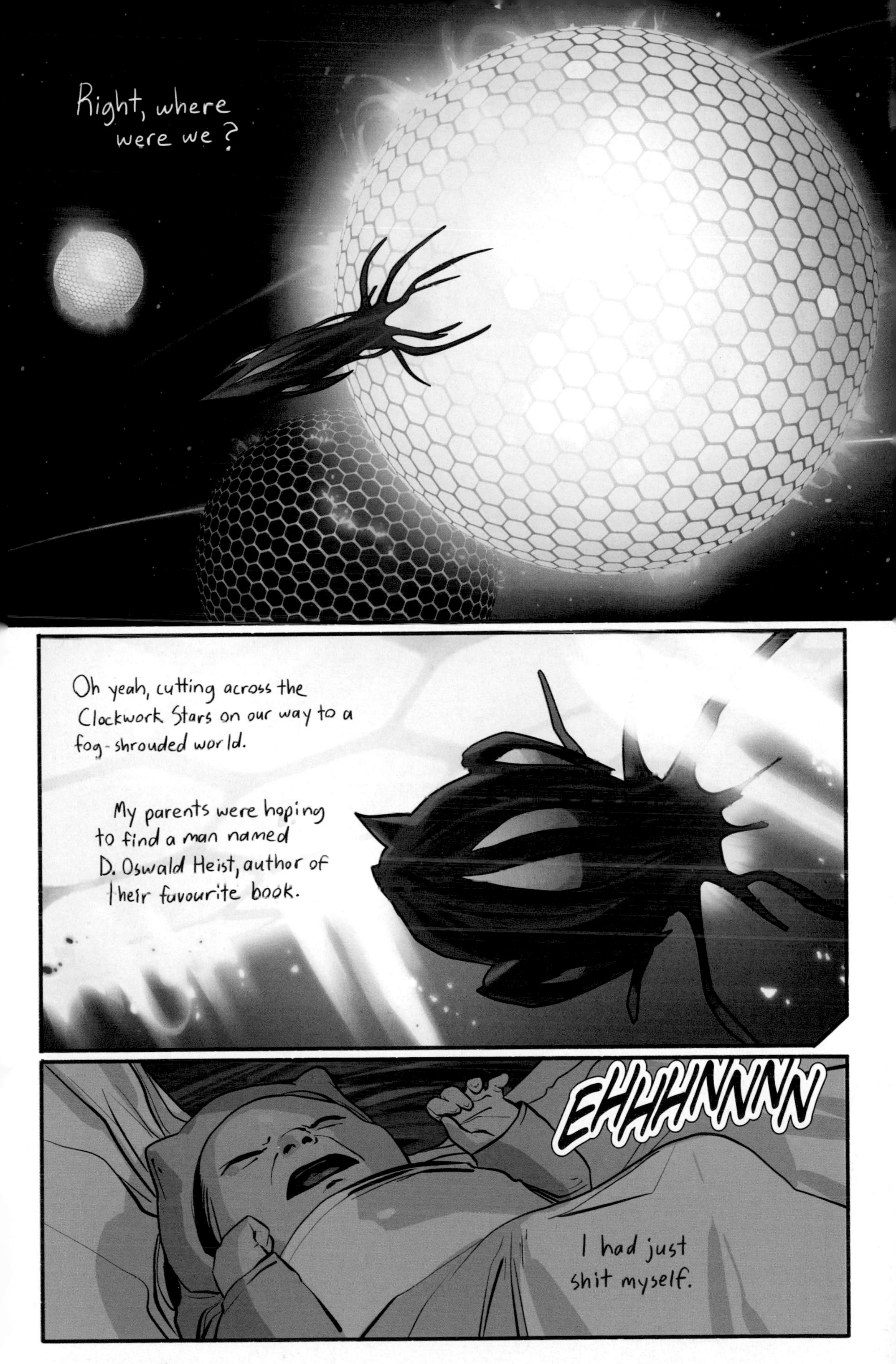
Right, where were we?
Oh yeah, cutting across the Clockwork Stars on our way to a fog-shrouded world.
My parents were hoping to find a man named D. Oswald Heist, author of their favourite book.
EHHHNNNN
I had just shit myself.

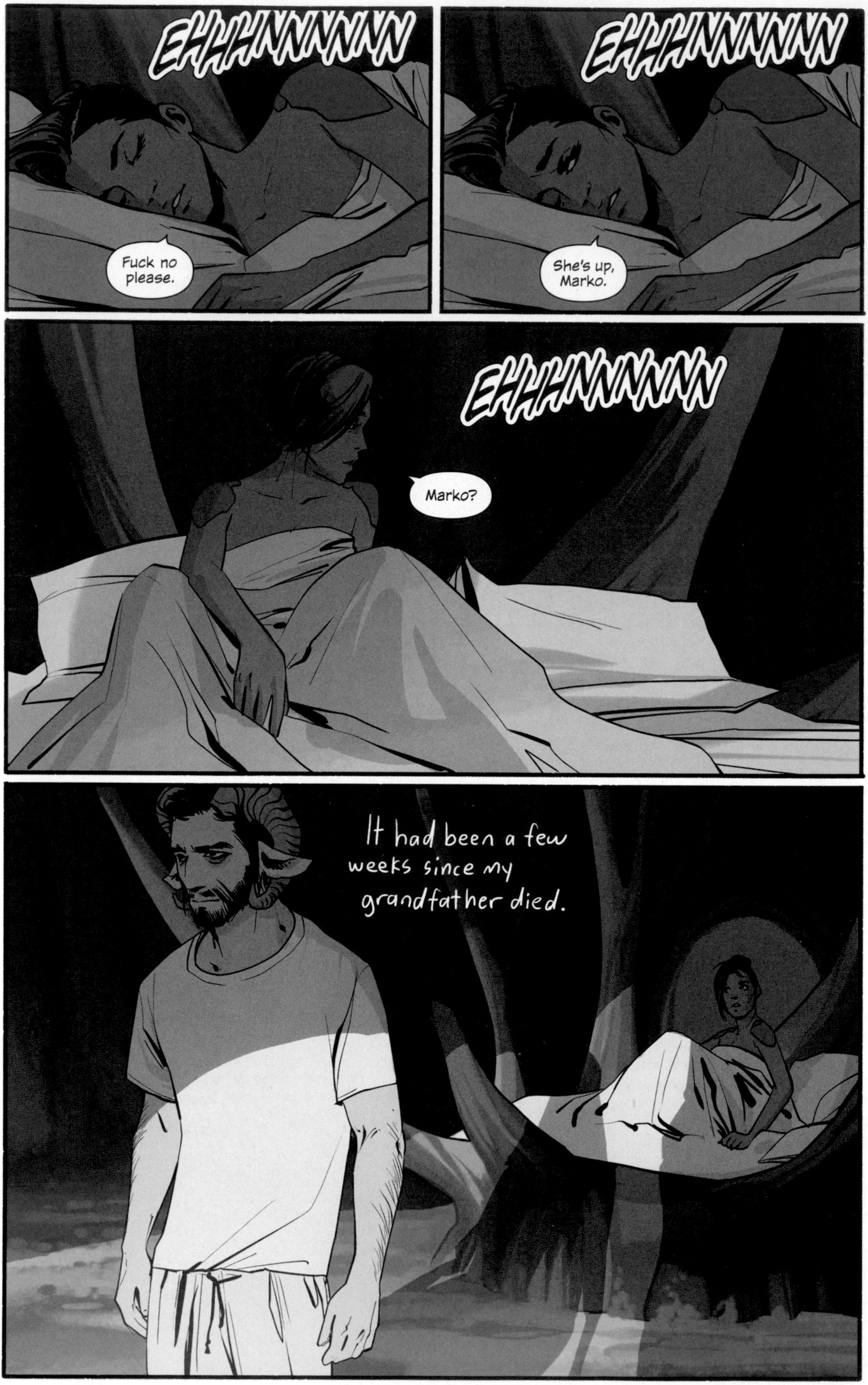
EHHHNNNNNNN
Fuck no please.
EHHHNNNNNNN
She's up, Marko.
EHHHNNNNNNN
Marko?
It had been a few weeks since my grandfather died.

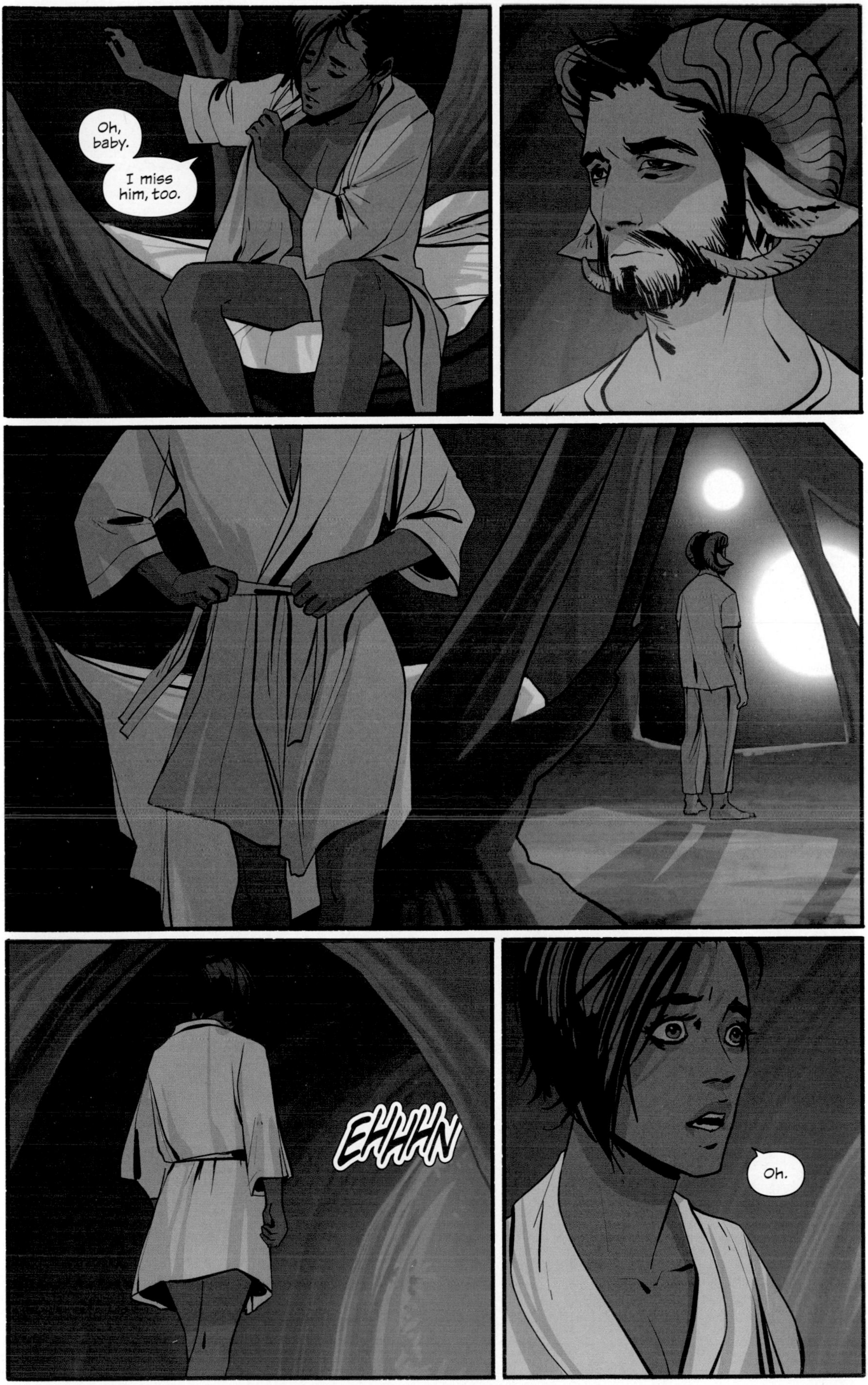
Oh, baby.
I miss him, too.
EHHHN
Oh.

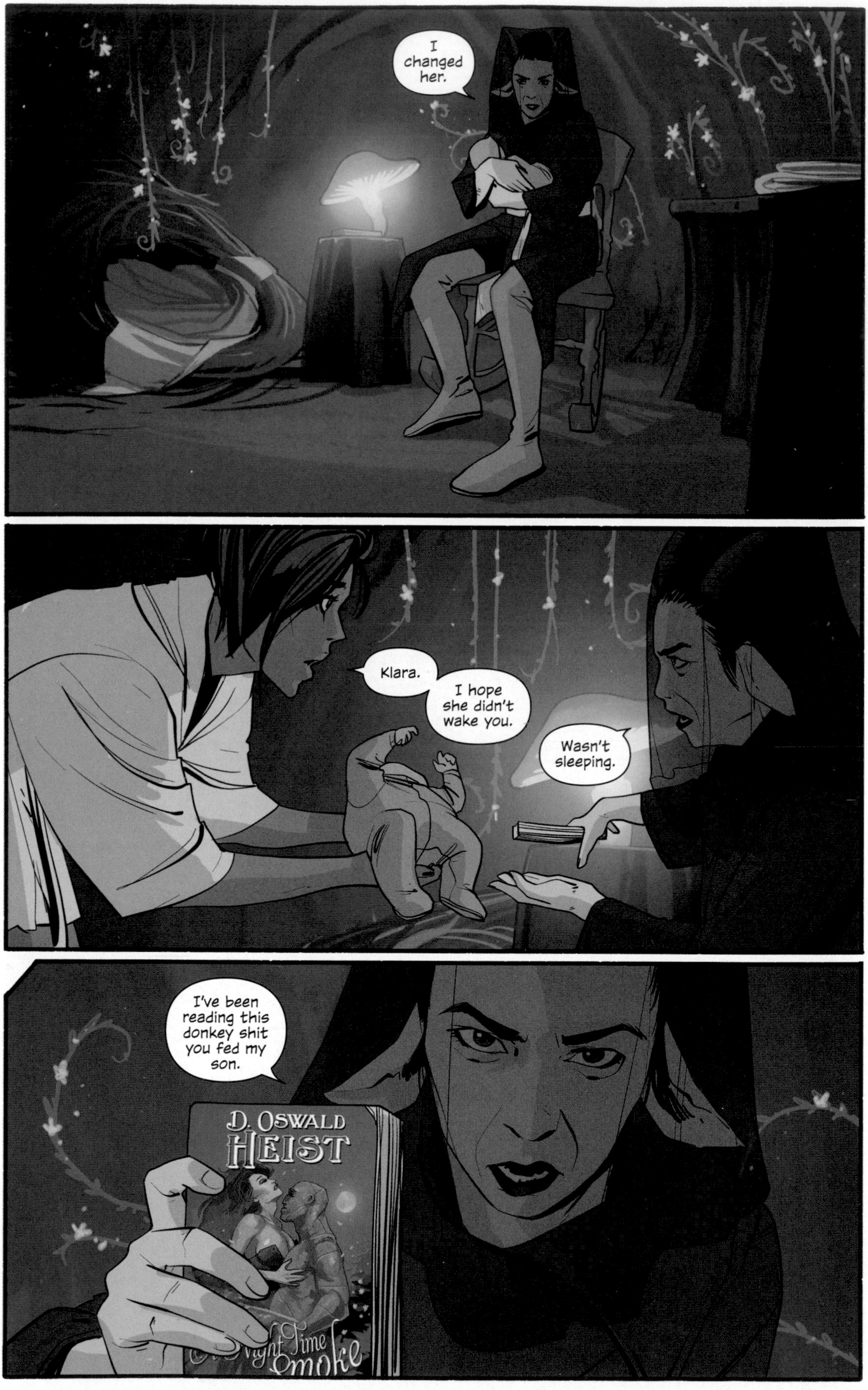
I changed her.
Klara.
I hope she didn't wake you.
Wasn't sleeping.
I've been reading this donkey shit you fed my son.
D. OSWALD HEIST
Night Time Smoke

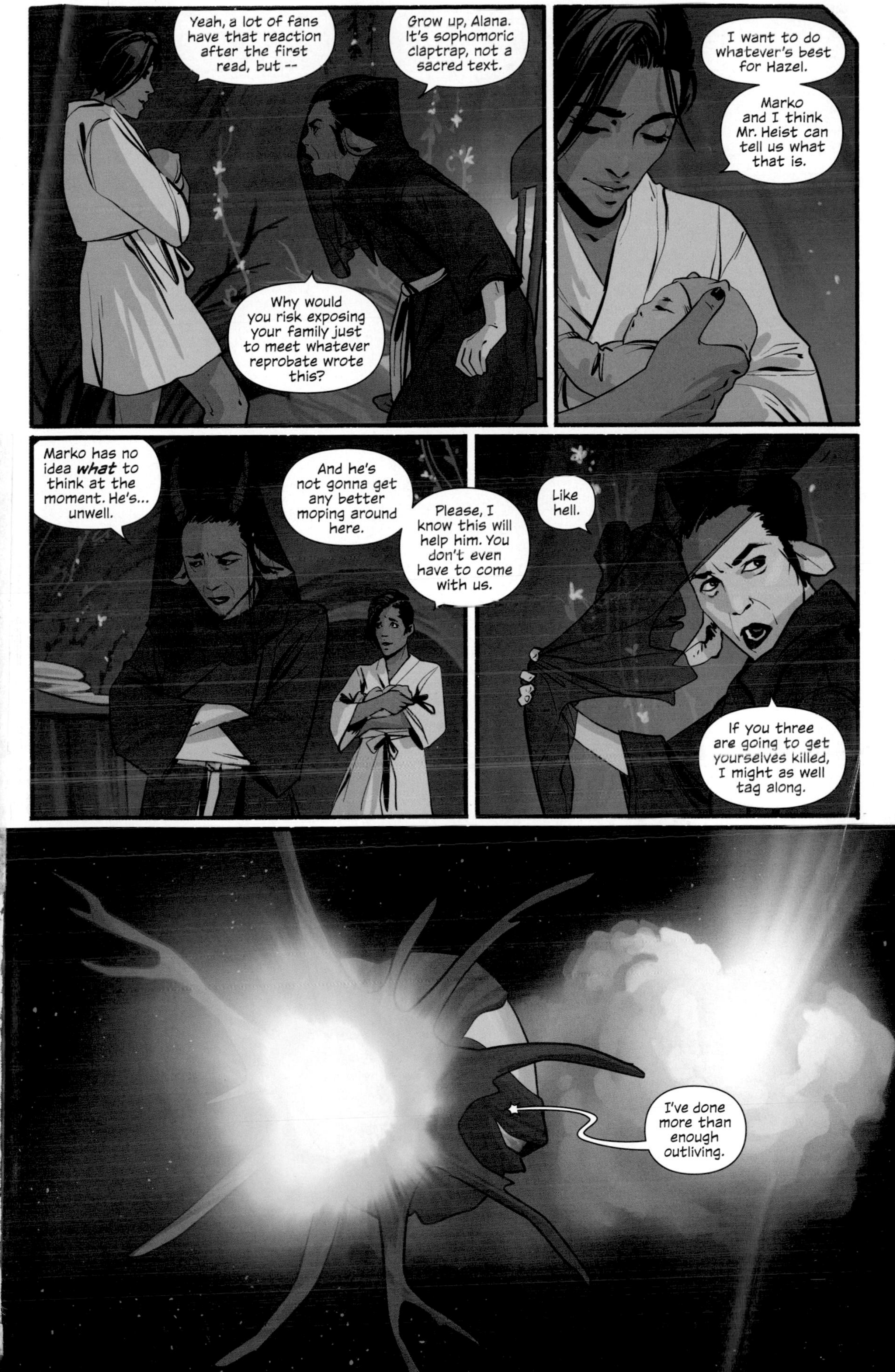
Yeah, a lot of fans have that reaction after the first read, but --
Grow up, Alana. It's sophomoric claptrap, not a sacred text.
Why would you risk exposing your family just to meet whatever reprobate wrote this?
I want to do whatever's best for Hazel.
Marko and I think Mr. Heist can tell us what that is.
Marko has no idea *what* to think at the moment. He's... unwell.
And he's not gonna get any better moping around here.
Please, I know this will help him. You don't even have to come with us.
Like hell.
If you three are going to get yourselves killed, I might as well tag along.
I've done more than enough outliving.

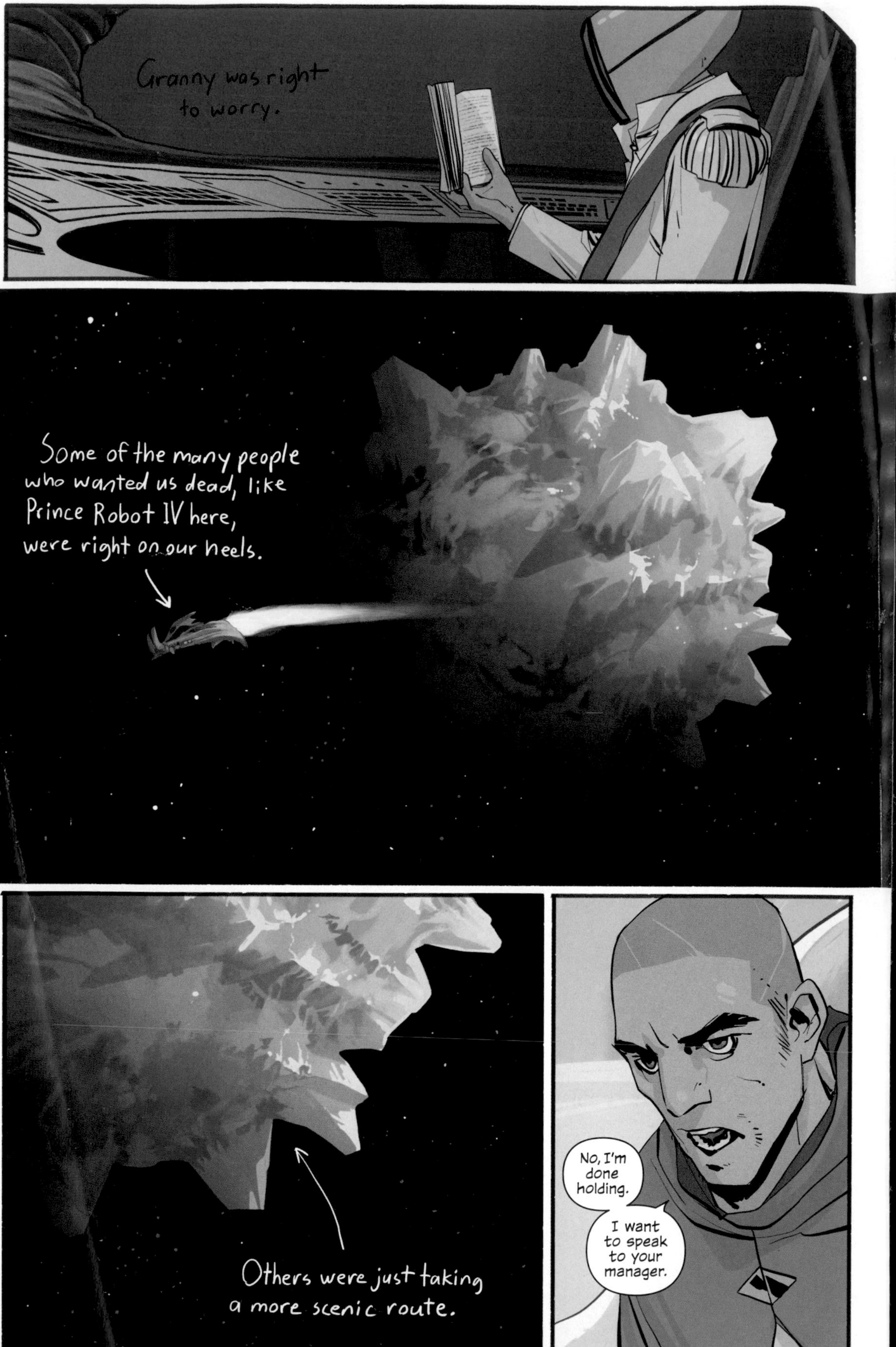

Granny was right to worry.
Some of the many people who wanted us dead, like Prince Robot IV here, were right on our heels.
Others were just taking a more scenic route.
No, I'm done holding.
I want to speak to your manager.

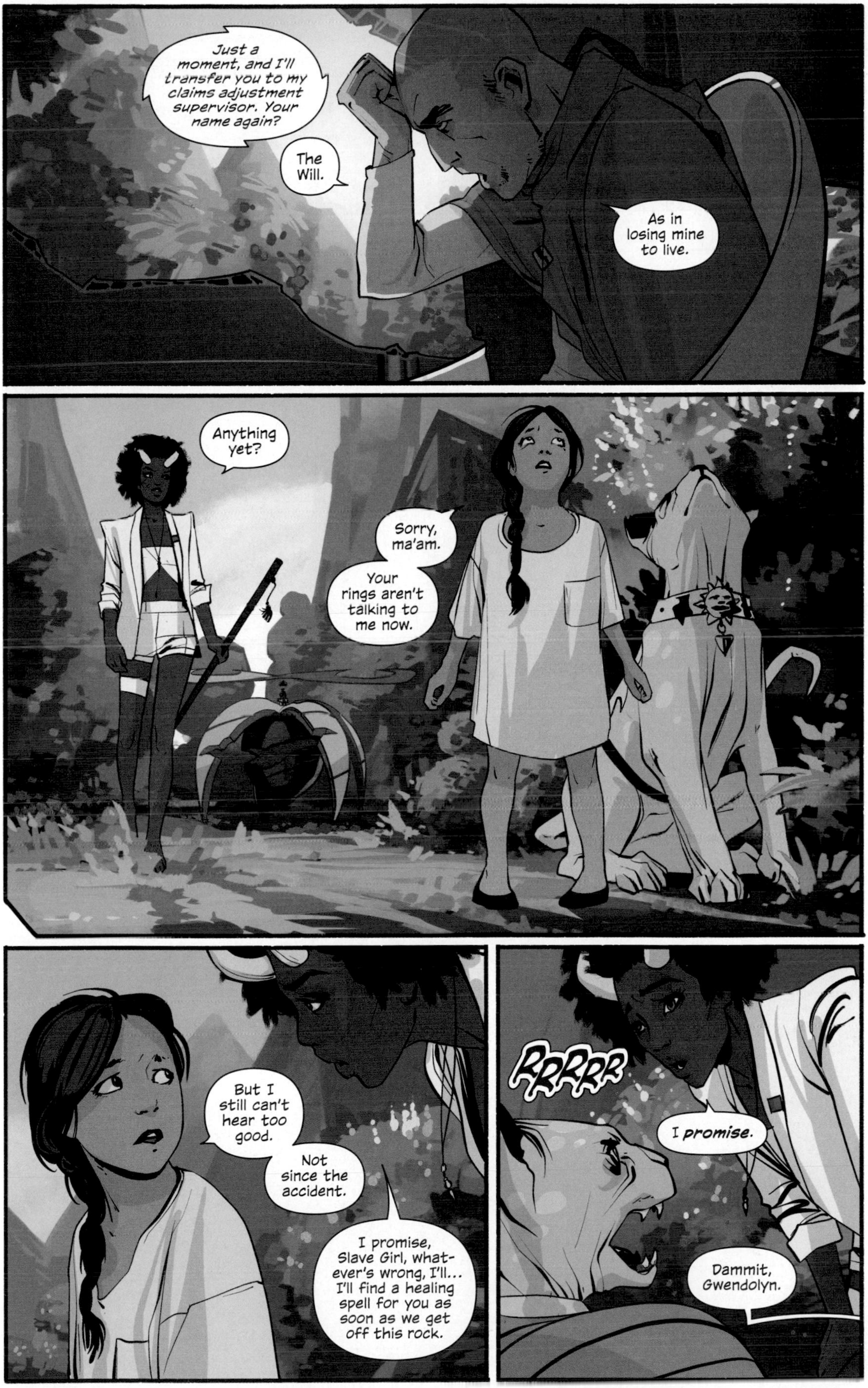
Just a moment, and I'll transfer you to my claims adjustment supervisor. Your name again?
The Will.
As in losing mine to live.
Anything yet?
Sorry, ma'am.
Your rings aren't talking to me now.
But I still can't hear too good.
Not since the accident.
I promise, Slave Girl, what-ever's wrong, I'll... I'll find a healing spell for you as soon as we get off this rock.
RRRRR
I *promise*.
Dammit, Gwendolyn.

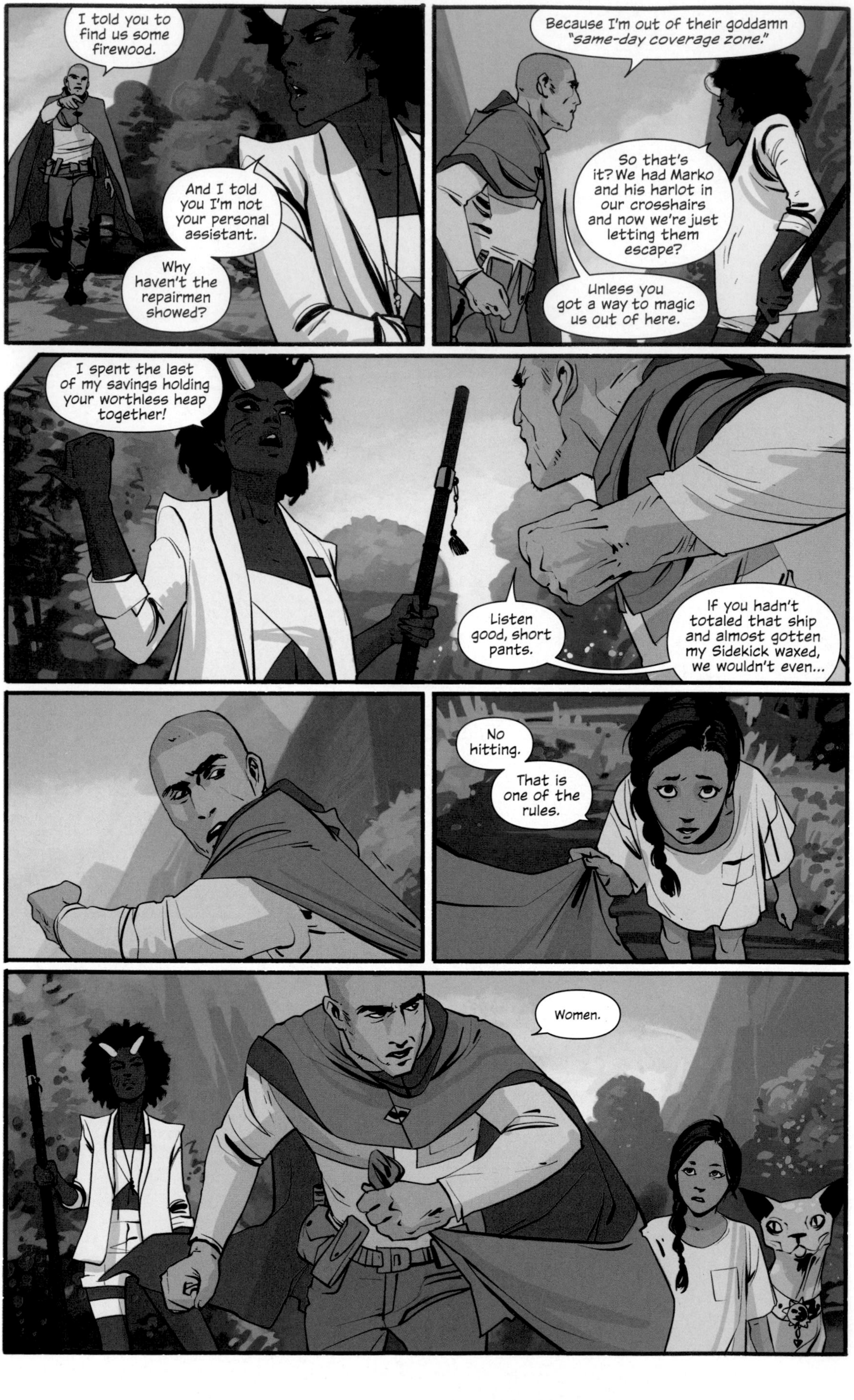
I told you to find us some firewood.
And I told you I'm not your personal assistant.
Why haven't the repairmen showed?
Because I'm out of their goddamn *"same-day coverage zone."*
So that's it? We had Marko and his harlot in our crosshairs and now we're just letting them escape?
Unless you got a way to magic us out of here.
I spent the last of my savings holding your worthless heap together!
Listen good, short pants.
If you hadn't totaled that ship and almost gotten my Sidekick waxed, we wouldn't even...
No hitting.
That is one of the rules.
Women.

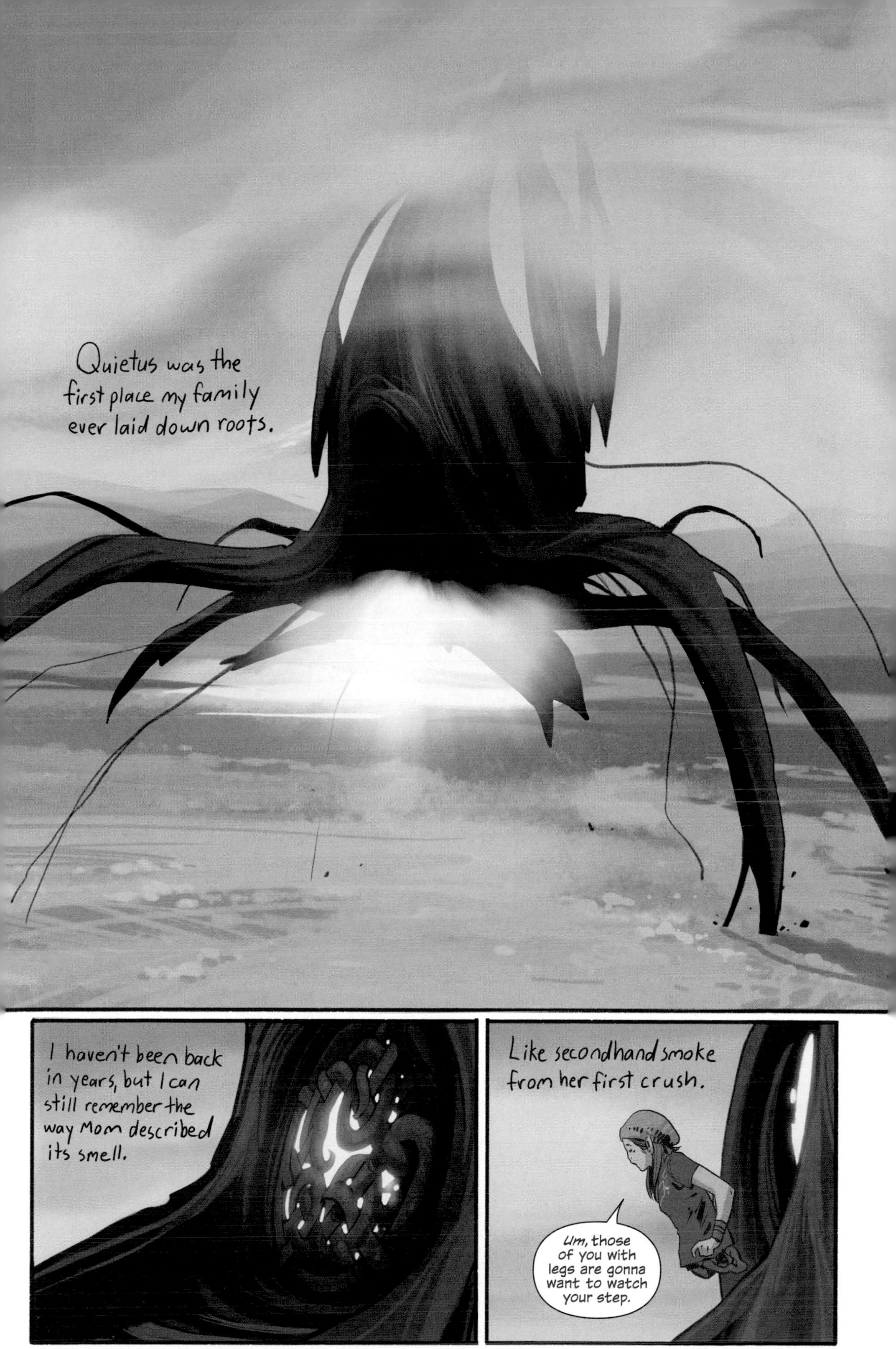
Quietus was the first place my family ever laid down roots.
I haven't been back in years, but I can still remember the way Mom described its smell.
Like secondhand smoke from her first crush.
Um, those of you with legs are gonna want to watch your step.

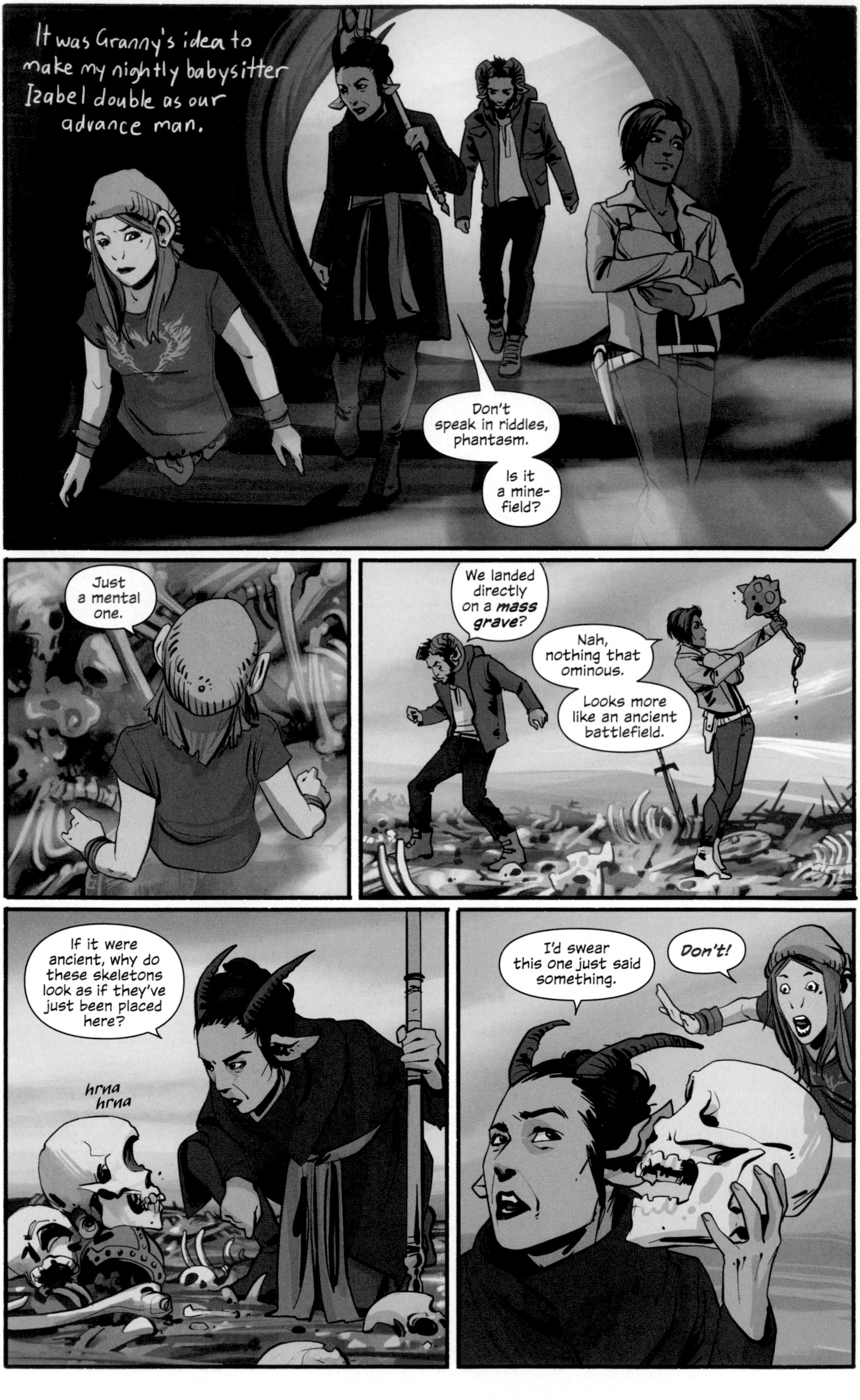
It was Granny's idea to make my nightly babysitter Izabel double as our advance man.
Don't speak in riddles, phantasm.
Is it a mine-field?
Just a mental one.
We landed directly on a *mass grave*?
Nah, nothing that ominous.
Looks more like an ancient battlefield.
If it were ancient, why do these skeletons look as if they've just been placed here?
hrna hrna
I'd swear this one just said something.
Don't!

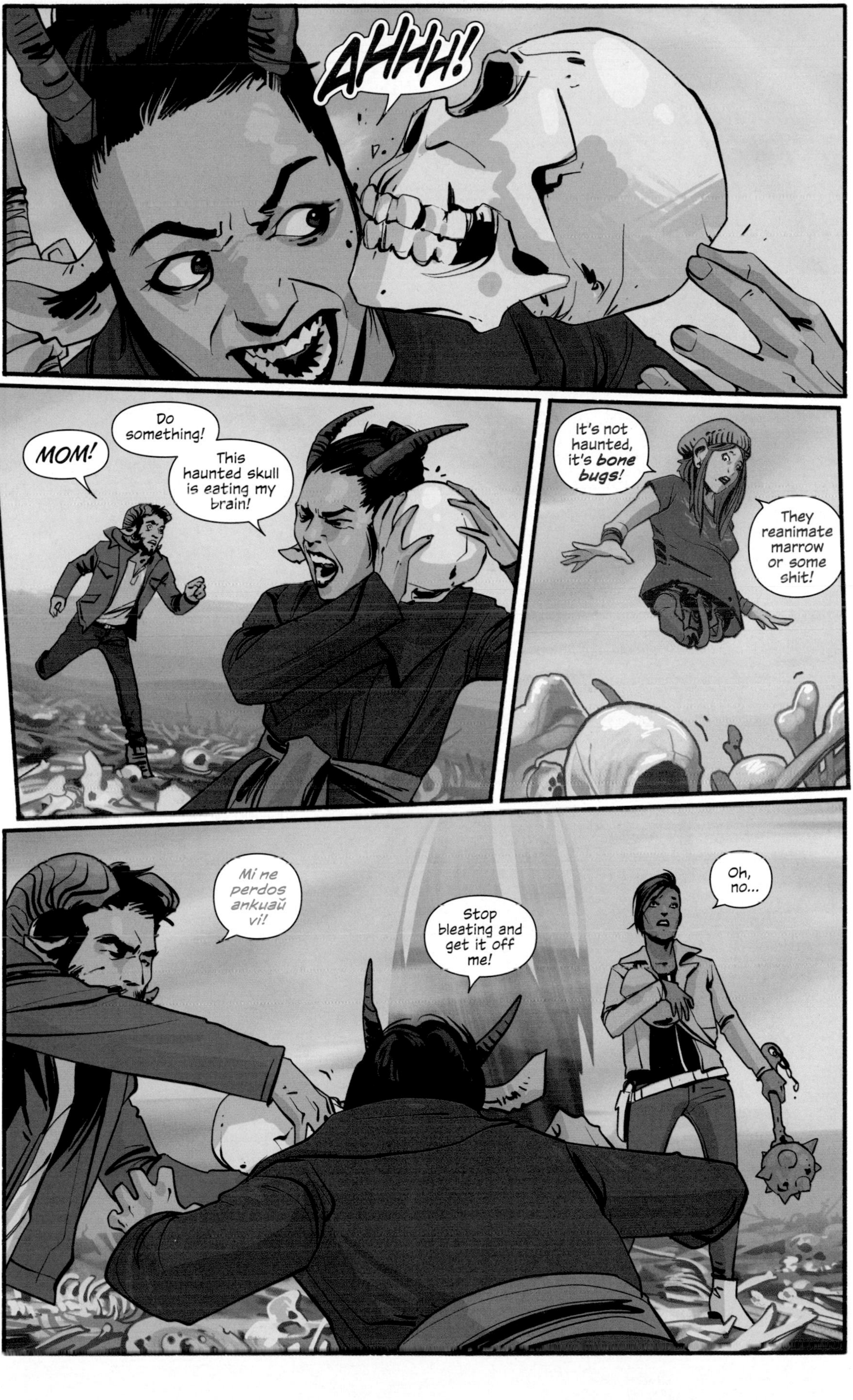
AHHH!
MOM!
Do something!
This haunted skull is eating my brain!
It's not haunted, it's **bone bugs!**
They reanimate marrow or some shit!
Mi ne perdos ankuaŭ vi!
Stop bleating and get it off me!
Oh, no...

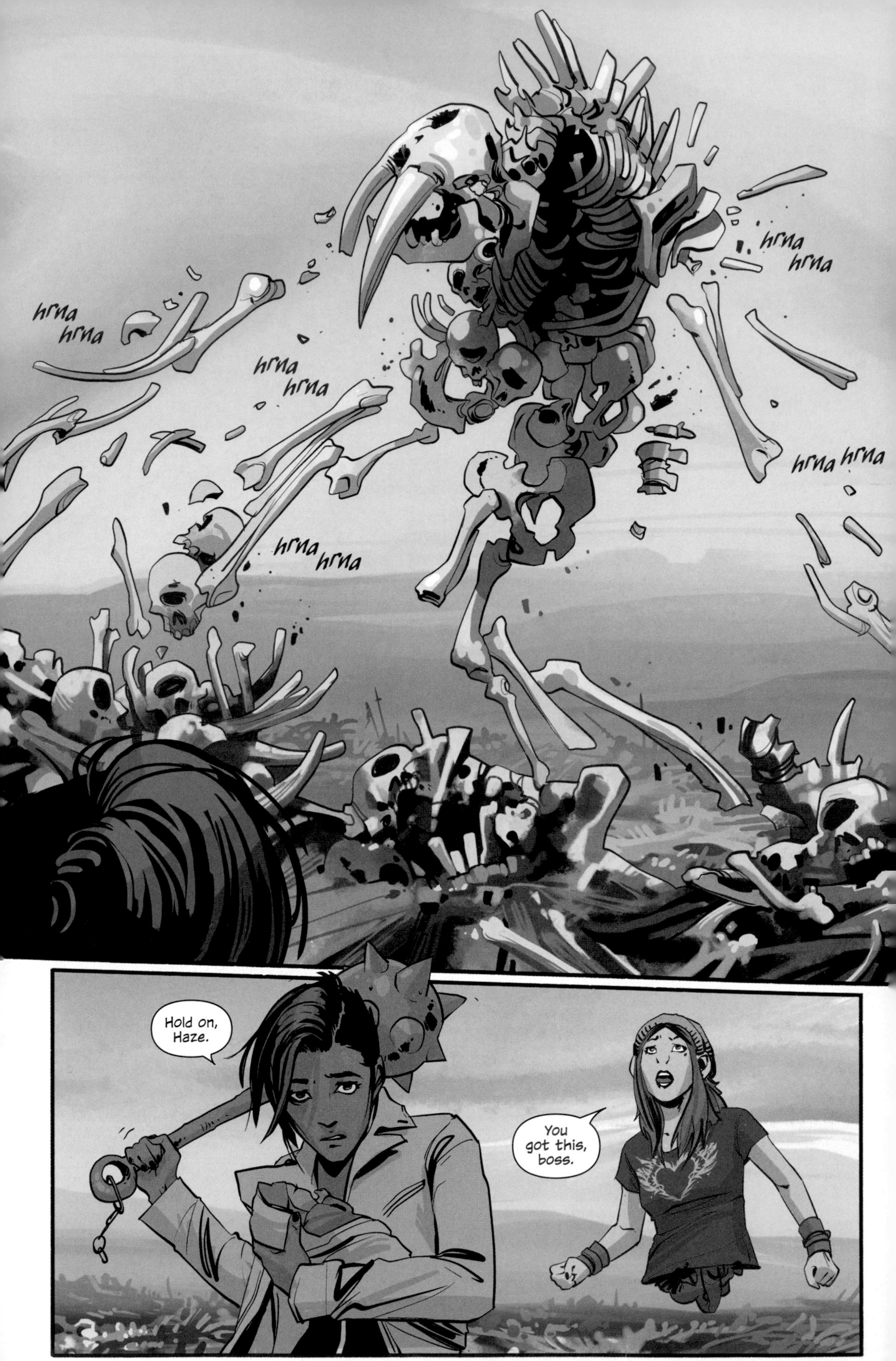
hrna hrna
hrna hrna
hrna hrna
hrna hrna
hrna hrna
hrna hrna
Hold on, Haze.
You got this, boss.

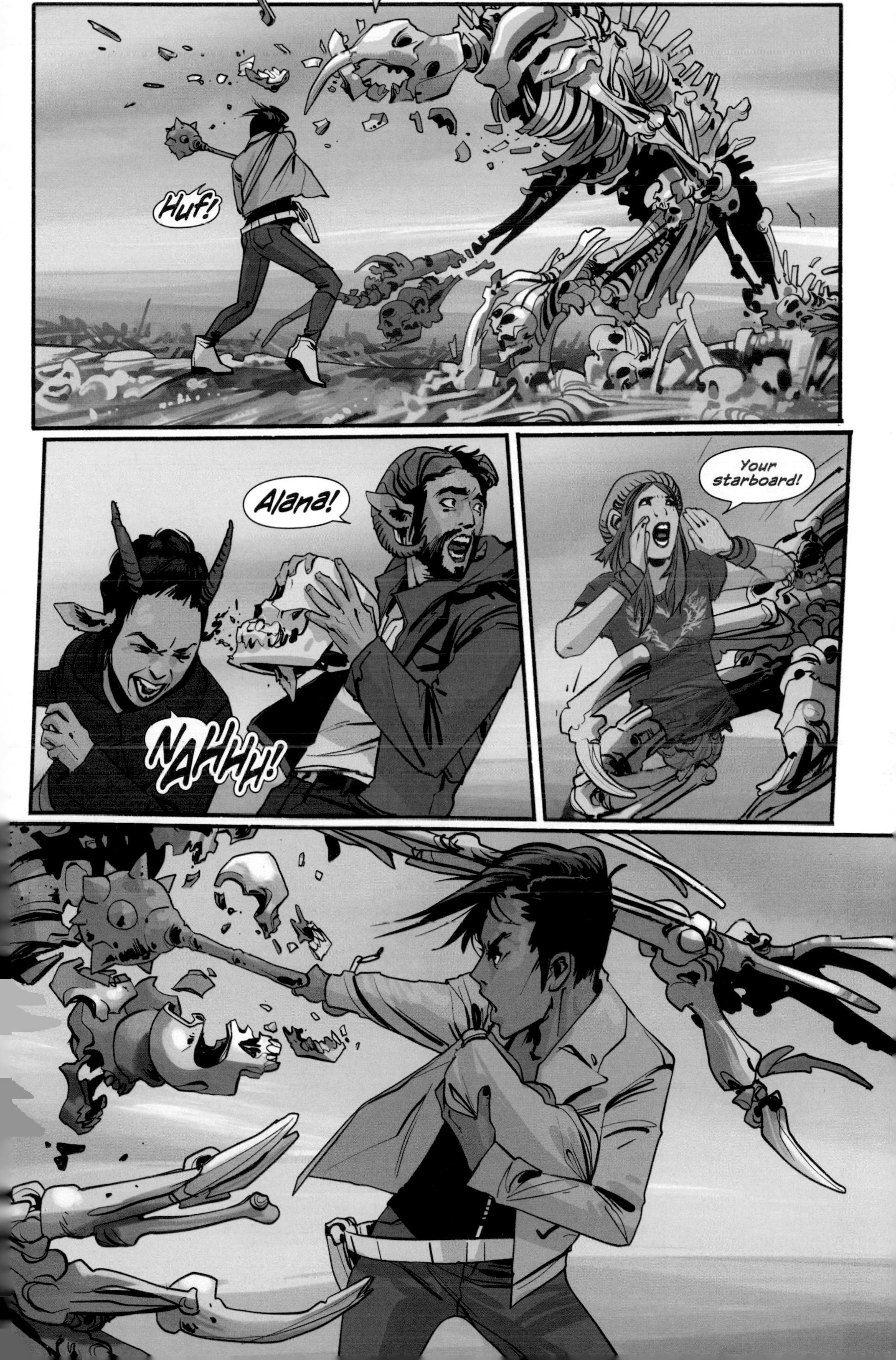
Huf!
Alana!
NAHHH!
Your starboard!

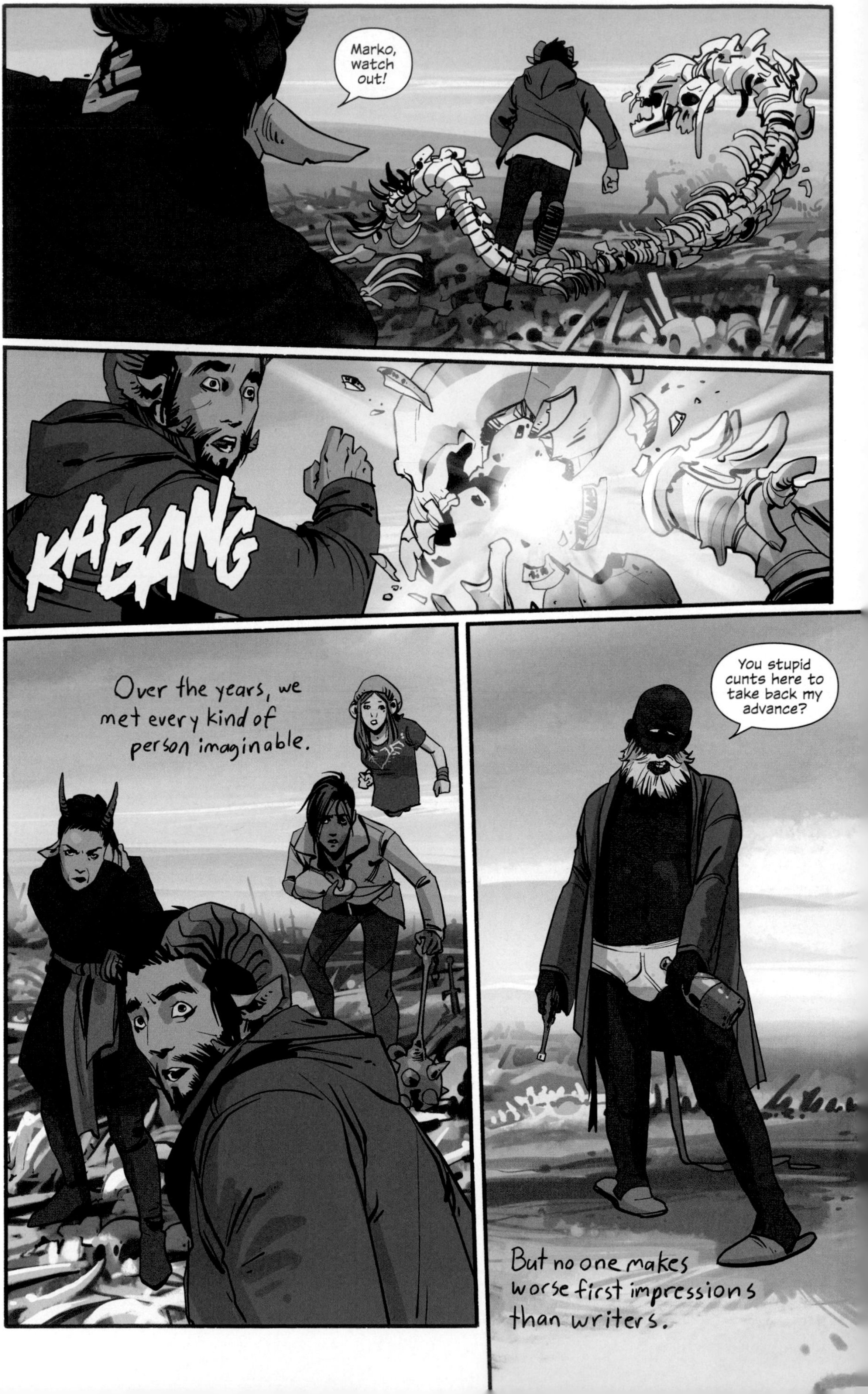
Marko, watch out!
KABANG
Over the years, we met every kind of person imaginable.
You stupid cunts here to take back my advance?
But no one makes worse first impressions than writers.

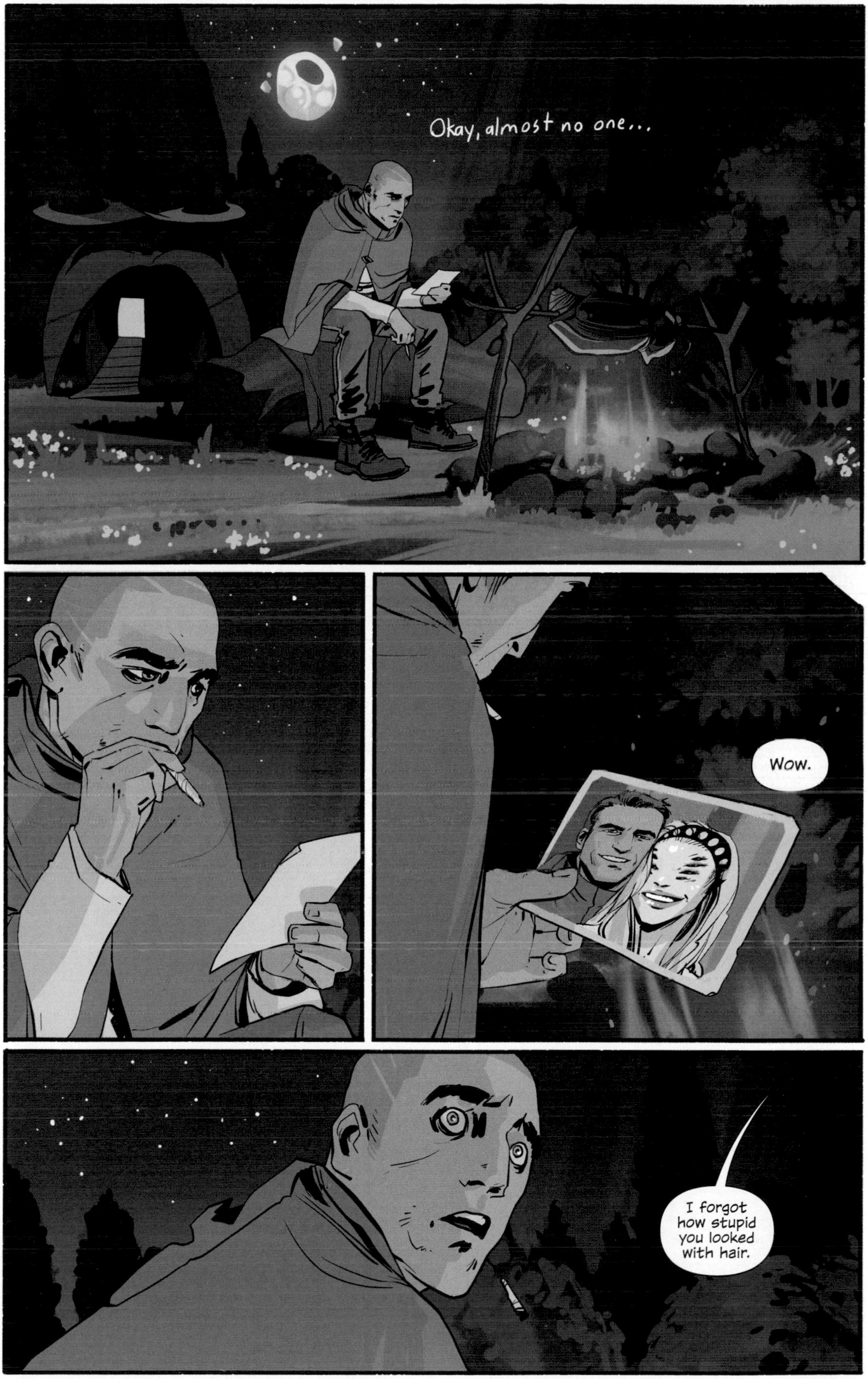
Okay, almost no one...
Wow.
I forgot how stupid you looked with hair.

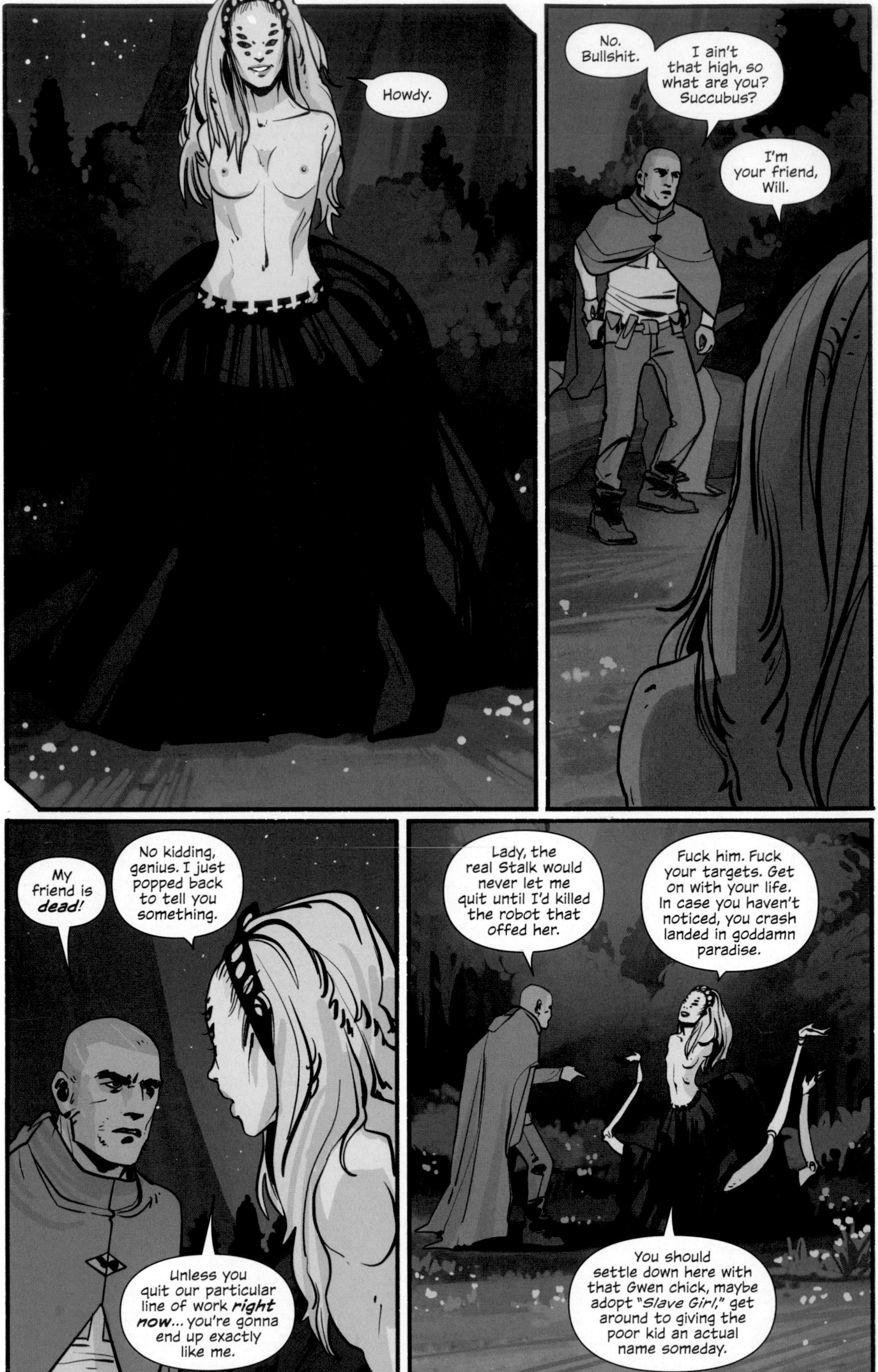
Howdy.
No. Bullshit.
I ain't that high, so what are you? Succubus?
I'm your friend, Will.
My friend is *dead!*
No kidding, genius. I just popped back to tell you something.
Unless you quit our particular line of work ***right now***... you're gonna end up exactly like me.
Lady, the real Stalk would never let me quit until I'd killed the robot that offed her.
Fuck him. Fuck your targets. Get on with your life. In case you haven't noticed, you crash landed in goddamn paradise.
You should settle down here with that Gwen chick, maybe adopt "*Slave Girl*," get around to giving the poor kid an actual name someday.

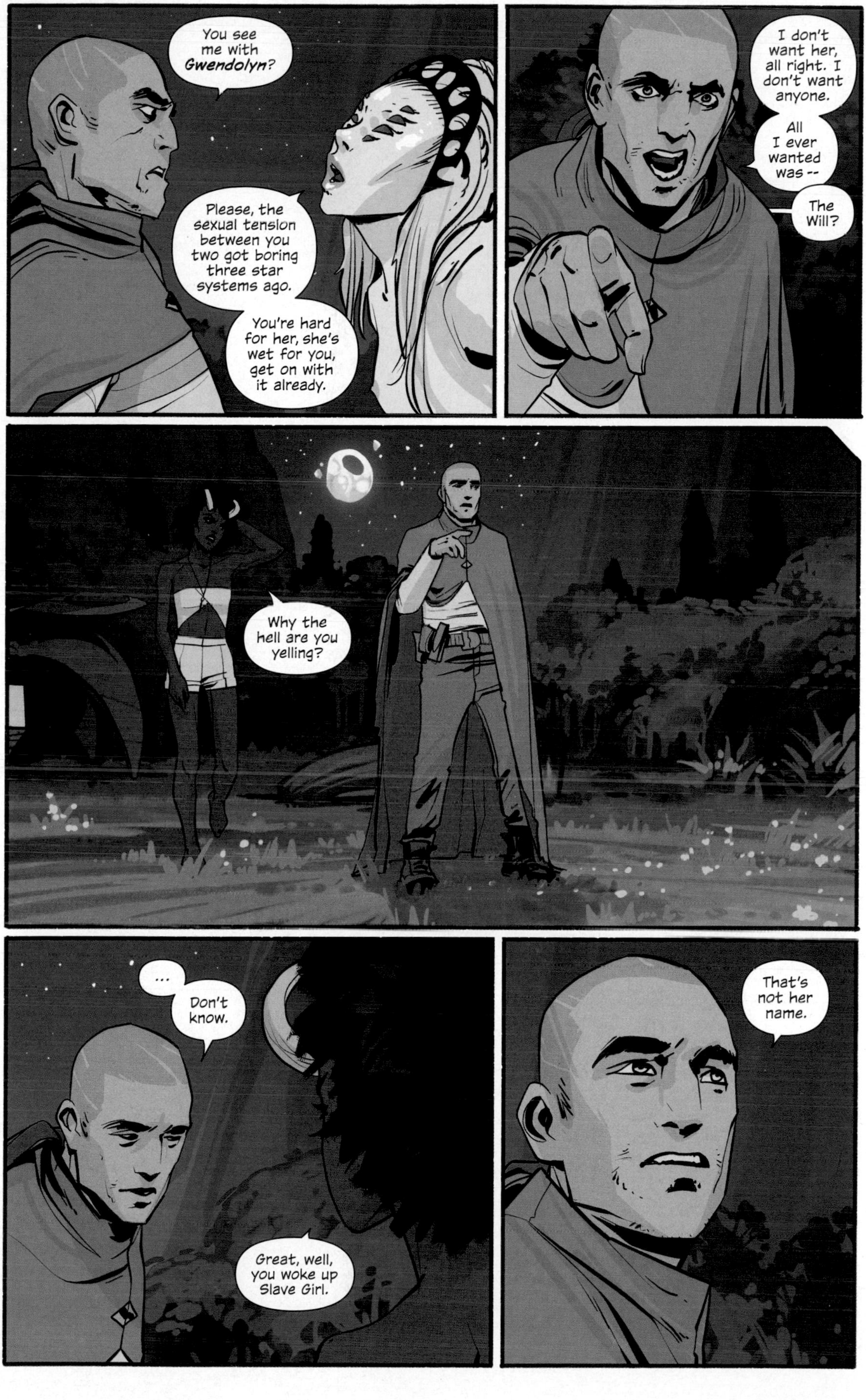
You see me with *Gwendolyn*?
Please, the sexual tension between you two got boring three star systems ago.
You're hard for her, she's wet for you, get on with it already.
I don't want her, all right. I don't want anyone.
All I ever wanted was --
The Will?
Why the hell are you yelling?
... Don't know.
Great, well, you woke up Slave Girl.
That's not her name.

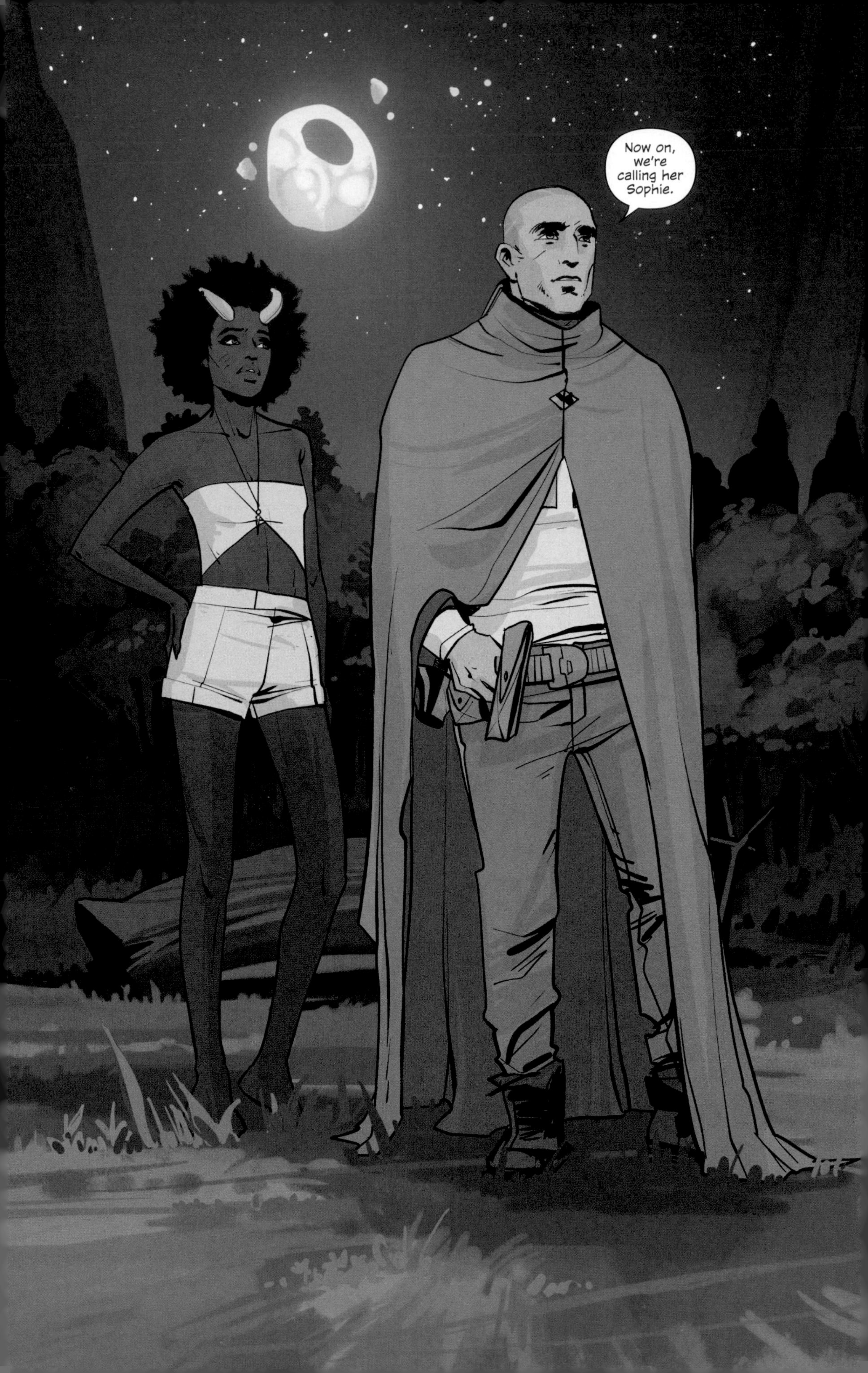
Now on, we're calling her Sophie.

end chapter thirteen

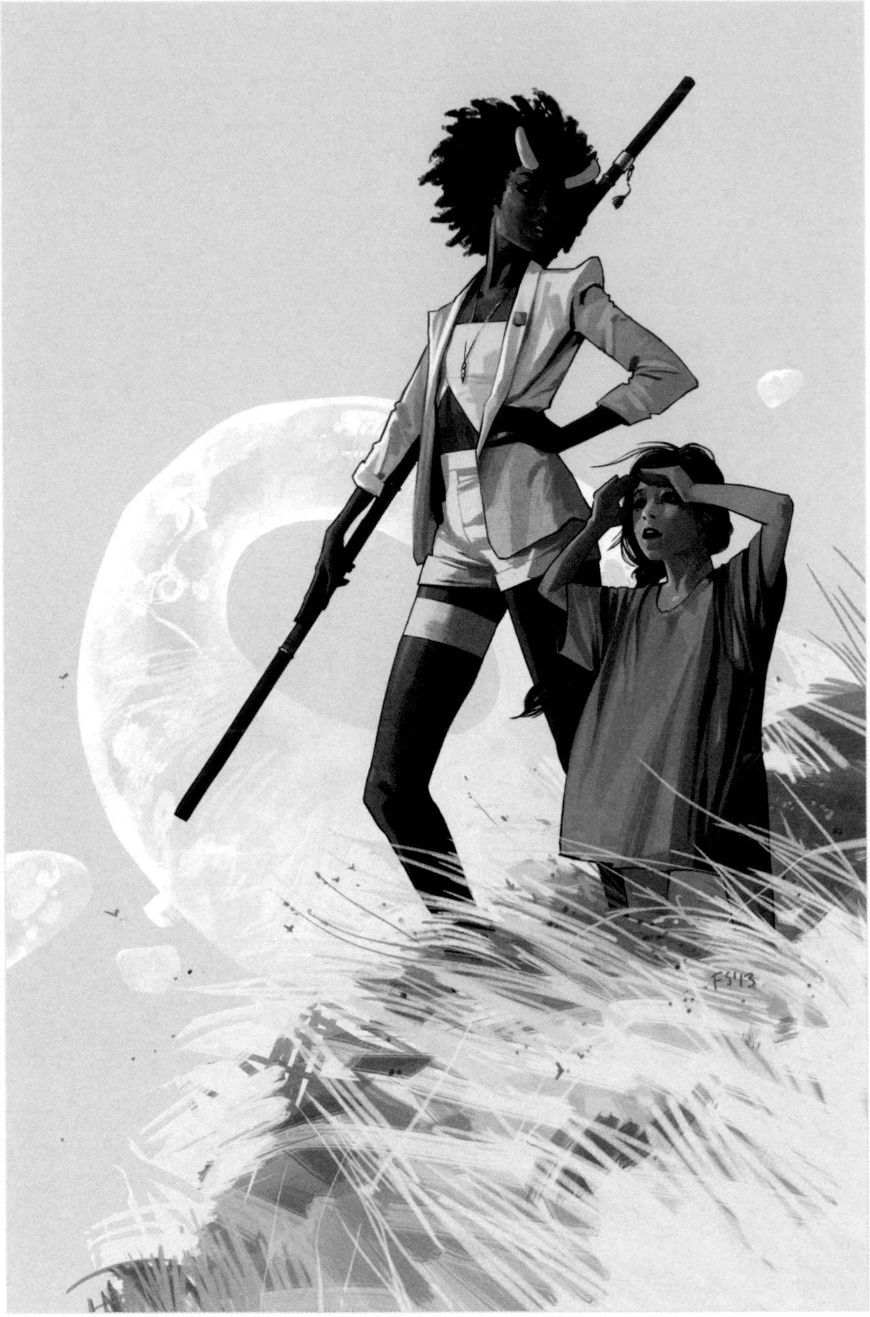
FS'13

CHAPTER
FOURTEEN

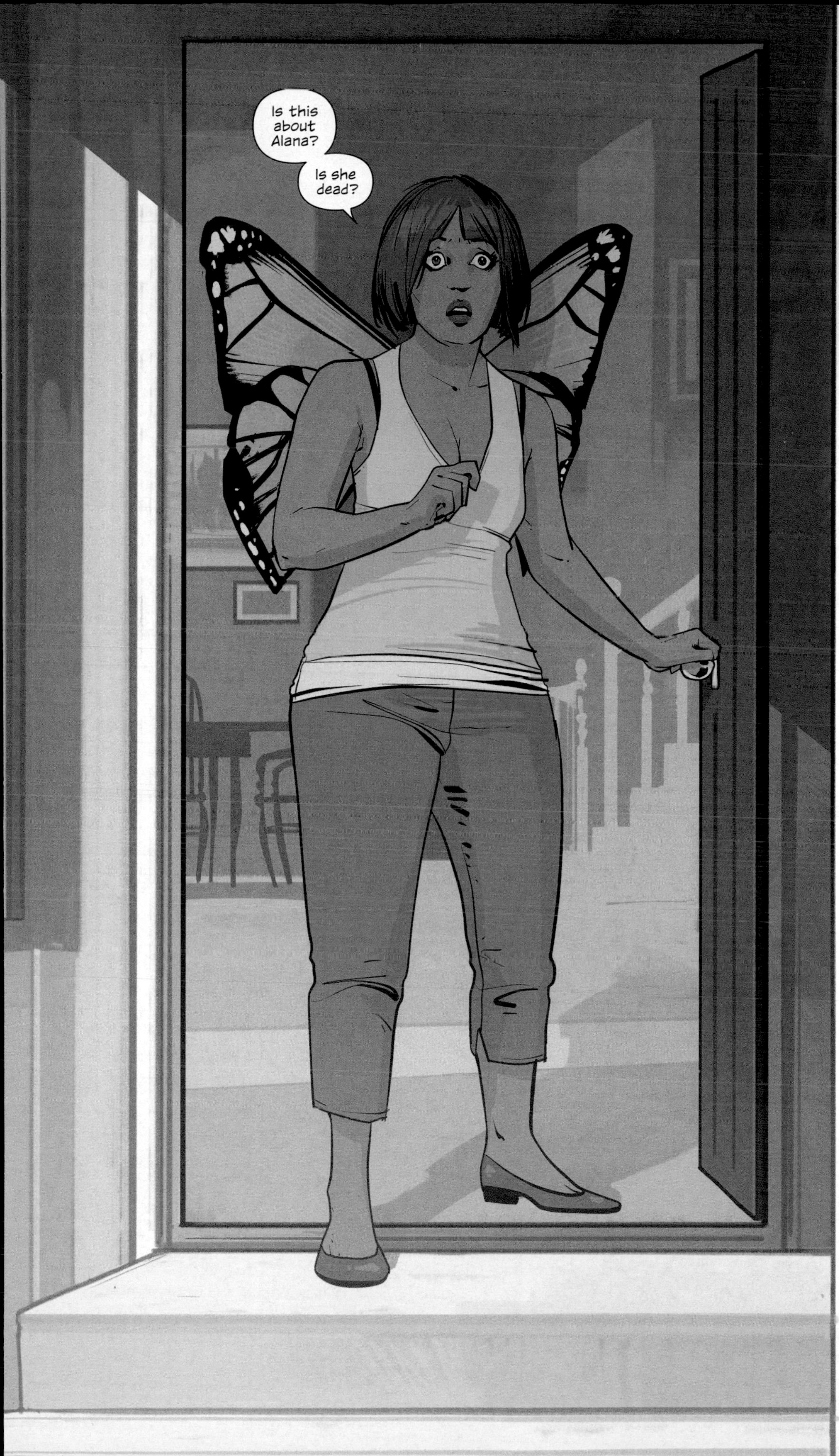
Is this about Alana?
Is she dead?

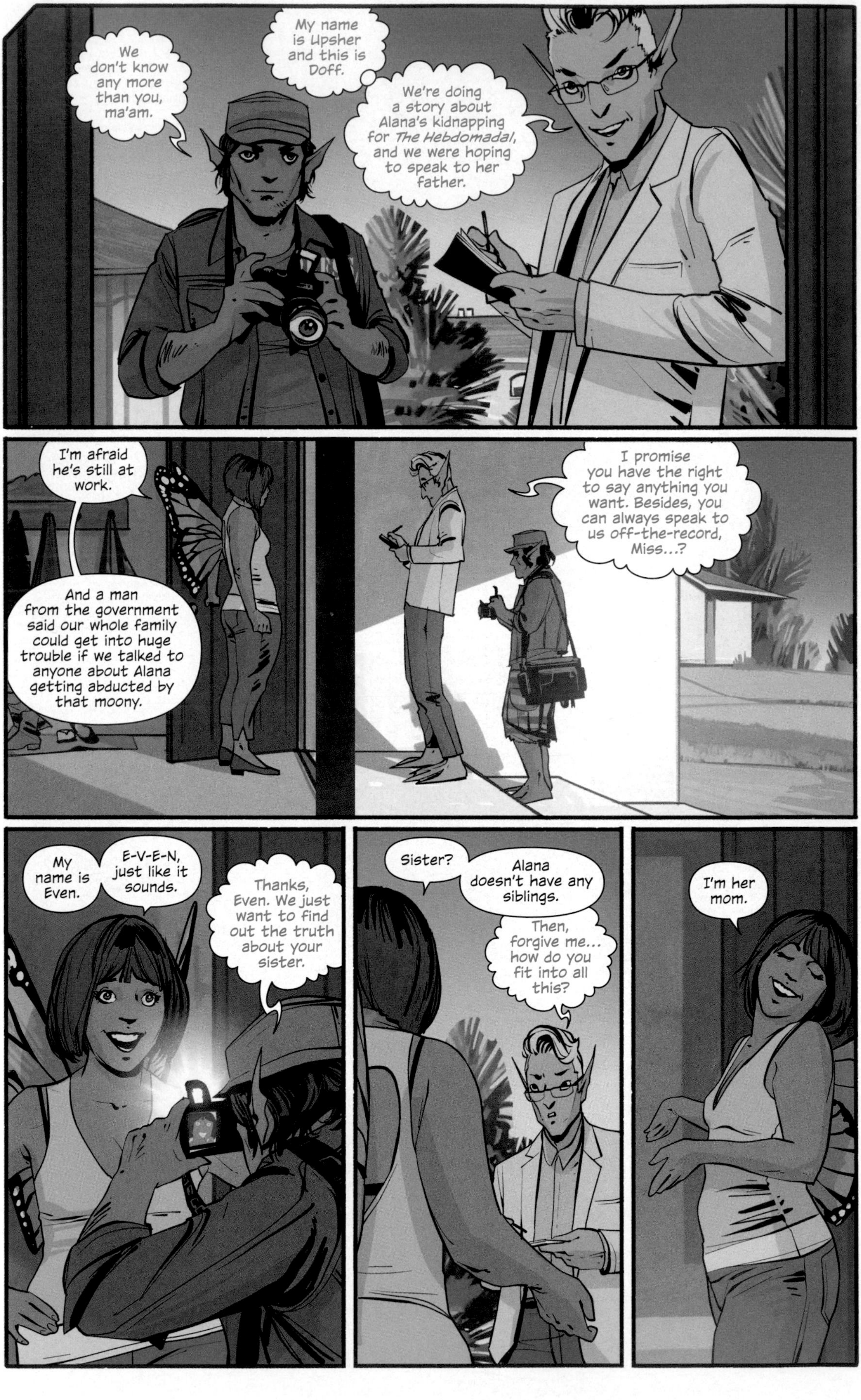
We don't know any more than you, ma'am.
My name is Upsher and this is Doff.
We're doing a story about Alana's kidnapping for *The Hebdomadal*, and we were hoping to speak to her father.
I'm afraid he's still at work.
And a man from the government said our whole family could get into huge trouble if we talked to anyone about Alana getting abducted by that moony.
I promise you have the right to say anything you want. Besides, you can always speak to us off-the-record, Miss...?
My name is Even.
E-V-E-N, just like it sounds.
Thanks, Even. We just want to find out the truth about your sister.
Sister?
Alana doesn't have any siblings.
Then, forgive me... how do you fit into all this?
I'm her mom.

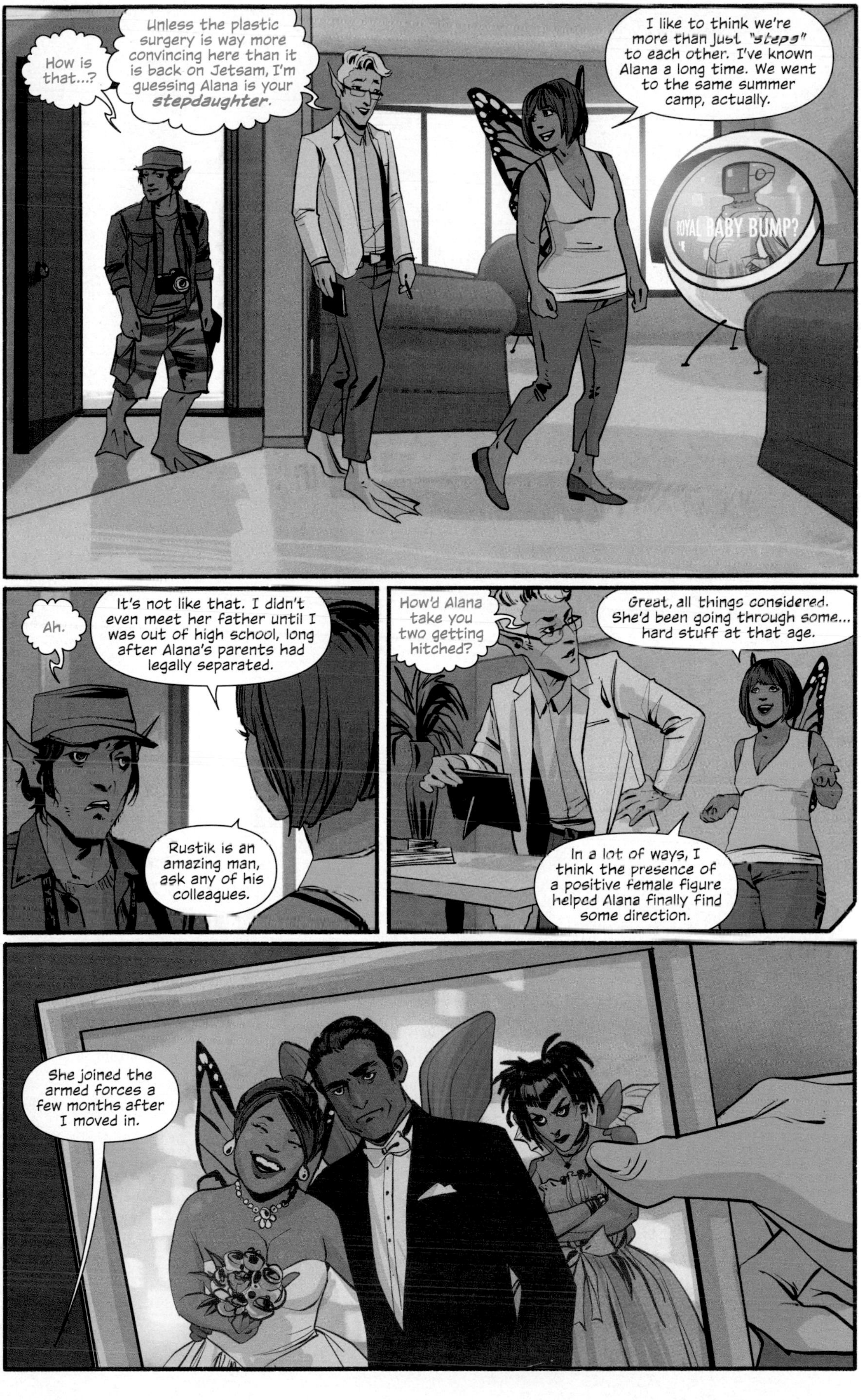
How is that...?
Unless the plastic surgery is way more convincing here than it is back on Jetsam, I'm guessing Alana is your *stepdaughter*.
I like to think we're more than just "*steps*" to each other. I've known Alana a long time. We went to the same summer camp, actually.
ROYAL BABY BUMP?
Ah.
It's not like that. I didn't even meet her father until I was out of high school, long after Alana's parents had legally separated.
Rustik is an amazing man, ask any of his colleagues.
How'd Alana take you two getting hitched?
Great, all things considered. She'd been going through some... hard stuff at that age.
In a lot of ways, I think the presence of a positive female figure helped Alana finally find some direction.
She joined the armed forces a few months after I moved in.

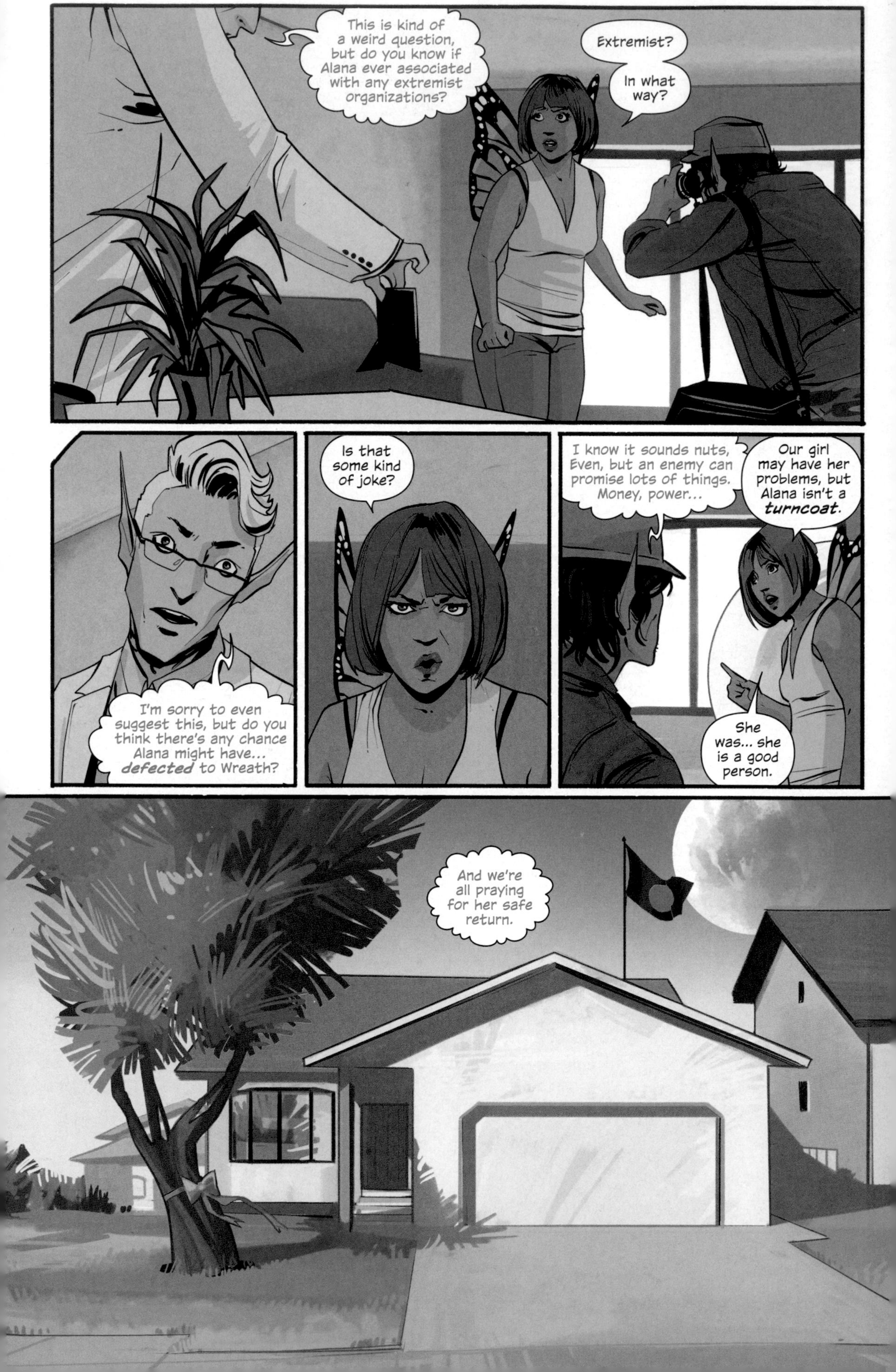
This is kind of a weird question, but do you know if Alana ever associated with any extremist organizations?
Extremist?
In what way?
I'm sorry to even suggest this, but do you think there's any chance Alana might have... *defected* to Wreath?
Is that some kind of joke?
I know it sounds nuts, Even, but an enemy can promise lots of things. Money, power...
Our girl may have her problems, but Alana isn't a *turncoat*.
She was... she is a good person.
And we're all praying for her safe return.

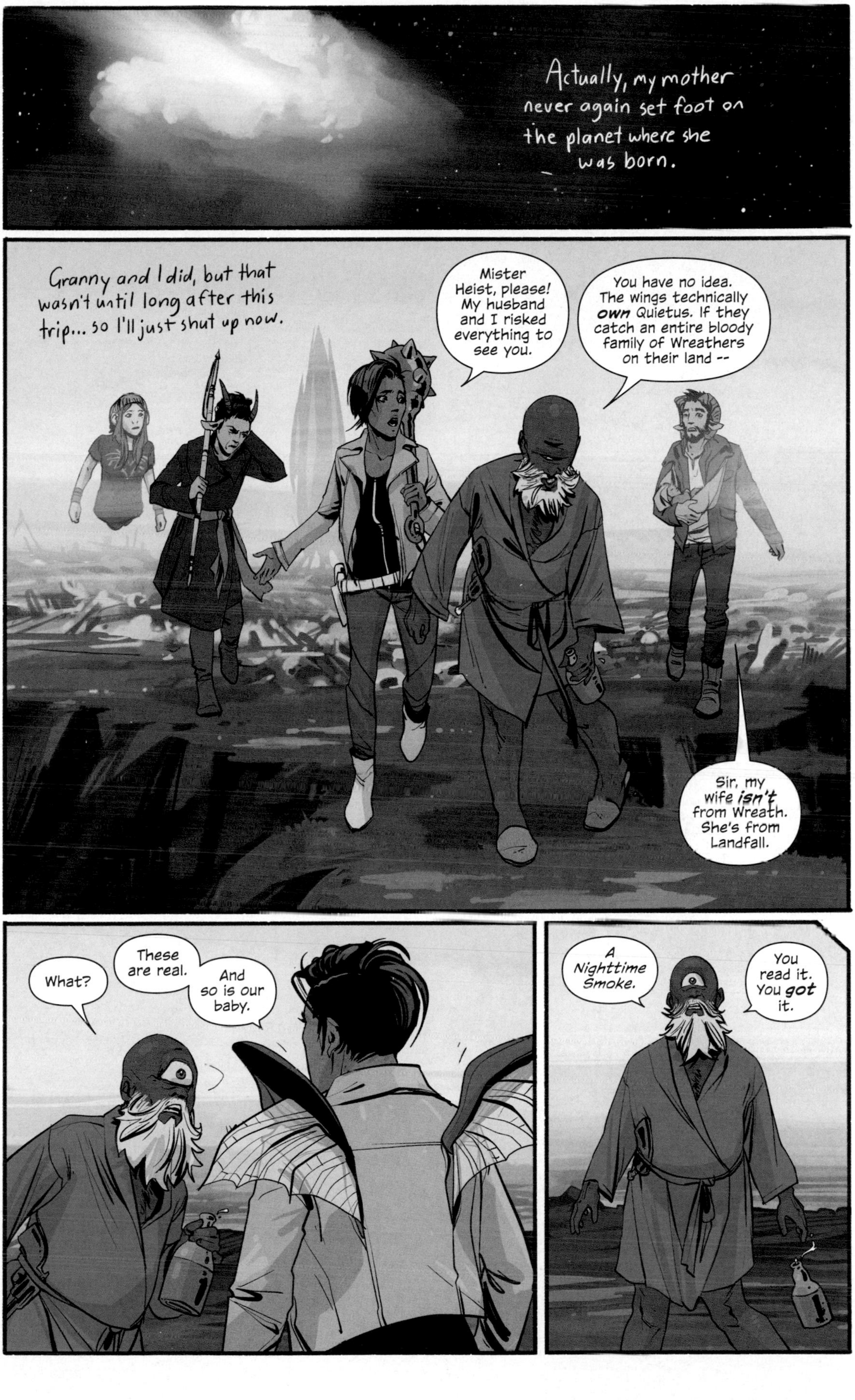
Actually, my mother never again set foot on the planet where she was born.
Granny and I did, but that wasn't until long after this trip... so I'll just shut up now.
Mister Heist, please! My husband and I risked everything to see you.
You have no idea. The wings technically own Quietus. If they catch an entire bloody family of Wreathers on their land --
Sir, my wife isn't from Wreath. She's from Landfall.
What?
These are real.
And so is our baby.
A Nighttime Smoke.
You read it. You got it.

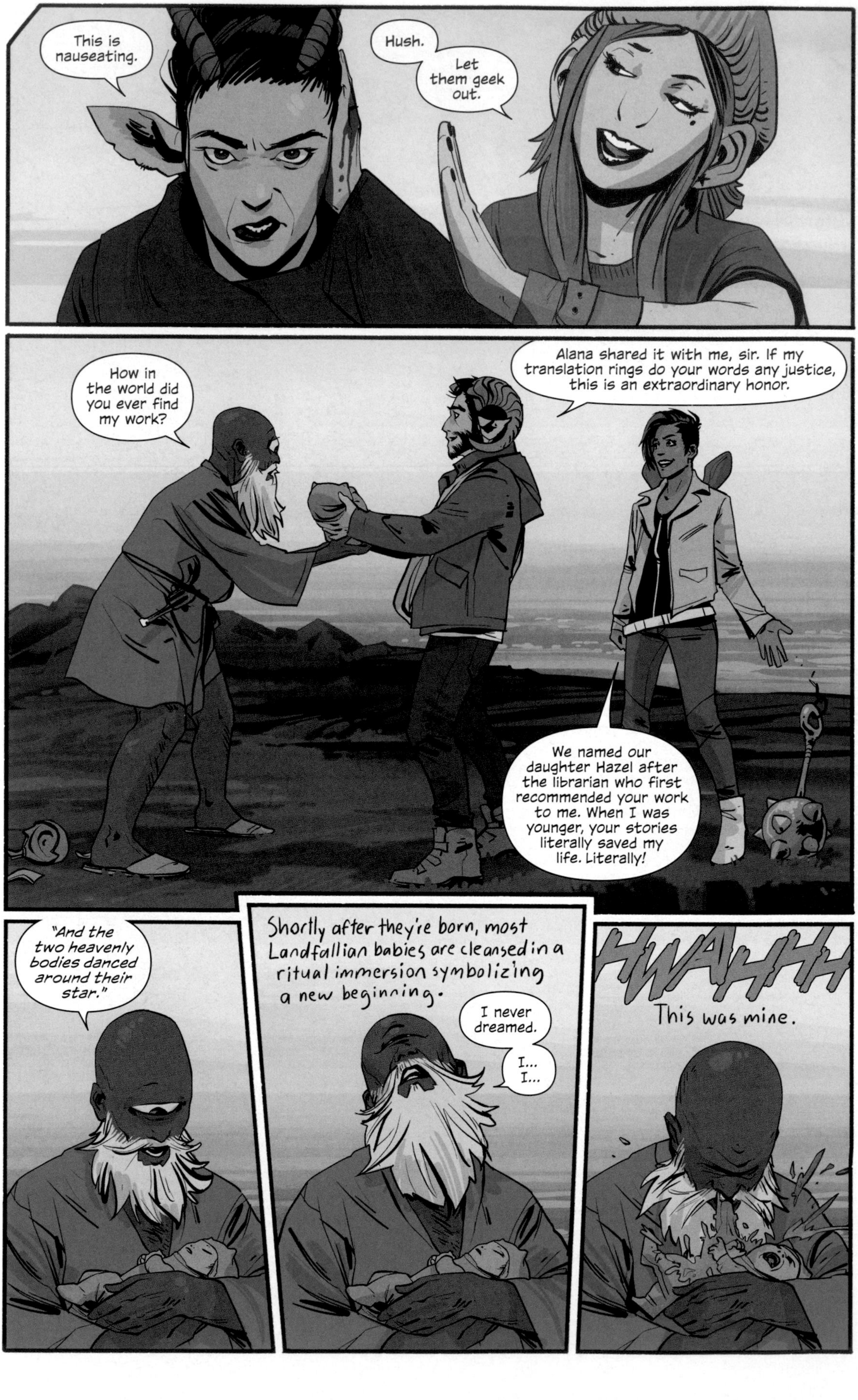
This is nauseating.
Hush.
Let them geek out.
How in the world did you ever find my work?
Alana shared it with me, sir. If my translation rings do your words any justice, this is an extraordinary honor.
We named our daughter Hazel after the librarian who first recommended your work to me. When I was younger, your stories literally saved my life. Literally!
"And the two heavenly bodies danced around their star."
Shortly after they're born, most Landfallian babies are cleansed in a ritual immersion symbolizing a new beginning.
I never dreamed.
I... I...
HWAHHH
This was mine.

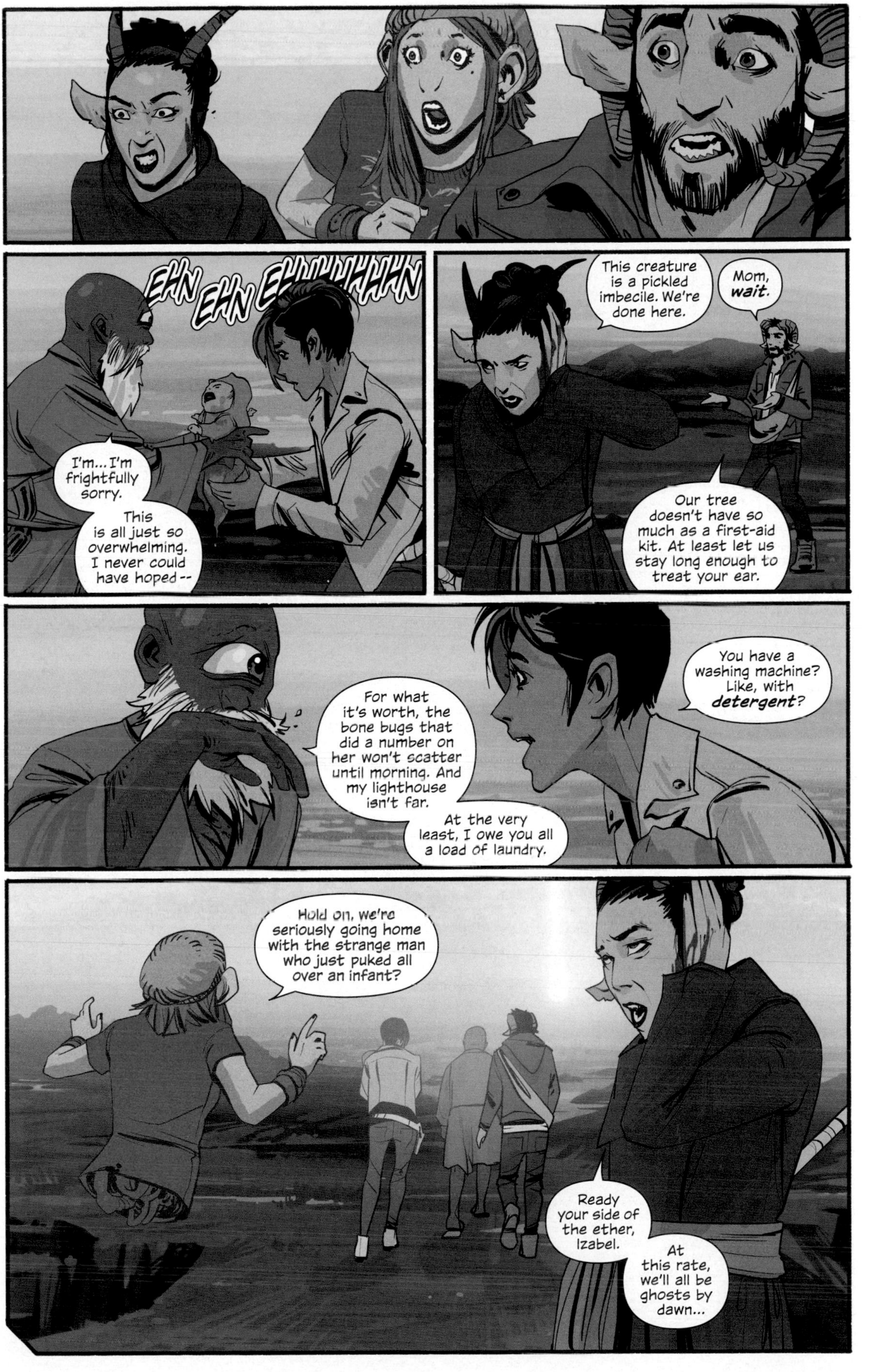
EHN EHN EHHHHHHHN
I'm... I'm frightfully sorry.
This is all just so overwhelming. I never could have hoped--
This creature is a pickled imbecile. We're done here.
Mom, *wait*.
Our tree doesn't have so much as a first-aid kit. At least let us stay long enough to treat your ear.
For what it's worth, the bone bugs that did a number on her won't scatter until morning. And my lighthouse isn't far.
At the very least, I owe you all a load of laundry.
You have a washing machine? Like, with ***detergent***?
Hold on, we're seriously going home with the strange man who just puked all over an infant?
Ready your side of the ether, Izabel.
At this rate, we'll all be ghosts by dawn...

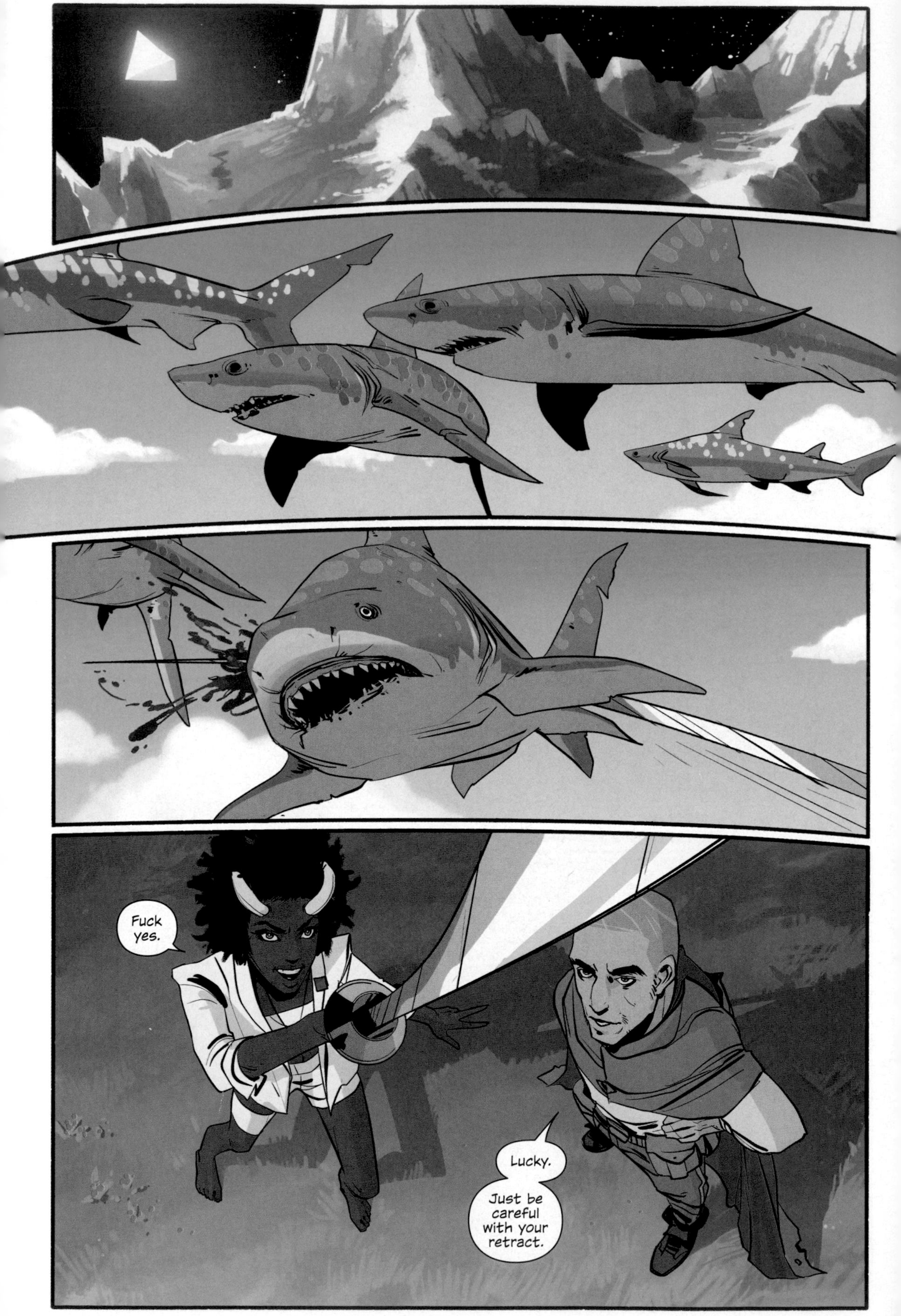
Fuck yes.
Lucky.
Just be careful with your retract.

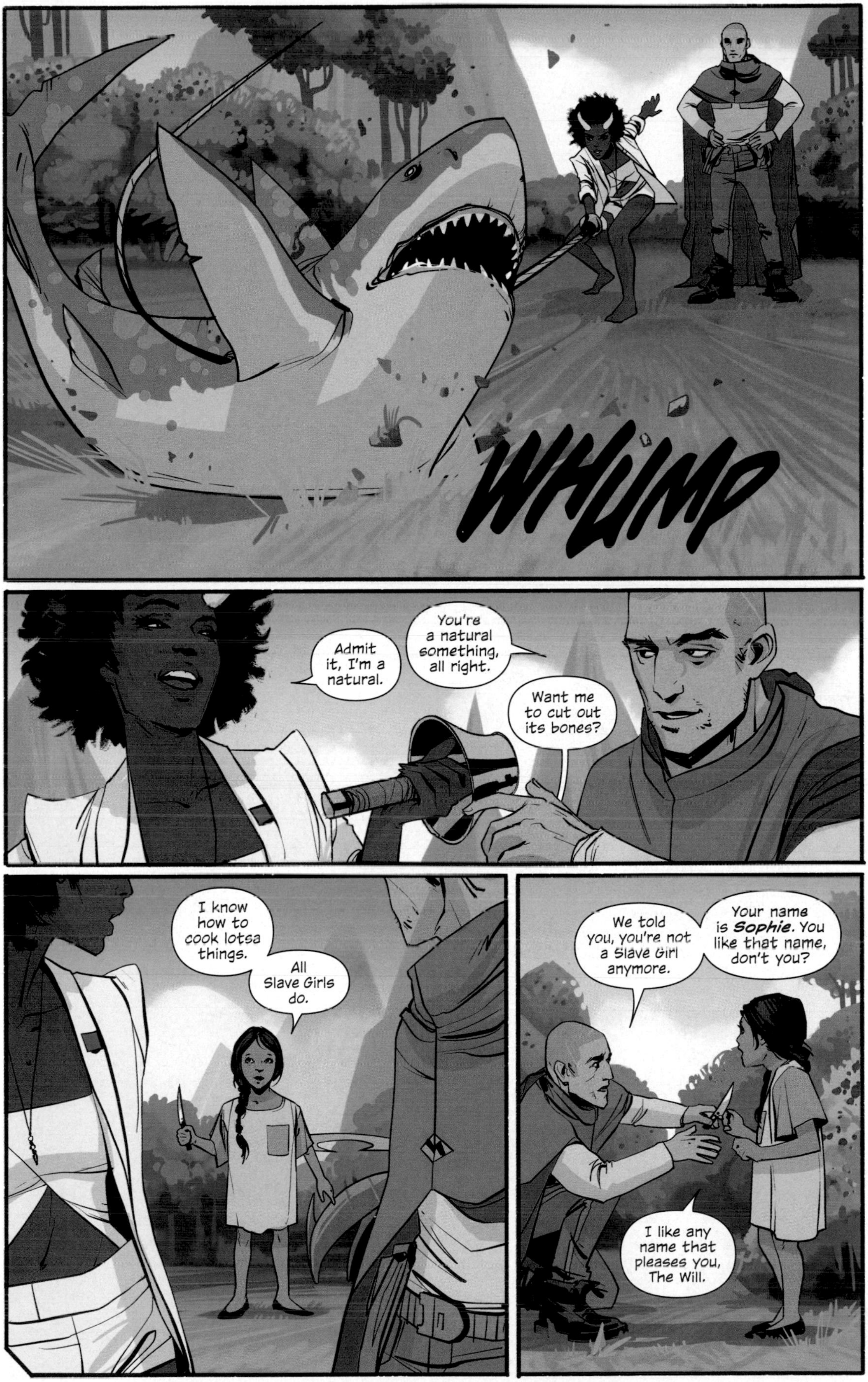
WHUMP
Admit it, I'm a natural.
You're a natural something, all right.
Want me to cut out its bones?
I know how to cook lotsa things.
All Slave Girls do.
We told you, you're not a Slave Girl anymore.
Your name is **Sophie**. You like that name, don't you?
I like any name that pleases you, The Will.

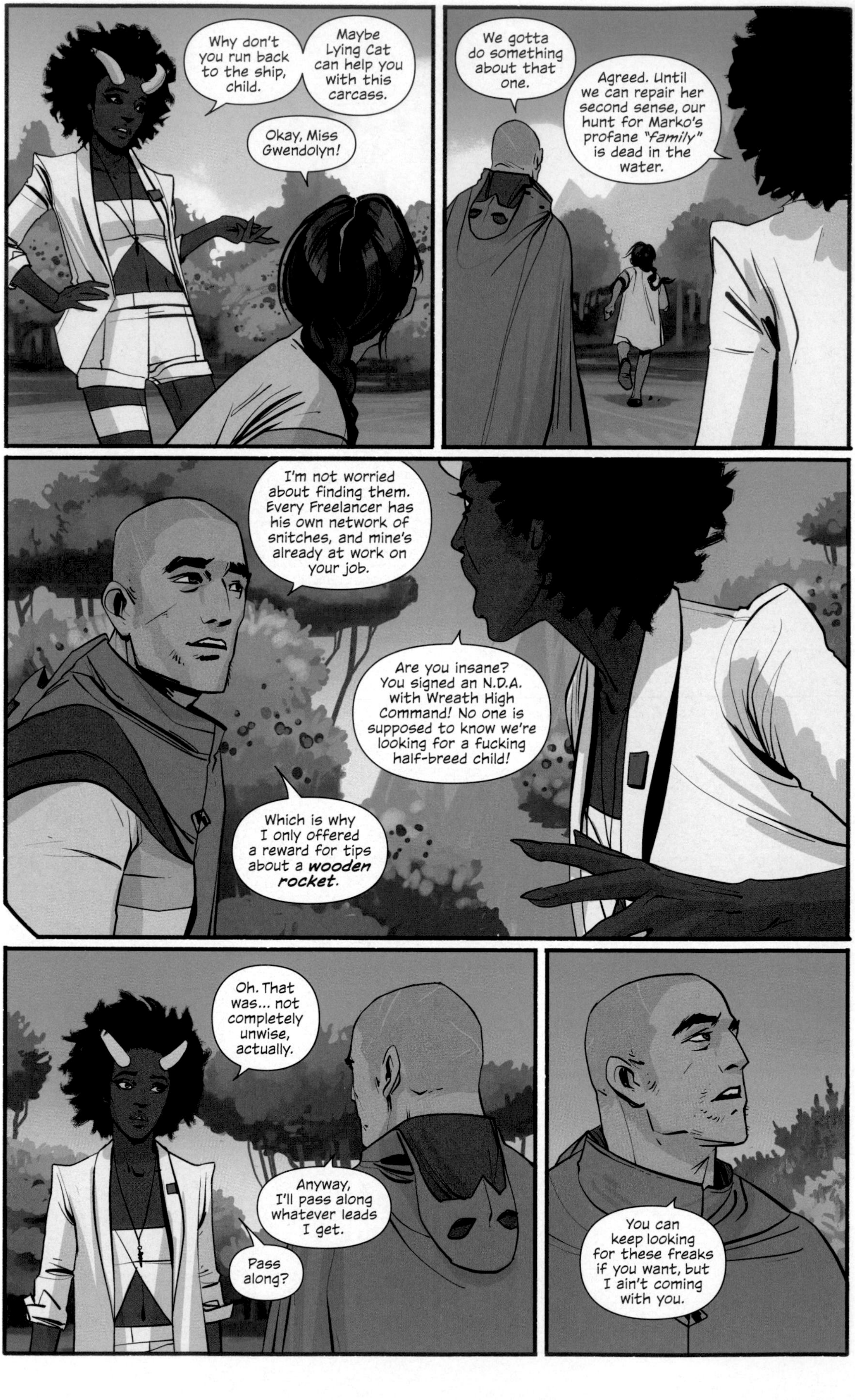

Why don't you run back to the ship, child.
Maybe Lying Cat can help you with this carcass.
Okay, Miss Gwendolyn!
We gotta do something about that one.
Agreed. Until we can repair her second sense, our hunt for Marko's profane *"family"* is dead in the water.
I'm not worried about finding them. Every Freelancer has his own network of snitches, and mine's already at work on your job.
Are you insane? You signed an N.D.A. with Wreath High Command! No one is supposed to know we're looking for a fucking half-breed child!
Which is why I only offered a reward for tips about a ***wooden rocket***.
Oh. That was... not completely unwise, actually.
Anyway, I'll pass along whatever leads I get.
Pass along?
You can keep looking for these freaks if you want, but I ain't coming with you.

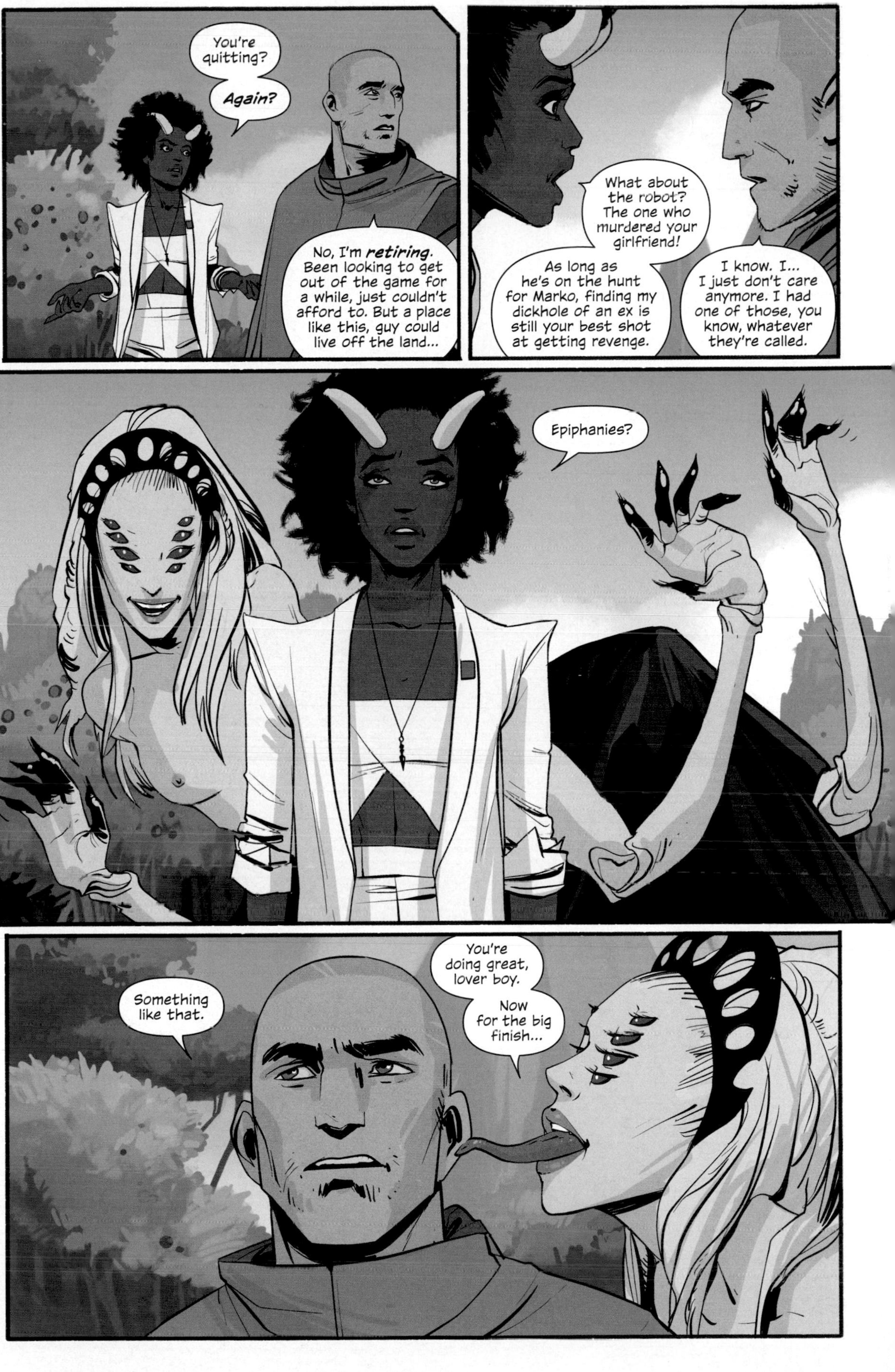
You're quitting?
Again?
No, I'm retiring. Been looking to get out of the game for a while, just couldn't afford to. But a place like this, guy could live off the land...
What about the robot? The one who murdered your girlfriend!
As long as he's on the hunt for Marko, finding my dickhole of an ex is still your best shot at getting revenge.
I know. I... I just don't care anymore. I had one of those, you know, whatever they're called.
Epiphanies?
Something like that.
You're doing great, lover boy.
Now for the big finish...

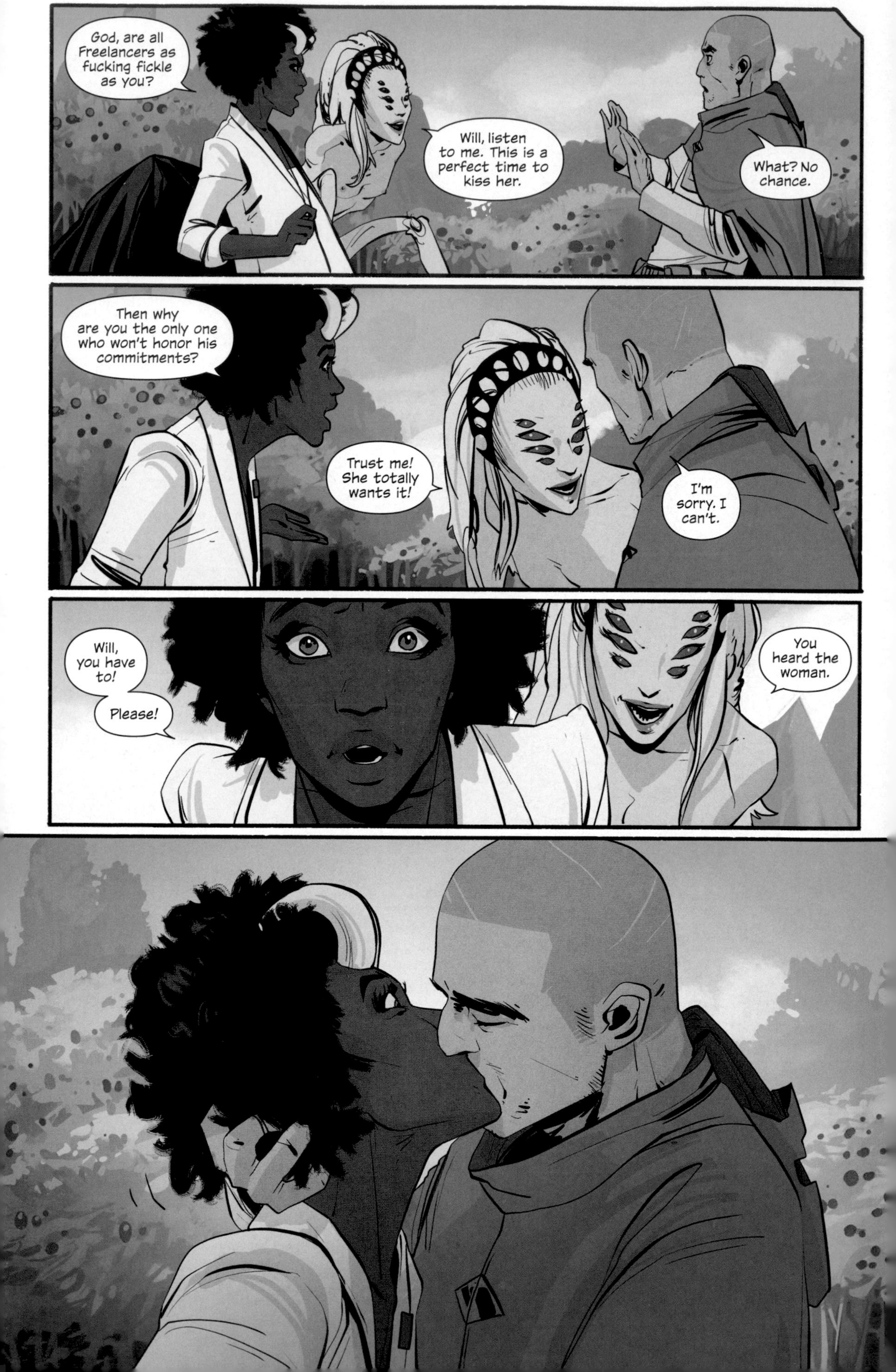
God, are all Freelancers as fucking fickle as you?
Will, listen to me. This is a perfect time to kiss her.
What? No chance.
Then why are you the only one who won't honor his commitments?
Trust me! She totally wants it!
I'm sorry. I can't.
Will, you have to!
Please!
You heard the woman.

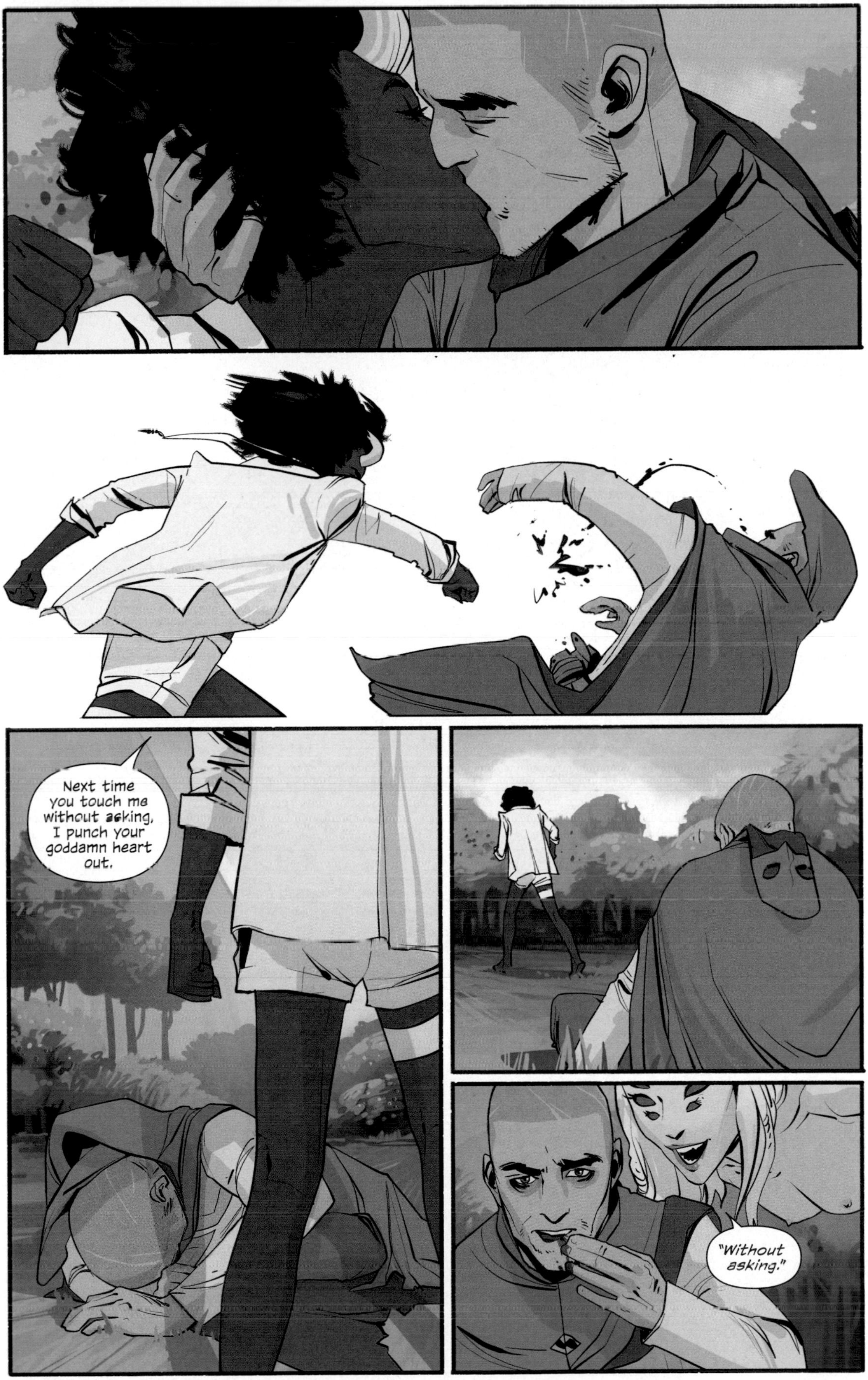
Next time you touch me without asking, I punch your goddamn heart out.
"Without asking."

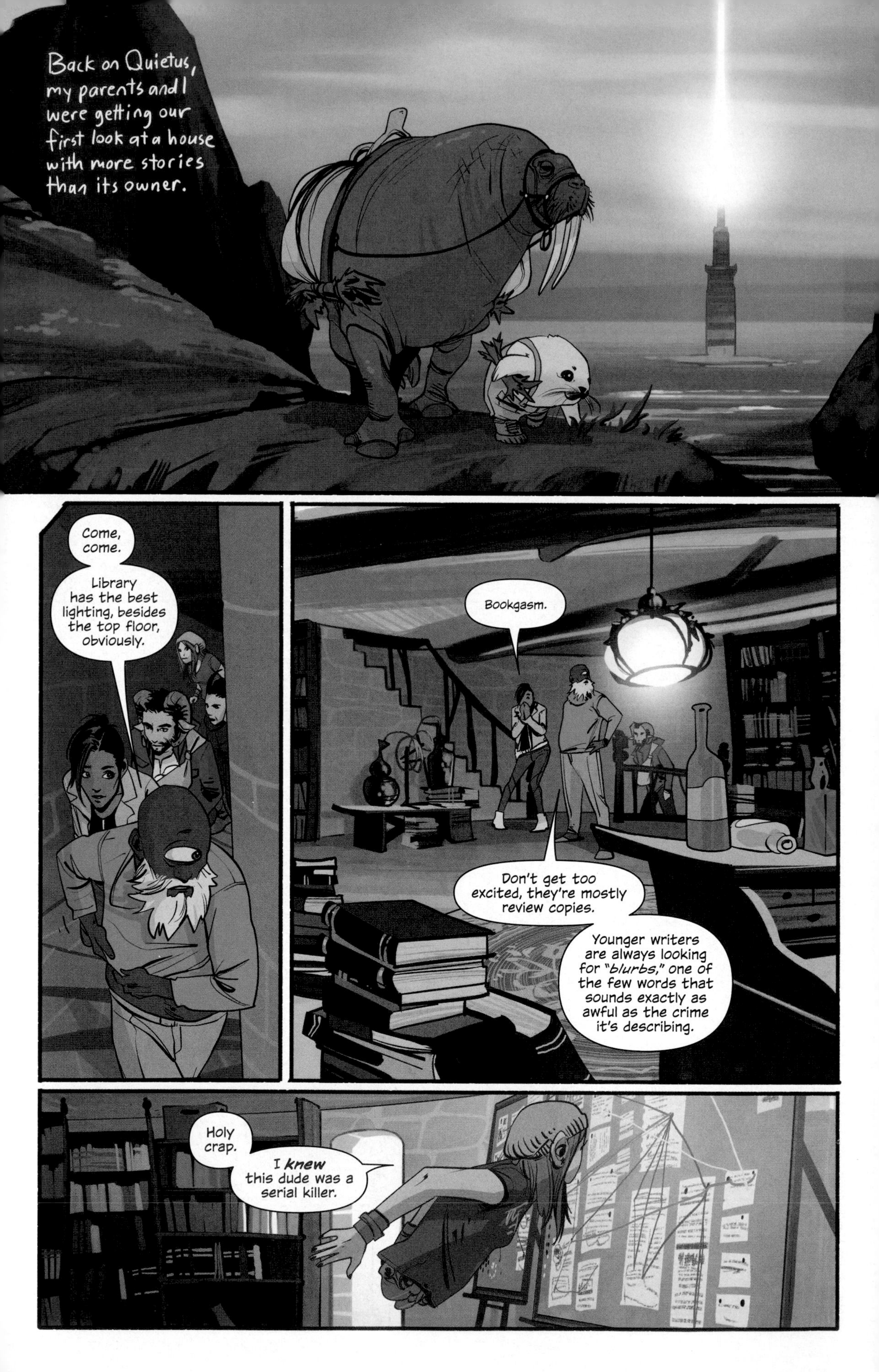
Back on Quietus, my parents and I were getting our first look at a house with more stories than its owner.
Come, come.
Library has the best lighting, besides the top floor, obviously.
Bookgasm.
Don't get too excited, they're mostly review copies.
Younger writers are always looking for "*blurbs*," one of the few words that sounds exactly as awful as the crime it's describing.
Holy crap.
I ***knew*** this dude was a serial killer.

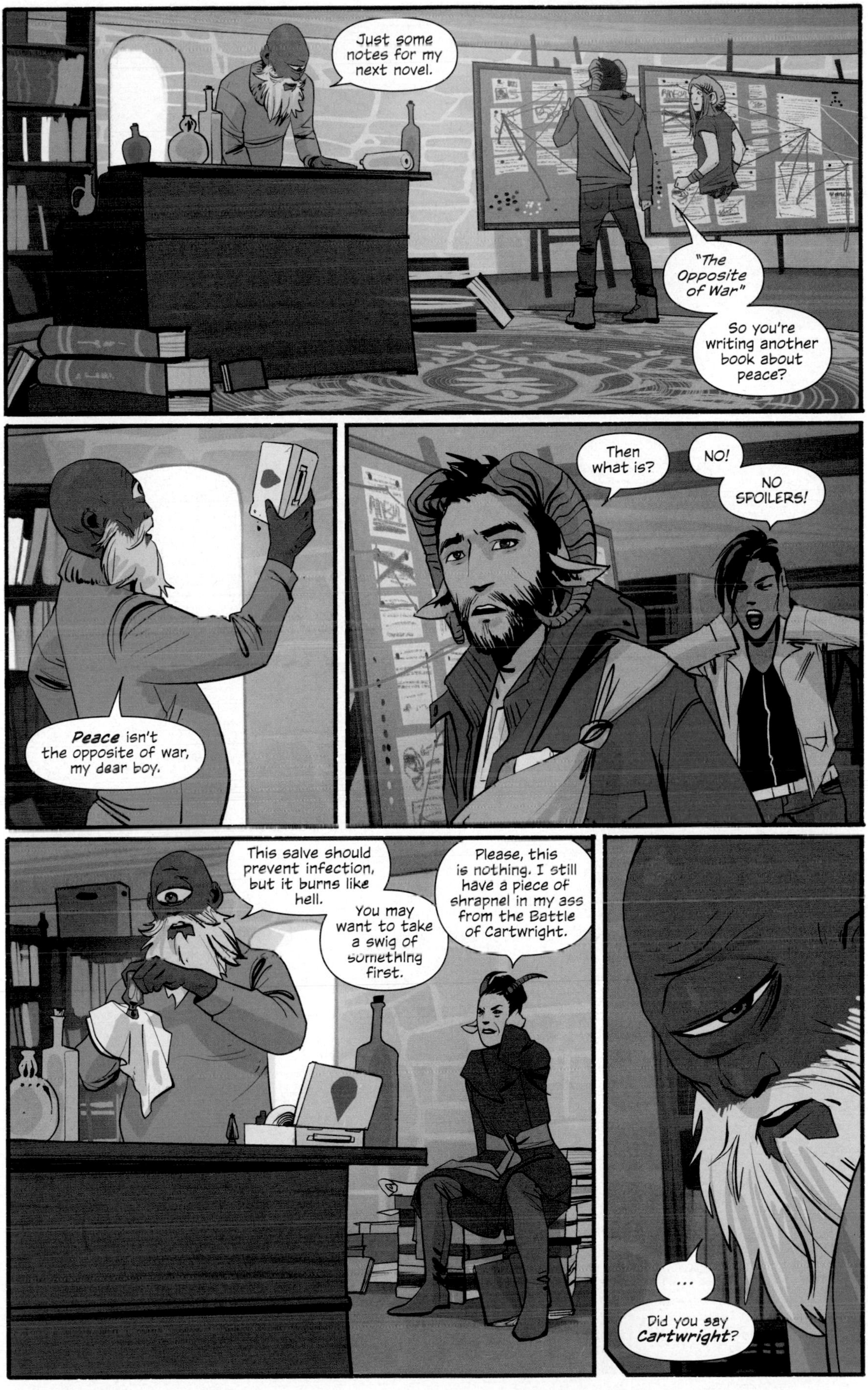
Just some notes for my next novel.
"The Opposite of War"
So you're writing another book about peace?
Peace isn't the opposite of war, my dear boy.
Then what is?
NO!
NO SPOILERS!
This salve should prevent infection, but it burns like hell.
You may want to take a swig of something first.
Please, this is nothing. I still have a piece of shrapnel in my ass from the Battle of Cartwright.
...
Did you say Cartwright?

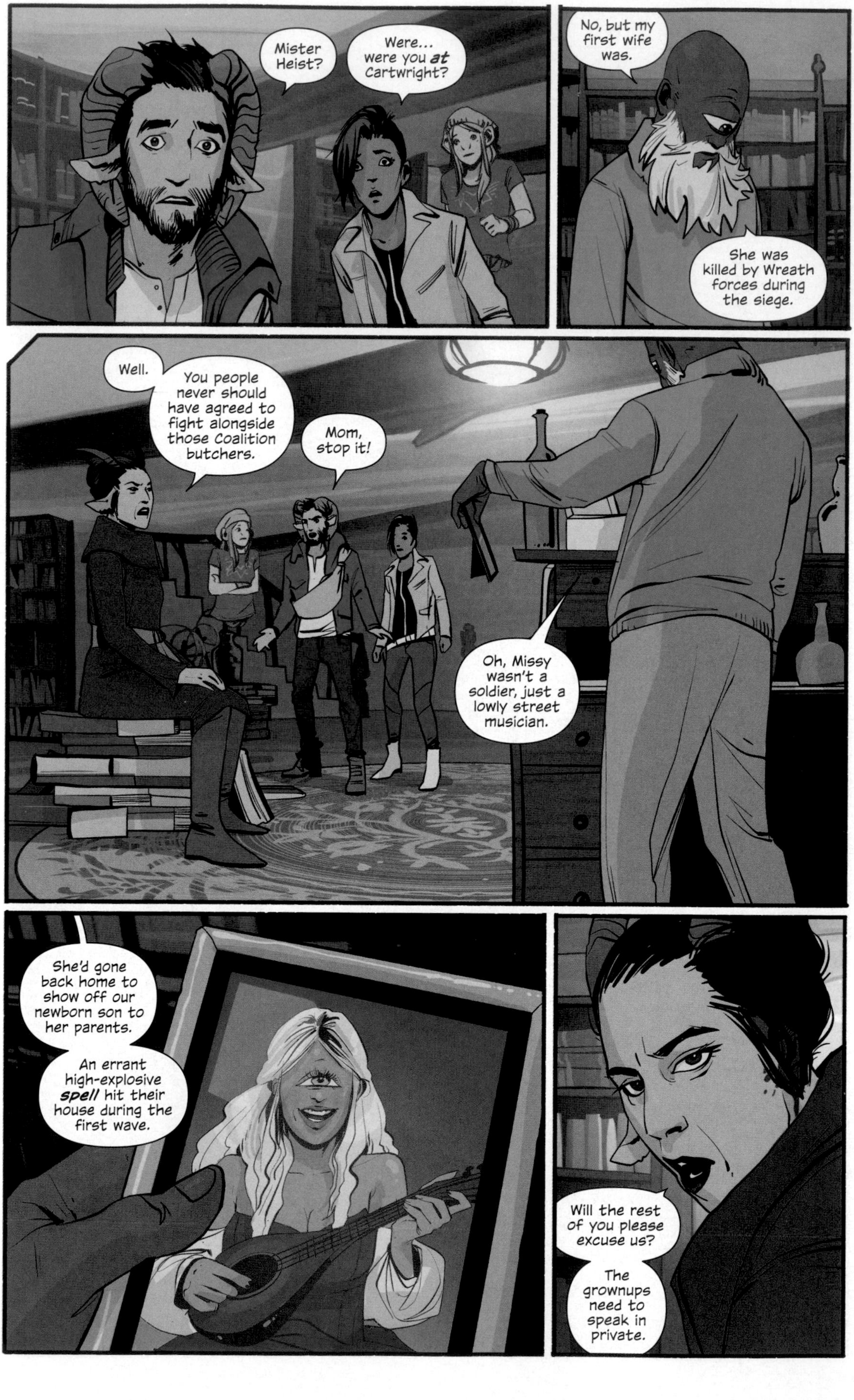
Mister Heist?
Were... were you at Cartwright?
No, but my first wife was.
She was killed by Wreath forces during the siege.
Well.
You people never should have agreed to fight alongside those Coalition butchers.
Mom, stop it!
Oh, Missy wasn't a soldier, just a lowly street musician.
She'd gone back home to show off our newborn son to her parents.
An errant high-explosive spell hit their house during the first wave.
Will the rest of you please excuse us?
The grownups need to speak in private.

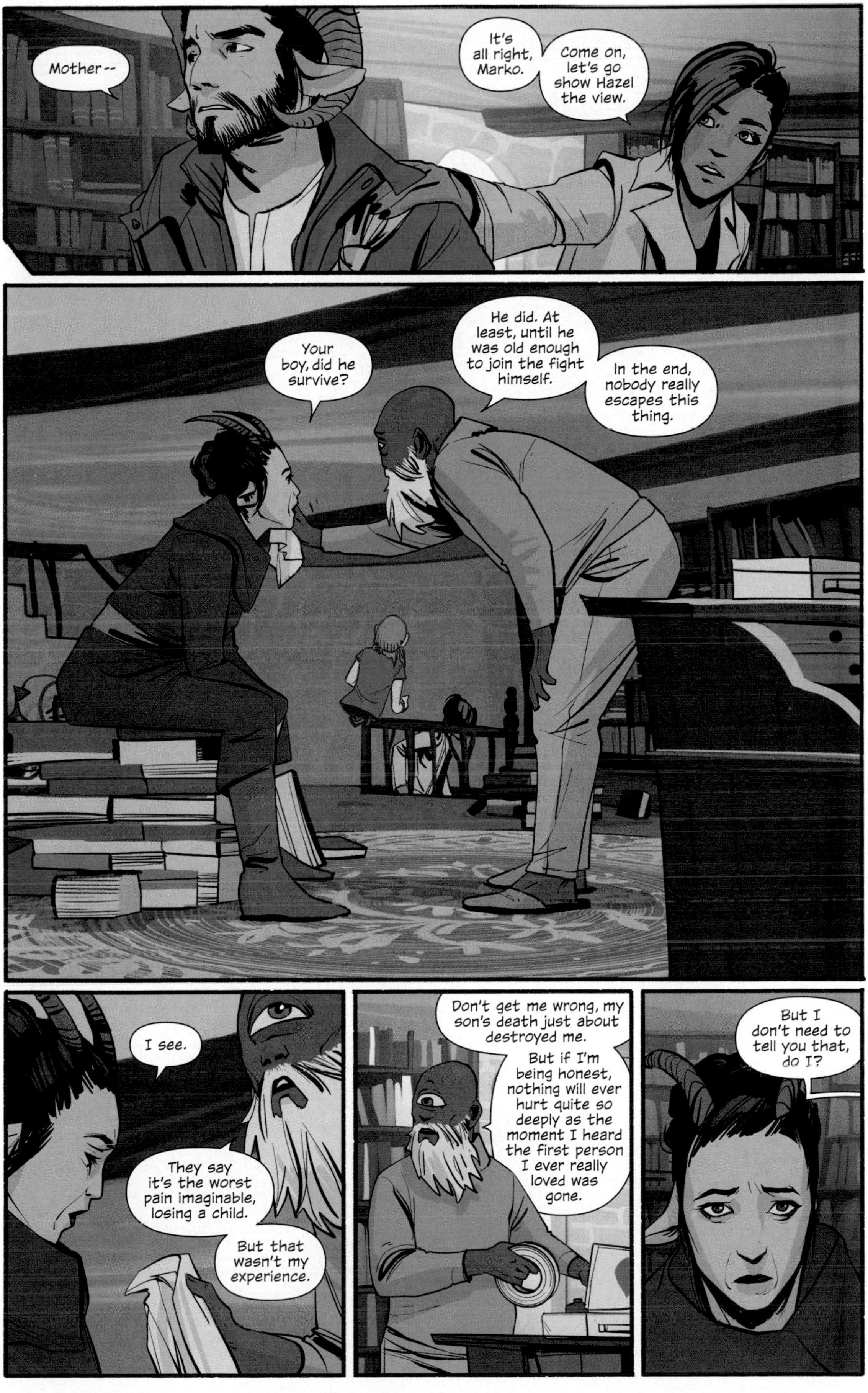
Mother--
It's all right, Marko.
Come on, let's go show Hazel the view.
Your boy, did he survive?
He did. At least, until he was old enough to join the fight himself.
In the end, nobody really escapes this thing.
I see.
They say it's the worst pain imaginable, losing a child.
But that wasn't my experience.
Don't get me wrong, my son's death just about destroyed me.
But if I'm being honest, nothing will ever hurt quite so deeply as the moment I heard the first person I ever really loved was gone.
But I don't need to tell you that, do I?

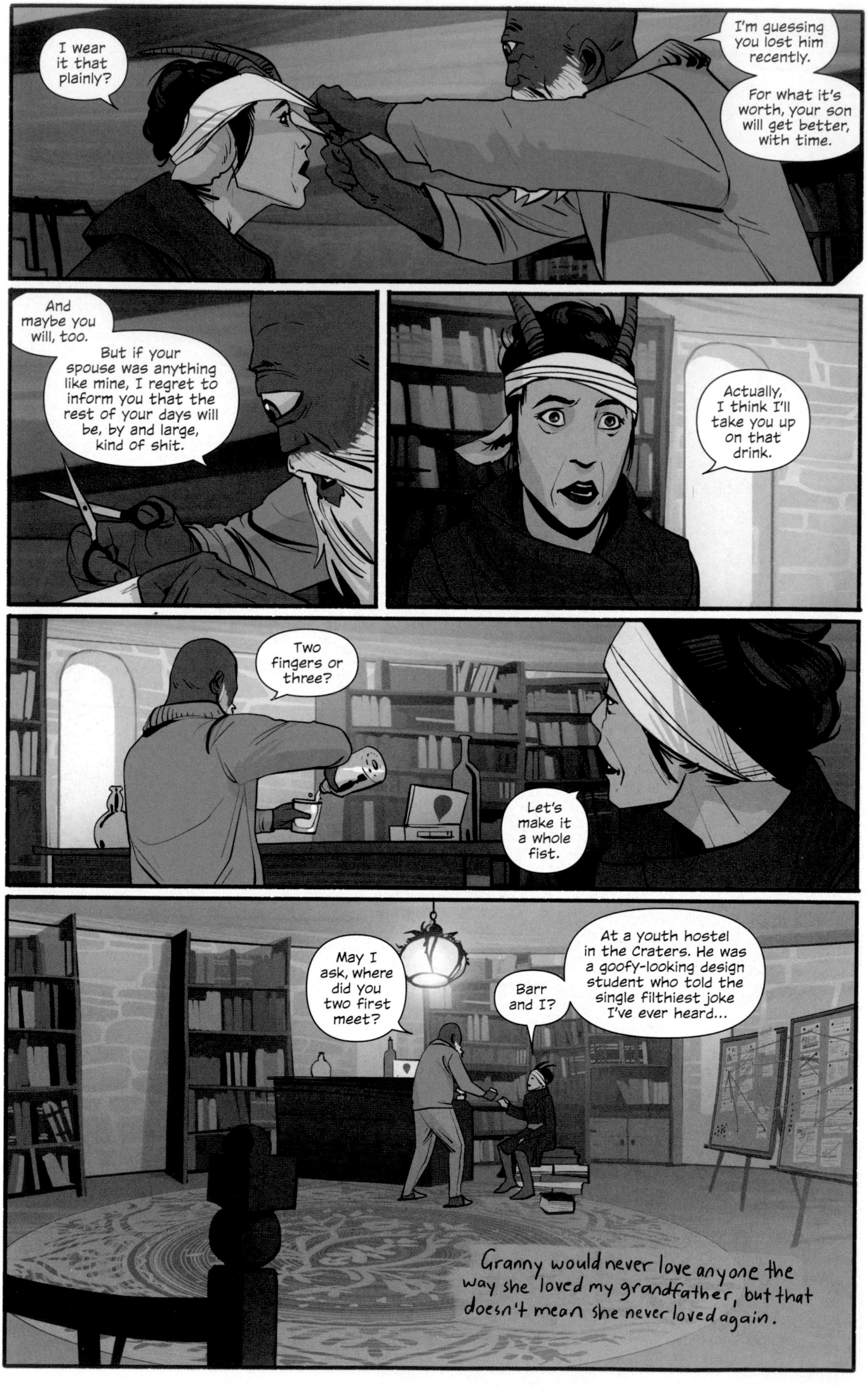
I wear it that plainly?
I'm guessing you lost him recently.
For what it's worth, your son will get better, with time.
And maybe you will, too.
But if your spouse was anything like mine, I regret to inform you that the rest of your days will be, by and large, kind of shit.
Actually, I think I'll take you up on that drink.
Two fingers or three?
Let's make it a whole fist.
May I ask, where did you two first meet?
Barr and I?
At a youth hostel in the Craters. He was a goofy-looking design student who told the single filthiest joke I've ever heard...
Granny would never love anyone the way she loved my grandfather, but that doesn't mean she never loved again.

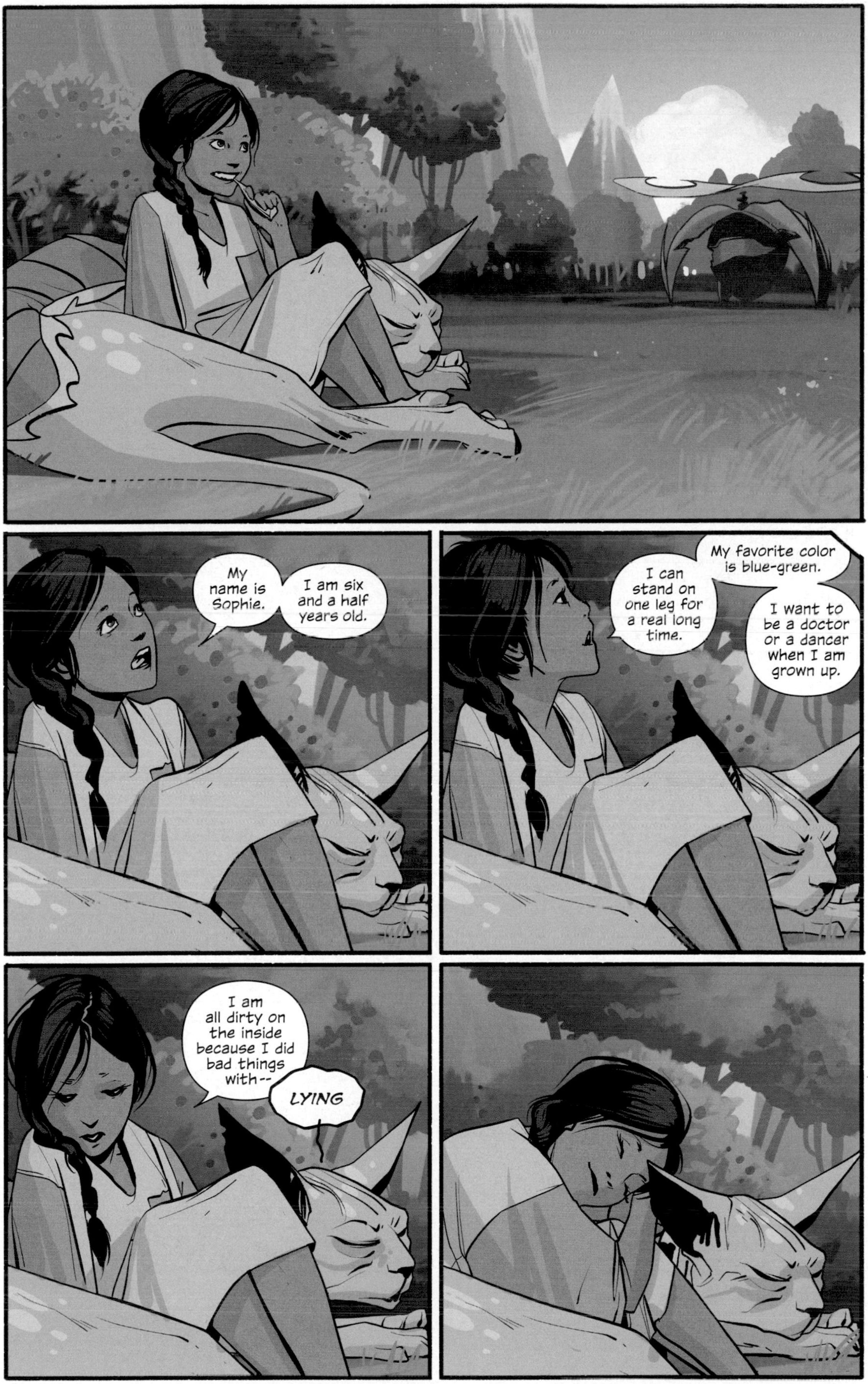
My name is Sophie.
I am six and a half years old.
I can stand on one leg for a real long time.
My favorite color is blue-green.
I want to be a doctor or a dancer when I am grown up.
I am all dirty on the inside because I did bad things with--
LYING

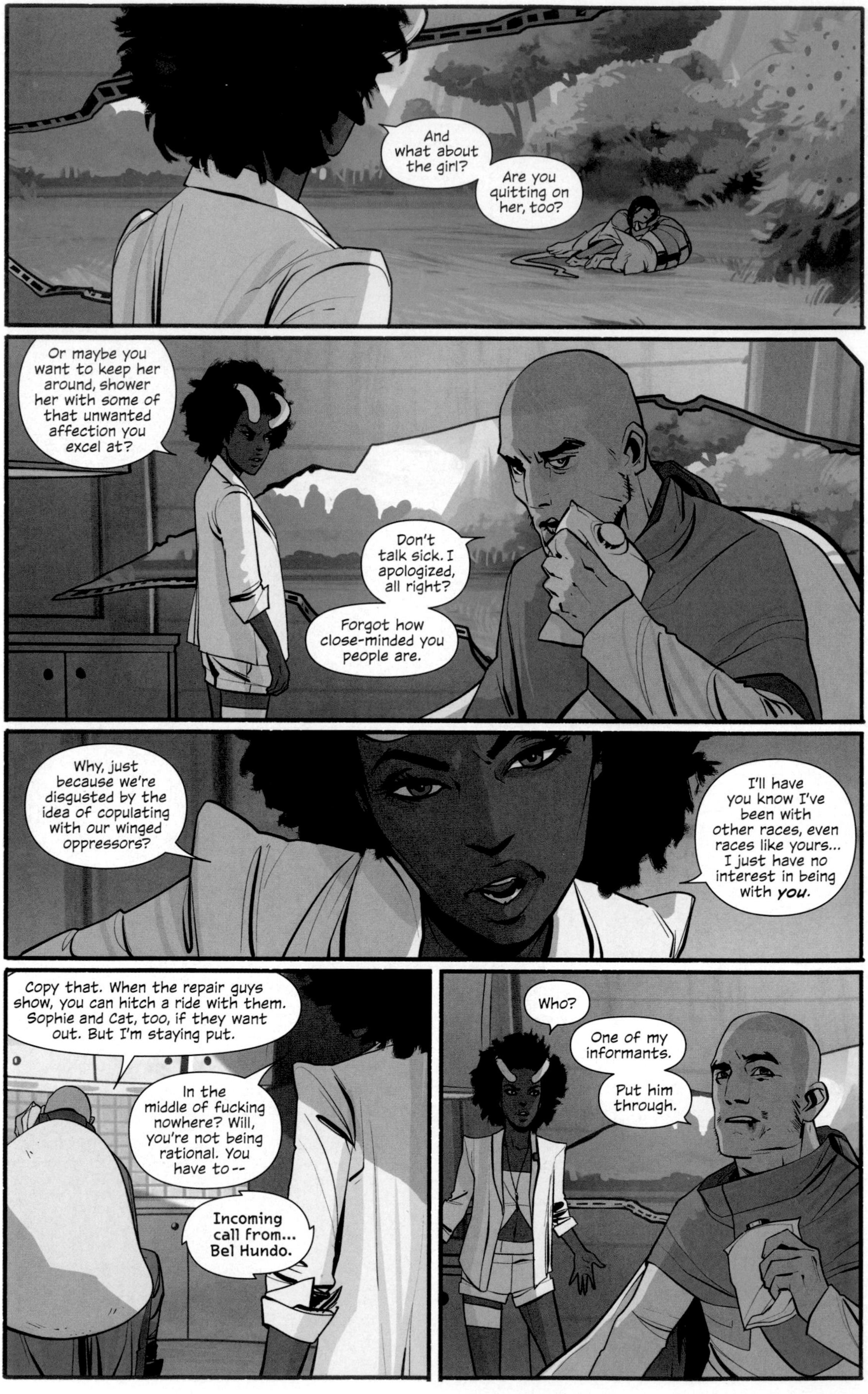
And what about the girl?
Are you quitting on her, too?
Or maybe you want to keep her around, shower her with some of that unwanted affection you excel at?
Don't talk sick. I apologized, all right?
Forgot how close-minded you people are.
Why, just because we're disgusted by the idea of copulating with our winged oppressors?
I'll have you know I've been with other races, even races like yours... I just have no interest in being with *you*.
Copy that. When the repair guys show, you can hitch a ride with them. Sophie and Cat, too, if they want out. But I'm staying put.
In the middle of fucking nowhere? Will, you're not being rational. You have to --
Incoming call from... Bel Hundo.
Who?
One of my informants.
Put him through.

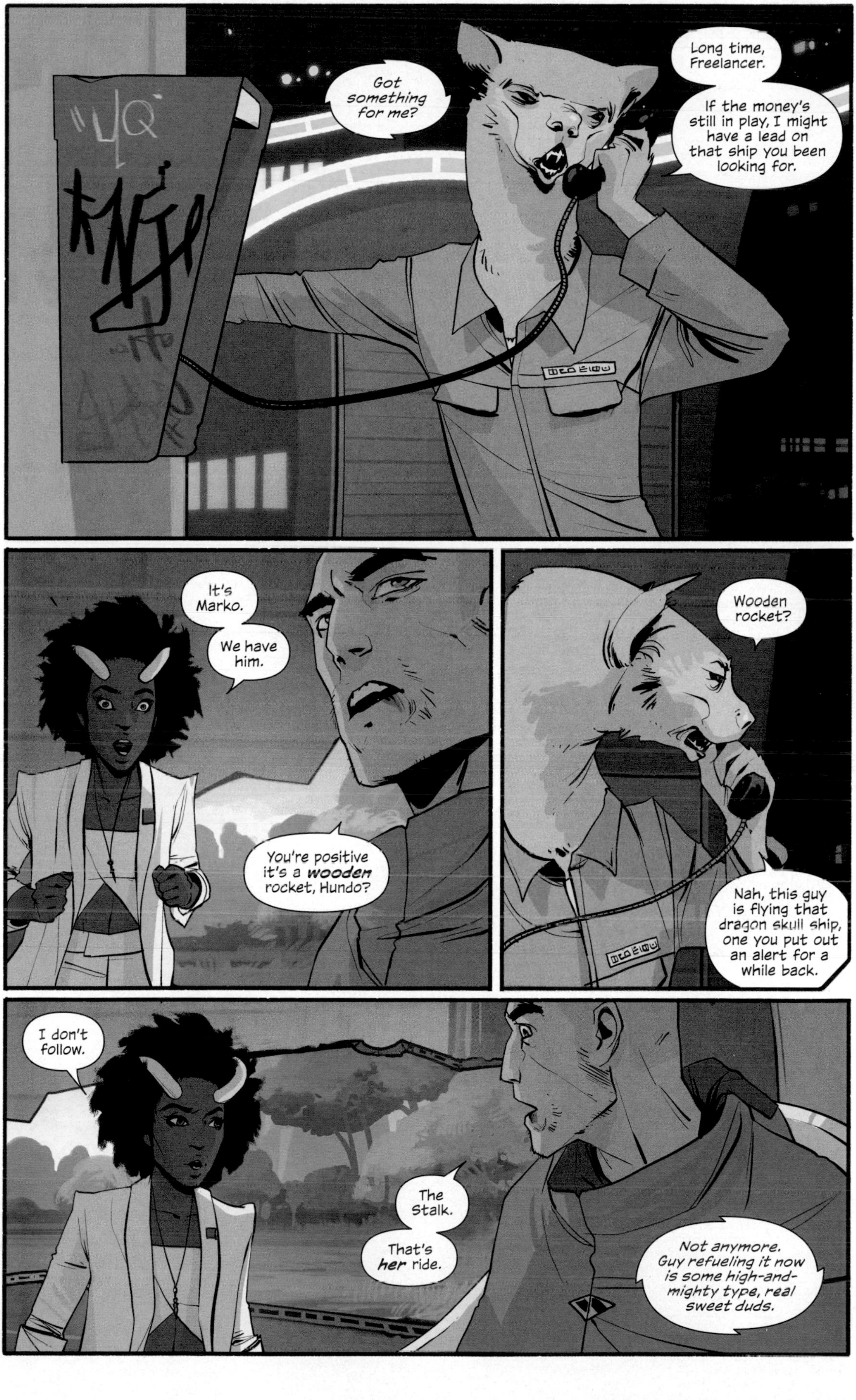
Got something for me?
Long time, Freelancer.
If the money's still in play, I might have a lead on that ship you been looking for.
It's Marko.
We have him.
You're positive it's a *wooden* rocket, Hundo?
Wooden rocket?
Nah, this guy is flying that dragon skull ship, one you put out an alert for a while back.
I don't follow.
The Stalk.
That's *her* ride.
Not anymore. Guy refueling it now is some high-and-mighty type, real sweet duds.

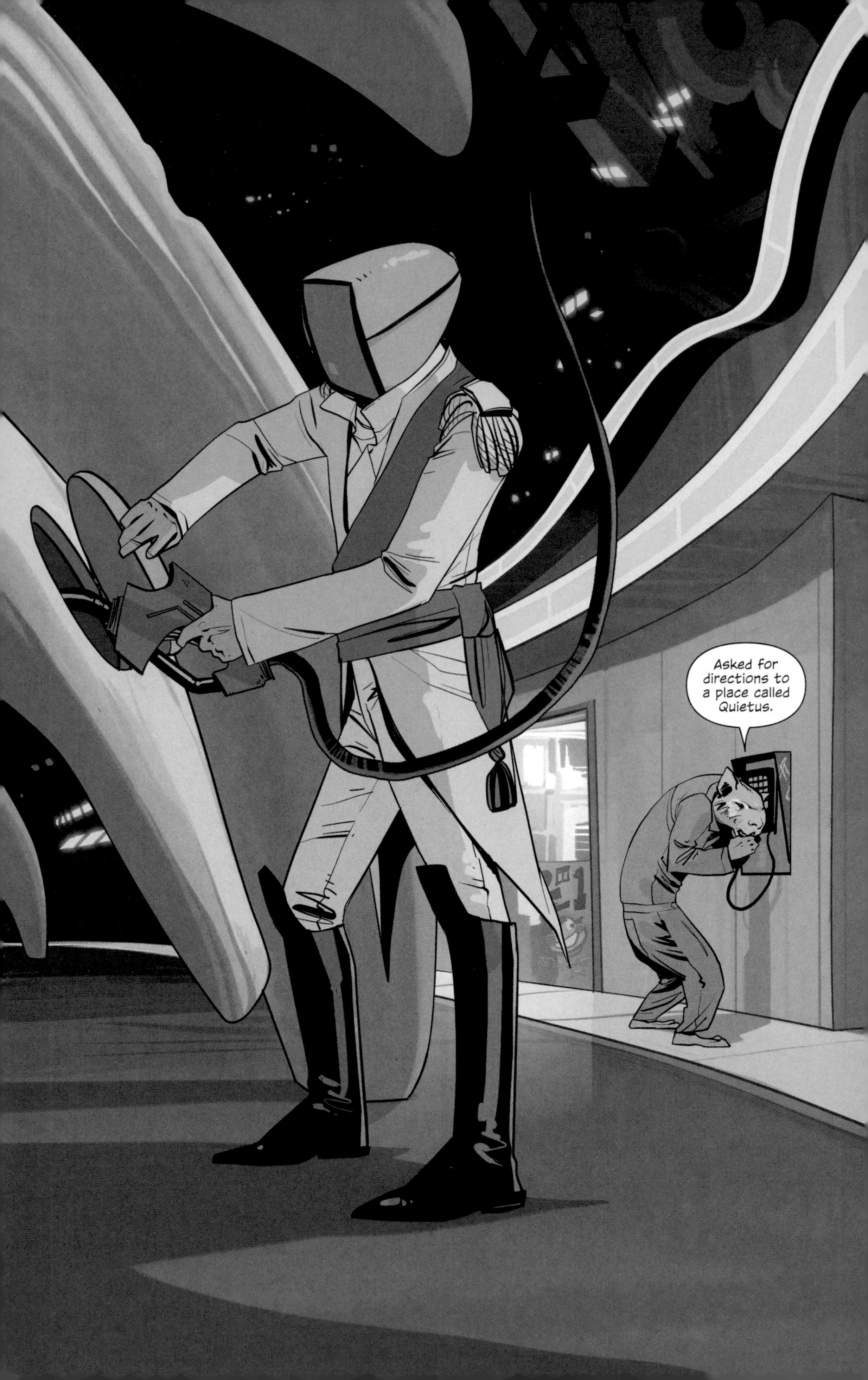
Asked for directions to a place called Quietus.

end chapter fourteen

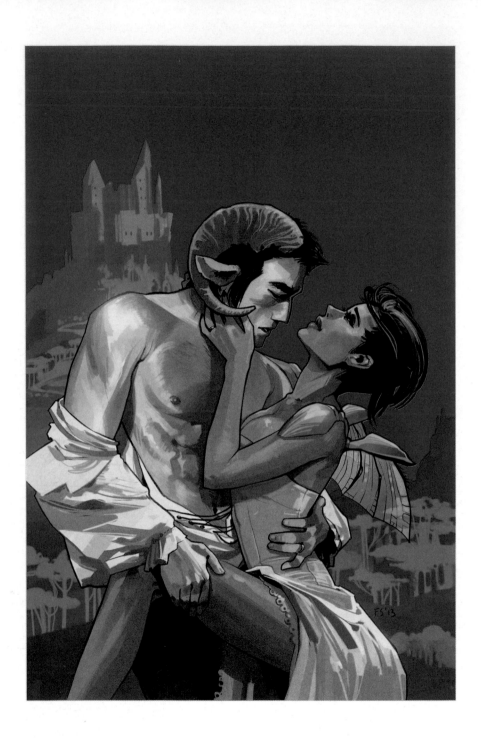

CHAPTER
FIFTEEN

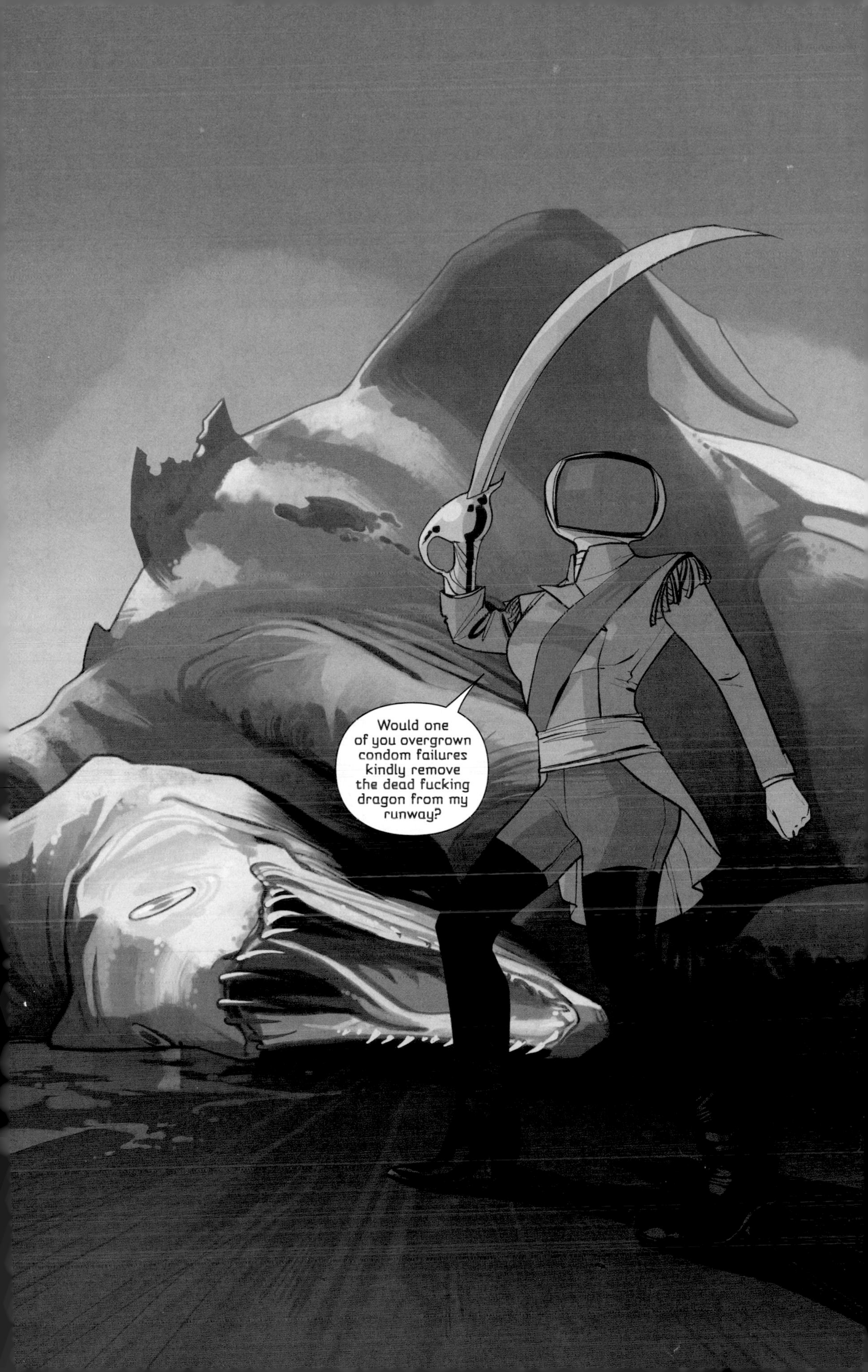
Would one of you overgrown condom failures kindly remove the dead fucking dragon from my runway?

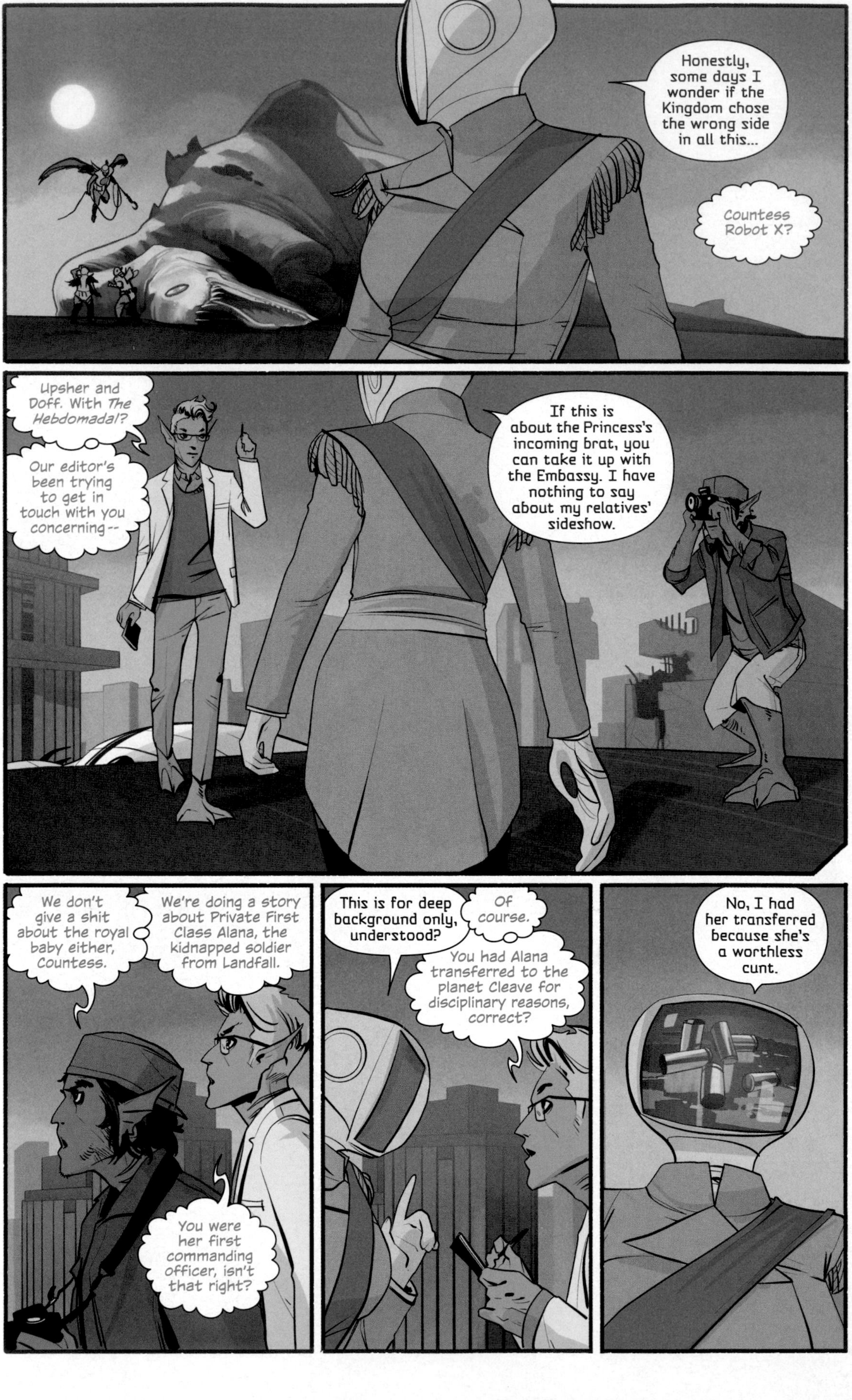

Honestly, some days I wonder if the Kingdom chose the wrong side in all this...
Countess Robot X?
Upsher and Doff. With *The Hebdomadal*?
Our editor's been trying to get in touch with you concerning--
If this is about the Princess's incoming brat, you can take it up with the Embassy. I have nothing to say about my relatives' sideshow.
We don't give a shit about the royal baby either, Countess.
We're doing a story about Private First Class Alana, the kidnapped soldier from Landfall.
You were her first commanding officer, isn't that right?
This is for deep background only, understood?
Of course.
You had Alana transferred to the planet Cleave for disciplinary reasons, correct?
No, I had her transferred because she's a worthless cunt.

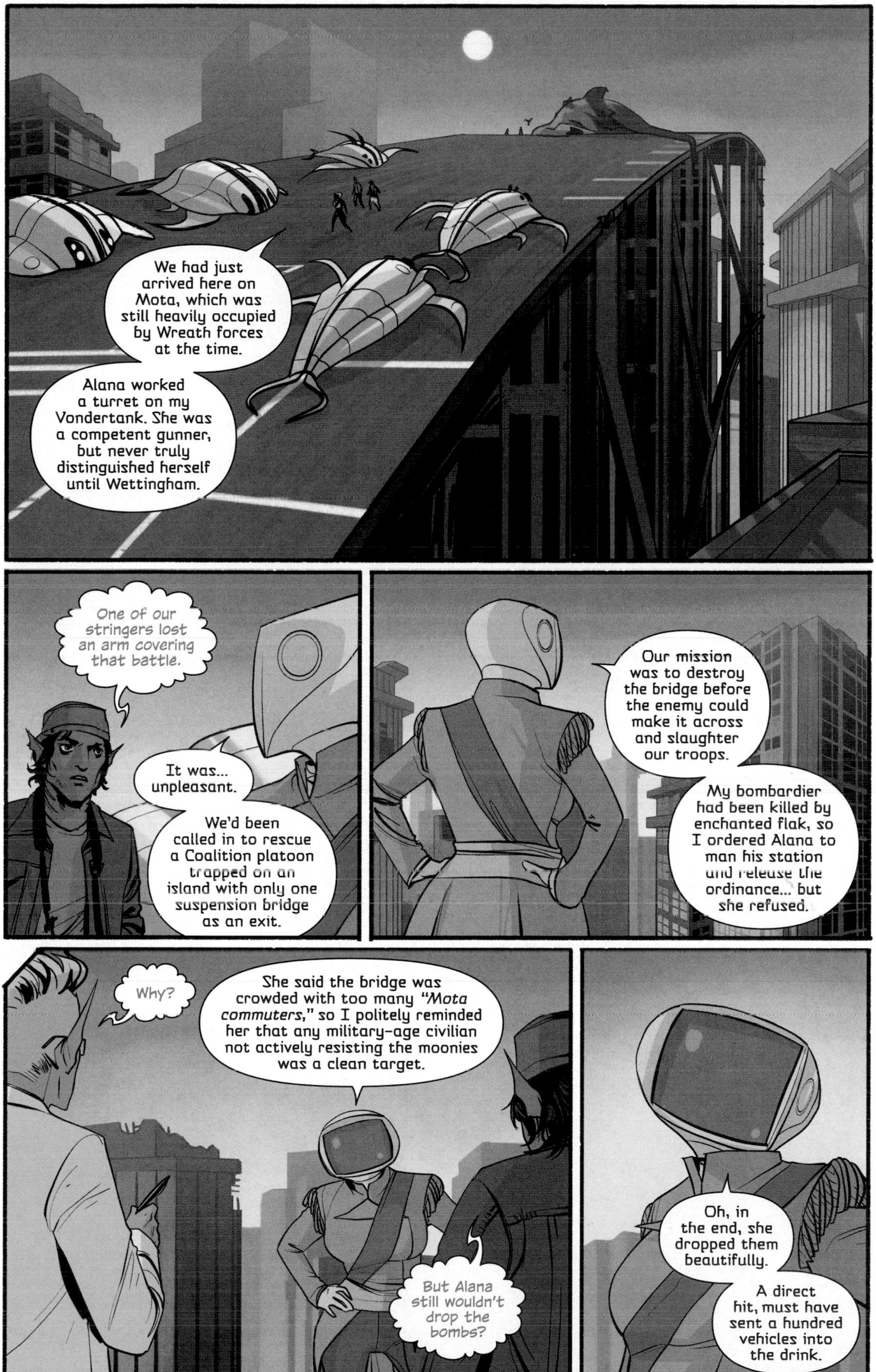
We had just arrived here on Mota, which was still heavily occupied by Wreath forces at the time.
Alana worked a turret on my Vondertank. She was a competent gunner, but never truly distinguished herself until Wettingham.
One of our stringers lost an arm covering that battle.
It was... unpleasant.
We'd been called in to rescue a Coalition platoon trapped on an island with only one suspension bridge as an exit.
Our mission was to destroy the bridge before the enemy could make it across and slaughter our troops.
My bombardier had been killed by enchanted flak, so I ordered Alana to man his station and release the ordinance... but she refused.
Why?
She said the bridge was crowded with too many *"Mota commuters,"* so I politely reminded her that any military-age civilian not actively resisting the moonies was a clean target.
But Alana still wouldn't drop the bombs?
Oh, in the end, she dropped them beautifully.
A direct hit, must have sent a hundred vehicles into the drink.

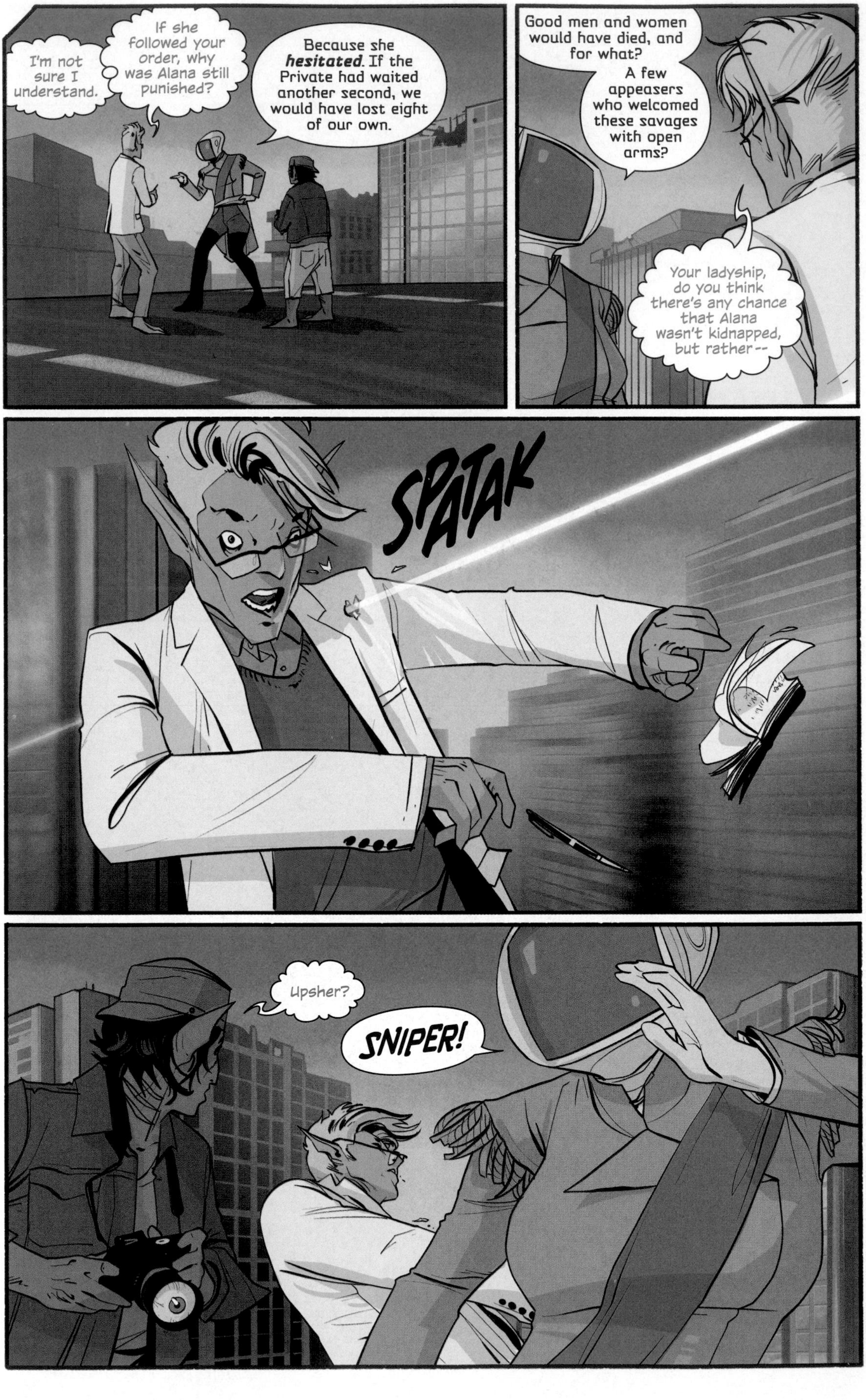
I'm not sure I understand.
If she followed your order, why was Alana still punished?
Because she ***hesitated***. If the Private had waited another second, we would have lost eight of our own.
Good men and women would have died, and for what?
A few appeasers who welcomed these savages with open arms?
Your ladyship, do you think there's any chance that Alana wasn't kidnapped, but rather--
SPATAK
Upsher?
SNIPER!

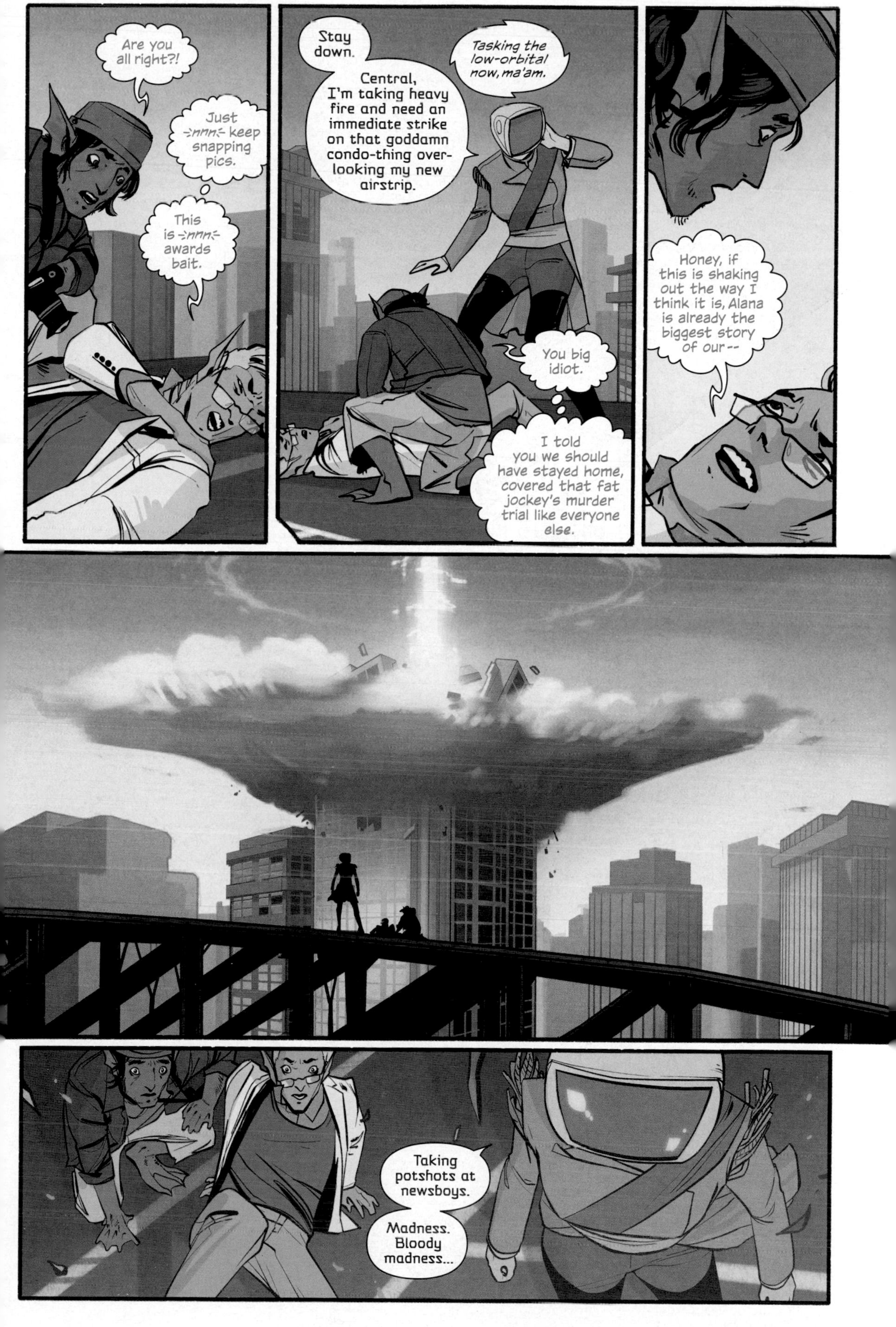
Are you all right?!
Just -nnn- keep snapping pics.
This is -nnn- awards bait.
Stay down.
Central, I'm taking heavy fire and need an immediate strike on that goddamn condo-thing over-looking my new airstrip.
Tasking the low-orbital now, ma'am.
You big idiot.
I told you we should have stayed home, covered that fat jockey's murder trial like everyone else.
Honey, if this is shaking out the way I think it is, Alana is already the biggest story of our--
Taking potshots at newsboys.
Madness. Bloody madness...

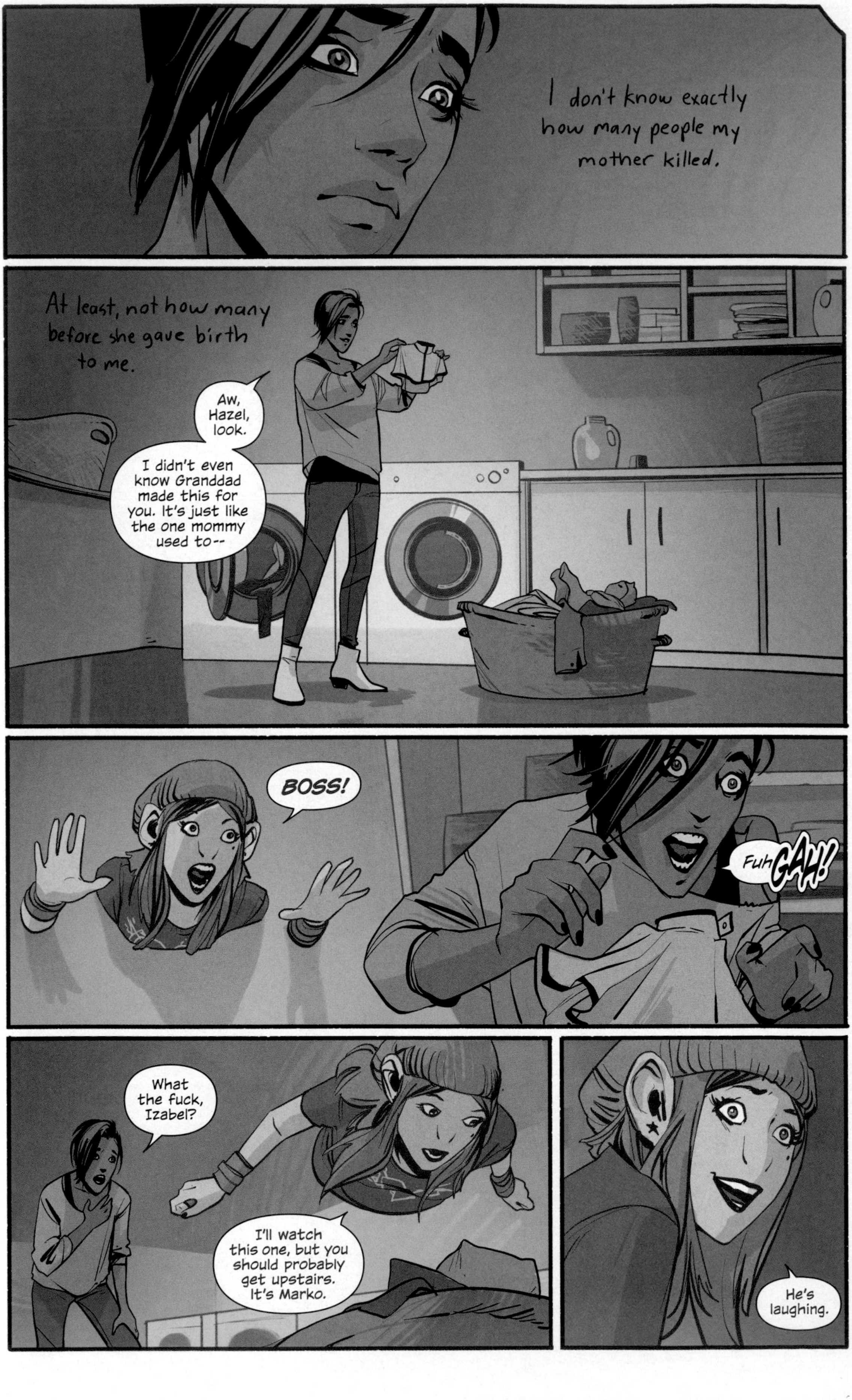
I don't know exactly how many people my mother killed.
At least, not how many before she gave birth to me.
Aw, Hazel, look.
I didn't even know Granddad made this for you. It's just like the one mommy used to--
BOSS!
FuhGAH!
What the fuck, Izabel?
I'll watch this one, but you should probably get upstairs. It's Marko.
He's laughing.

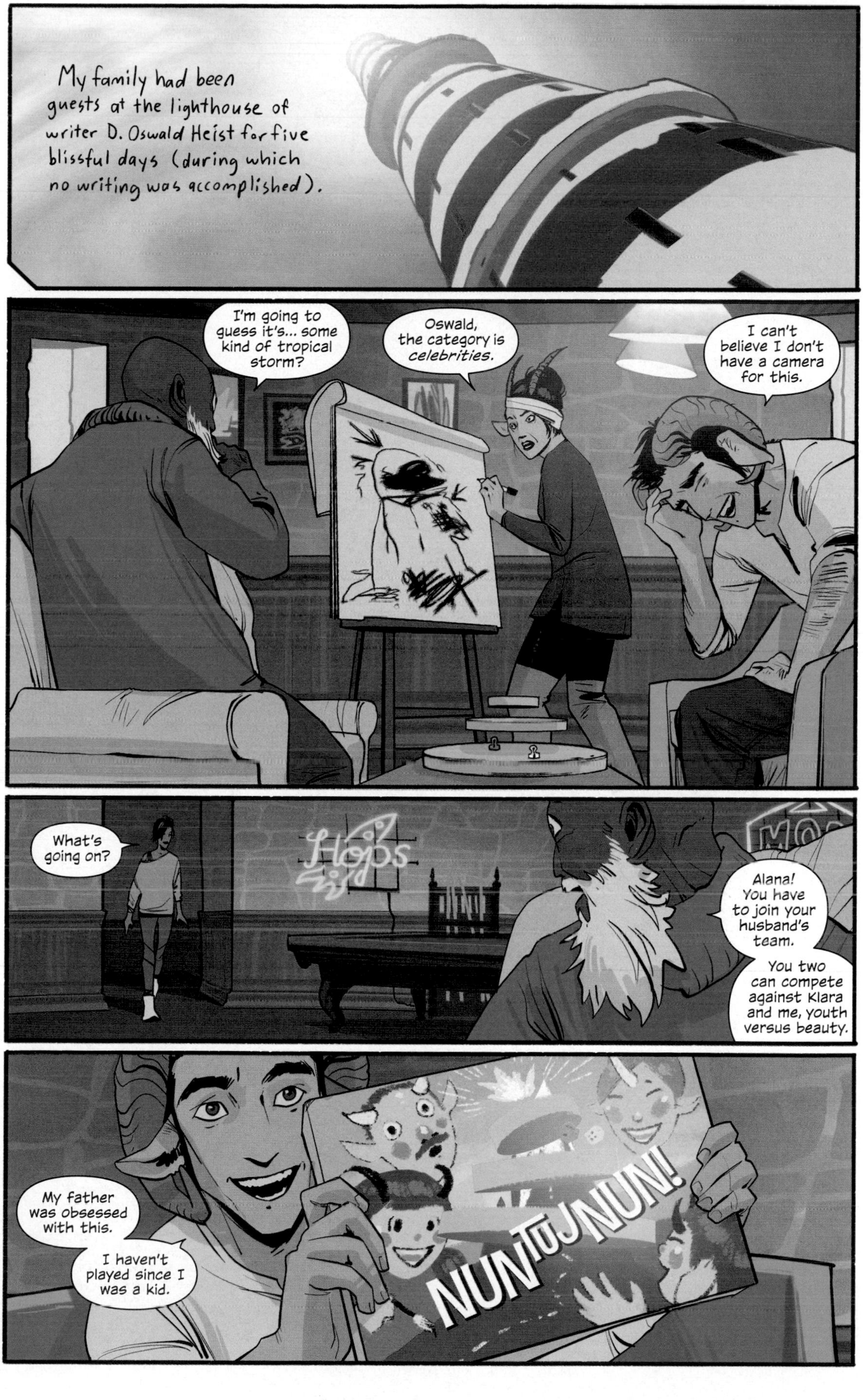
My family had been guests at the lighthouse of writer D. Oswald Heist for five blissful days (during which no writing was accomplished).
I'm going to guess it's... some kind of tropical storm?
Oswald, the category is *celebrities.*
I can't believe I don't have a camera for this.
What's going on?
Alana! You have to join your husband's team.
You two can compete against Klara and me, youth versus beauty.
My father was obsessed with this.
I haven't played since I was a kid.
NUN TU NUN!

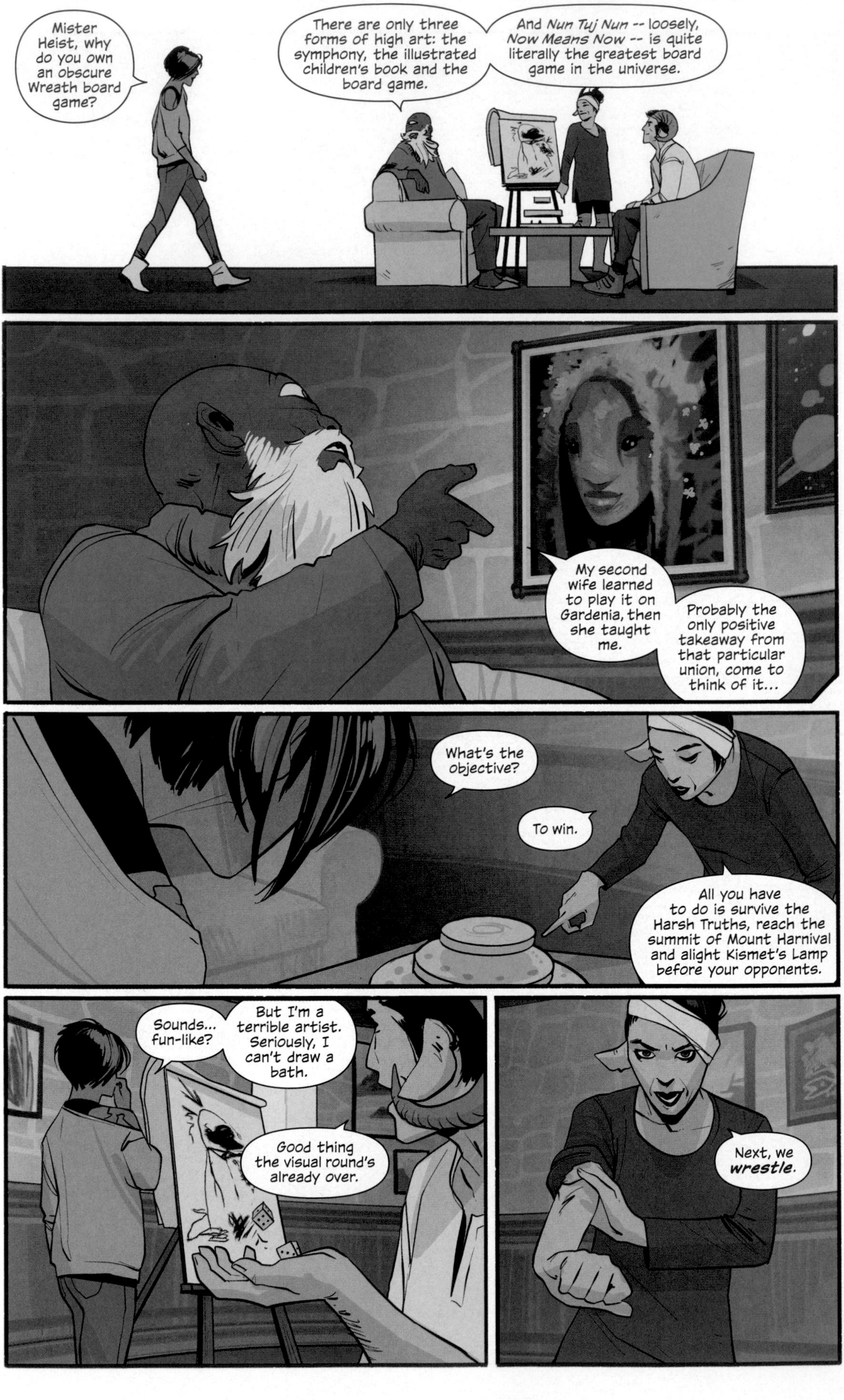
Mister Heist, why do you own an obscure Wreath board game?
There are only three forms of high art: the symphony, the illustrated children's book and the board game.
And *Nun Tuj Nun* -- loosely, *Now Means Now* -- is quite literally the greatest board game in the universe.
My second wife learned to play it on Gardenia, then she taught me.
Probably the only positive takeaway from that particular union, come to think of it...
What's the objective?
To win.
All you have to do is survive the Harsh Truths, reach the summit of Mount Harnival and alight Kismet's Lamp before your opponents.
Sounds... fun-like?
But I'm a terrible artist. Seriously, I can't draw a bath.
Good thing the visual round's already over.
Next, we ***wrestle***.

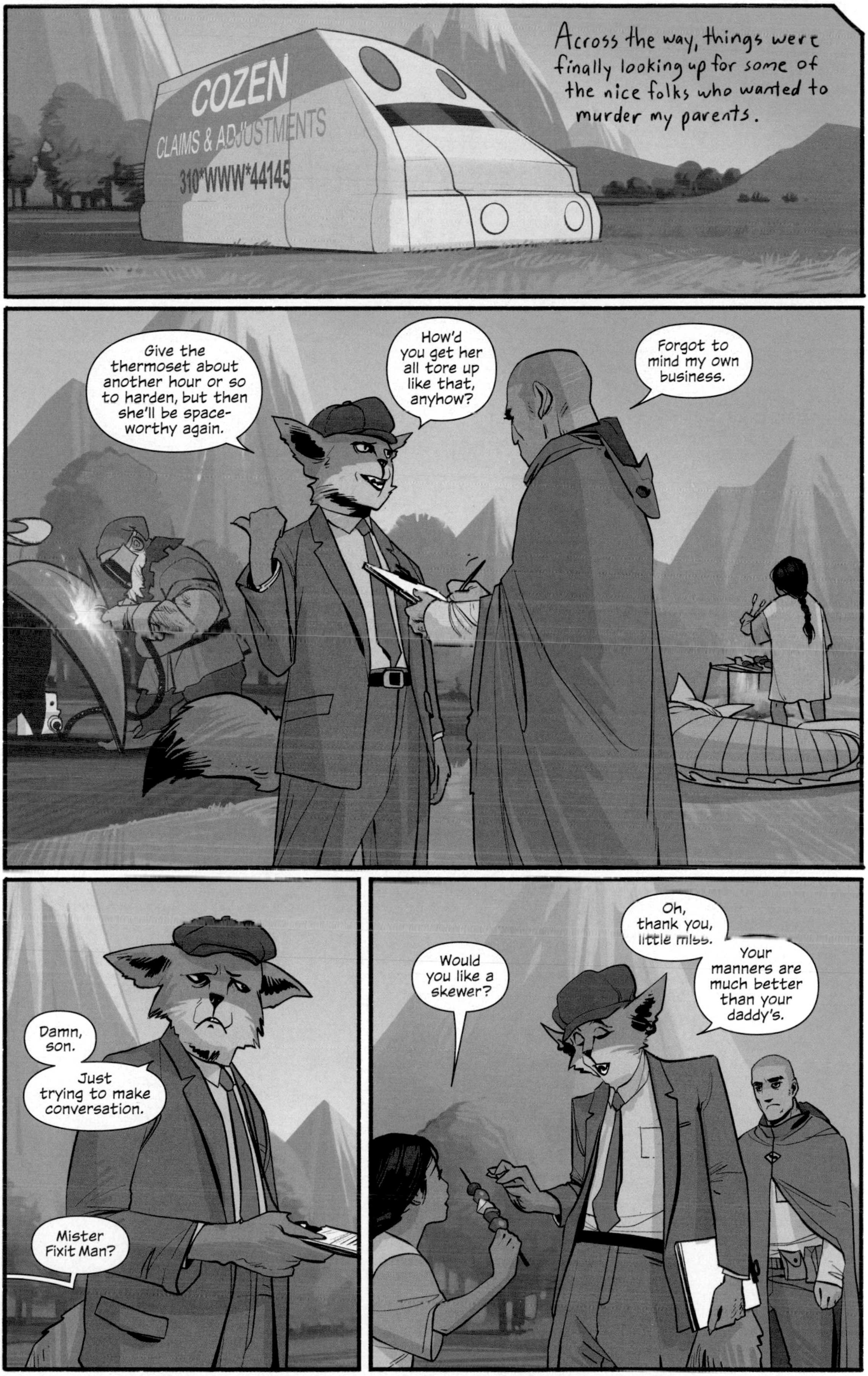

COZEN
CLAIMS & ADJUSTMENTS
310*WWW*44145
Across the way, things were finally looking up for some of the nice folks who wanted to murder my parents.
Give the thermoset about another hour or so to harden, but then she'll be space-worthy again.
How'd you get her all tore up like that, anyhow?
Forgot to mind my own business.
Damn, son.
Just trying to make conversation.
Mister Fixit Man?
Would you like a skewer?
Oh, thank you, little miss.
Your manners are much better than your daddy's.

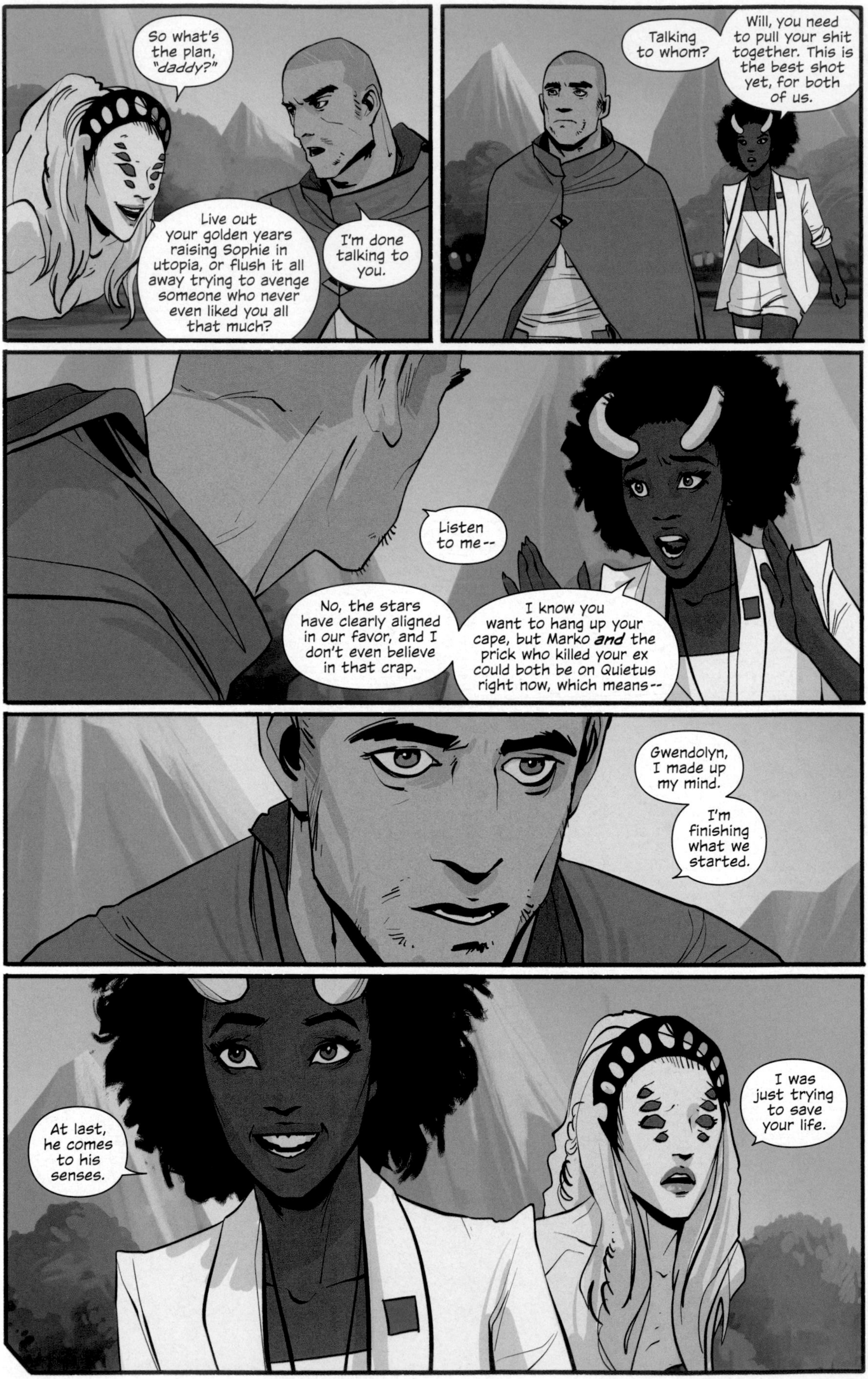
So what's the plan, "daddy?"
Live out your golden years raising Sophie in utopia, or flush it all away trying to avenge someone who never even liked you all that much?
I'm done talking to you.
Talking to whom?
Will, you need to pull your shit together. This is the best shot yet, for both of us.
Listen to me--
No, the stars have clearly aligned in our favor, and I don't even believe in that crap.
I know you want to hang up your cape, but Marko *and* the prick who killed your ex could both be on Quietus right now, which means--
Gwendolyn, I made up my mind.
I'm finishing what we started.
At last, he comes to his senses.
I was just trying to save your life.

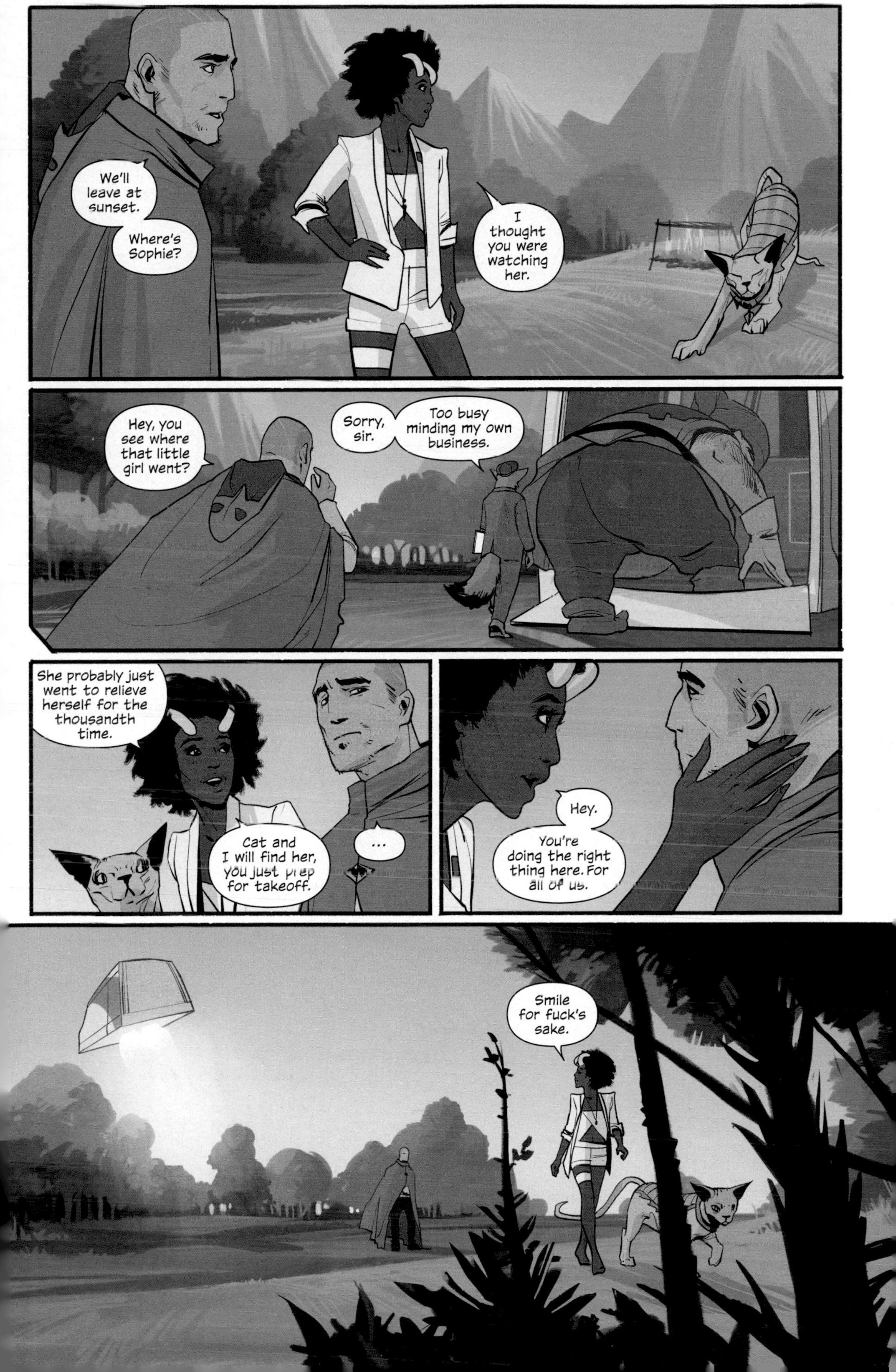

We'll leave at sunset.
Where's Sophie?
I thought you were watching her.
Hey, you see where that little girl went?
Sorry, sir.
Too busy minding my own business.
She probably just went to relieve herself for the thousandth time.
Cat and I will find her, you just prep for takeoff.
...
Hey.
You're doing the right thing here. For all of us.
Smile for fuck's sake.

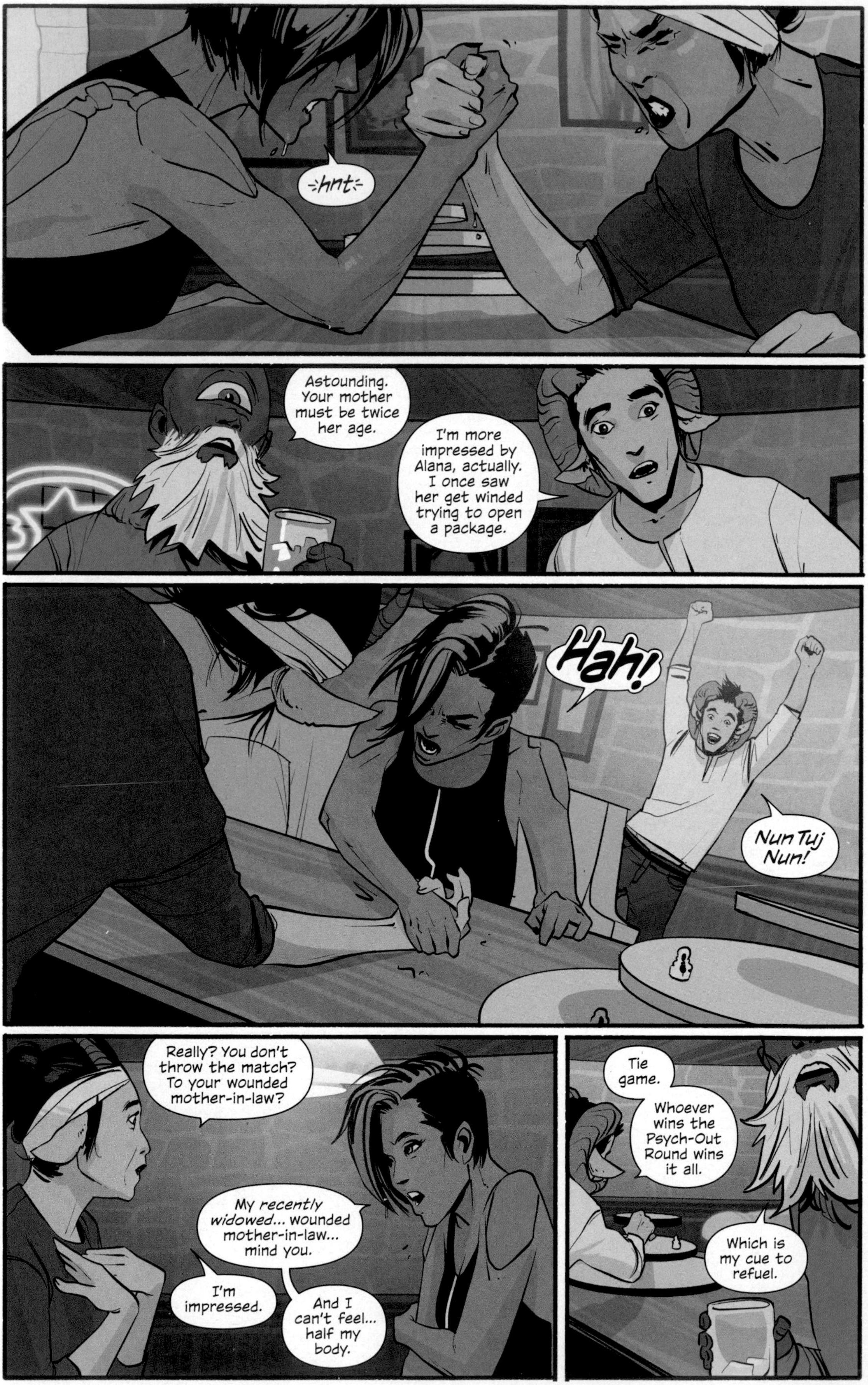
hnt
Astounding. Your mother must be twice her age.
I'm more impressed by Alana, actually. I once saw her get winded trying to open a package.
Hah!
Nun Tuj Nun!
Really? You don't throw the match? To your wounded mother-in-law?
My *recently widowed*... wounded mother-in-law... mind you.
I'm impressed.
And I can't feel... half my body.
Tie game.
Whoever wins the Psych-Out Round wins it all.
Which is my cue to refuel.

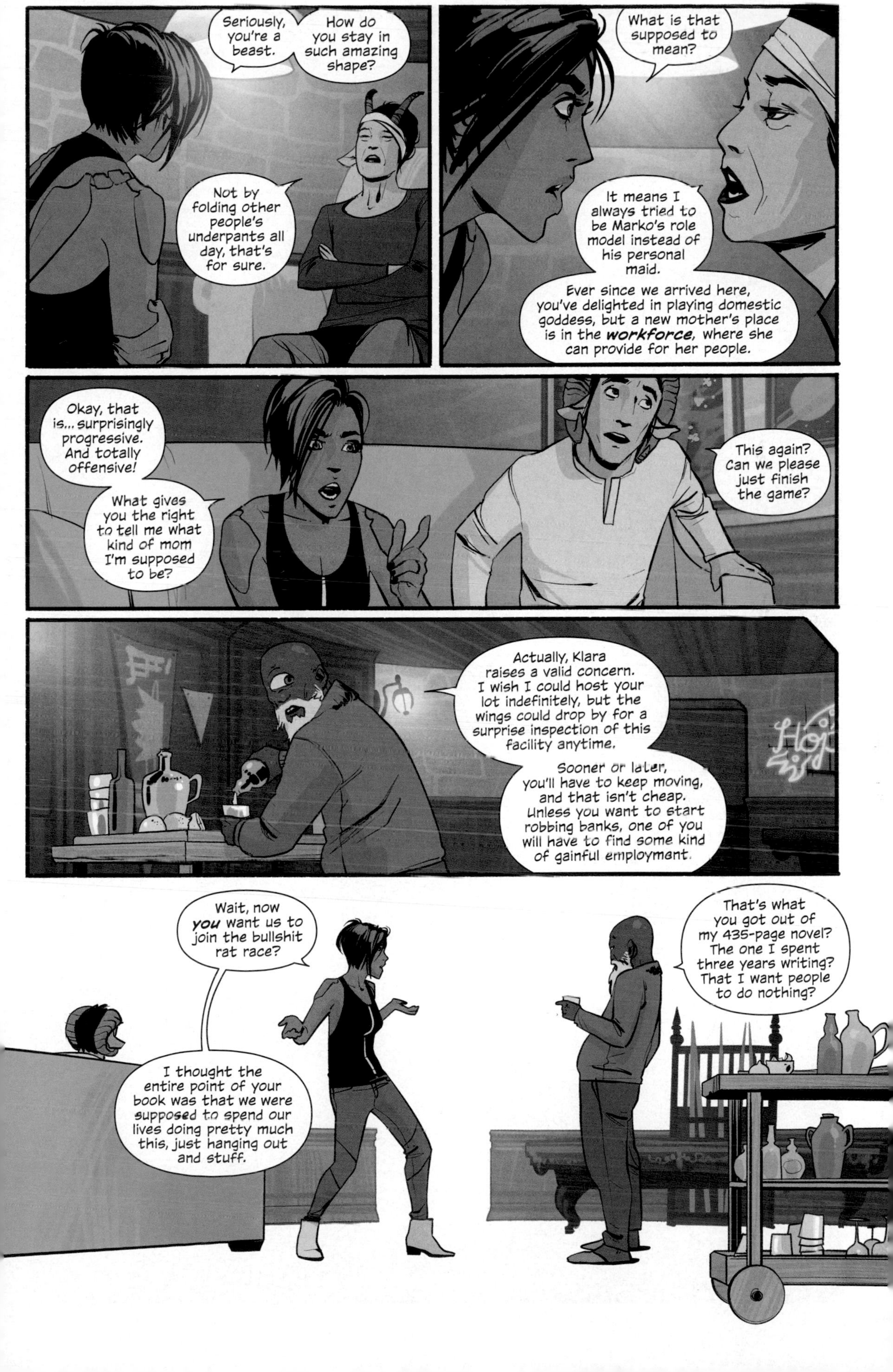
Seriously, you're a beast.
How do you stay in such amazing shape?
Not by folding other people's underpants all day, that's for sure.
What is that supposed to mean?
It means I always tried to be Marko's role model instead of his personal maid.
Ever since we arrived here, you've delighted in playing domestic goddess, but a new mother's place is in the *workforce*, where she can provide for her people.
Okay, that is... surprisingly progressive. And totally offensive!
What gives you the right to tell me what kind of mom I'm supposed to be?
This again? Can we please just finish the game?
Actually, Klara raises a valid concern. I wish I could host your lot indefinitely, but the wings could drop by for a surprise inspection of this facility anytime.
Sooner or later, you'll have to keep moving, and that isn't cheap. Unless you want to start robbing banks, one of you will have to find some kind of gainful employment.
Wait, now *you* want us to join the bullshit rat race?
I thought the entire point of your book was that we were supposed to spend our lives doing pretty much this, just hanging out and stuff.
That's what you got out of my 435-page novel? The one I spent three years writing? That I want people to do nothing?

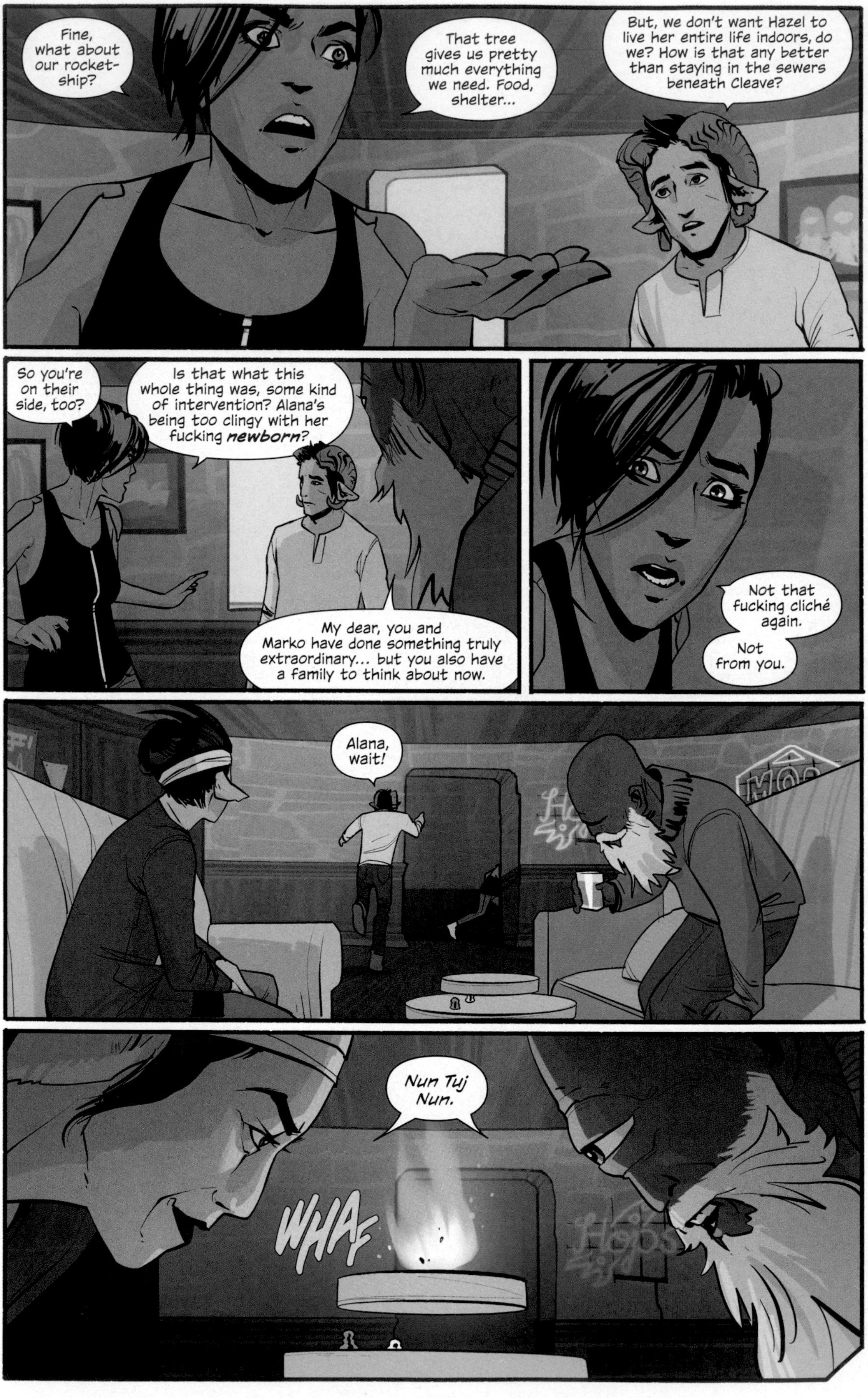
Fine, what about our rocket-ship?
That tree gives us pretty much everything we need. Food, shelter...
But, we don't want Hazel to live her entire life indoors, do we? How is that any better than staying in the sewers beneath Cleave?
So you're on their side, too?
Is that what this whole thing was, some kind of intervention? Alana's being too clingy with her fucking ***newborn***?
My dear, you and Marko have done something truly extraordinary... but you also have a family to think about now.
Not that fucking cliché again.
Not from you.
Alana, wait!
Nun Tuj Nun.
WHAF

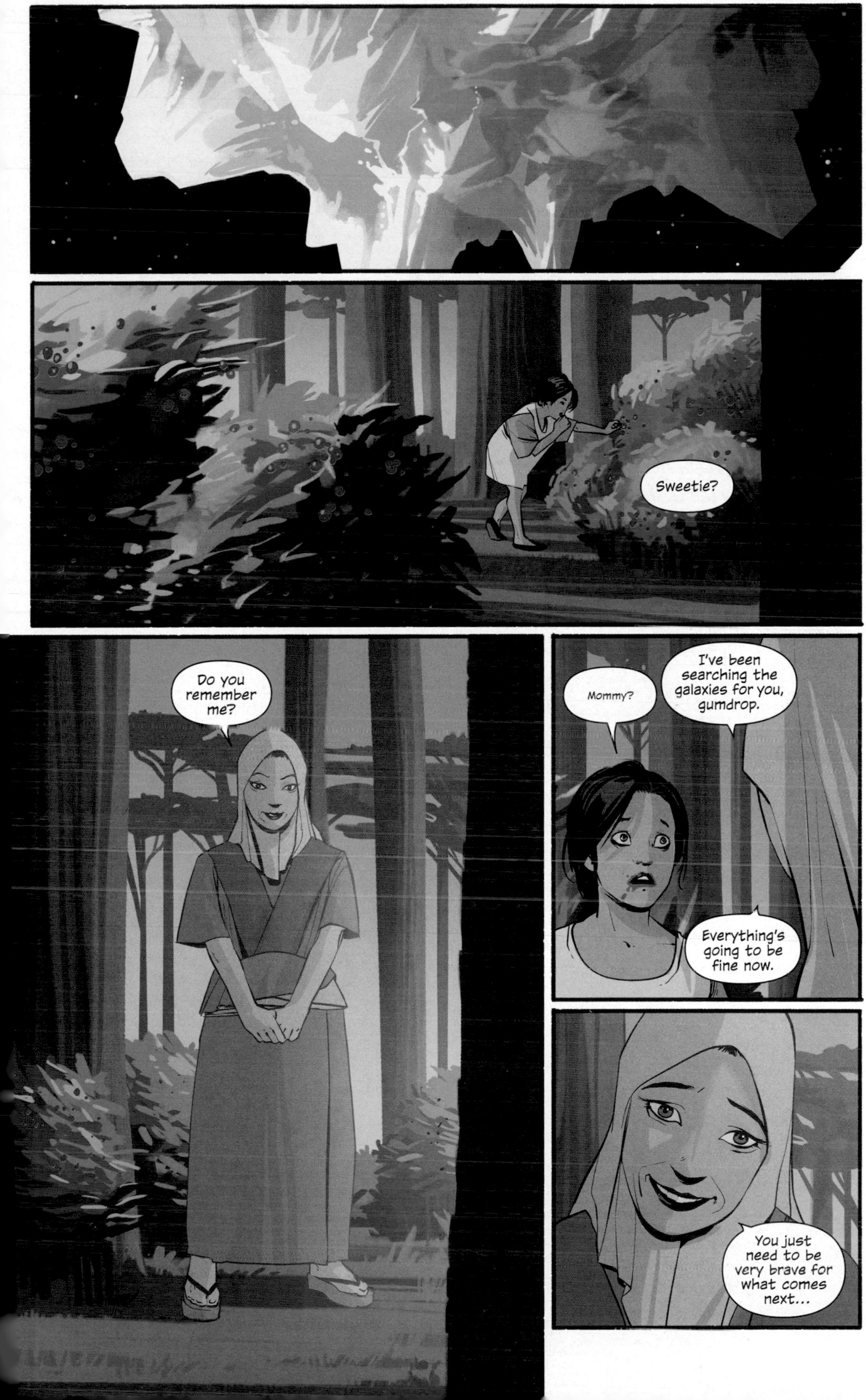

Sweetie?
Do you remember me?
Mommy?
I've been searching the galaxies for you, gumdrop.
Everything's going to be fine now.
You just need to be very brave for what comes next...

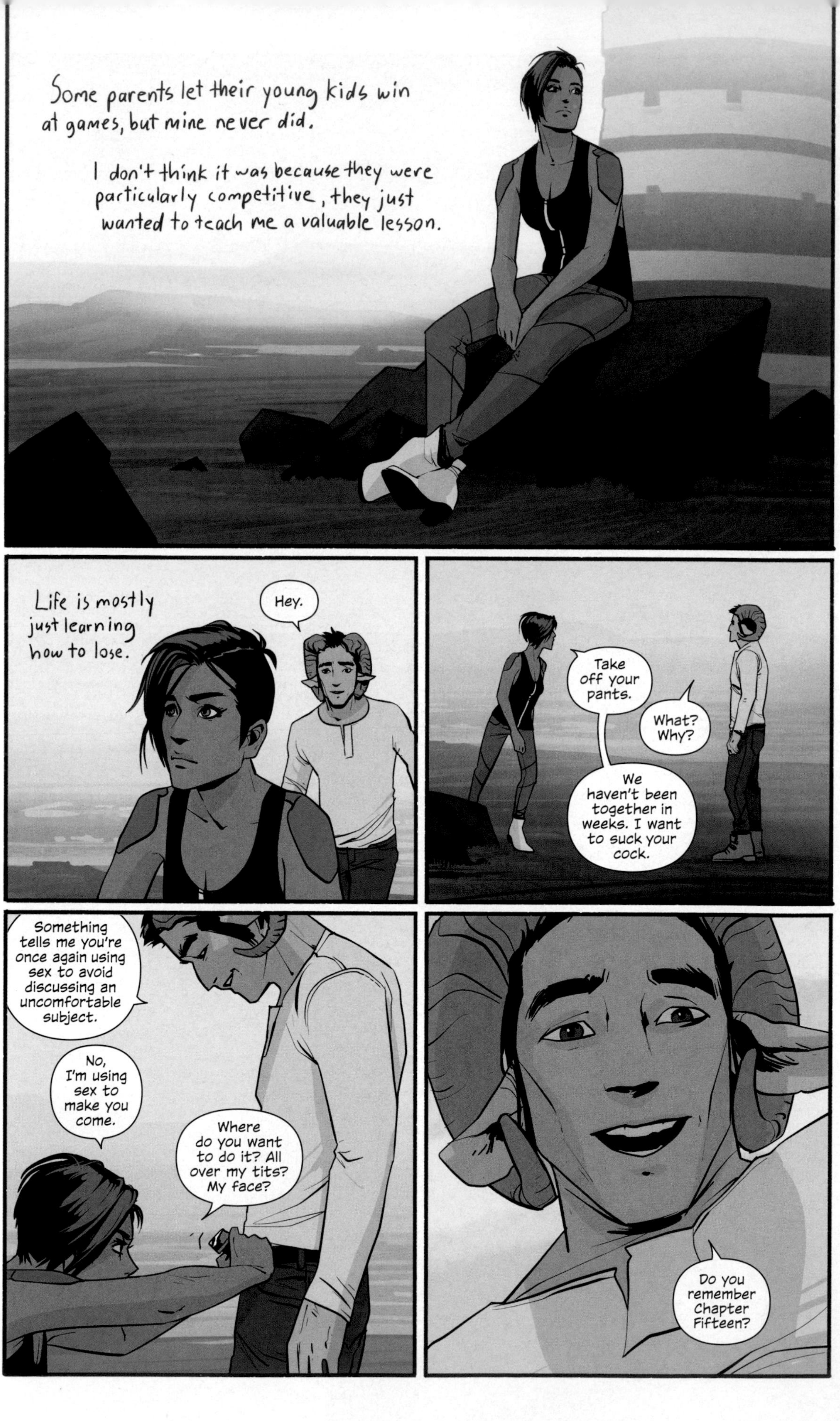
Some parents let their young kids win at games, but mine never did.
I don't think it was because they were particularly competitive, they just wanted to teach me a valuable lesson.
Life is mostly just learning how to lose.
Hey.
Take off your pants.
What? Why?
We haven't been together in weeks. I want to suck your cock.
Something tells me you're once again using sex to avoid discussing an uncomfortable subject.
No, I'm using sex to make you come.
Where do you want to do it? All over my tits? My face?
Do you remember Chapter Fifteen?

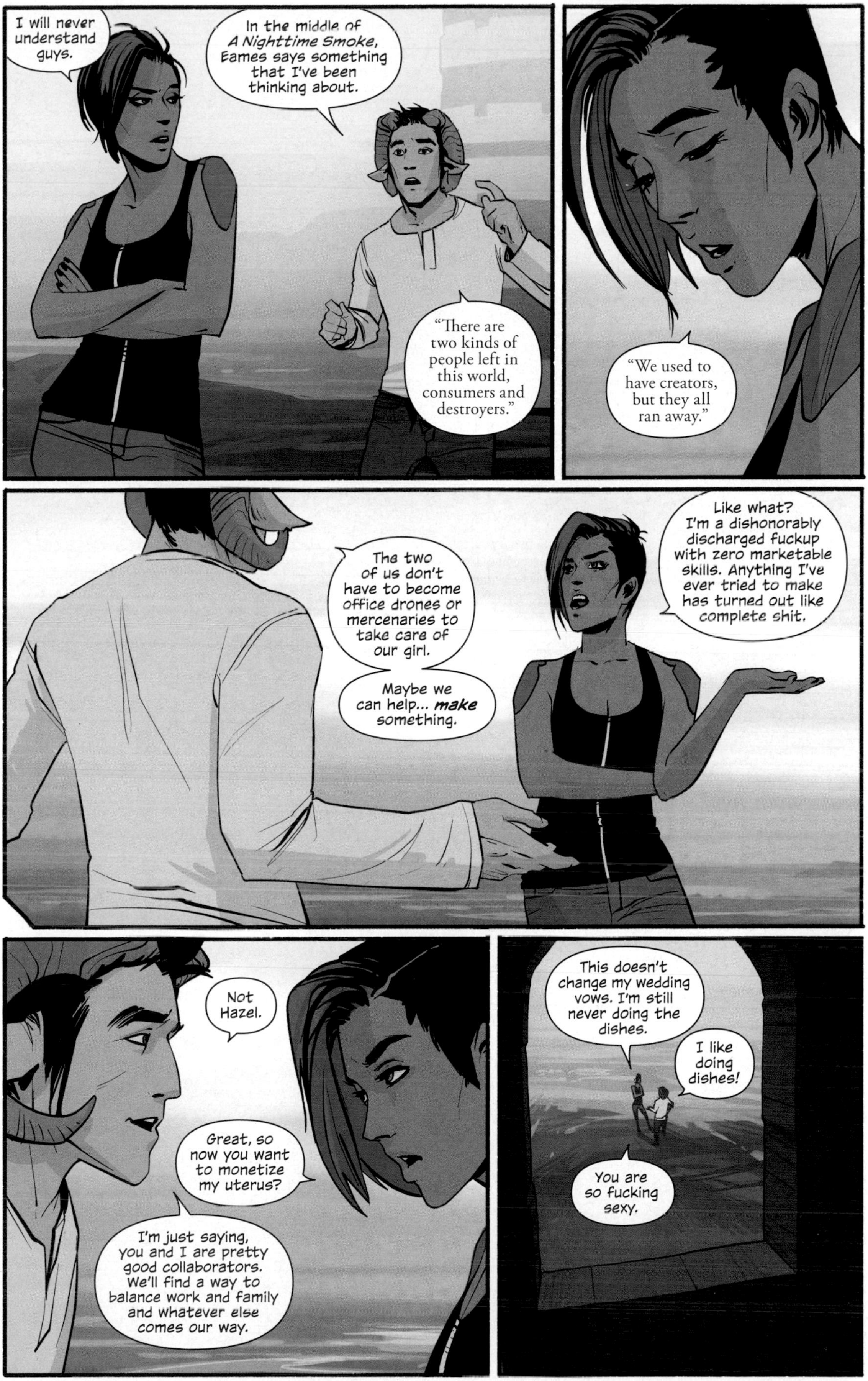
I will never understand guys.
In the middle of *A Nighttime Smoke*, Eames says something that I've been thinking about.
"There are two kinds of people left in this world, consumers and destroyers."
"We used to have creators, but they all ran away."
The two of us don't have to become office drones or mercenaries to take care of our girl.
Maybe we can help... ***make*** something.
Like what? I'm a dishonorably discharged fuckup with zero marketable skills. Anything I've ever tried to make has turned out like complete shit.
Not Hazel.
Great, so now you want to monetize my uterus?
I'm just saying, you and I are pretty good collaborators. We'll find a way to balance work and family and whatever else comes our way.
This doesn't change my wedding vows. I'm still never doing the dishes.
I like doing dishes!
You are so fucking sexy.

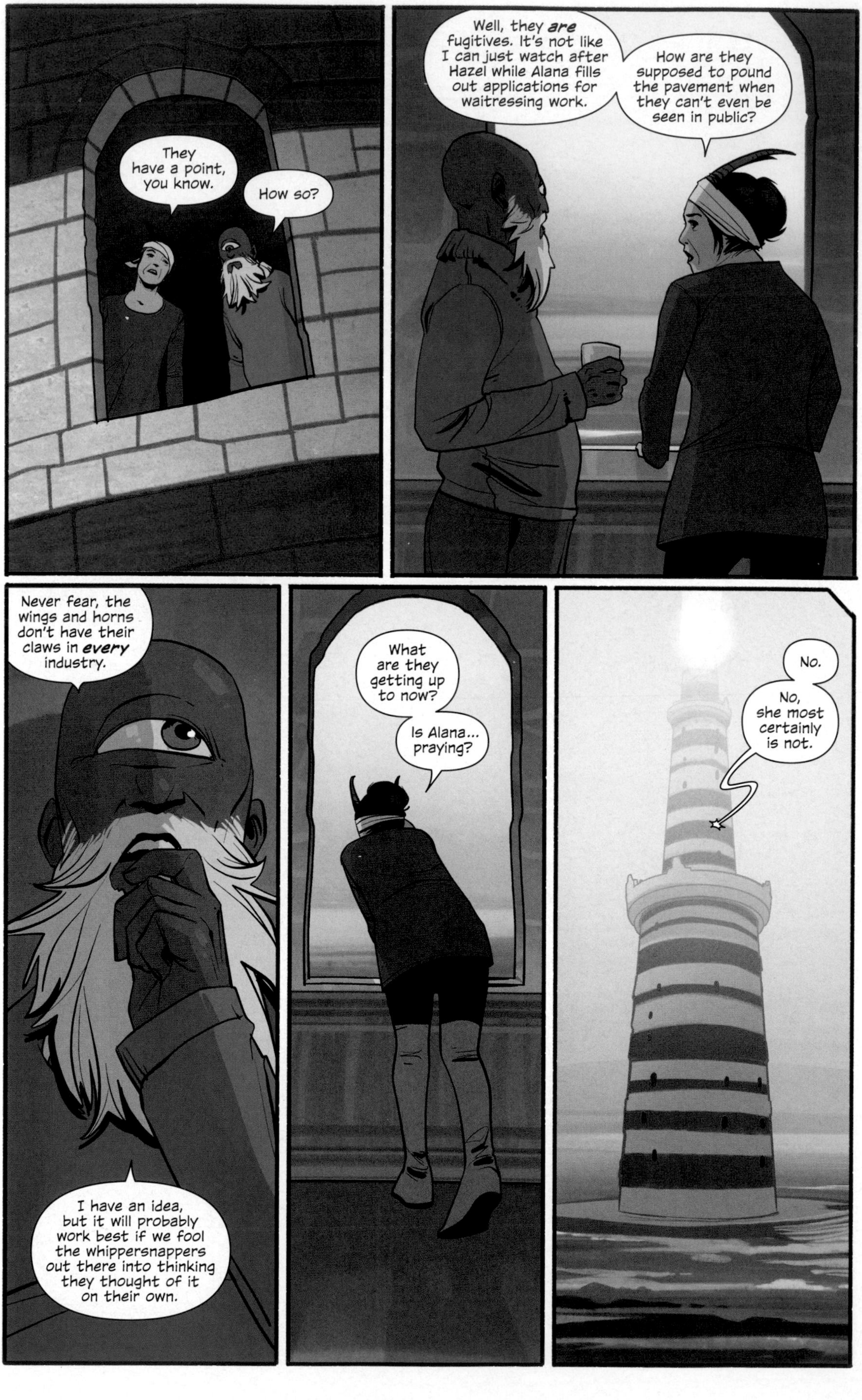
They have a point, you know.
How so?
Well, they *are* fugitives. It's not like I can just watch after Hazel while Alana fills out applications for waitressing work.
How are they supposed to pound the pavement when they can't even be seen in public?
Never fear, the wings and horns don't have their claws in *every* industry.
I have an idea, but it will probably work best if we fool the whippersnappers out there into thinking they thought of it on their own.
What are they getting up to now?
Is Alana... praying?
No.
No, she most certainly is not.

Gwen? You back yet?

Incoming call from... Cozen Claims & Adjustments.

I don't have time to take your damn customer satisfaction survey so--

Sorry to bother, sir, but would you happen to know if our employees ate any native meat or produce while assisting you?

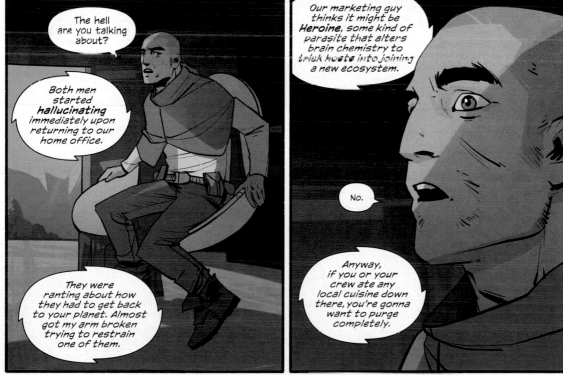

The hell are you talking about?

Both men started **hallucinating** immediately upon returning to our home office.

They were ranting about how they had to get back to your planet. Almost got my arm broken trying to restrain one of them.

Our marketing guy thinks it might be **Heroine**, some kind of parasite that alters brain chemistry to trick hosts into joining a new ecosystem.

No.

Anyway, if you or your crew ate any local cuisine down there, you're gonna want to purge completely.

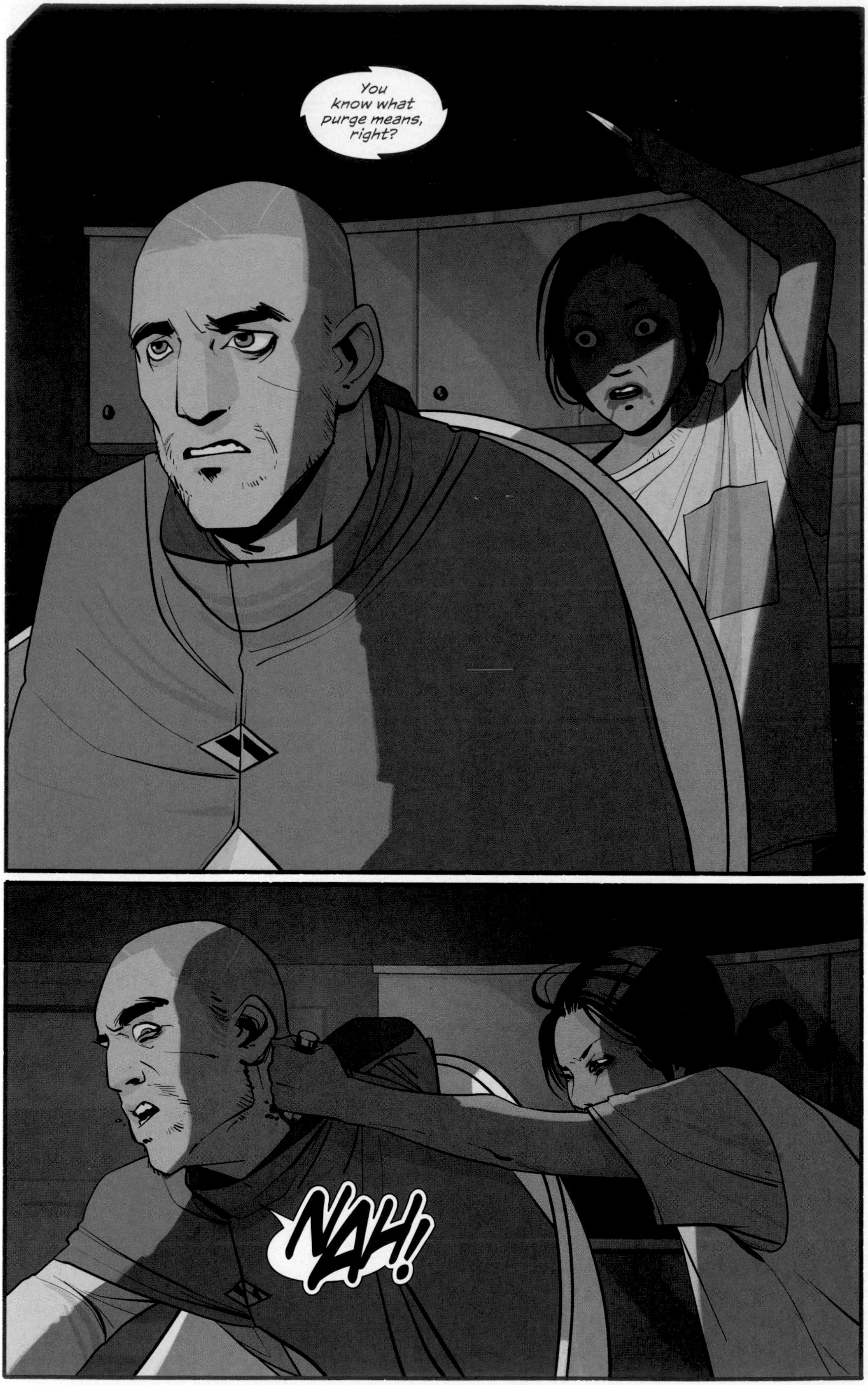
You know what purge means, right?
NAH!

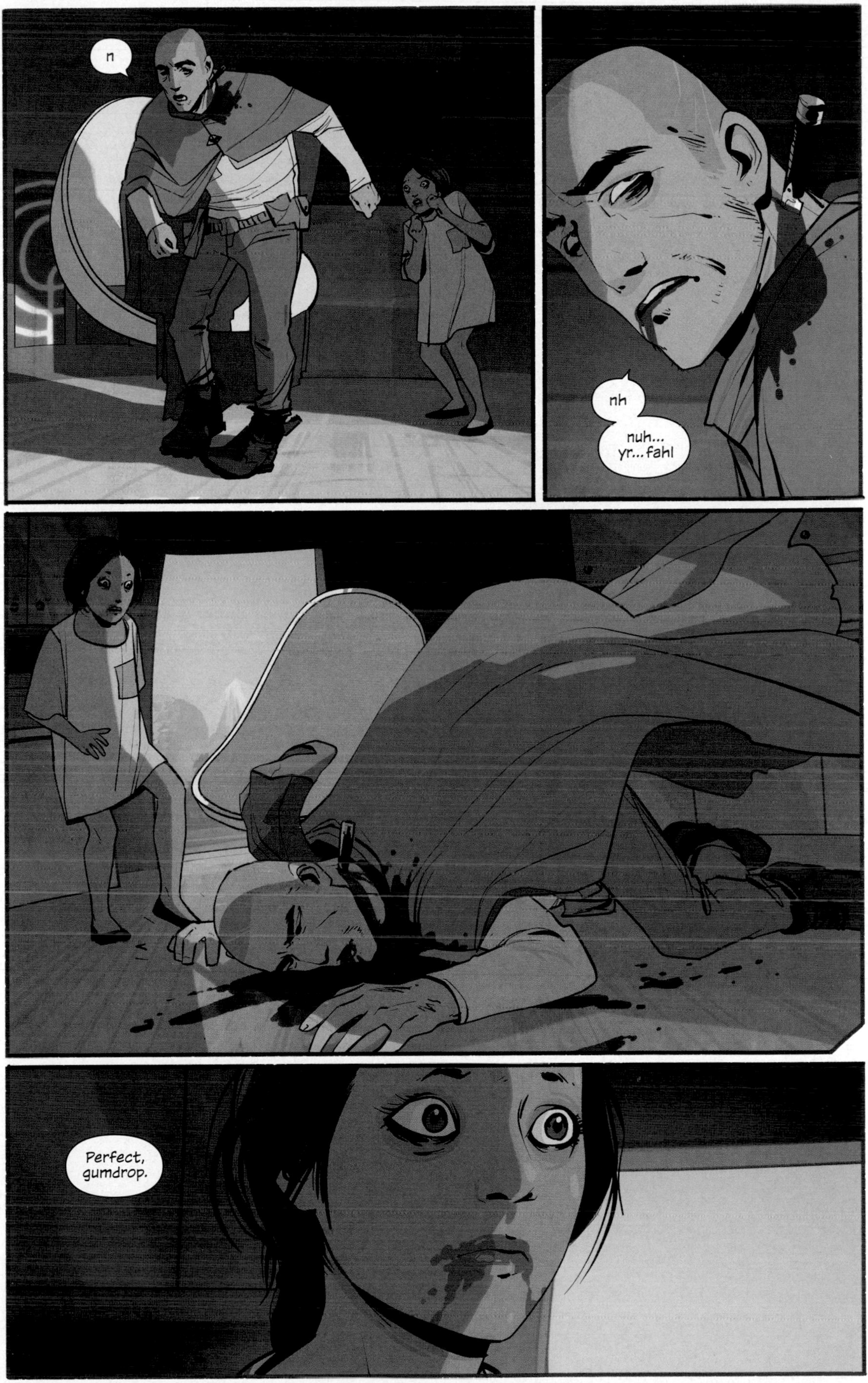
n
nh
nuh... yr...fahl
Perfect, gumdrop.

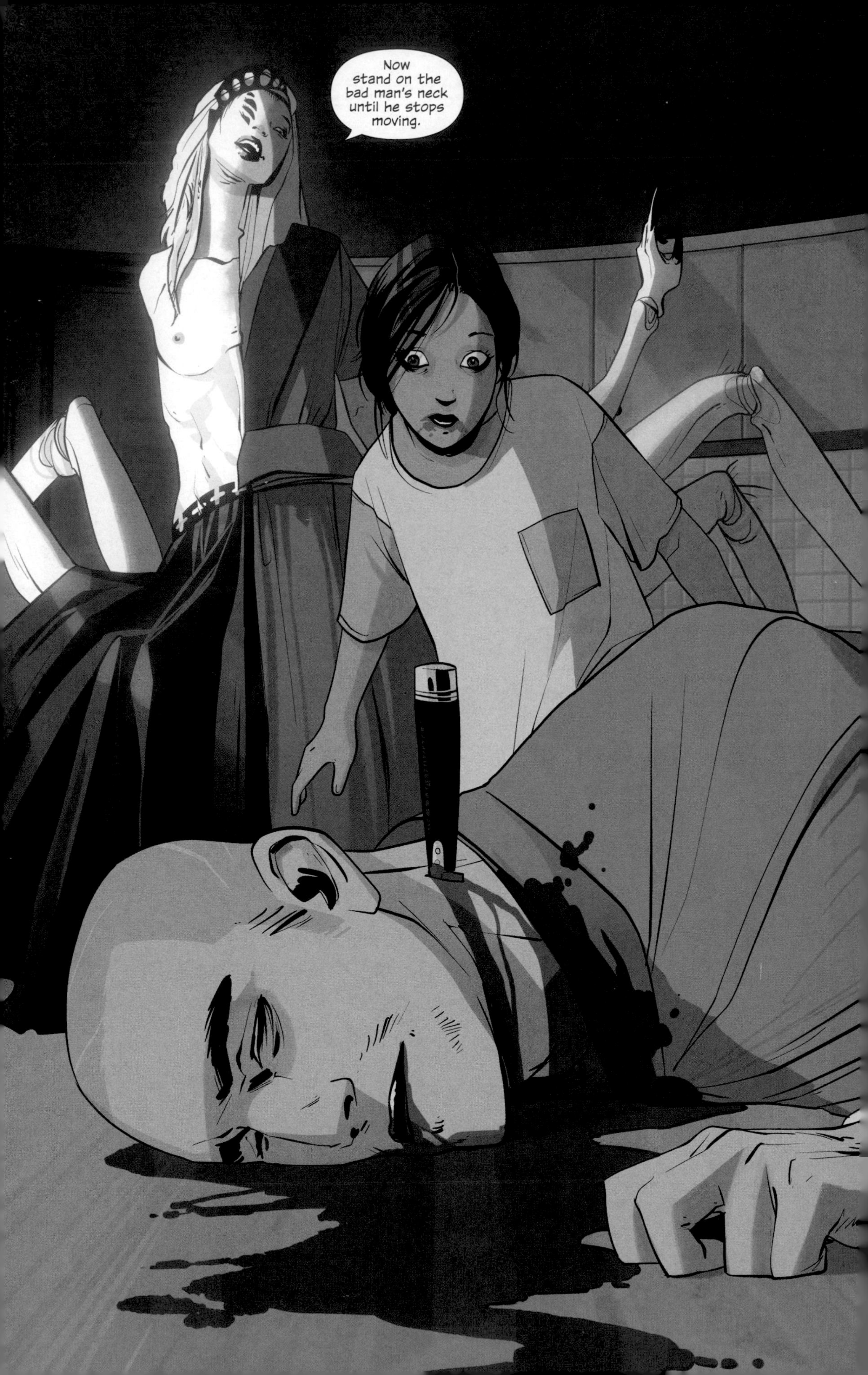
Now stand on the bad man's neck until he stops moving.

end chapter fifteen

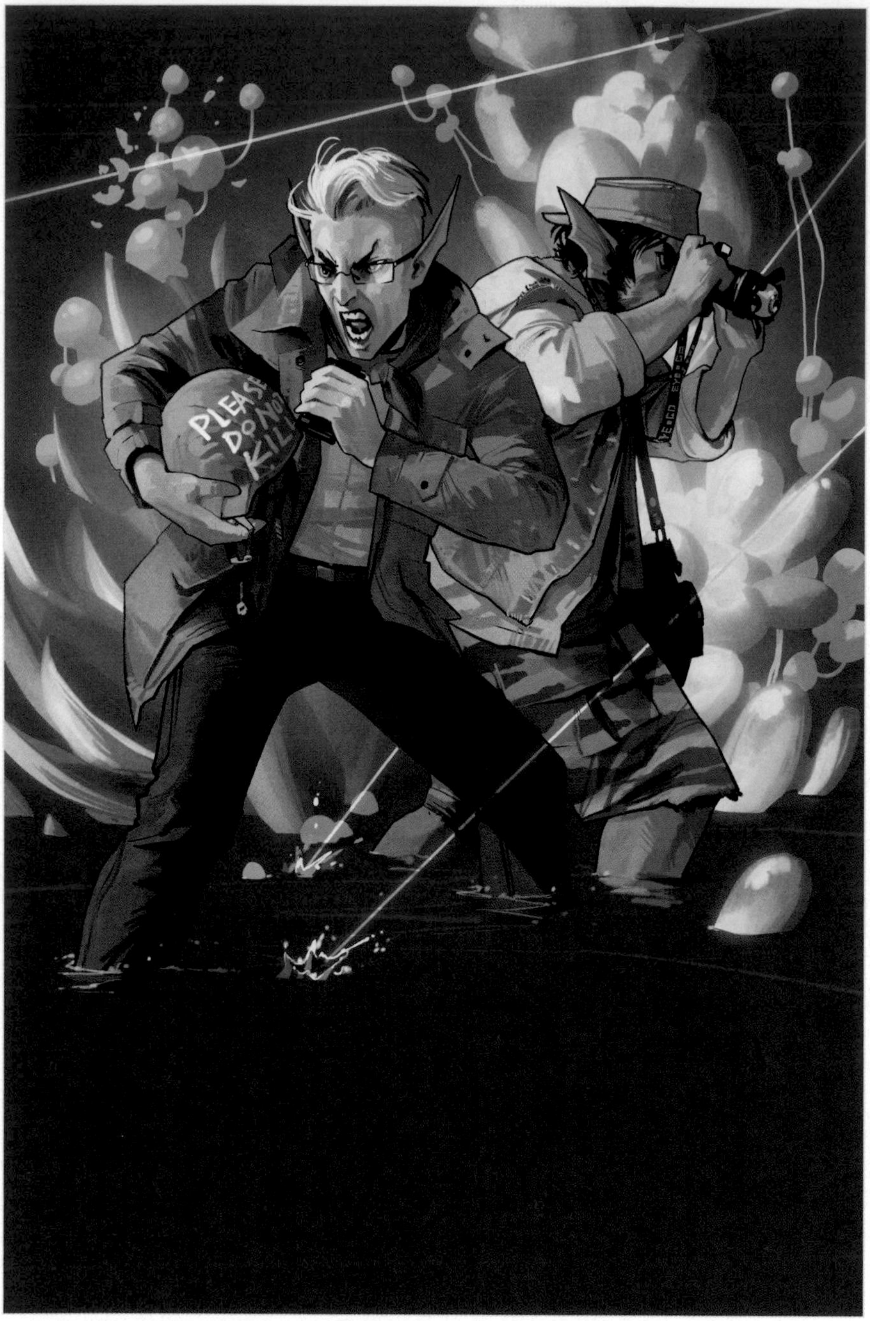
PLEASE DO NOT KILL

CHAPTER
SIXTEEN

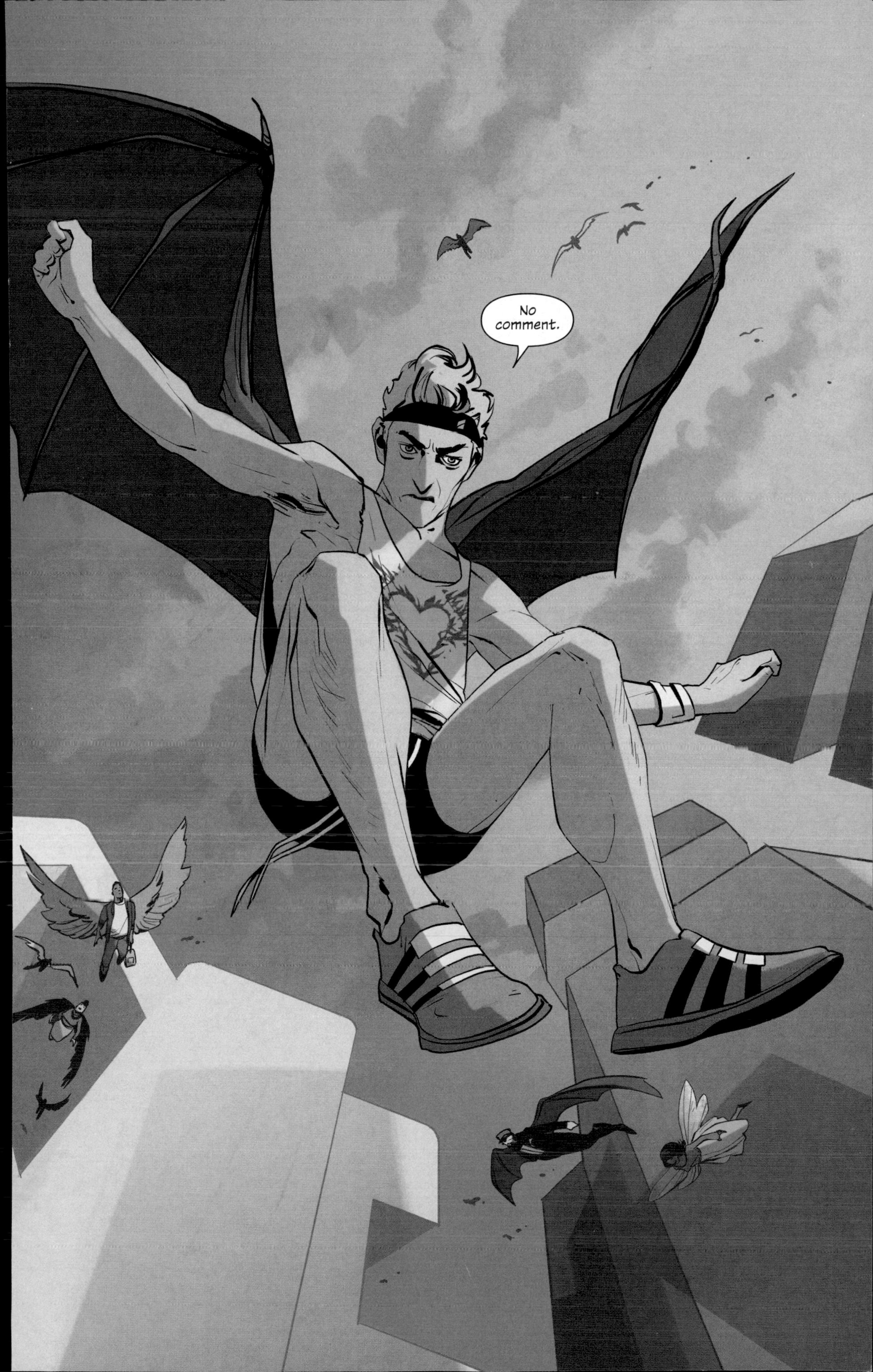
No comment.

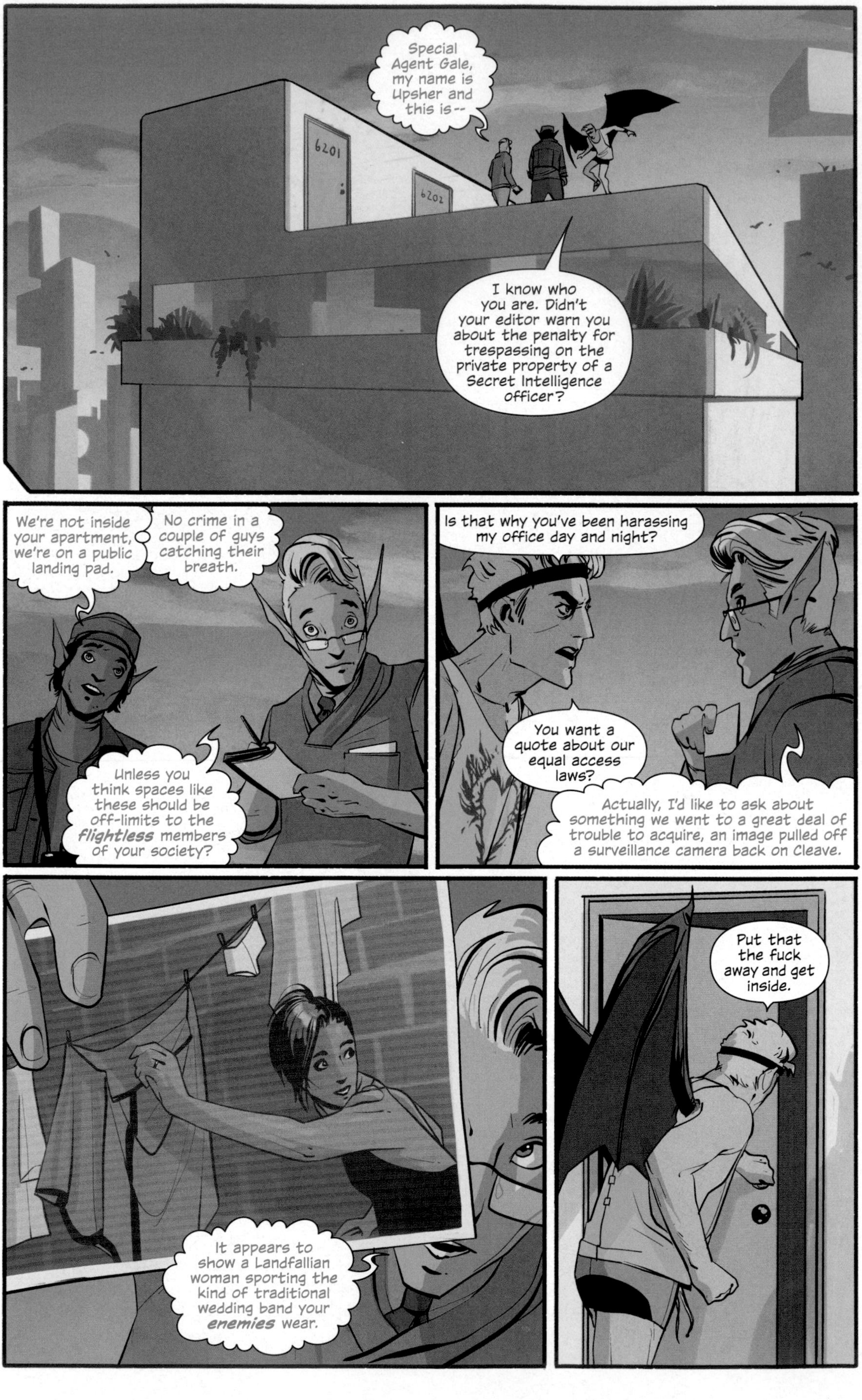
Special Agent Gale, my name is Upsher and this is--
I know who you are. Didn't your editor warn you about the penalty for trespassing on the private property of a Secret Intelligence officer?
We're not inside your apartment, we're on a public landing pad.
No crime in a couple of guys catching their breath.
Unless you think spaces like these should be off-limits to the *flightless* members of your society?
Is that why you've been harassing my office day and night?
You want a quote about our equal access laws?
Actually, I'd like to ask about something we went to a great deal of trouble to acquire, an image pulled off a surveillance camera back on Cleave.
It appears to show a Landfallian woman sporting the kind of traditional wedding band your *enemies* wear.
Put that the fuck away and get inside.

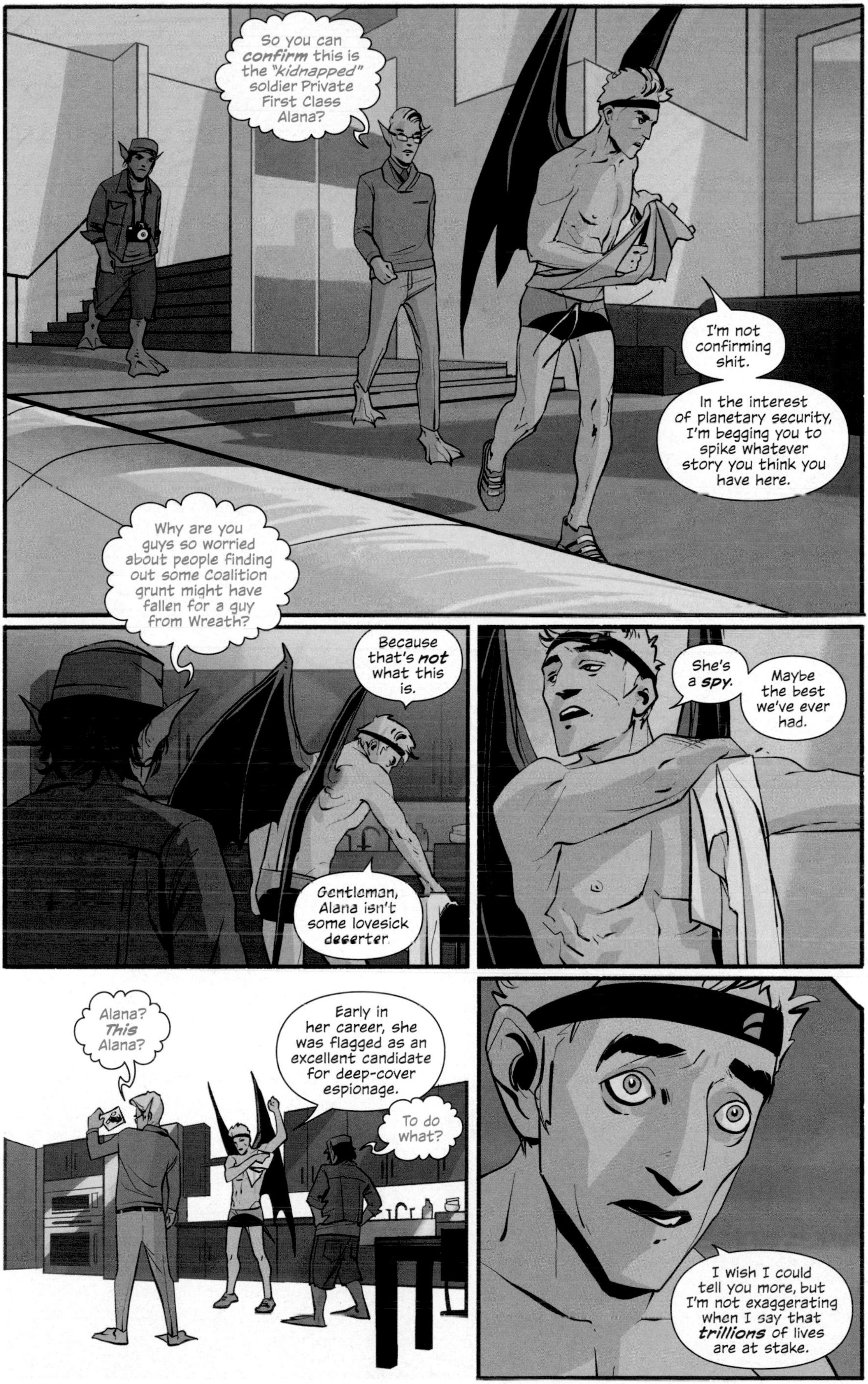
So you can *confirm* this is the *"kidnapped"* soldier Private First Class Alana?
I'm not confirming shit.
In the interest of planetary security, I'm begging you to spike whatever story you think you have here.
Why are you guys so worried about people finding out some Coalition grunt might have fallen for a guy from Wreath?
Because that's *not* what this is.
Gentleman, Alana isn't some lovesick *deserter*.
She's a *spy*.
Maybe the best we've ever had.
Alana? *This* Alana?
Early in her career, she was flagged as an excellent candidate for deep-cover espionage.
To do what?
I wish I could tell you more, but I'm not exaggerating when I say that *trillions* of lives are at stake.

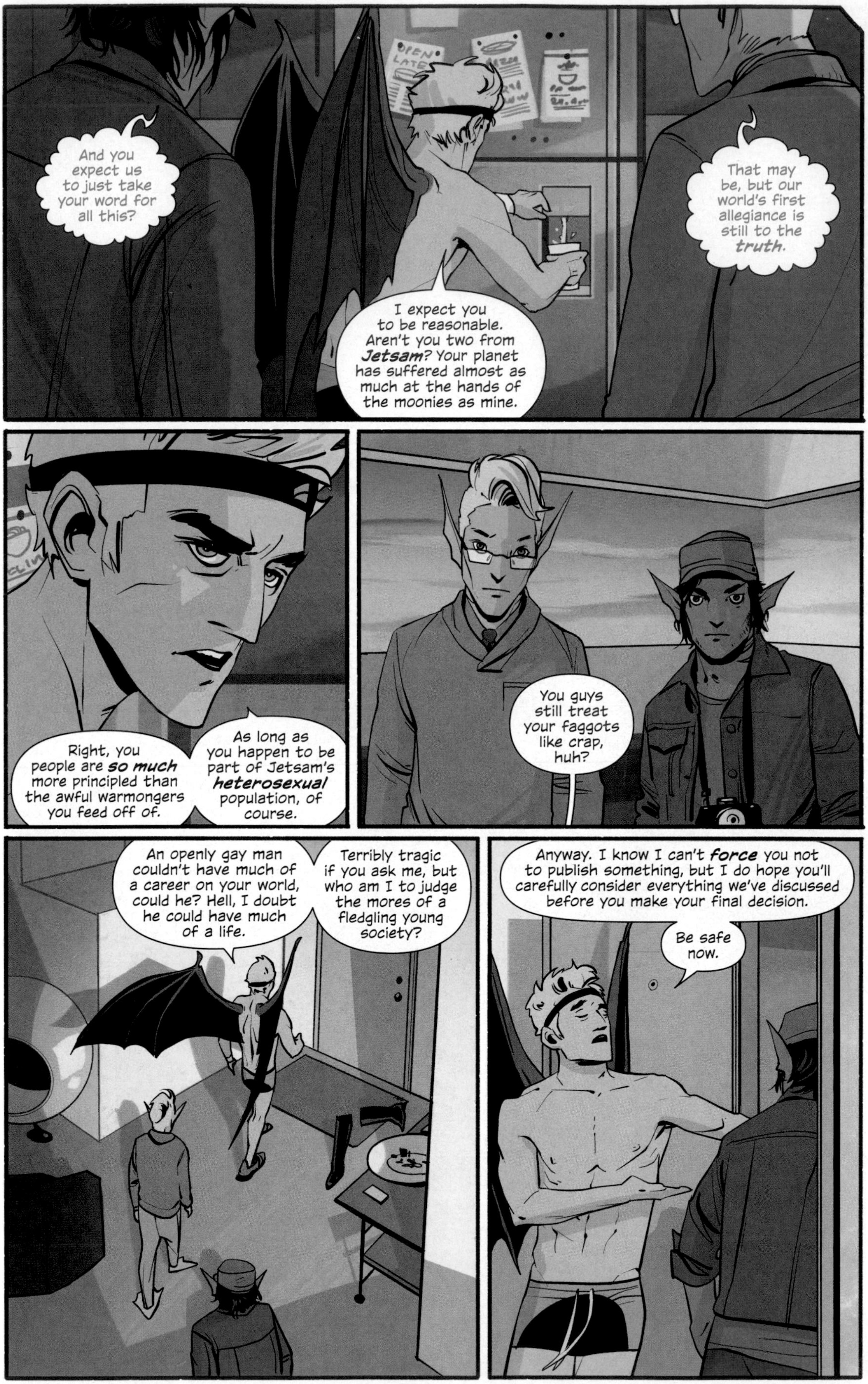
And you expect us to just take your word for all this?
That may be, but our world's first allegiance is still to the *truth*.
I expect you to be reasonable. Aren't you two from *Jetsam*? Your planet has suffered almost as much at the hands of the moonies as mine.
Right, you people are *so much* more principled than the awful warmongers you feed off of.
As long as you happen to be part of Jetsam's *heterosexual* population, of course.
You guys still treat your faggots like crap, huh?
An openly gay man couldn't have much of a career on your world, could he? Hell, I doubt he could have much of a life.
Terribly tragic if you ask me, but who am I to judge the mores of a fledgling young society?
Anyway. I know I can't *force* you not to publish something, but I do hope you'll carefully consider everything we've discussed before you make your final decision.
Be safe now.

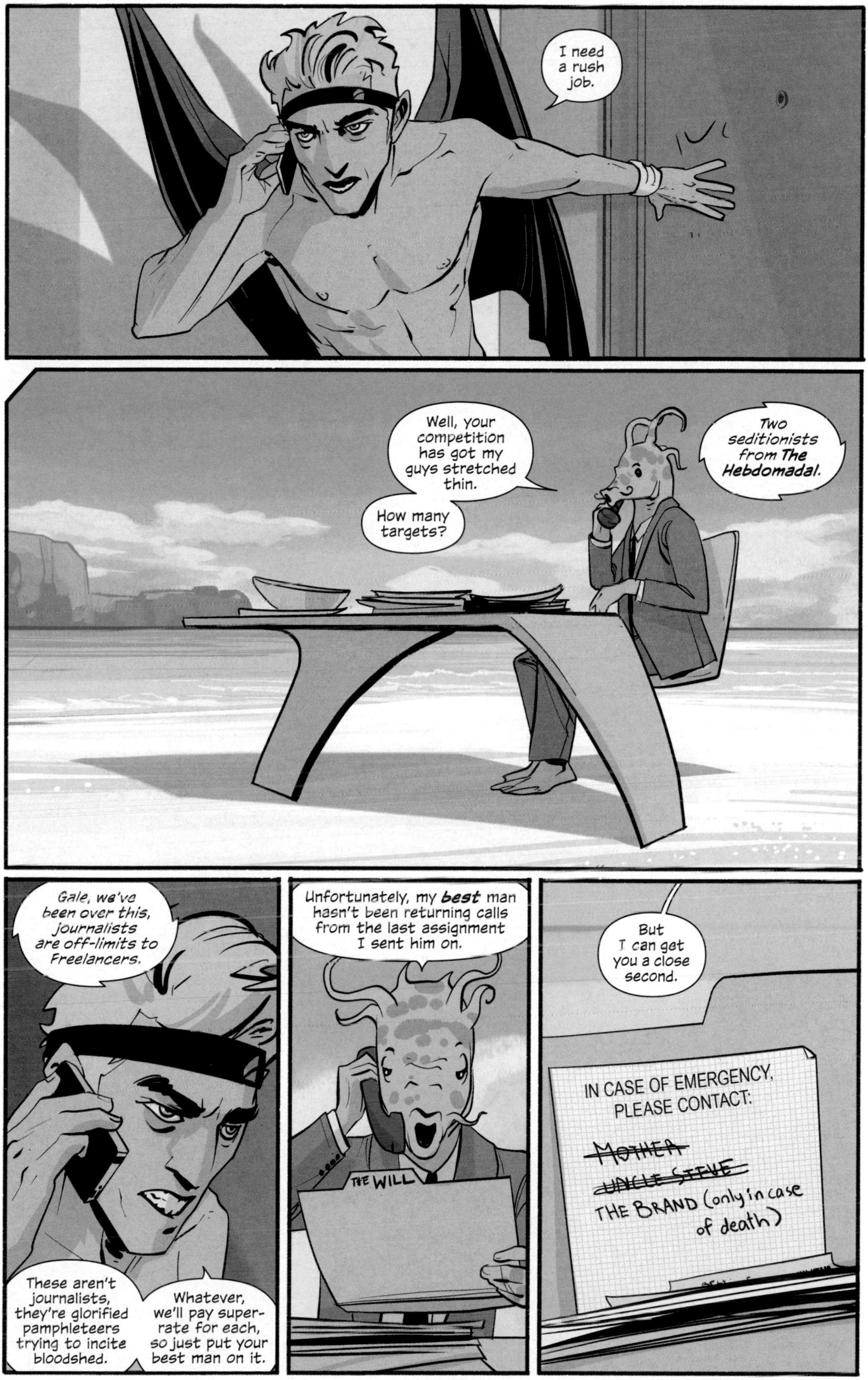
I need a rush job.
Well, your competition has got my guys stretched thin.
How many targets?
Two seditionists from **The Hebdomadal.**
Gale, we've been over this, journalists are off-limits to Freelancers.
These aren't journalists, they're glorified pamphleteers trying to incite bloodshed.
Whatever, we'll pay super-rate for each, so just put your best man on it.
Unfortunately, my **best** man hasn't been returning calls from the last assignment I sent him on.
THE WILL
But I can get you a close second.
IN CASE OF EMERGENCY, PLEASE CONTACT:
~~MOTHER~~
~~UNCLE STEVE~~
THE BRAND (only in case of death)

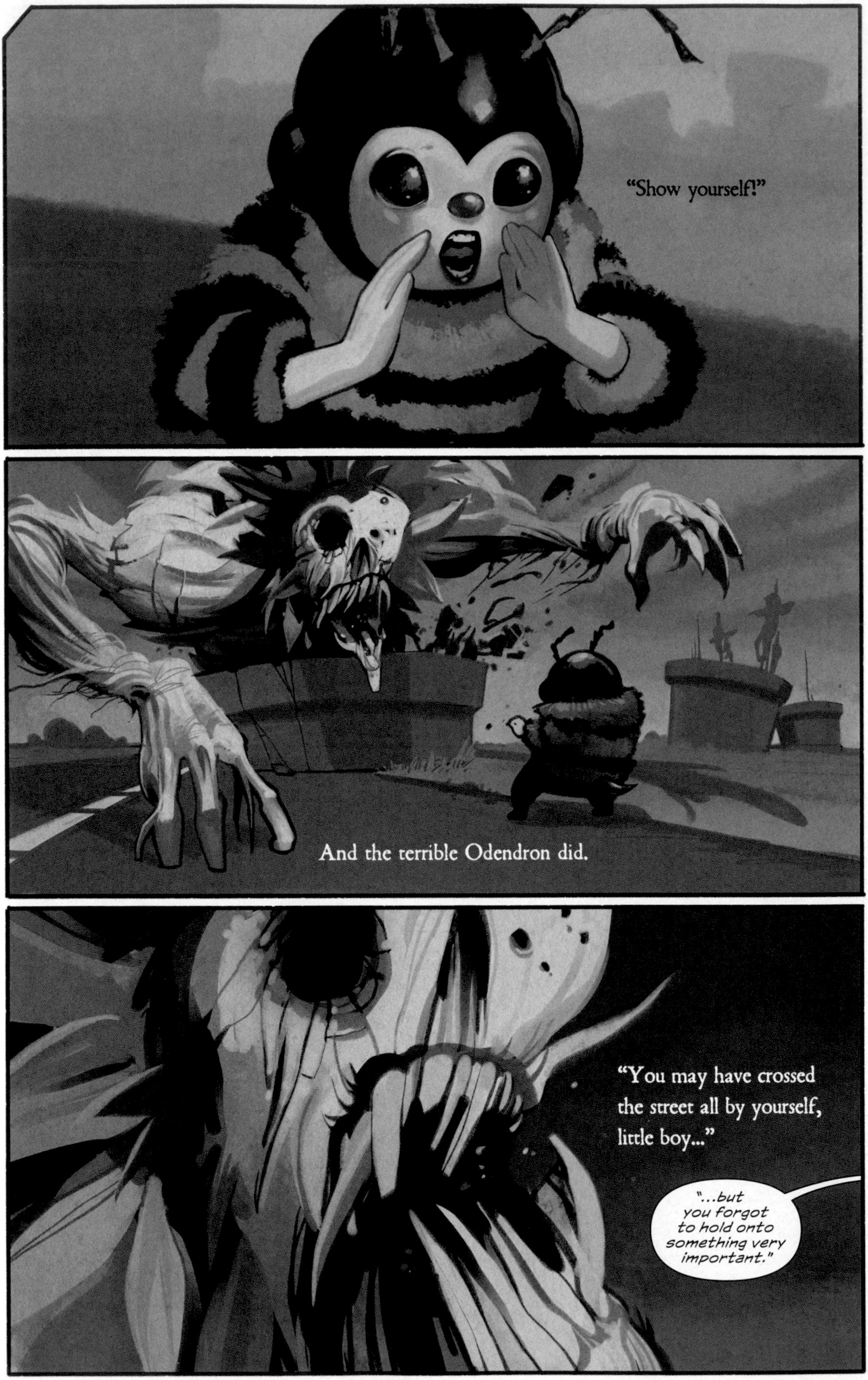

"Show yourself!"
And the terrible Odendron did.
"You may have crossed the street all by yourself, little boy..."
"...but you forgot to hold onto something very important."

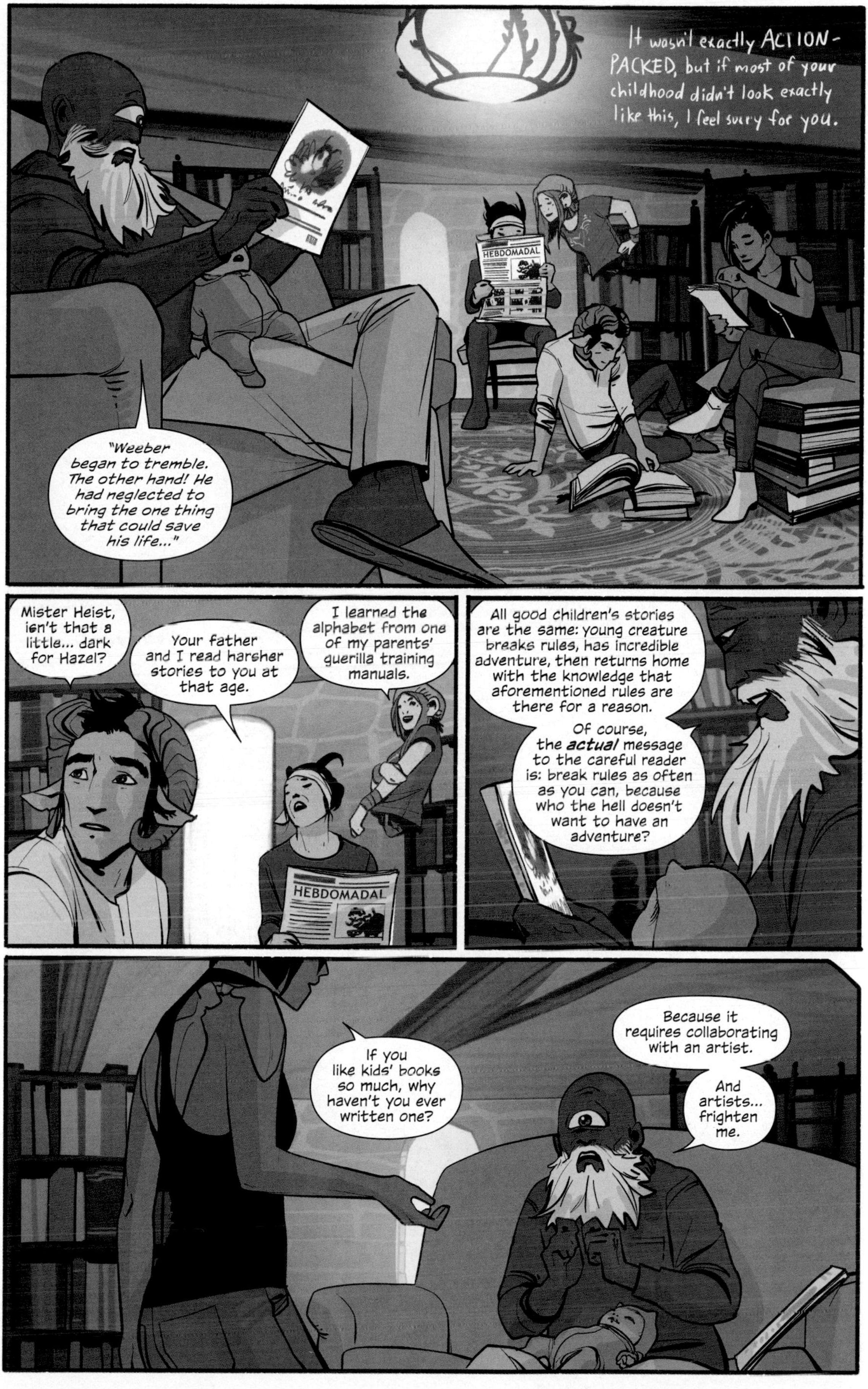

It wasn't exactly ACTION-PACKED, but if most of your childhood didn't look exactly like this, I feel sorry for you.
"Weeber began to tremble. The other hand! He had neglected to bring the one thing that could save his life..."
HEBDOMADAL
Mister Heist, isn't that a little... dark for Hazel?
Your father and I read harsher stories to you at that age.
I learned the alphabet from one of my parents' guerilla training manuals.
HEBDOMADAL
All good children's stories are the same: young creature breaks rules, has incredible adventure, then returns home with the knowledge that aforementioned rules are there for a reason.
Of course, the *actual* message to the careful reader is: break rules as often as you can, because who the hell doesn't want to have an adventure?
If you like kids' books so much, why haven't you ever written one?
Because it requires collaborating with an artist.
And artists... frighten me.

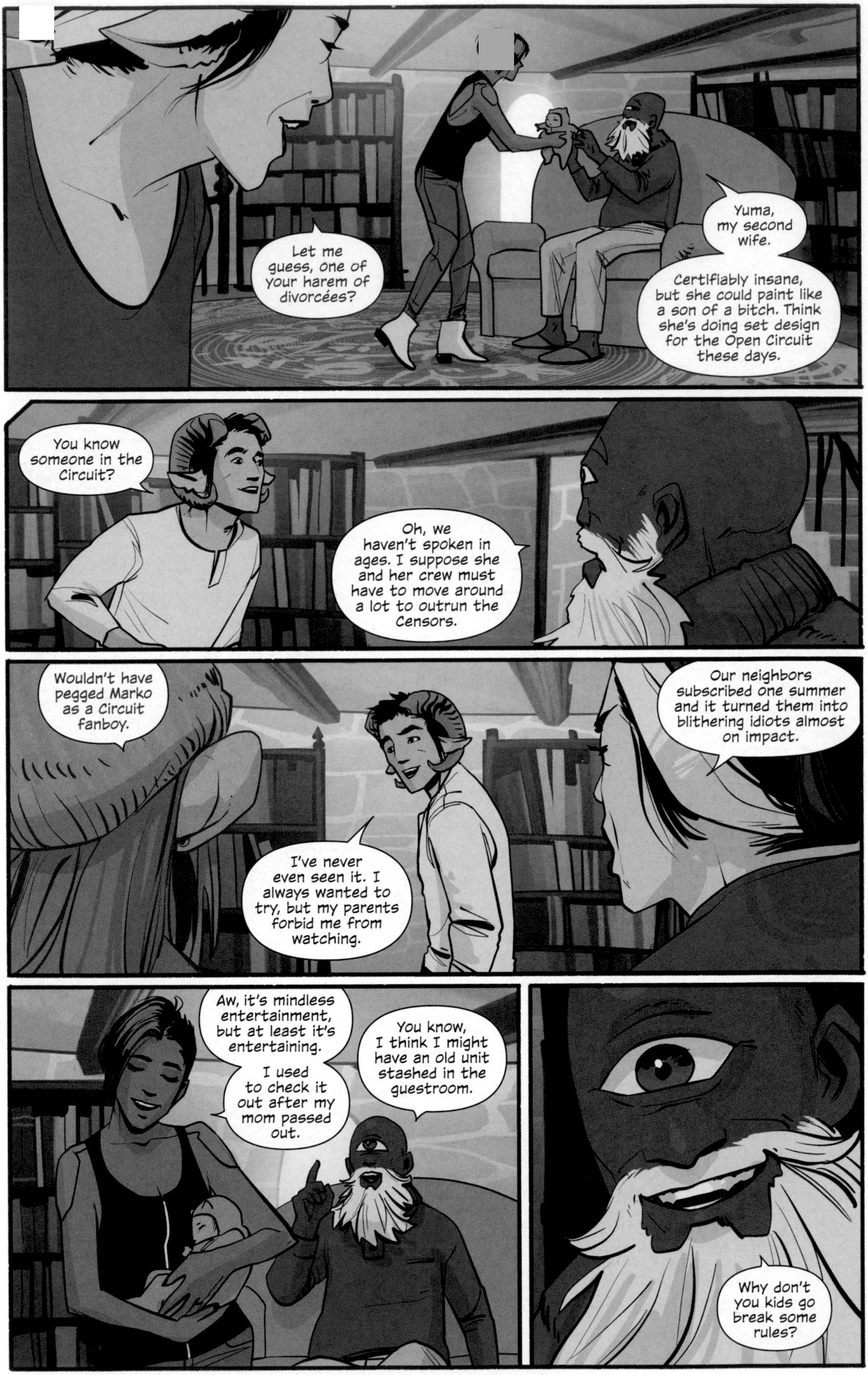
Let me guess, one of your harem of divorcées?
Yuma, my second wife.
Certifiably insane, but she could paint like a son of a bitch. Think she's doing set design for the Open Circuit these days.
You know someone in the Circuit?
Oh, we haven't spoken in ages. I suppose she and her crew must have to move around a lot to outrun the Censors.
Wouldn't have pegged Marko as a Circuit fanboy.
Our neighbors subscribed one summer and it turned them into blithering idiots almost on impact.
I've never even seen it. I always wanted to try, but my parents forbid me from watching.
Aw, it's mindless entertainment, but at least it's entertaining.
I used to check it out after my mom passed out.
You know, I think I might have an old unit stashed in the guestroom.
Why don't you kids go break some rules?

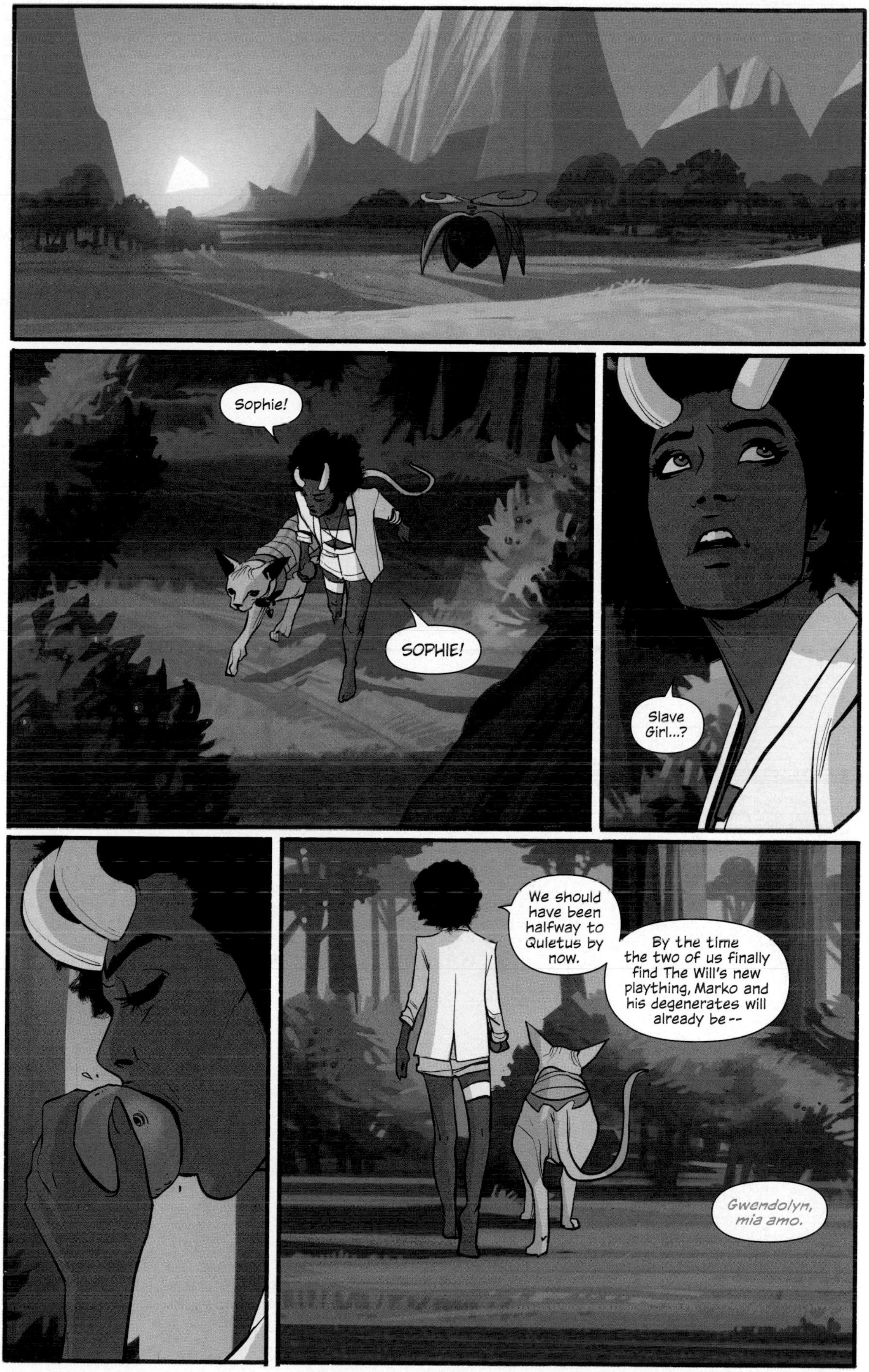
Sophie!
SOPHIE!
Slave Girl...?
We should have been halfway to Quletus by now.
By the time the two of us finally find The Will's new plaything, Marko and his degenerates will already be --
Gwendolyn, mia amo.

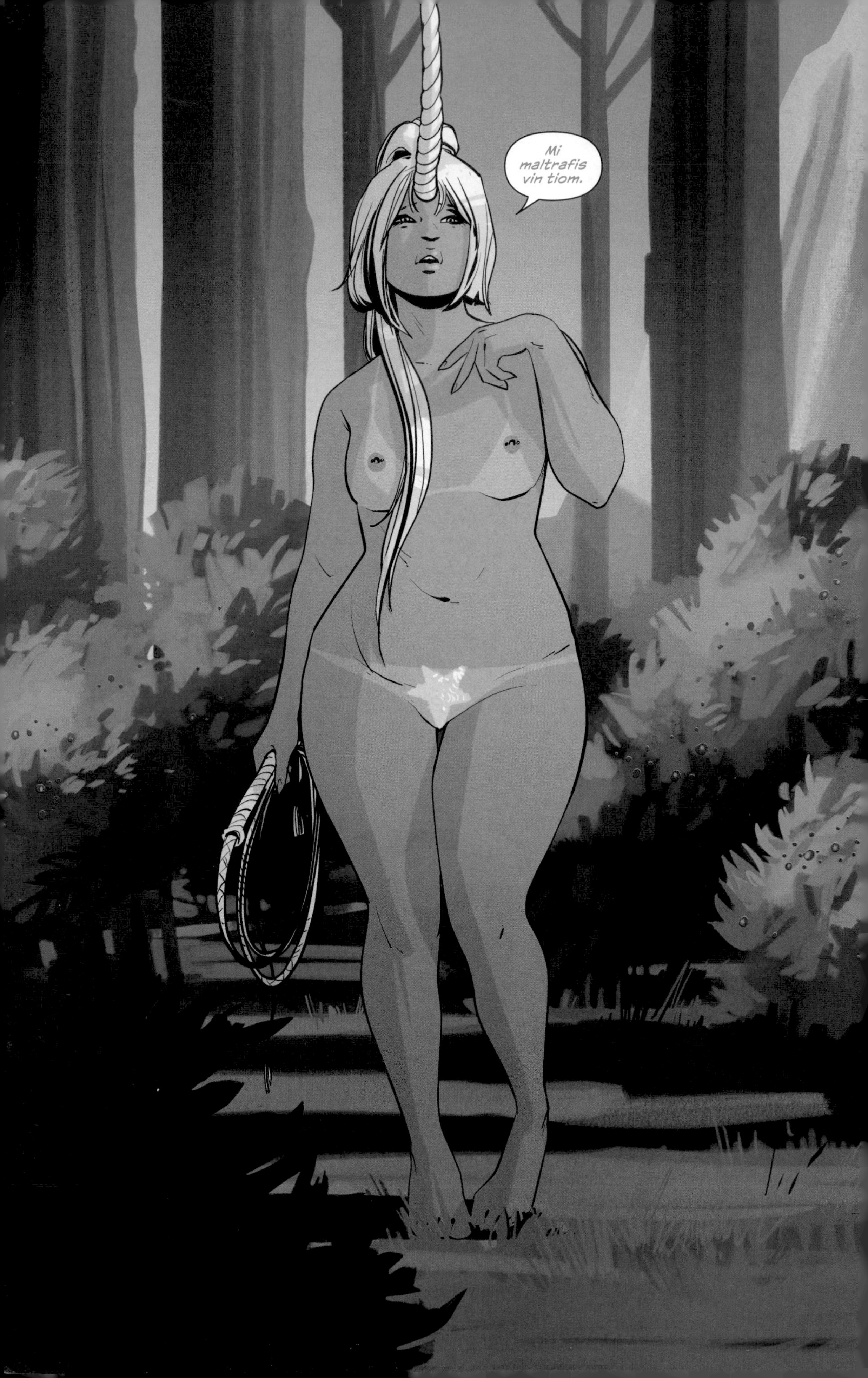
Mi maltrafis vin tiom.

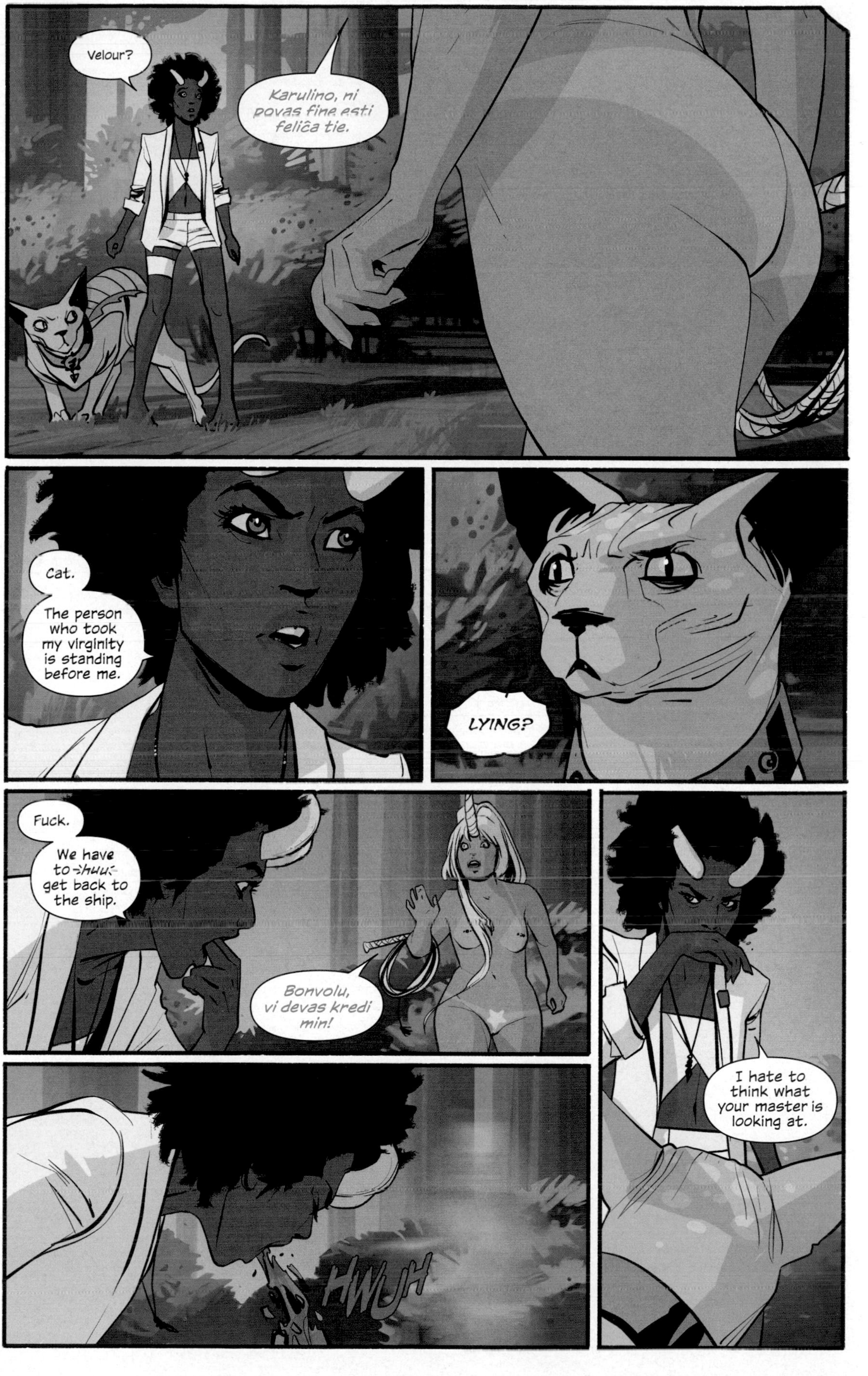

Velour?
Karulino, ni povas fine esti feliĉa tie.
Cat.
The person who took my virginity is standing before me.
LYING?
Fuck.
We have to -hwu- get back to the ship.
Bonvolu, vi devas kredi min!
I hate to think what your master is looking at.
HWUH

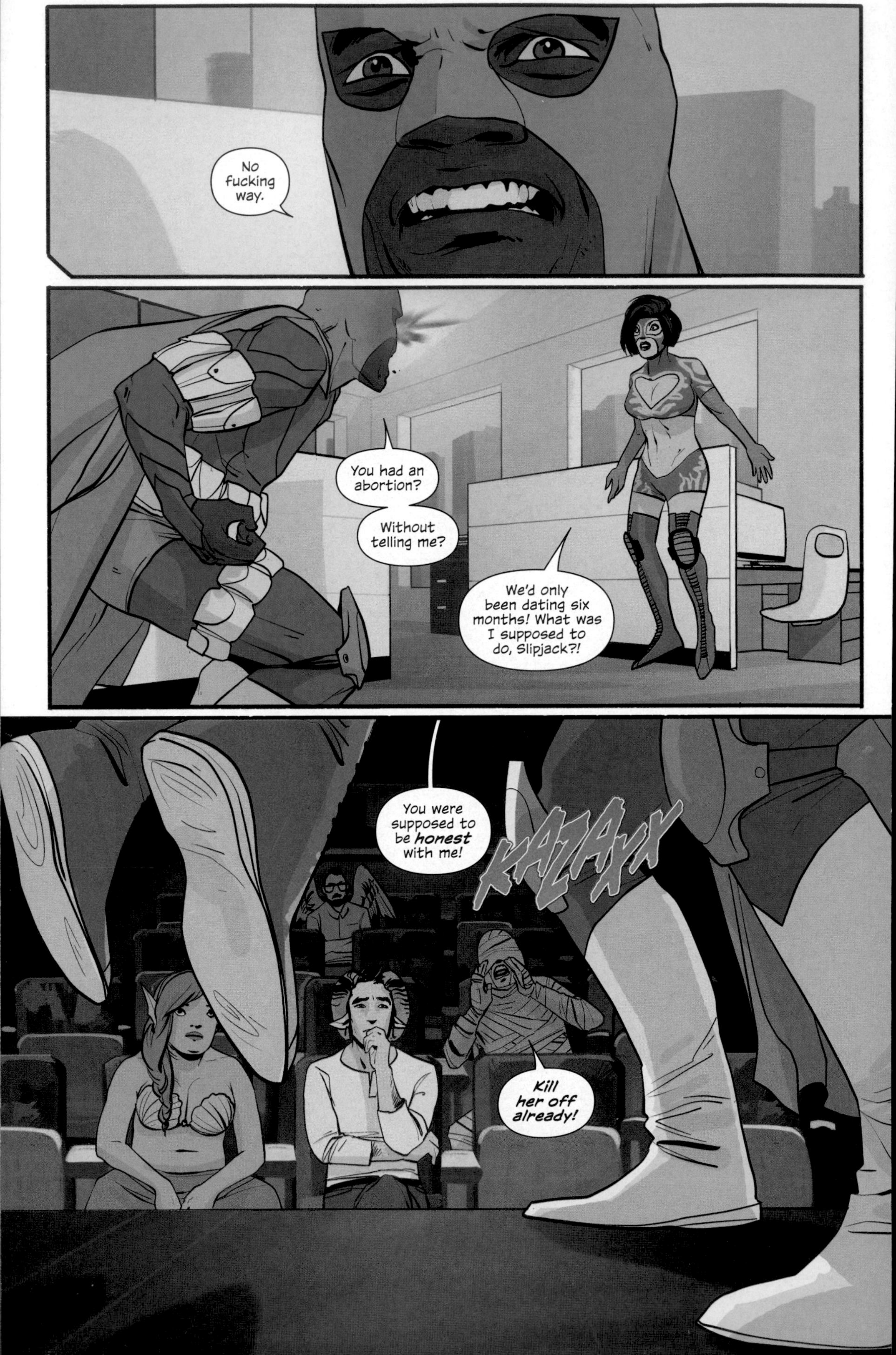

No fucking way.
You had an abortion?
Without telling me?
We'd only been dating six months! What was I supposed to do, Slipjack?!
You were supposed to be **honest** with me!
KAZAXX
Kill her off already!

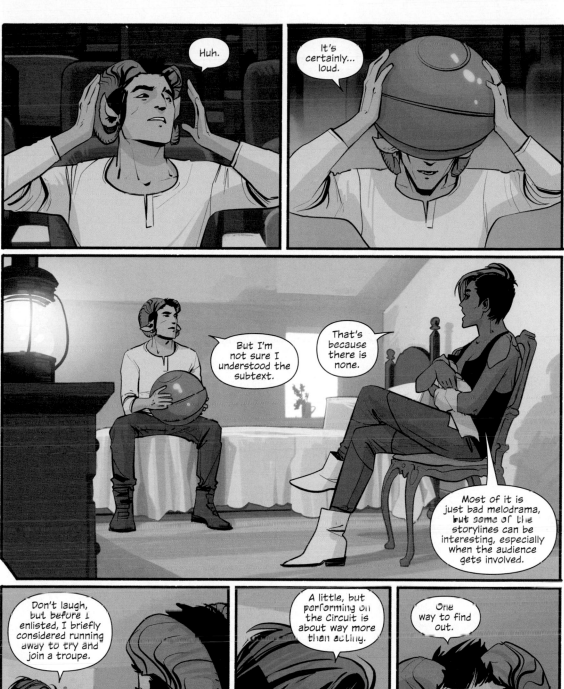

Huh.

It's certainly... loud.

But I'm not sure I understood the subtext.

That's because there is none.

Most of it is just bad melodrama, but some of the storylines can be interesting, especially when the audience gets involved.

Don't laugh, but before I enlisted, I briefly considered running away to try and join a troupe.

Are you kidding? Why the hell didn't you? I mean, you're passable as one of their kind with your wings retracted. And you used to act in high school, right?

A little, but performing on the Circuit is about way more than acting.

I doubt I could have survived the audition.

One way to find out.

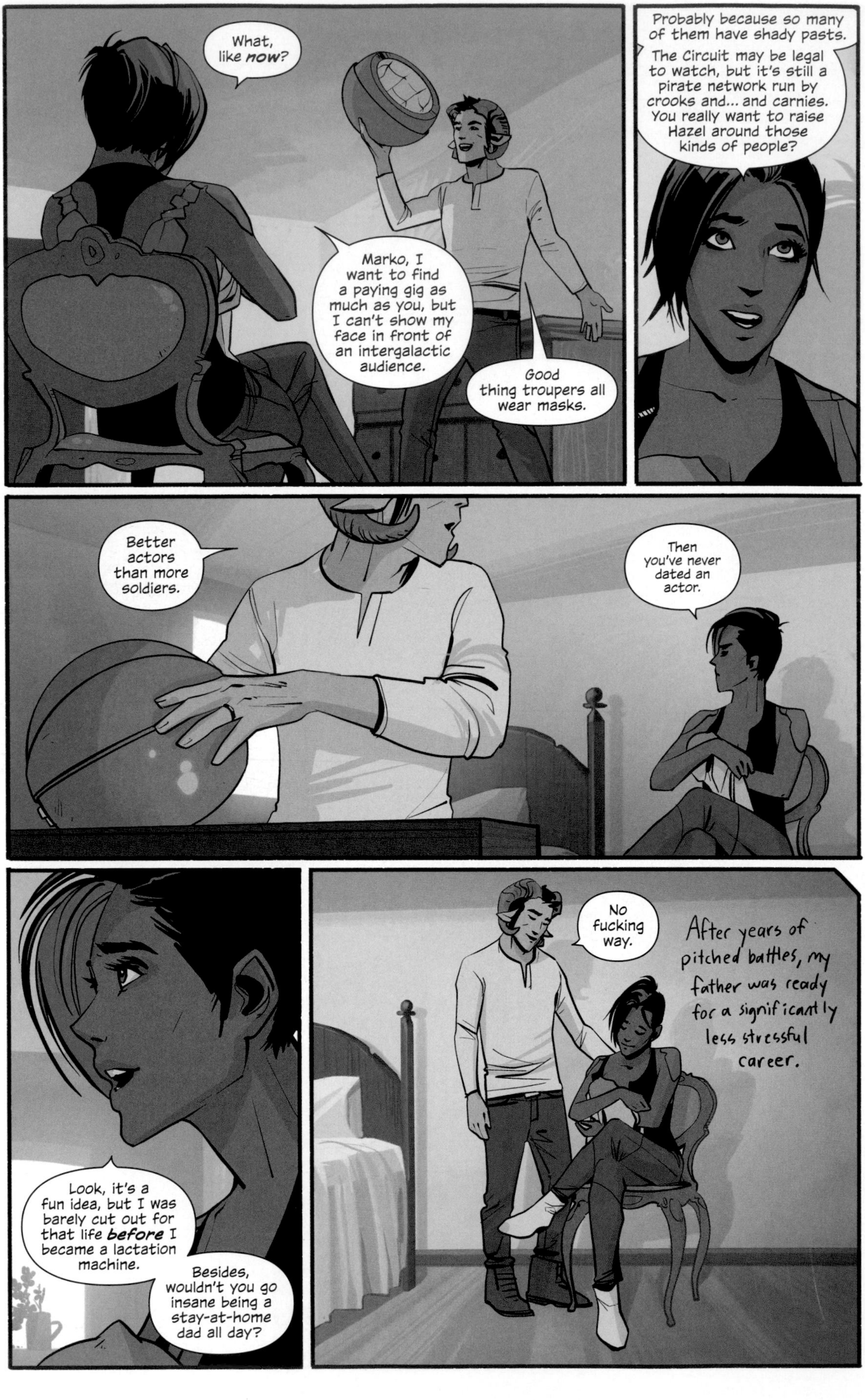

What, like *now*?
Marko, I want to find a paying gig as much as you, but I can't show my face in front of an intergalactic audience.
Good thing troupers all wear masks.
Probably because so many of them have shady pasts.
The Circuit may be legal to watch, but it's still a pirate network run by crooks and... and carnies. You really want to raise Hazel around those kinds of people?
Better actors than more soldiers.
Then you've never dated an actor.
Look, it's a fun idea, but I was barely cut out for that life *before* I became a lactation machine.
Besides, wouldn't you go insane being a stay-at-home dad all day?
No fucking way.
After years of pitched battles, my father was ready for a significantly less stressful career.

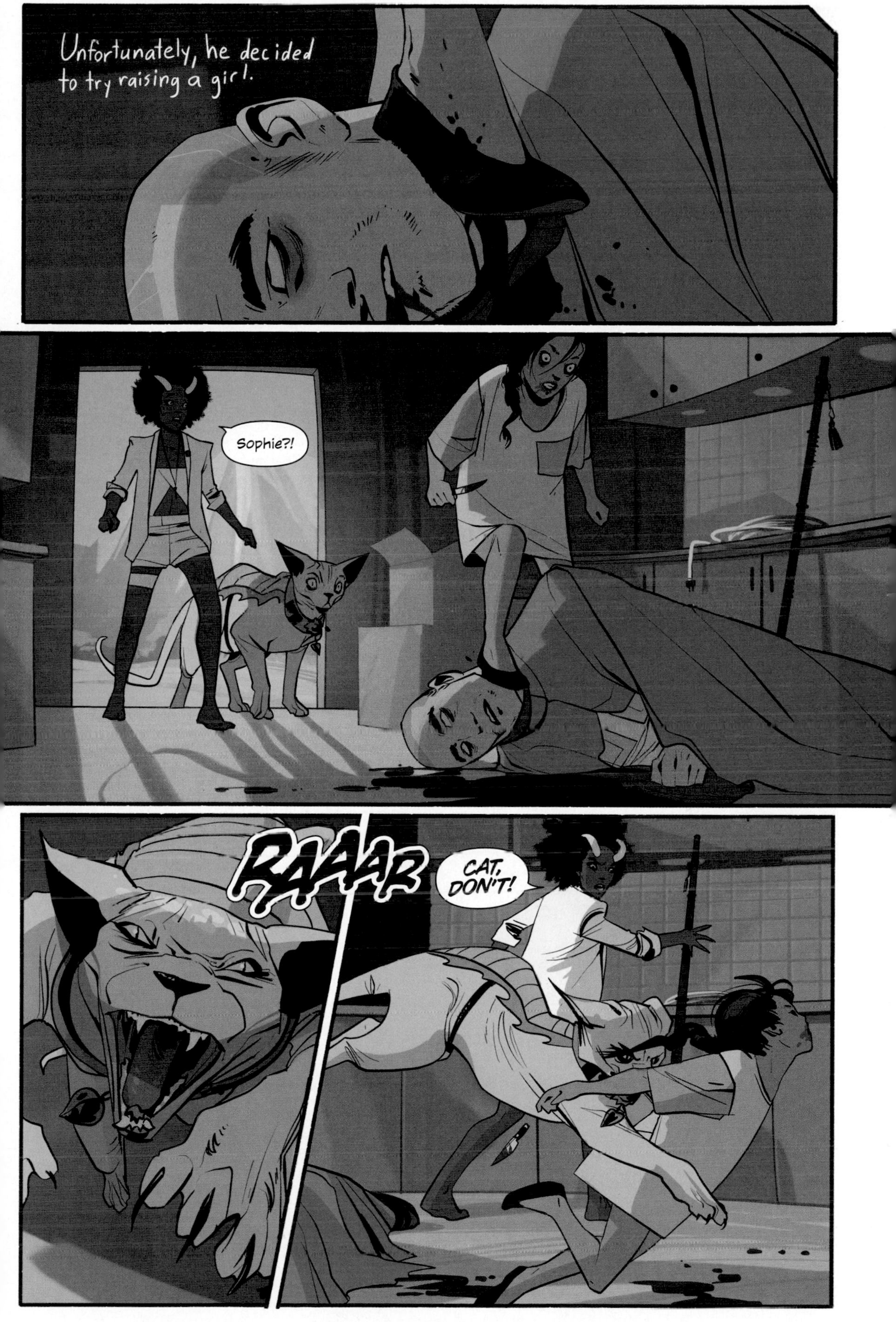
Unfortunately, he decided to try raising a girl.
Sophie?!
RAAAR
CAT, DON'T!

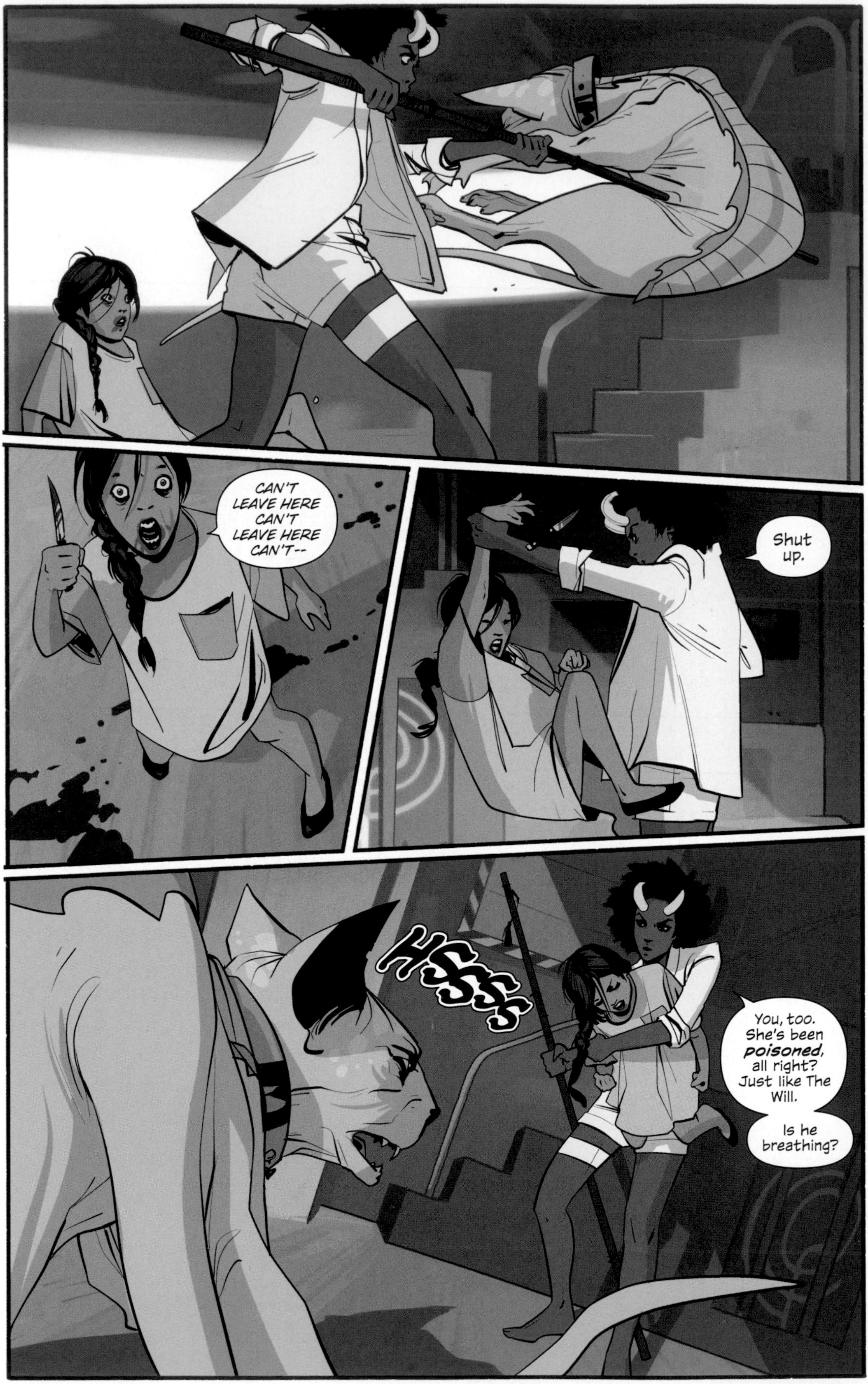
CAN'T LEAVE HERE CAN'T LEAVE HERE CAN'T--
Shut up.
HSSSS
You, too. She's been *poisoned*, all right? Just like The Will.
Is he breathing?

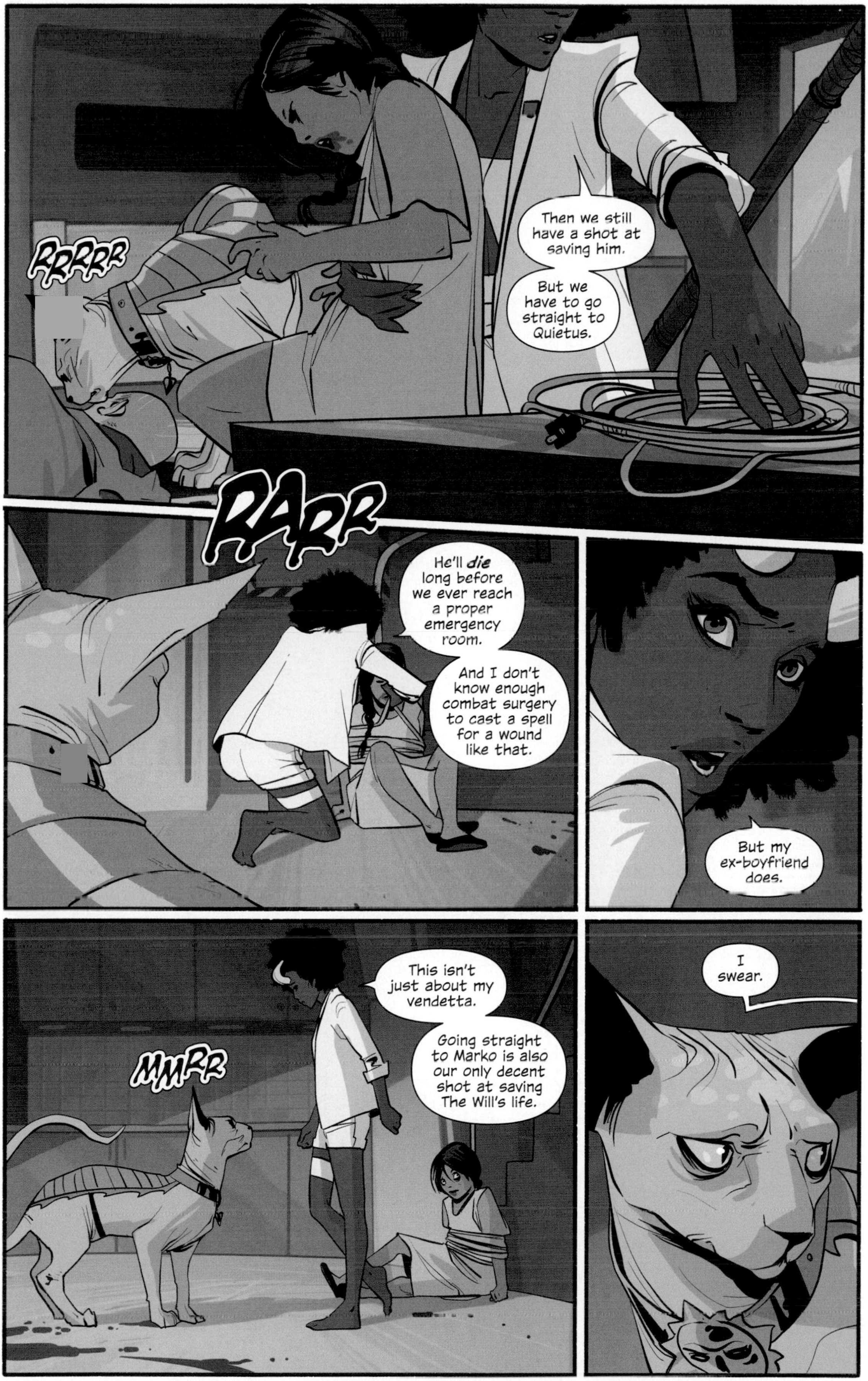
RRRRR
Then we still have a shot at saving him.
But we have to go straight to Quietus.
RARR
He'll *die* long before we ever reach a proper emergency room.
And I don't know enough combat surgery to cast a spell for a wound like that.
But my ex-boyfriend does.
This isn't just about my vendetta.
Going straight to Marko is also our only decent shot at saving The Will's life.
MMRR
I swear.

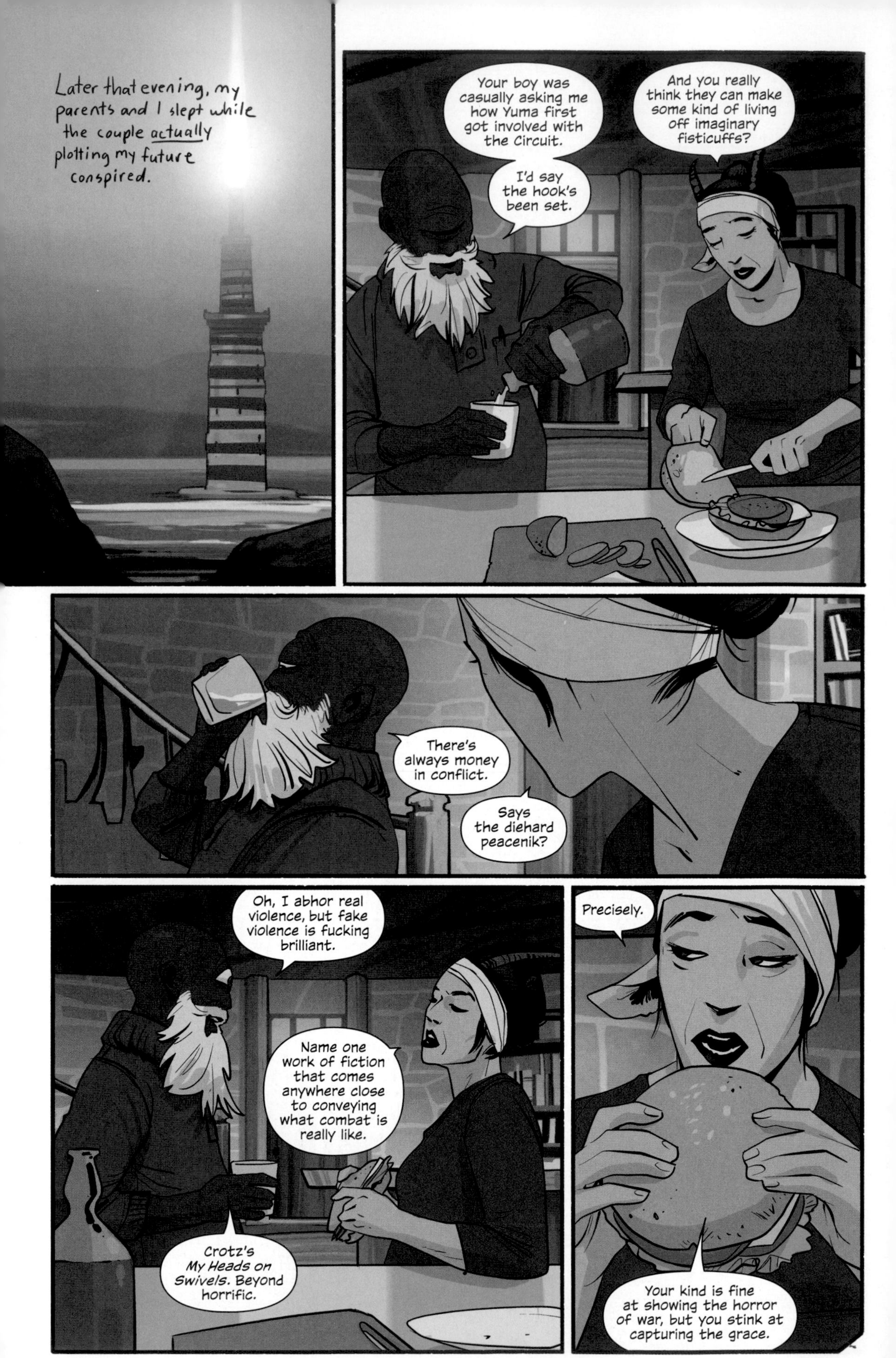
Later that evening, my parents and I slept while the couple actually plotting my future conspired.
Your boy was casually asking me how Yuma first got involved with the Circuit.
I'd say the hook's been set.
And you really think they can make some kind of living off imaginary fisticuffs?
There's always money in conflict.
Says the diehard peacenik?
Oh, I abhor real violence, but fake violence is fucking brilliant.
Name one work of fiction that comes anywhere close to conveying what combat is really like.
Crotz's *My Heads on Swivels*. Beyond horrific.
Precisely.
Your kind is fine at showing the horror of war, but you stink at capturing the grace.

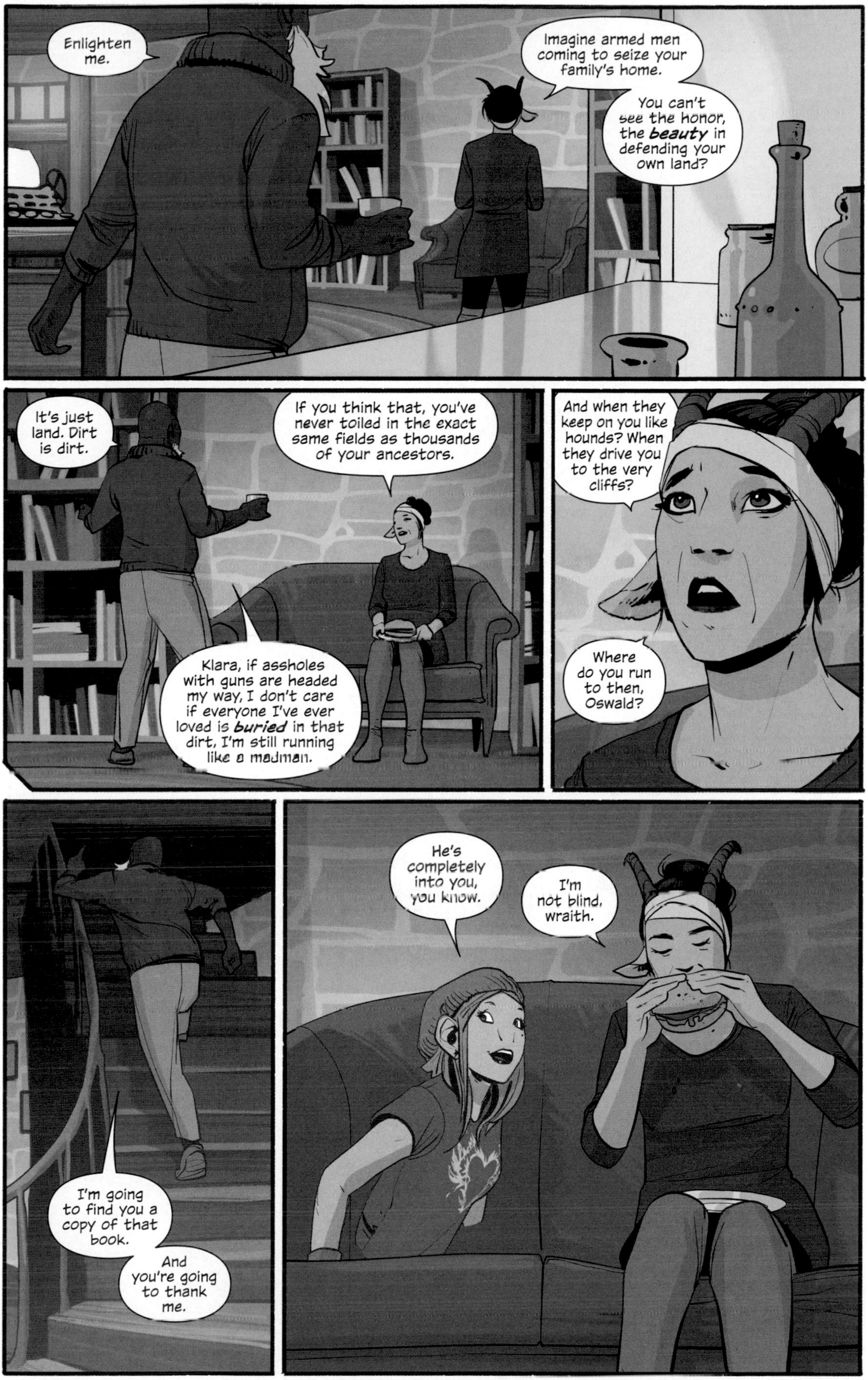
Enlighten me.
Imagine armed men coming to seize your family's home.
You can't see the honor, the ***beauty*** in defending your own land?
It's just land. Dirt is dirt.
If you think that, you've never toiled in the exact same fields as thousands of your ancestors.
Klara, if assholes with guns are headed my way, I don't care if everyone I've ever loved is ***buried*** in that dirt, I'm still running like a madman.
And when they keep on you like hounds? When they drive you to the very cliffs?
Where do you run to then, Oswald?
I'm going to find you a copy of that book.
And you're going to thank me.
He's completely into you, you know.
I'm not blind, wraith.

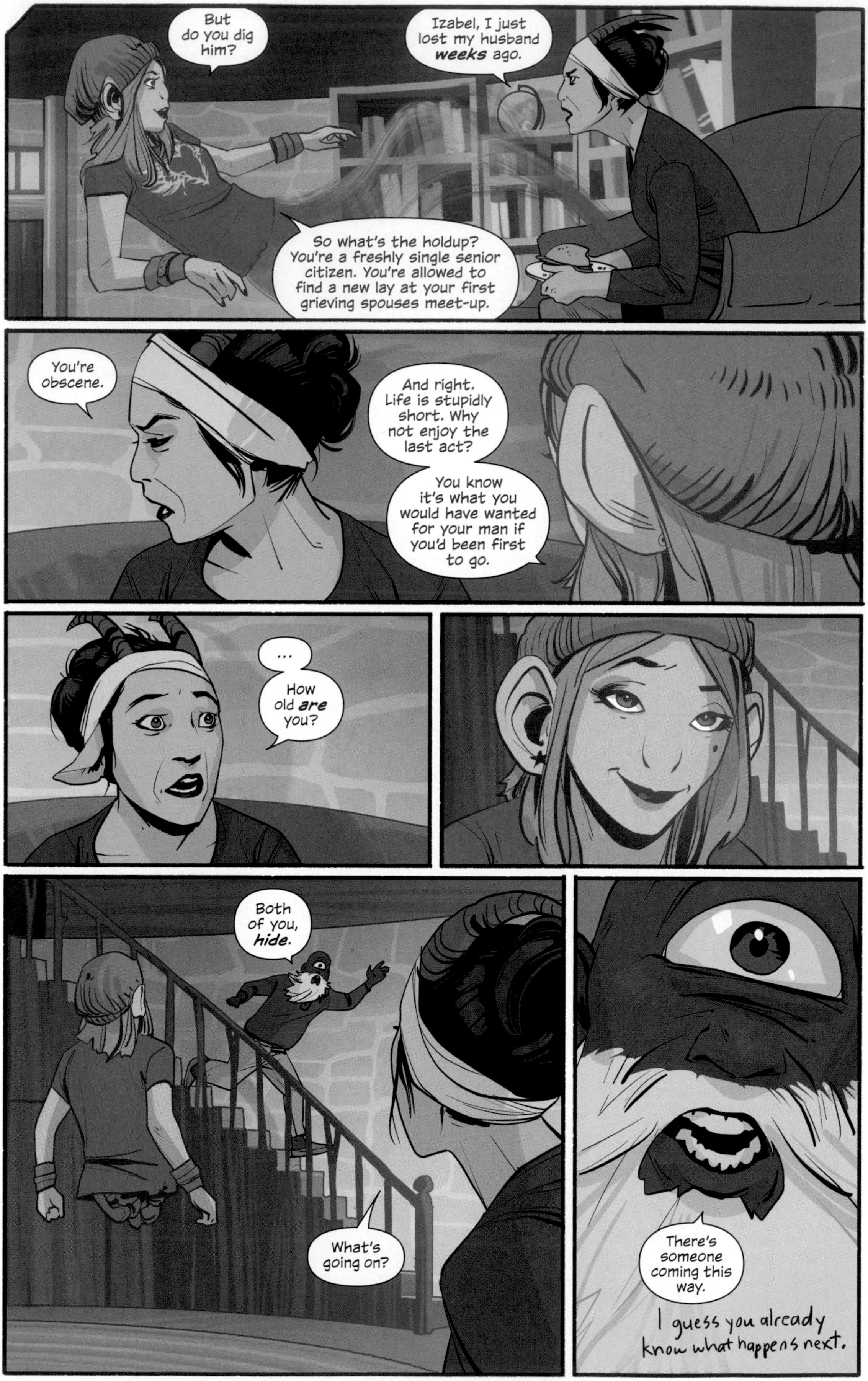
But do you dig him?
Izabel, I just lost my husband *weeks* ago.
So what's the holdup? You're a freshly single senior citizen. You're allowed to find a new lay at your first grieving spouses meet-up.
You're obscene.
And right. Life is stupidly short. Why not enjoy the last act?
You know it's what you would have wanted for your man if you'd been first to go.
...
How old *are* you?
Both of you, *hide*.
What's going on?
There's someone coming this way.
I guess you already know what happens next.

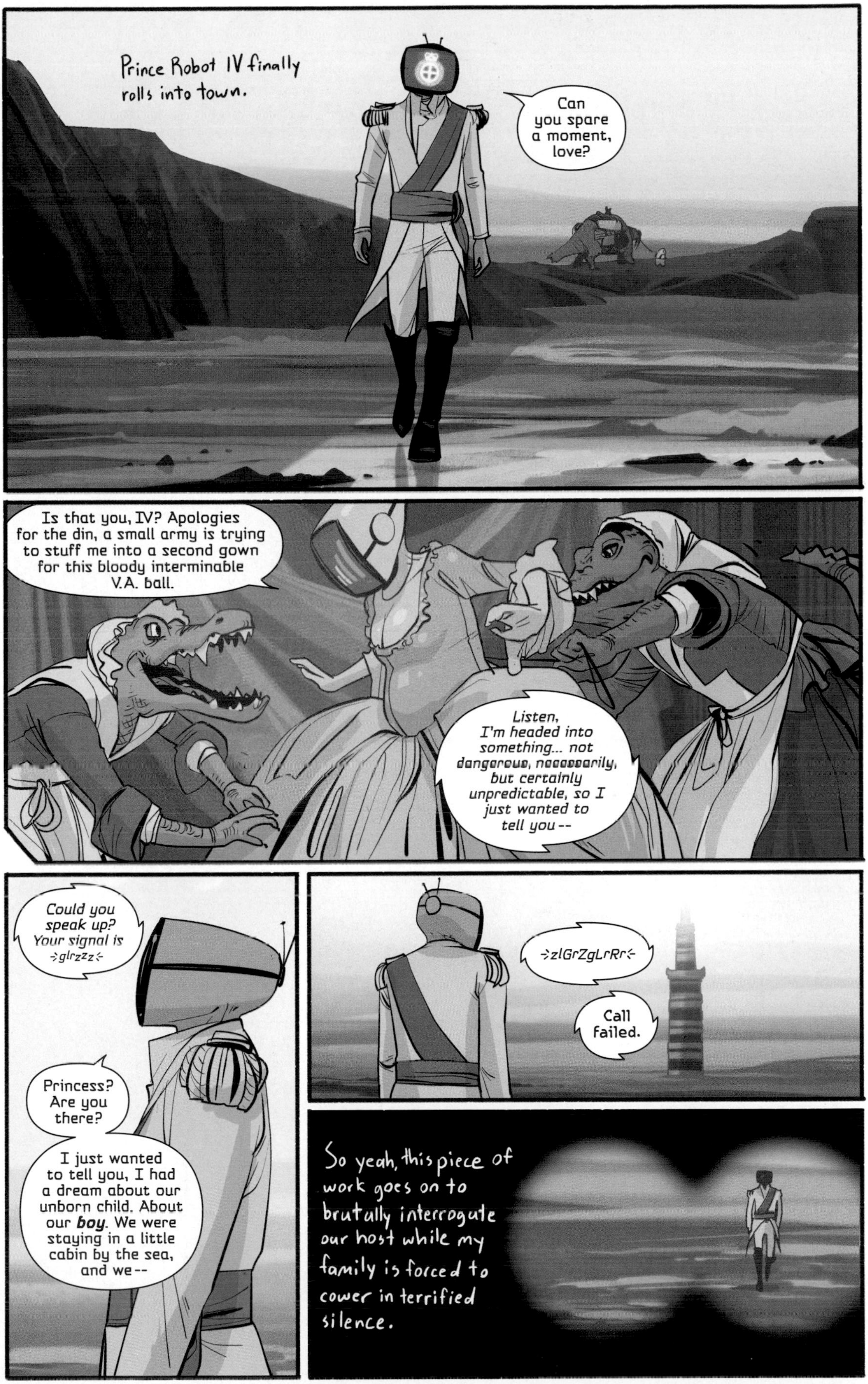
Prince Robot IV finally rolls into town.
Can you spare a moment, love?
Is that you, IV? Apologies for the din, a small army is trying to stuff me into a second gown for this bloody interminable V.A. ball.
Listen, I'm headed into something... not dangerous, necessarily, but certainly unpredictable, so I just wanted to tell you--
Could you speak up? Your signal is glrzzz
Princess? Are you there?
I just wanted to tell you, I had a dream about our unborn child. About our **boy**. We were staying in a little cabin by the sea, and we--
zlGrZgLrRr
Call failed.
So yeah, this piece of work goes on to brutally interrogate our host while my family is forced to cower in terrified silence.

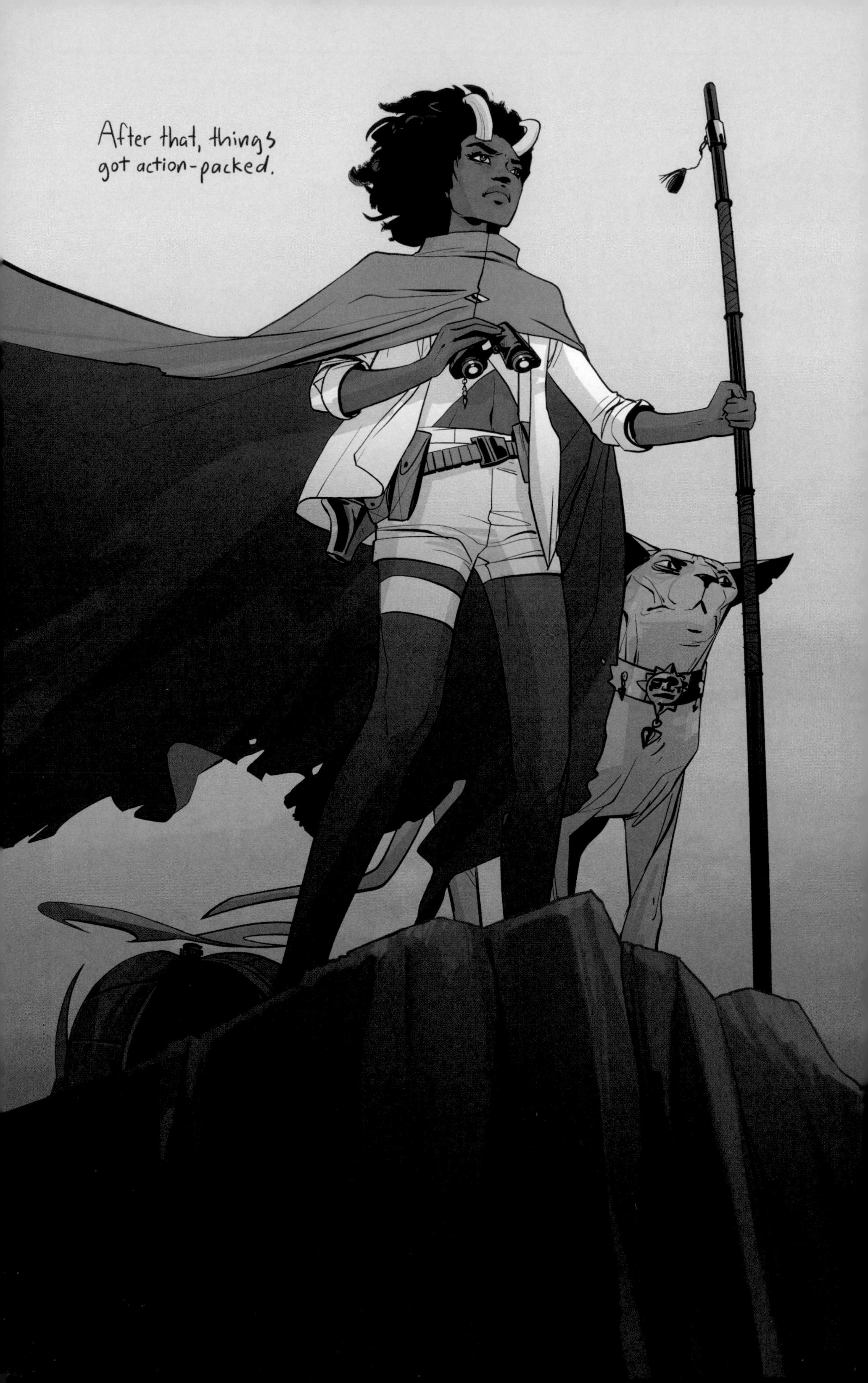
After that, things
got action-packed.

end chapter sixteen

CHAPTER
SEVENTEEN

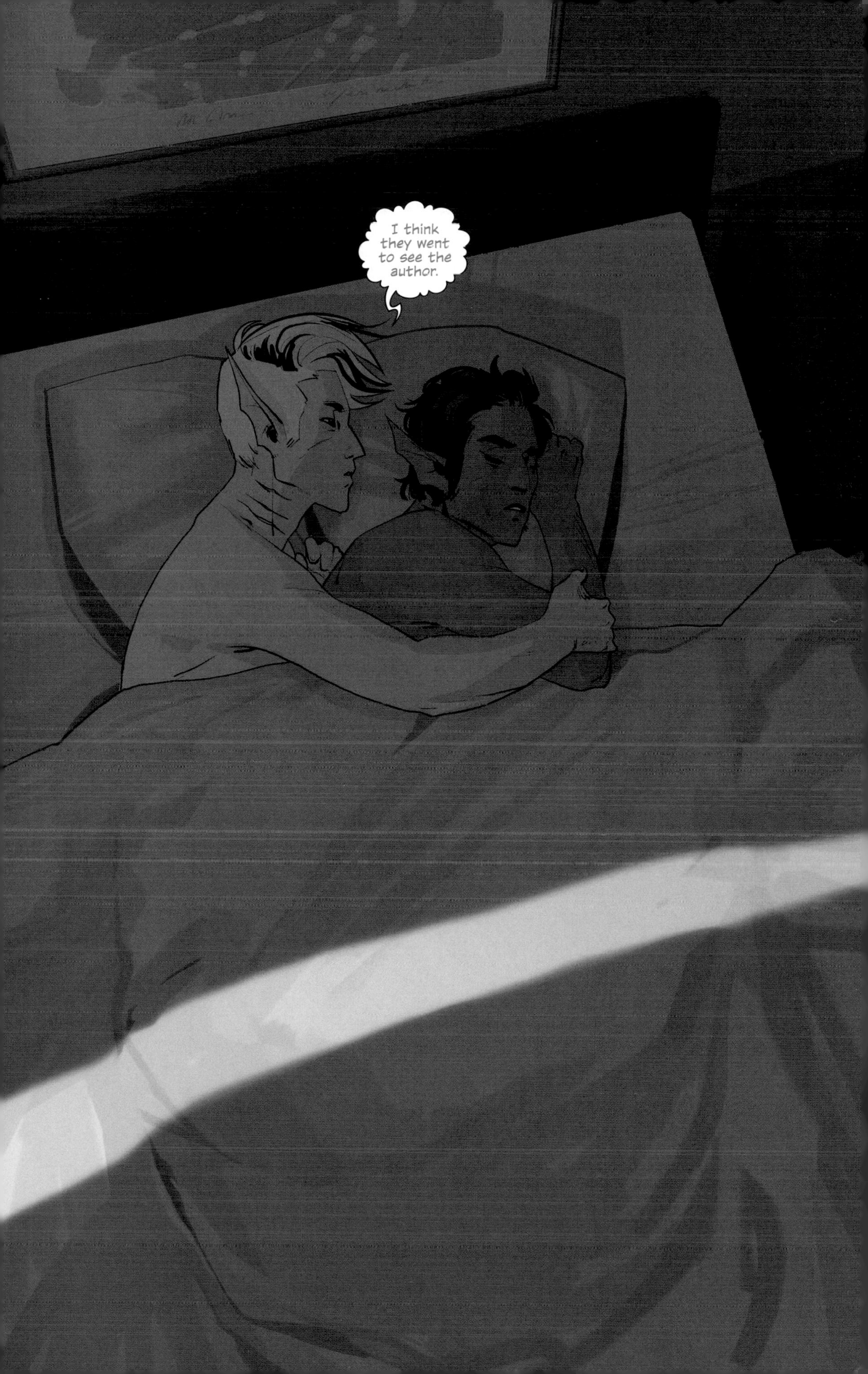
I think they went to see the author.

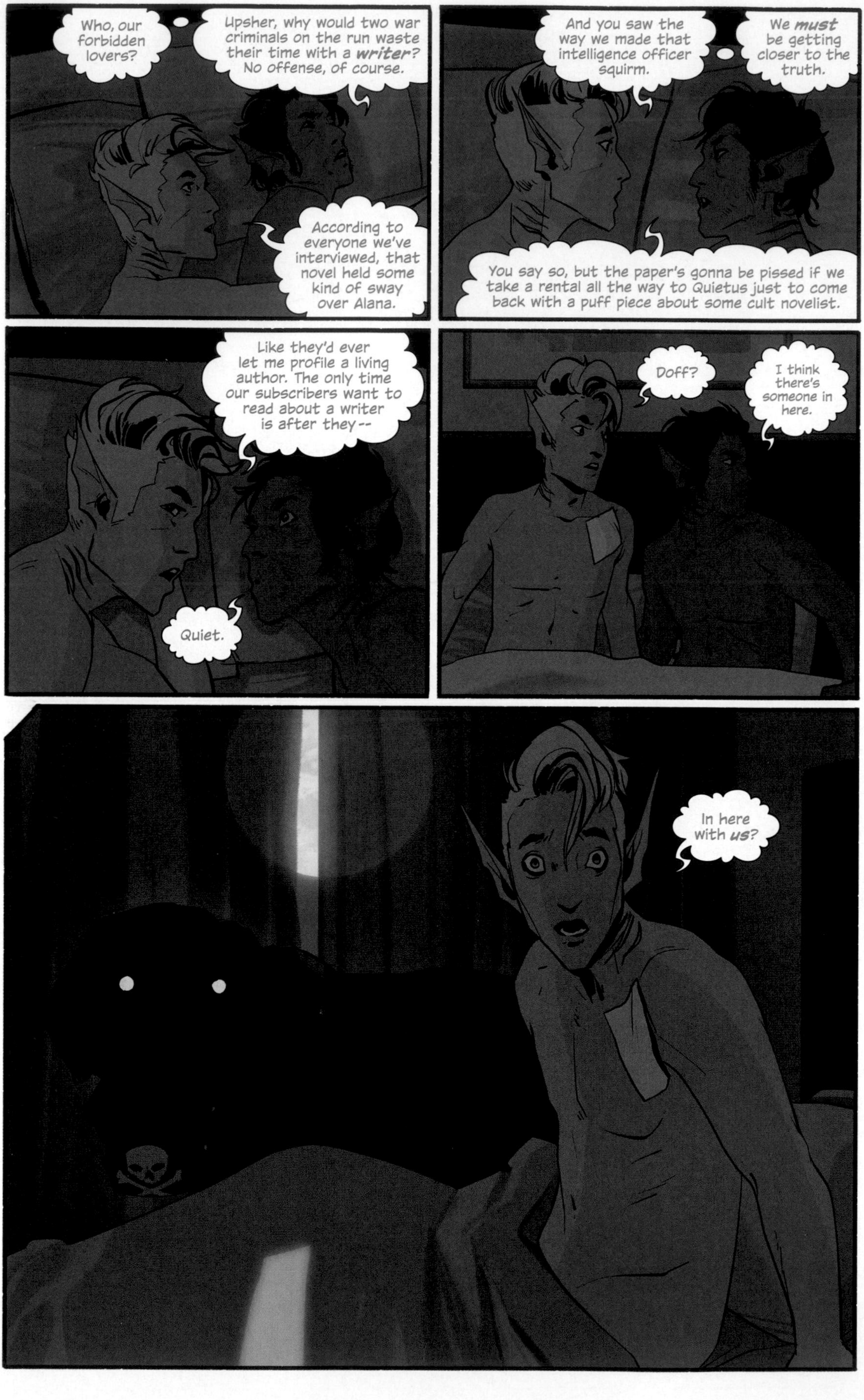
Who, our forbidden lovers?
Upsher, why would two war criminals on the run waste their time with a *writer*? No offense, of course.
According to everyone we've interviewed, that novel held some kind of sway over Alana.
And you saw the way we made that intelligence officer squirm.
We *must* be getting closer to the truth.
You say so, but the paper's gonna be pissed if we take a rental all the way to Quietus just to come back with a puff piece about some cult novelist.
Like they'd ever let me profile a living author. The only time our subscribers want to read about a writer is after they--
Quiet.
Doff?
I think there's someone in here.
In here with *us*?

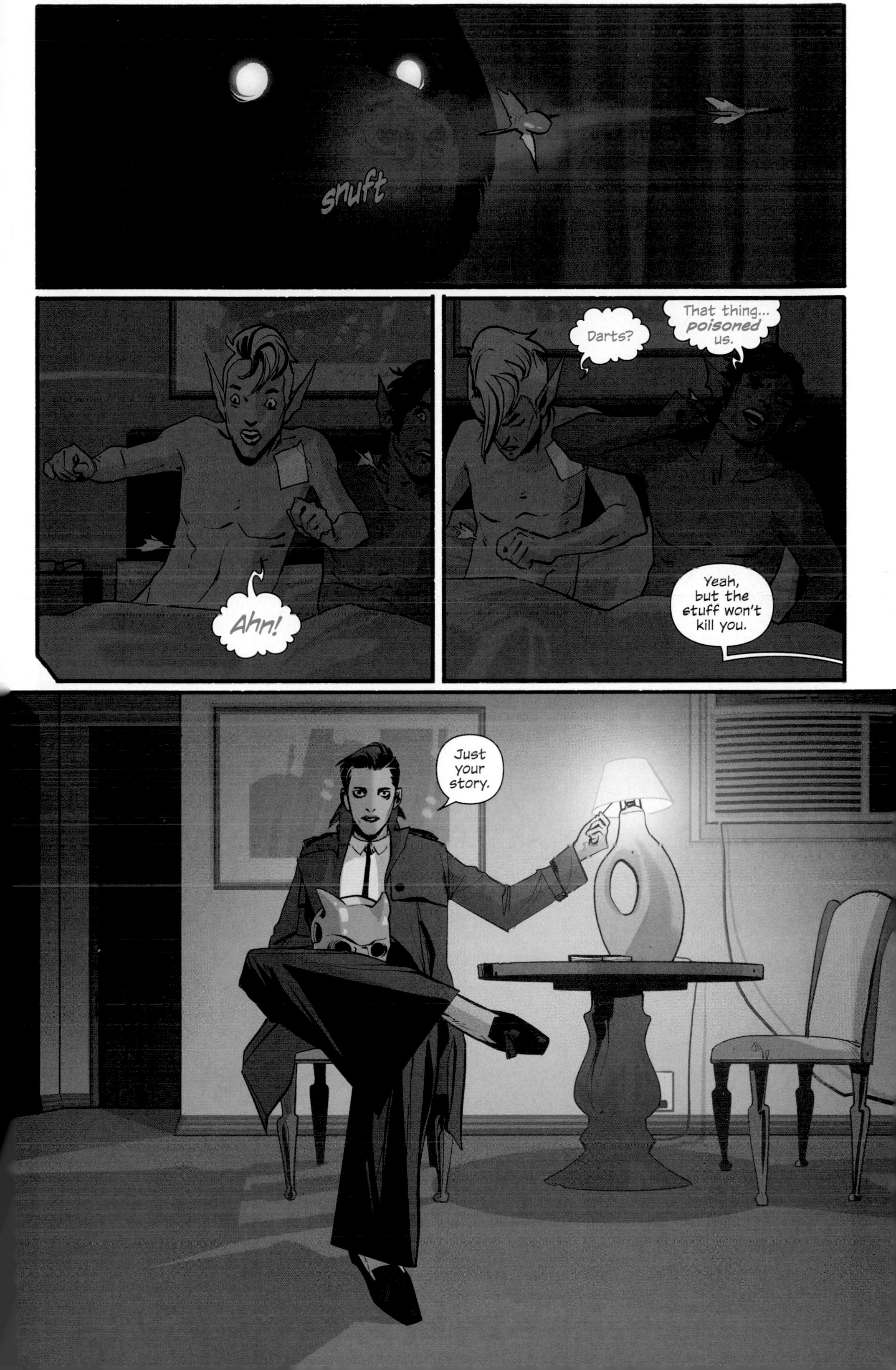
snuft
Ahn!
Darts?
That thing... poisoned us.
Yeah, but the stuff won't kill you.
Just your story.

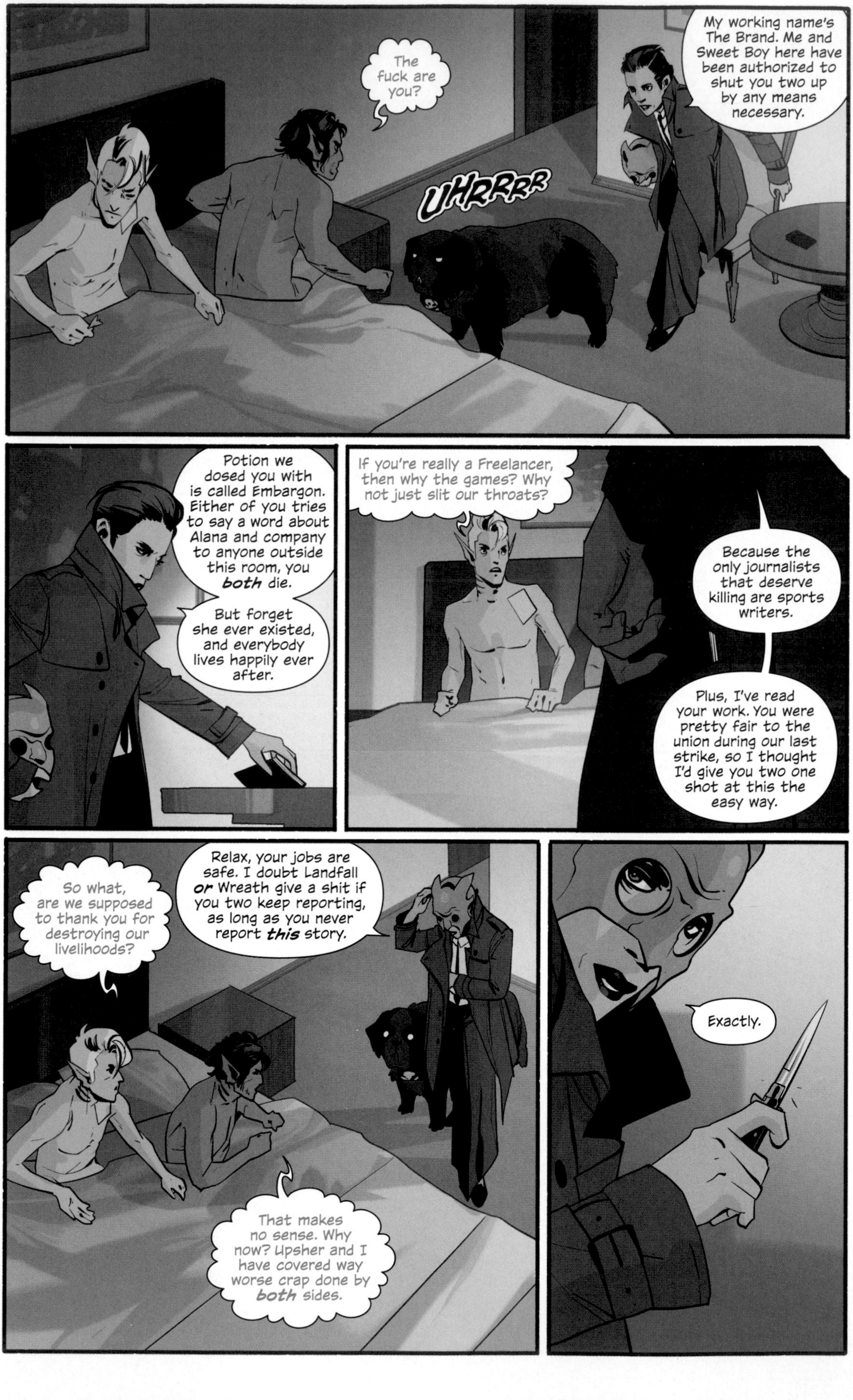
The fuck are you?
My working name's The Brand. Me and Sweet Boy here have been authorized to shut you two up by any means necessary.
UHRRRR
Potion we dosed you with is called Embargon. Either of you tries to say a word about Alana and company to anyone outside this room, you both die.
But forget she ever existed, and everybody lives happily ever after.
If you're really a Freelancer, then why the games? Why not just slit our throats?
Because the only journalists that deserve killing are sports writers.
Plus, I've read your work. You were pretty fair to the union during our last strike, so I thought I'd give you two one shot at this the easy way.
So what, are we supposed to thank you for destroying our livelihoods?
Relax, your jobs are safe. I doubt Landfall or Wreath give a shit if you two keep reporting, as long as you never report this story.
That makes no sense. Why now? Upsher and I have covered way worse crap done by both sides.
Exactly.

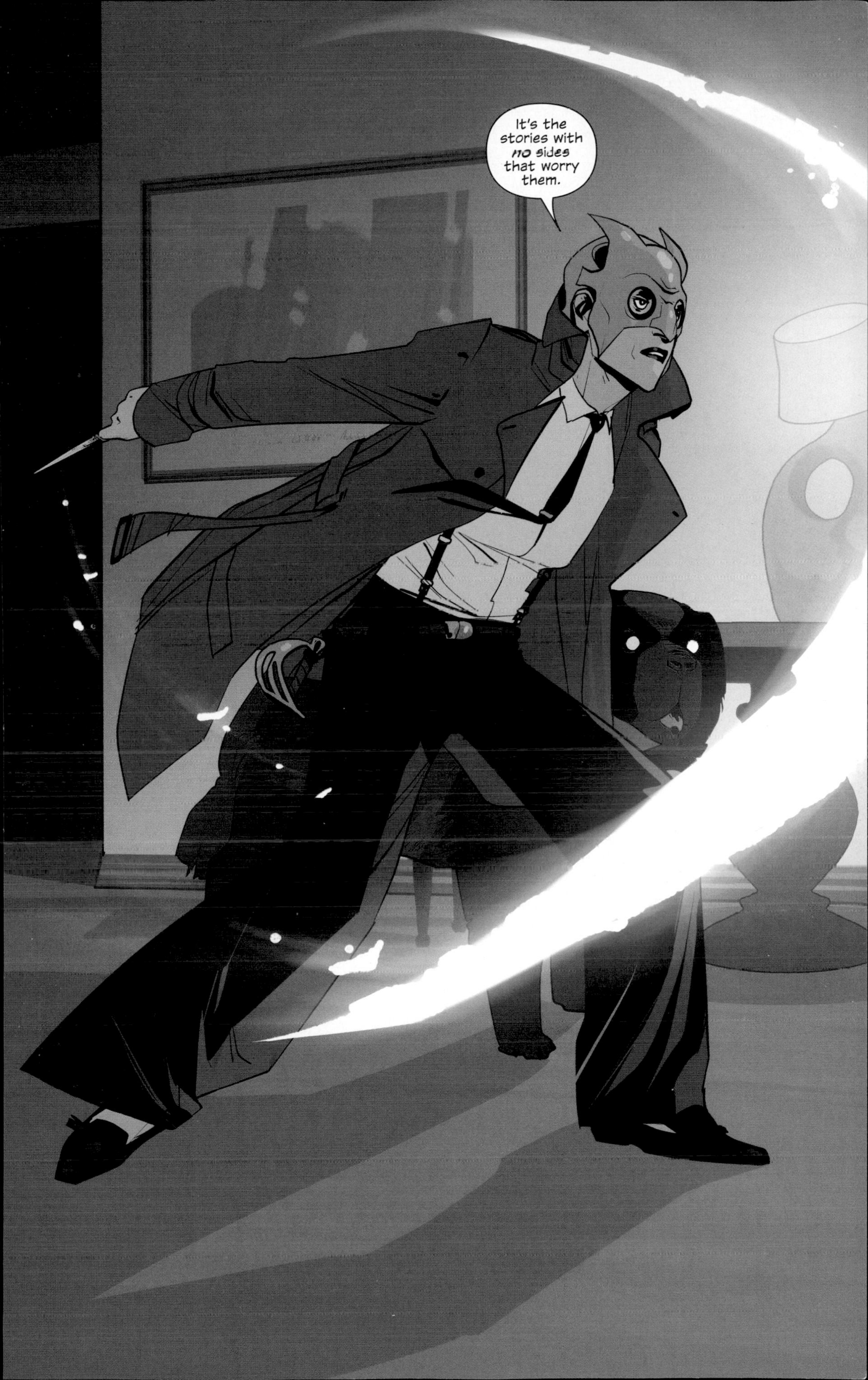
It's the stories with *no* sides that worry them.

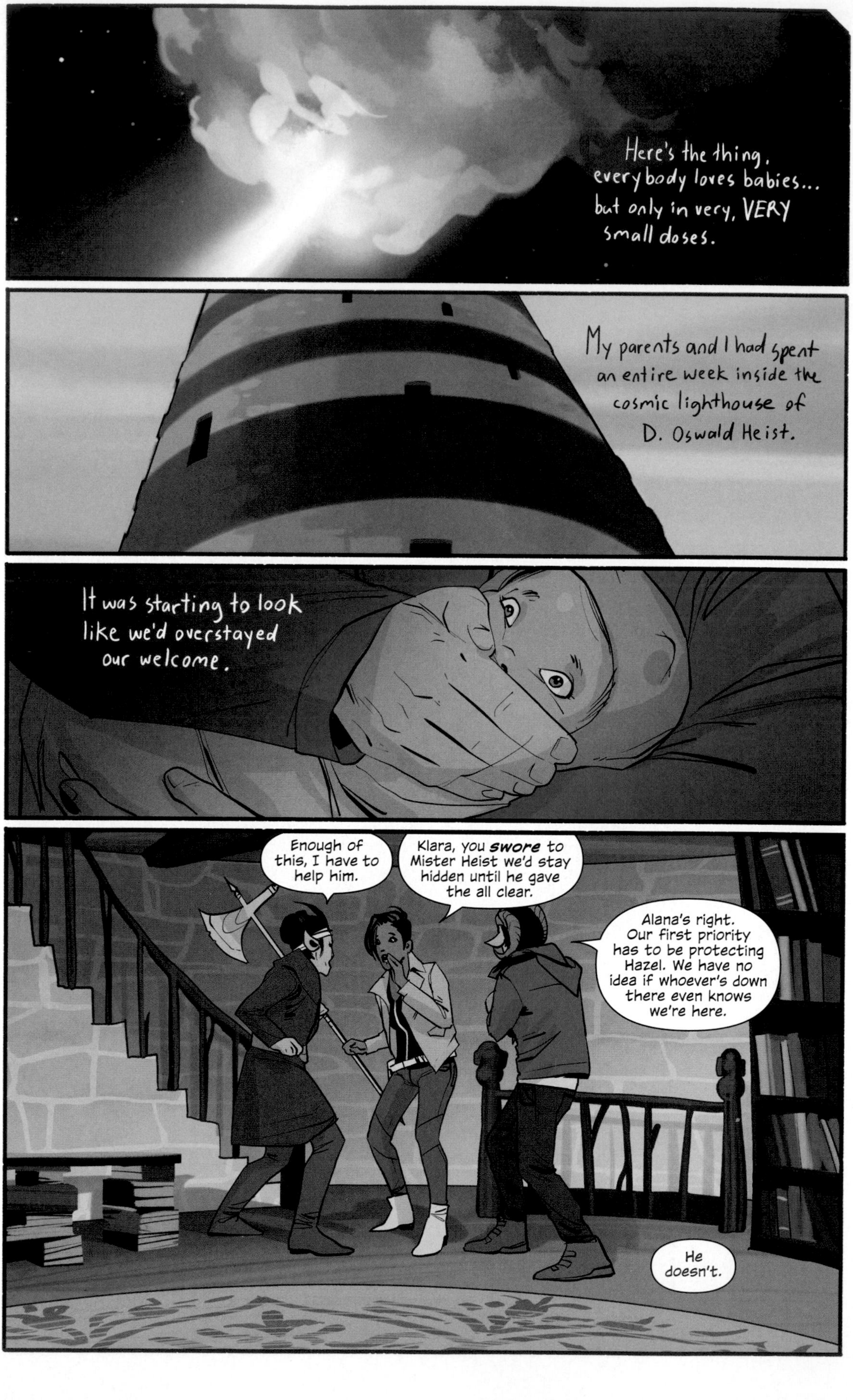
Here's the thing, everybody loves babies... but only in very, VERY small doses.
My parents and I had spent an entire week inside the cosmic lighthouse of D. Oswald Heist.
It was starting to look like we'd overstayed our welcome.
Enough of this, I have to help him.
Klara, you **swore** to Mister Heist we'd stay hidden until he gave the all clear.
Alana's right. Our first priority has to be protecting Hazel. We have no idea if whoever's down there even knows we're here.
He doesn't.

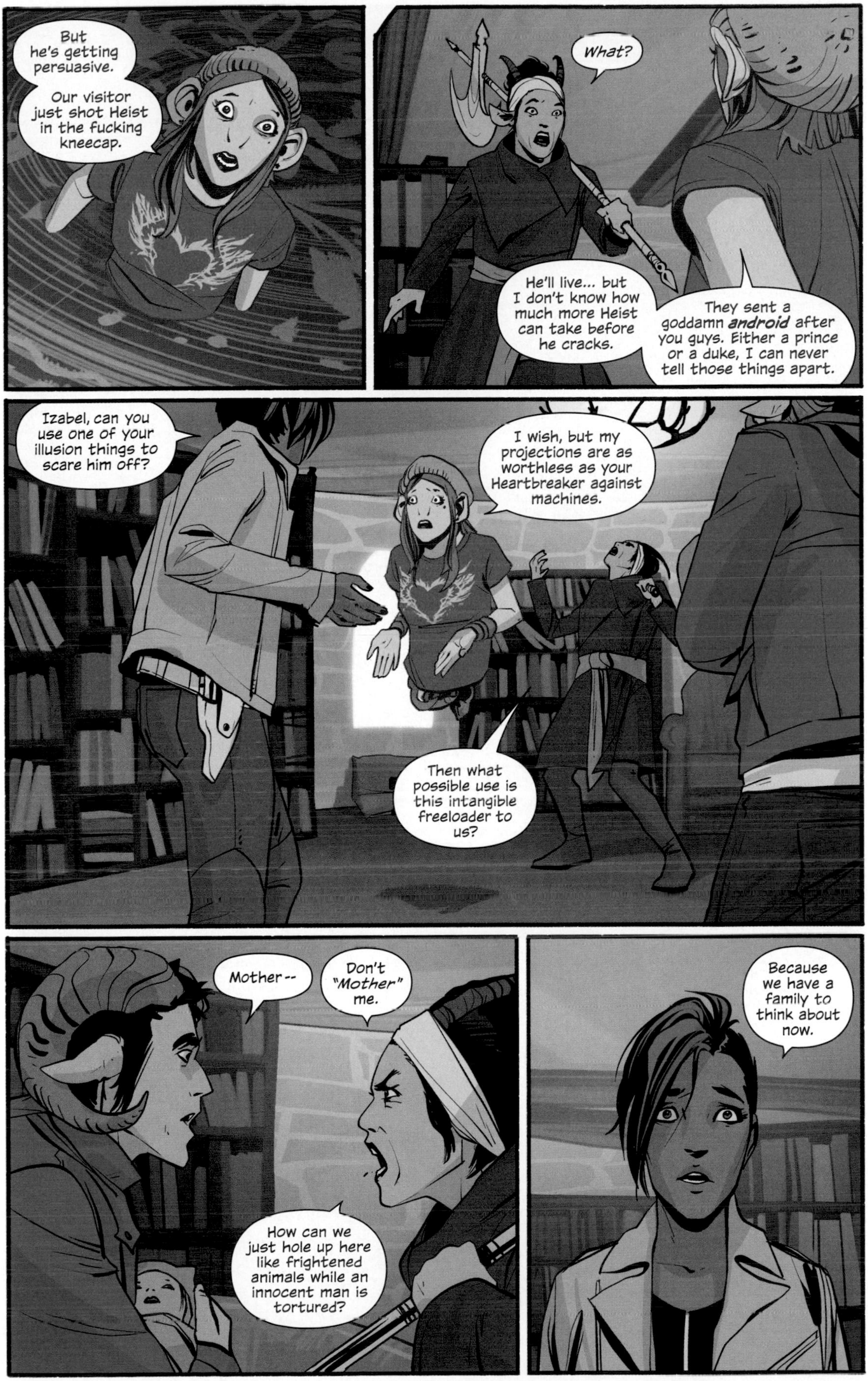
But he's getting persuasive.
Our visitor just shot Heist in the fucking kneecap.
What?
He'll live... but I don't know how much more Heist can take before he cracks.
They sent a goddamn *android* after you guys. Either a prince or a duke, I can never tell those things apart.
Izabel, can you use one of your illusion things to scare him off?
I wish, but my projections are as worthless as your Heartbreaker against machines.
Then what possible use is this intangible freeloader to us?
Mother--
Don't "*Mother*" me.
How can we just hole up here like frightened animals while an innocent man is tortured?
Because we have a family to think about now.

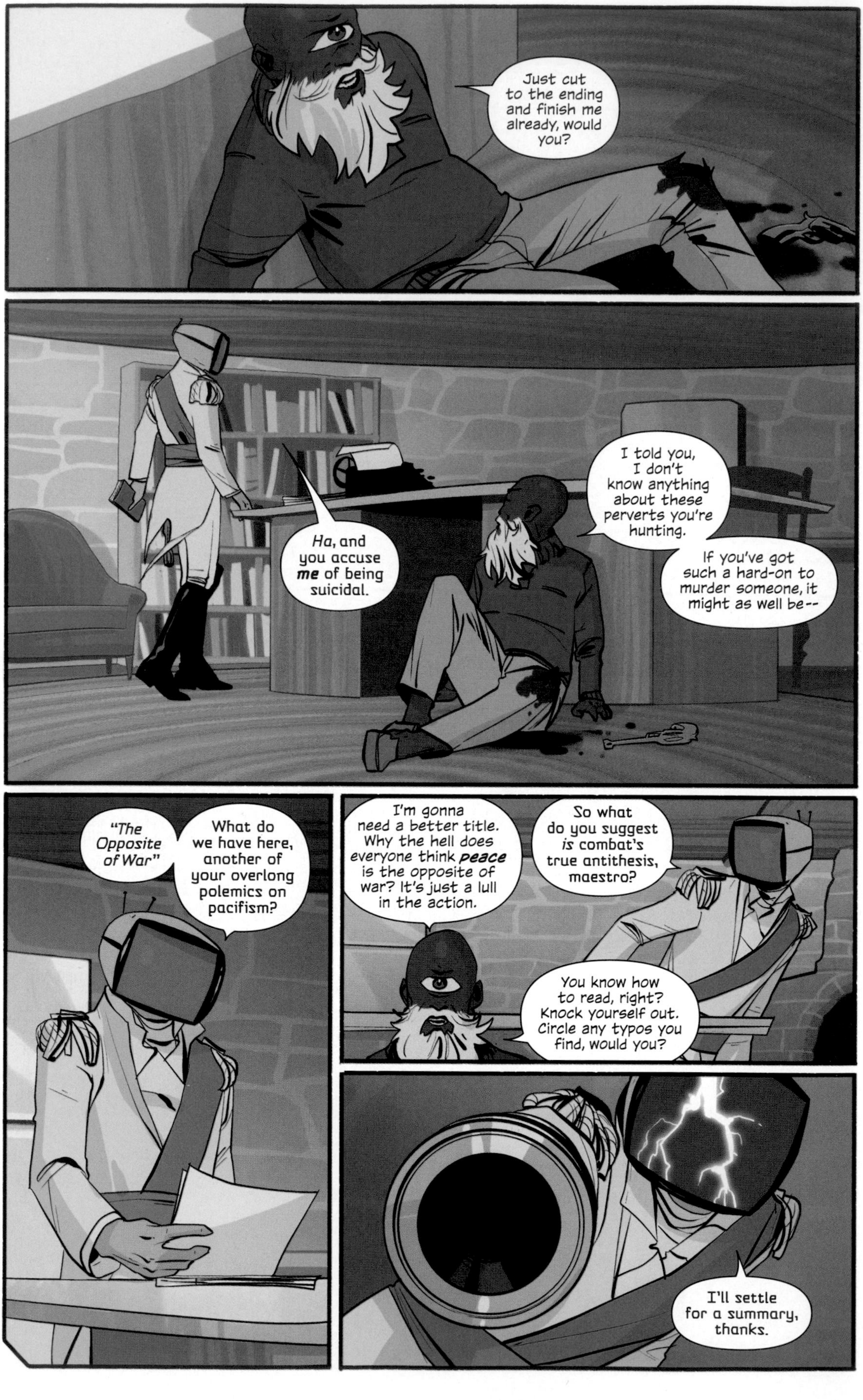

Just cut to the ending and finish me already, would you?
I told you, I don't know anything about these perverts you're hunting.
If you've got such a hard-on to murder someone, it might as well be--
Ha, and you accuse **me** of being suicidal.
"The Opposite of War"
What do we have here, another of your overlong polemics on pacifism?
I'm gonna need a better title. Why the hell does everyone think **peace** is the opposite of war? It's just a lull in the action.
So what do you suggest *is* combat's true antithesis, maestro?
You know how to read, right? Knock yourself out. Circle any typos you find, would you?
I'll settle for a summary, thanks.

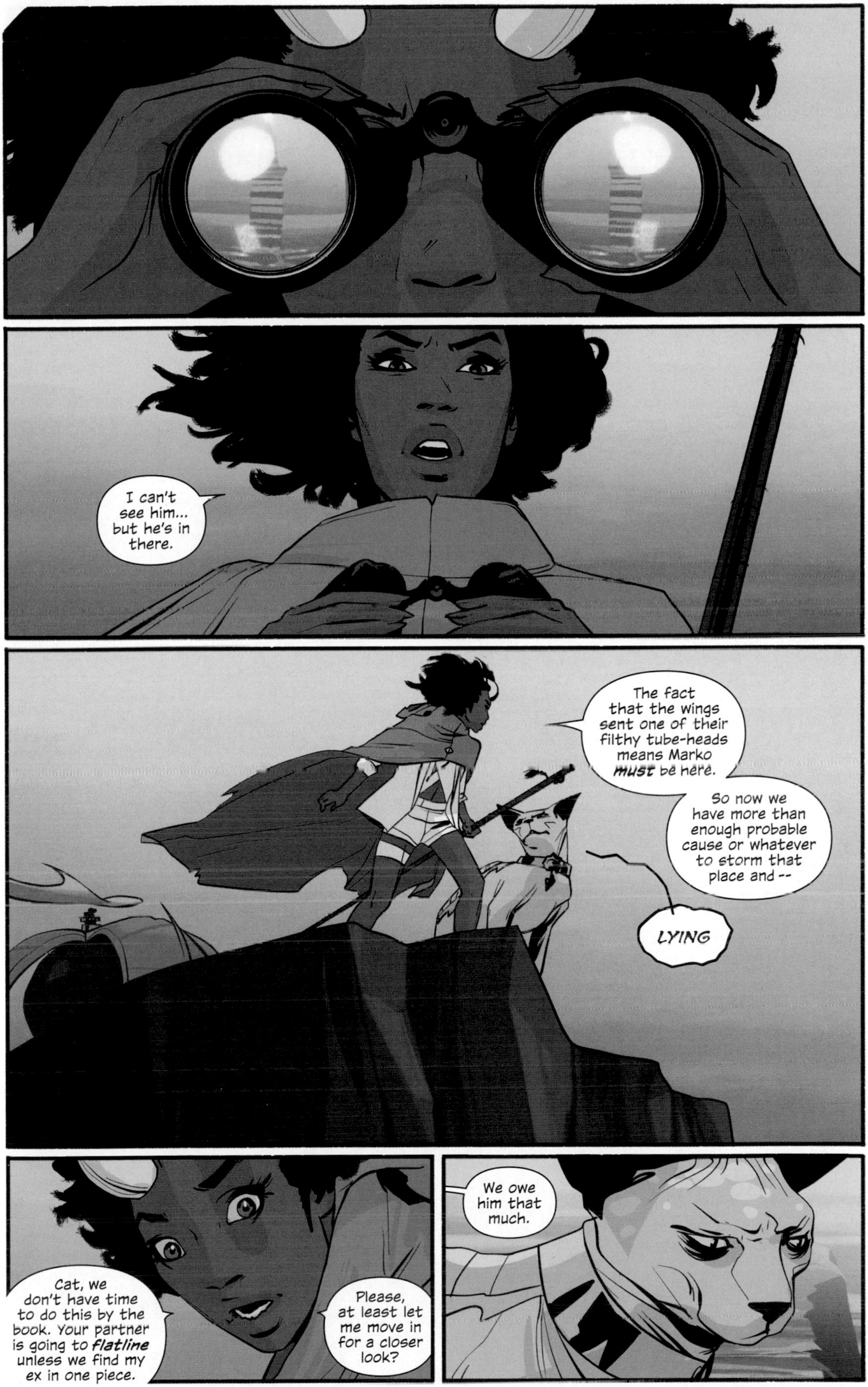
I can't see him... but he's in there.
The fact that the wings sent one of their filthy tube-heads means Marko *must* be here.
So now we have more than enough probable cause or whatever to storm that place and --
LYING
Cat, we don't have time to do this by the book. Your partner is going to *flatline* unless we find my ex in one piece.
Please, at least let me move in for a closer look?
We owe him that much.

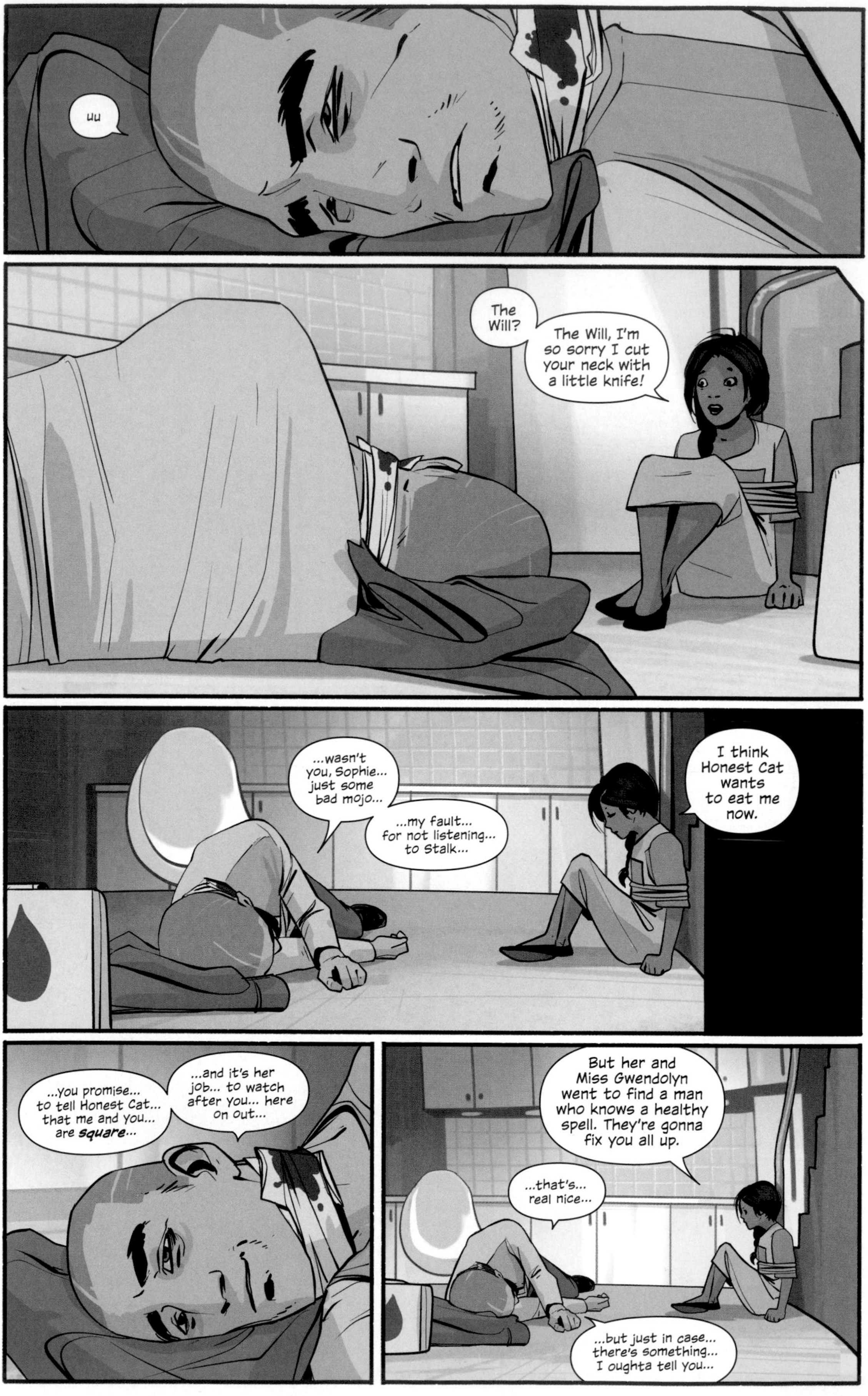
uu
The Will?
The Will, I'm so sorry I cut your neck with a little knife!
...wasn't you, Sophie... just some bad mojo...
...my fault... for not listening... to Stalk...
I think Honest Cat wants to eat me now.
...you promise... to tell Honest Cat... that me and you... are *square*...
...and it's her job... to watch after you... here on out...
But her and Miss Gwendolyn went to find a man who knows a healthy spell. They're gonna fix you all up.
...that's... real nice...
...but just in case... there's something... I oughta tell you...

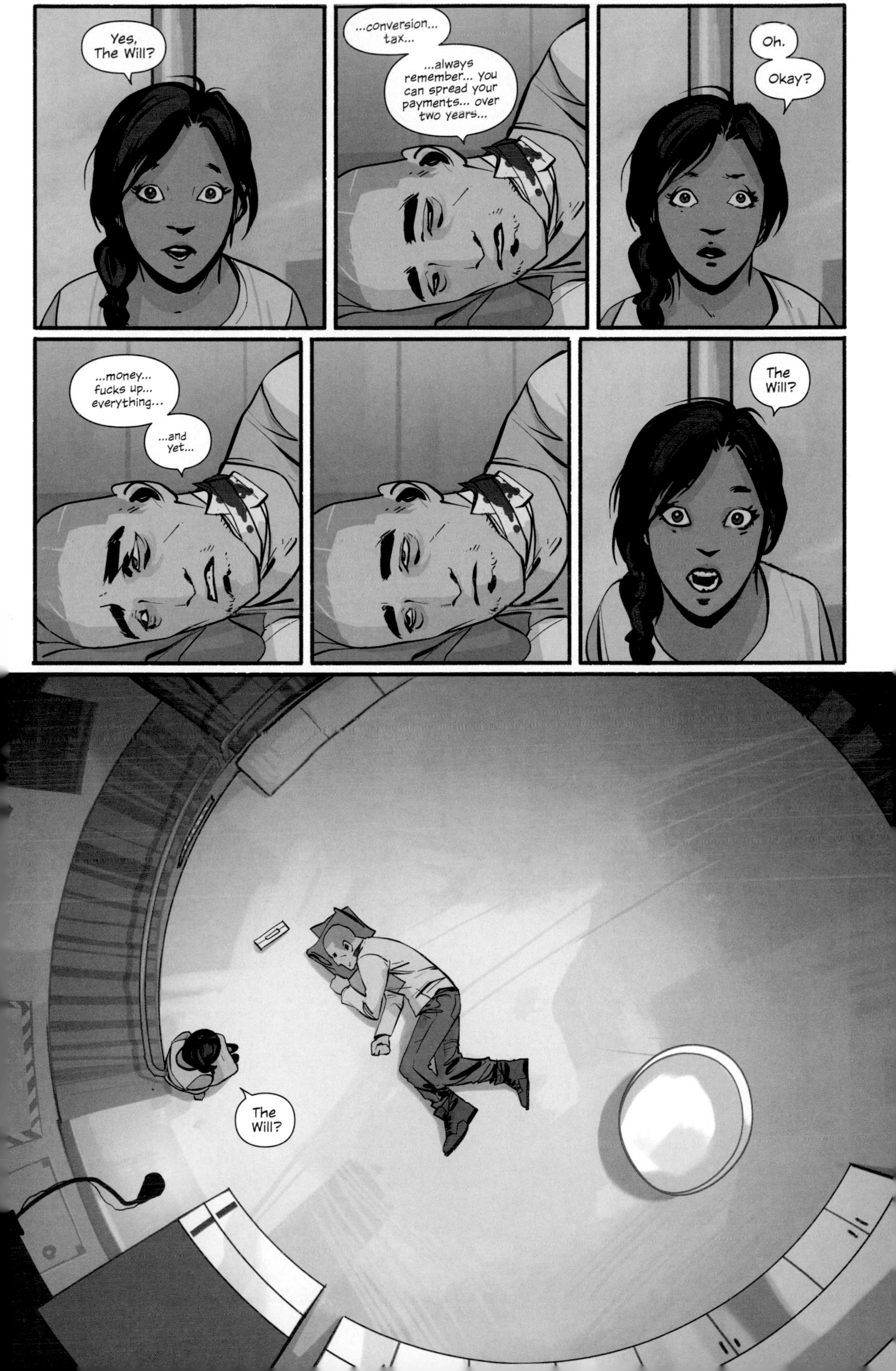
Yes, The Will?
...conversion... tax...
...always remember... You can spread your payments... over two years...
Oh.
Okay?
...money... fucks up... everything...
...and yet...
The Will?
The Will?

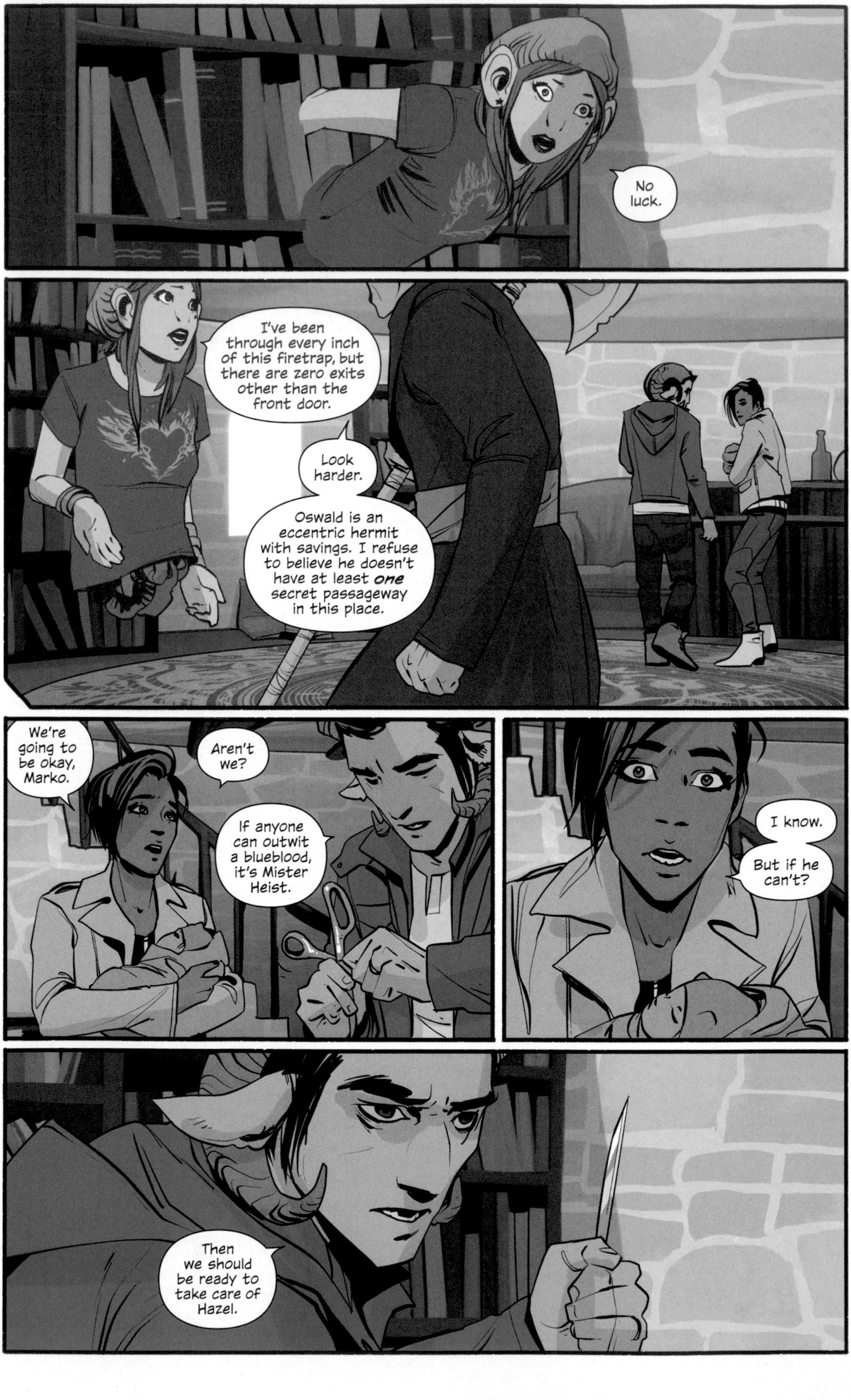
No luck.
I've been through every inch of this firetrap, but there are zero exits other than the front door.
Look harder.
Oswald is an eccentric hermit with savings. I refuse to believe he doesn't have at least ***one*** secret passageway in this place.
We're going to be okay, Marko.
Aren't we?
If anyone can outwit a blueblood, it's Mister Heist.
I know.
But if he can't?
Then we should be ready to take care of Hazel.

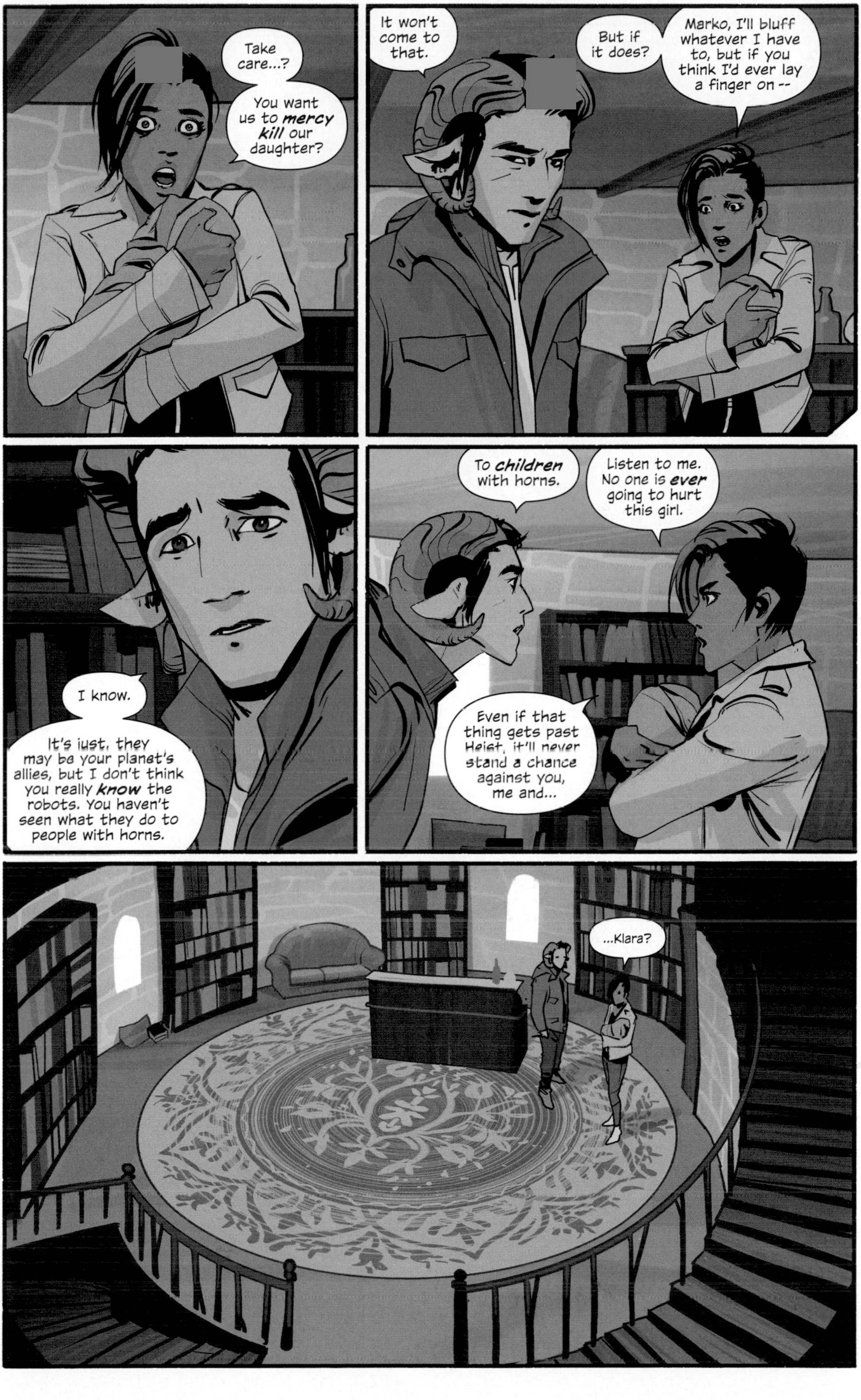
Take care...?
You want us to *mercy kill* our daughter?
It won't come to that.
But if it does?
Marko, I'll bluff whatever I have to, but if you think I'd ever lay a finger on --
I know.
It's just, they may be your planet's allies, but I don't think you really *know* the robots. You haven't seen what they do to people with horns.
To *children* with horns.
Listen to me. No one is *ever* going to hurt this girl.
Even if that thing gets past Heist, it'll never stand a chance against you, me and...
...Klara?

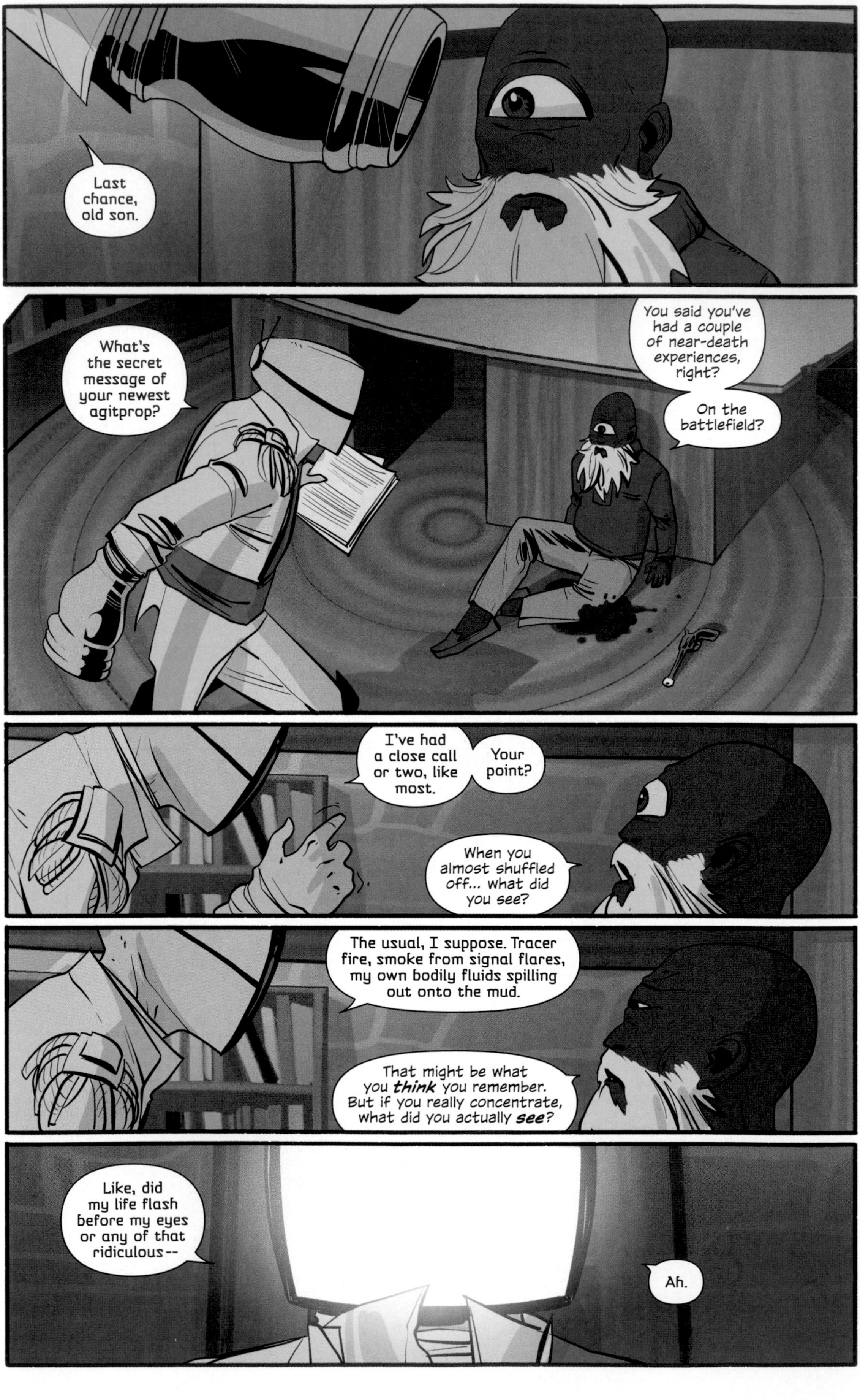
Last chance, old son.
What's the secret message of your newest agitprop?
You said you've had a couple of near-death experiences, right?
On the battlefield?
I've had a close call or two, like most.
Your point?
When you almost shuffled off... what did you see?
The usual, I suppose. Tracer fire, smoke from signal flares, my own bodily fluids spilling out onto the mud.
That might be what you *think* you remember. But if you really concentrate, what did you actually *see*?
Like, did my life flash before my eyes or any of that ridiculous--
Ah.

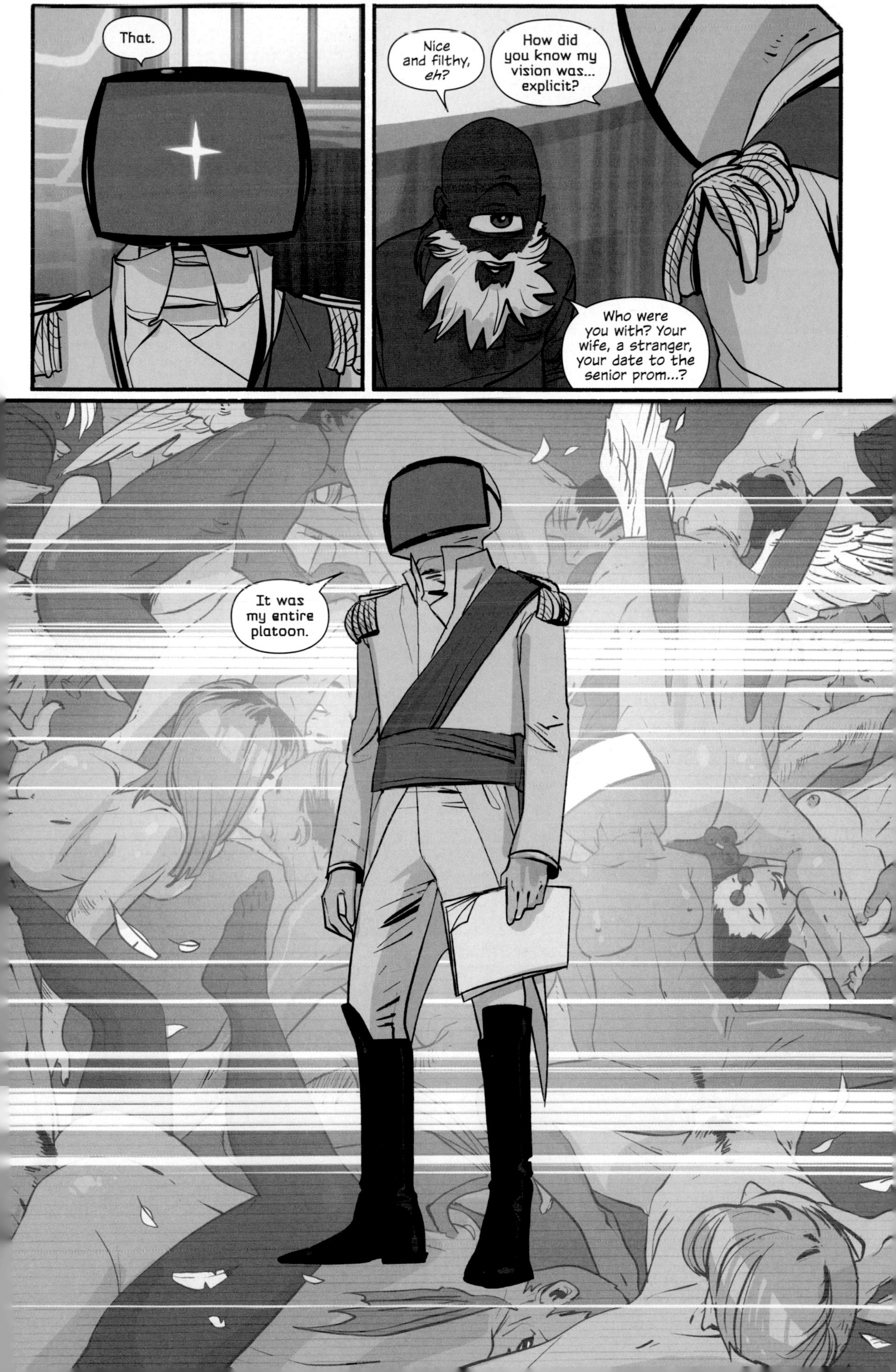
That.
Nice and filthy, *eh?*
How did you know my vision was... explicit?
Who were you with? Your wife, a stranger, your date to the senior prom...?
It was my entire platoon.

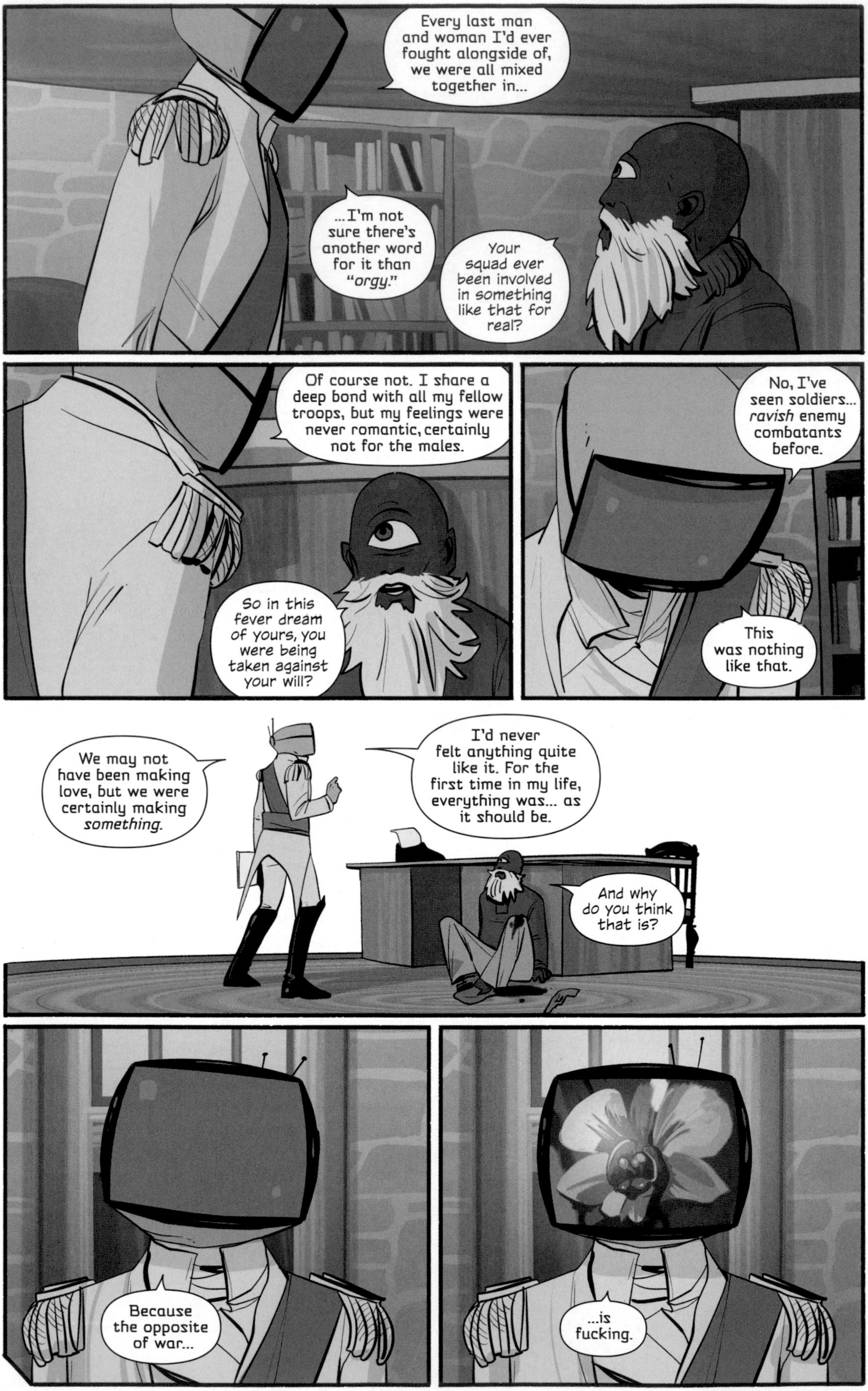
Every last man and woman I'd ever fought alongside of, we were all mixed together in...
...I'm not sure there's another word for it than "orgy."
Your squad ever been involved in something like that for real?
Of course not. I share a deep bond with all my fellow troops, but my feelings were never romantic, certainly not for the males.
So in this fever dream of yours, you were being taken against your will?
No, I've seen soldiers... ravish enemy combatants before.
This was nothing like that.
We may not have been making love, but we were certainly making something.
I'd never felt anything quite like it. For the first time in my life, everything was... as it should be.
And why do you think that is?
Because the opposite of war...
...is fucking.

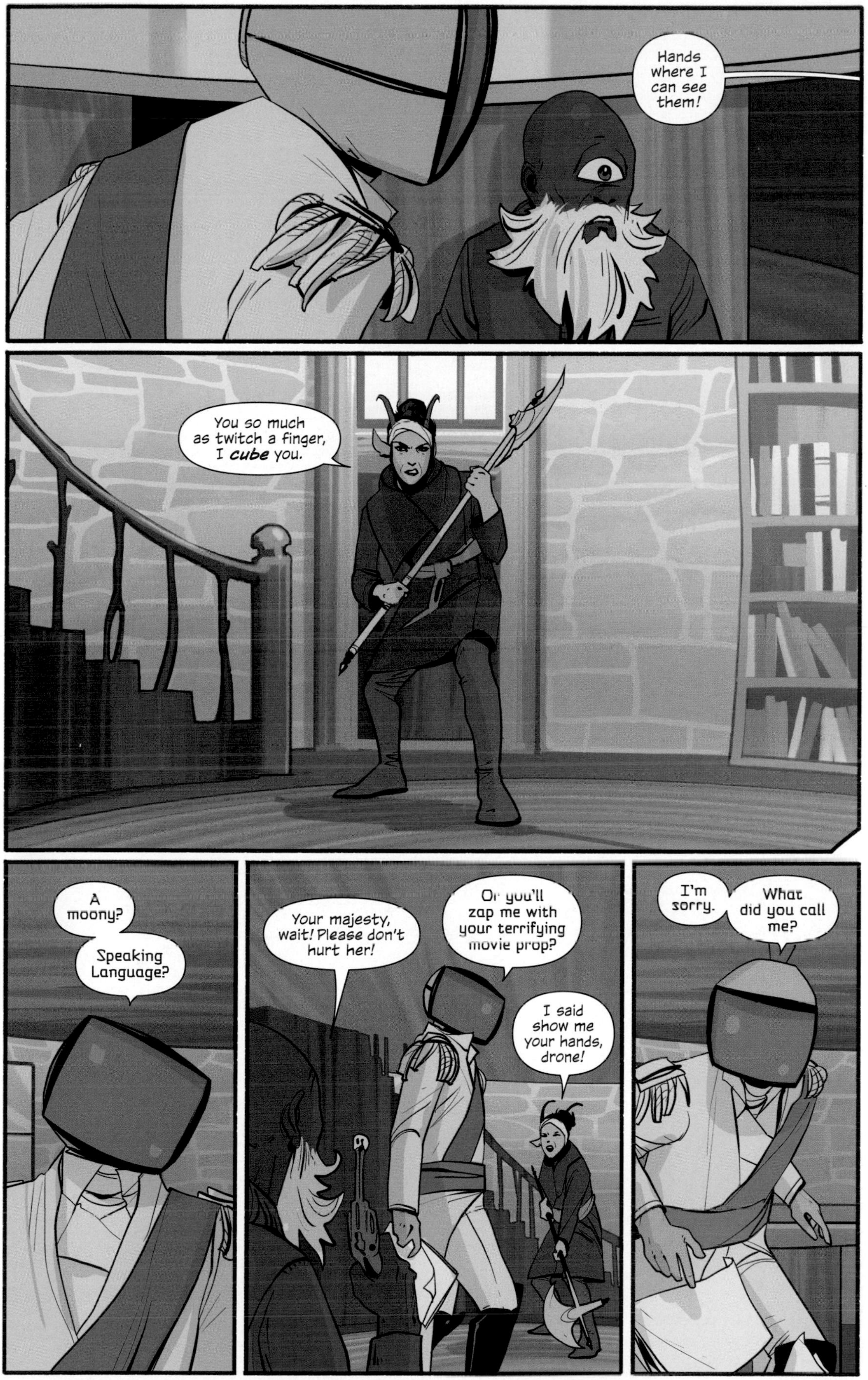
Hands where I can see them!
You so much as twitch a finger, I *cube* you.
A moony?
Speaking Language?
Your majesty, wait! Please don't hurt her!
Or you'll zap me with your terrifying movie prop?
I said show me your hands, drone!
I'm sorry.
What did you call me?

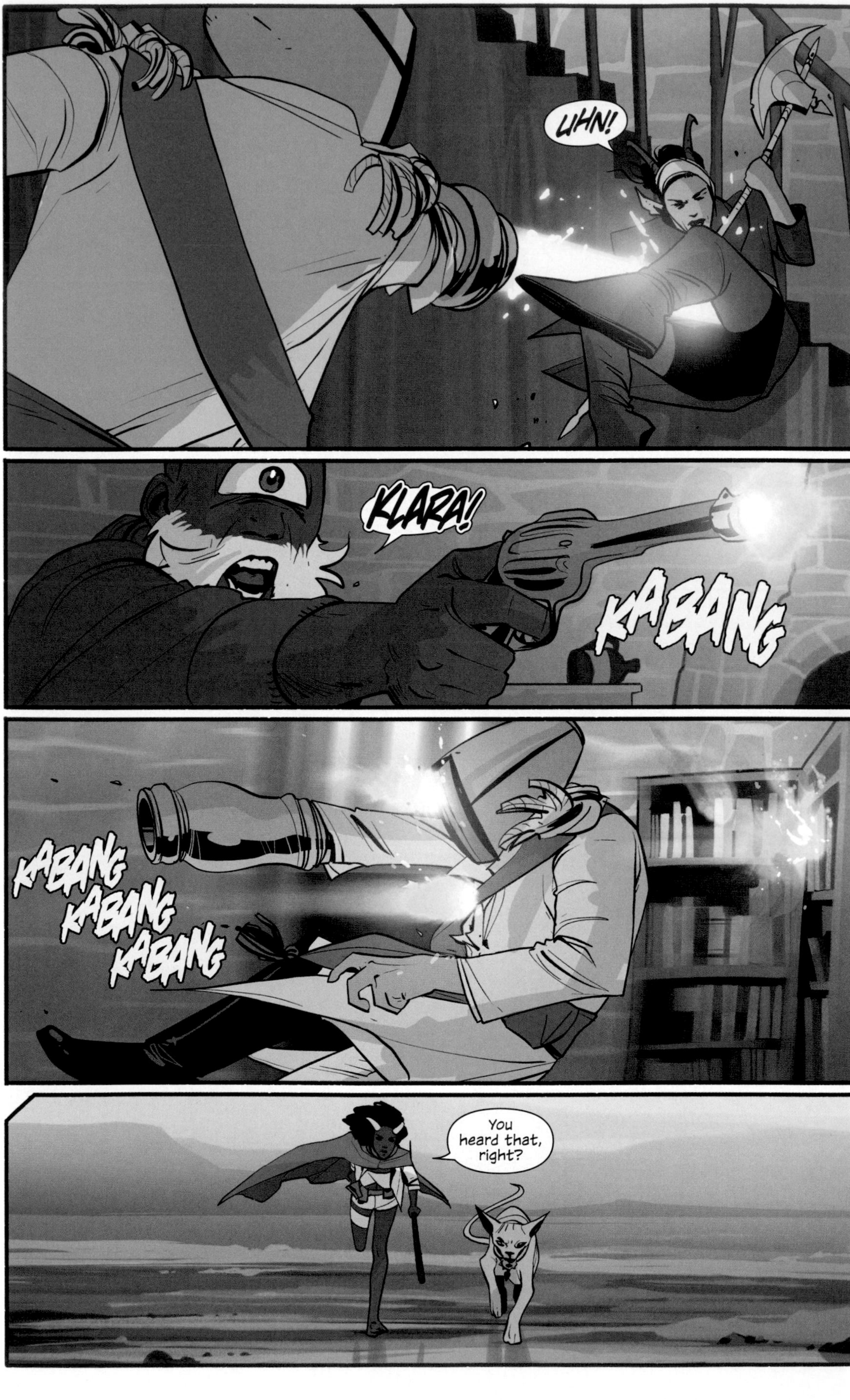
UHN!
KLARA!
KABANG
KABANG
KABANG
KABANG
You heard that, right?

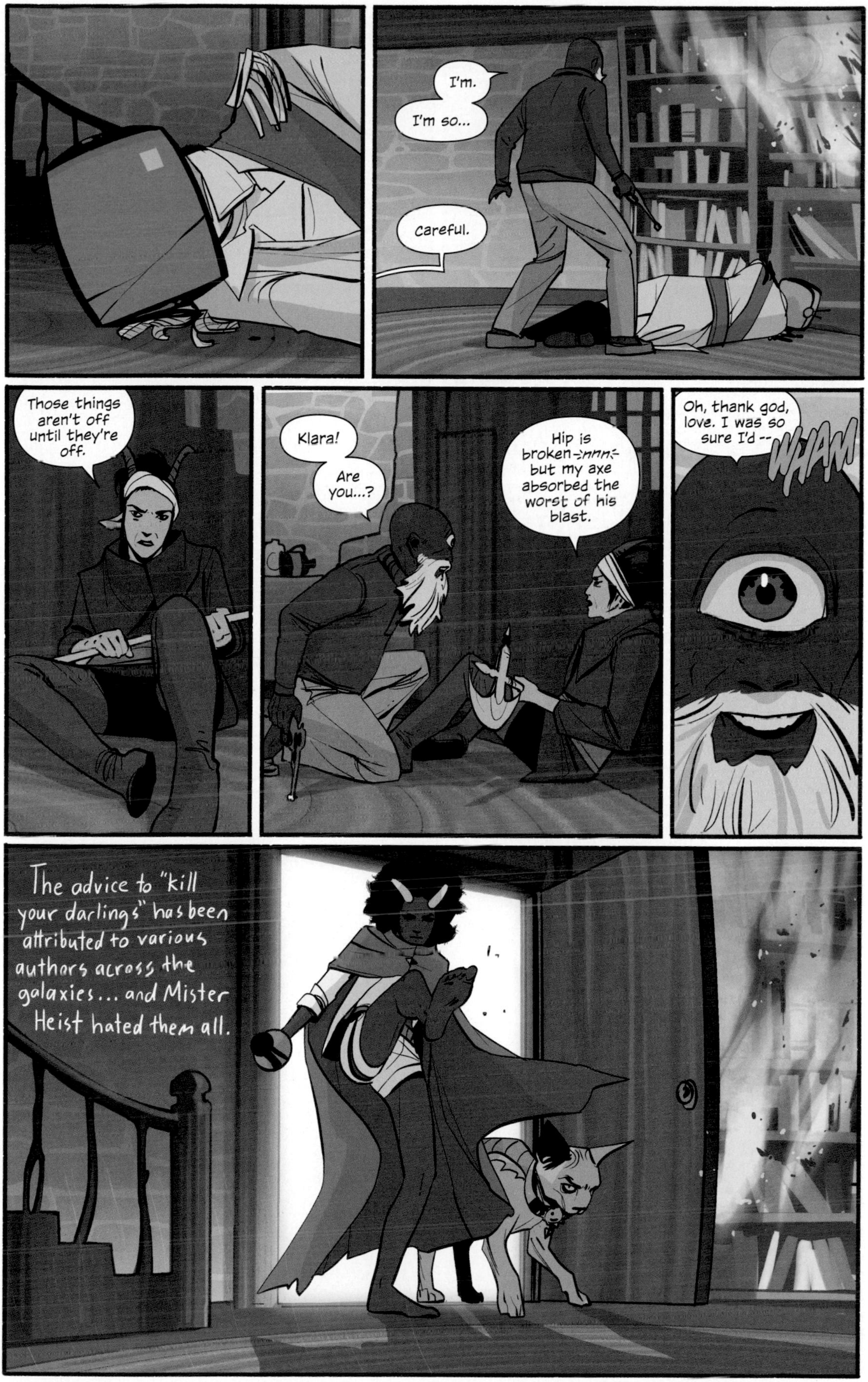
I'm.
I'm so...
Careful.
Those things aren't off until they're off.
Klara!
Are you...?
Hip is broken-=nnn=- but my axe absorbed the worst of his blast.
Oh, thank god, love. I was so sure I'd --
WHAM
The advice to "kill your darlings" has been attributed to various authors across the galaxies... and Mister Heist hated them all.
!

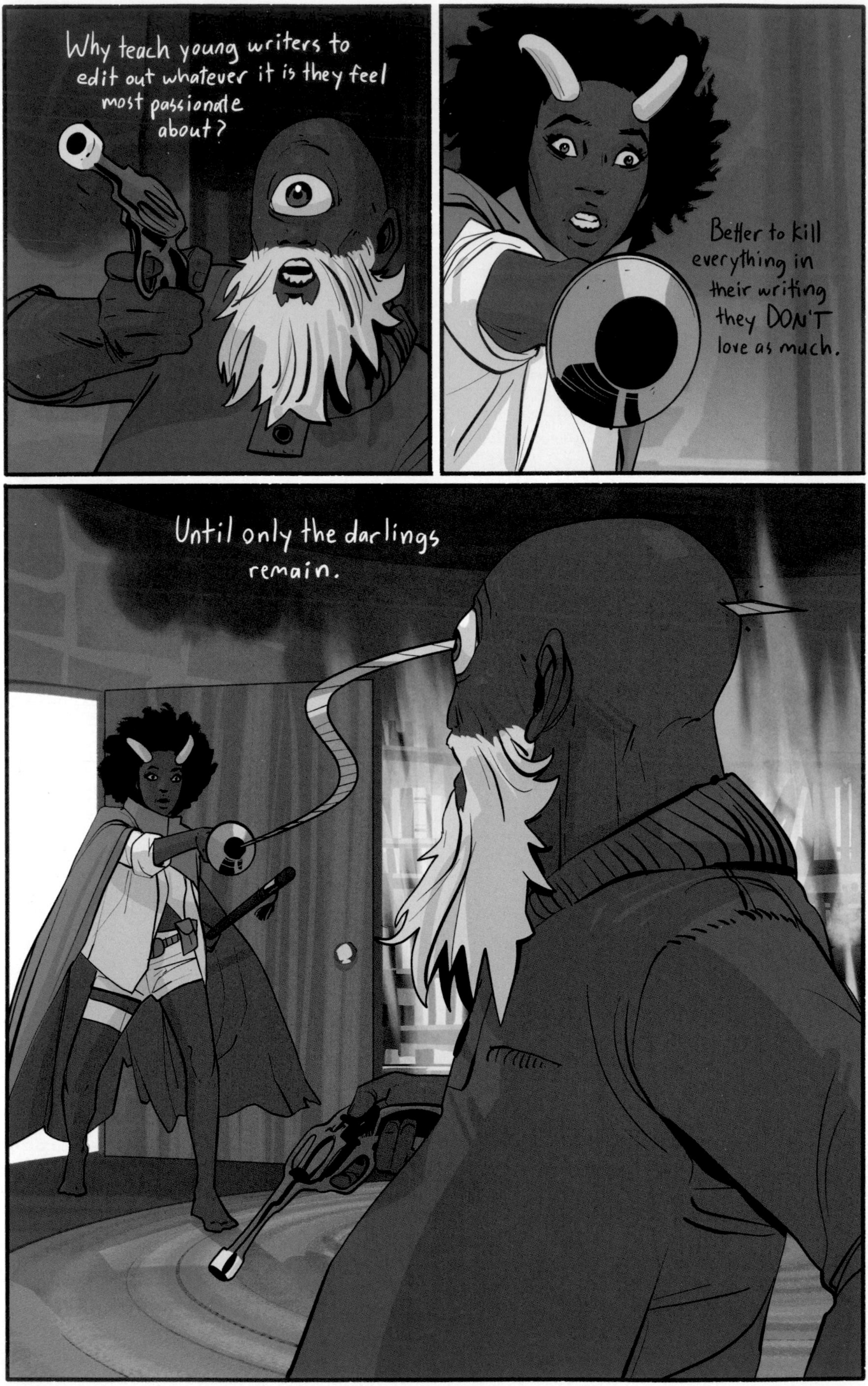
Why teach young writers to edit out whatever it is they feel most passionate about?
Better to kill everything in their writing they DON'T love as much.
Until only the darlings remain.

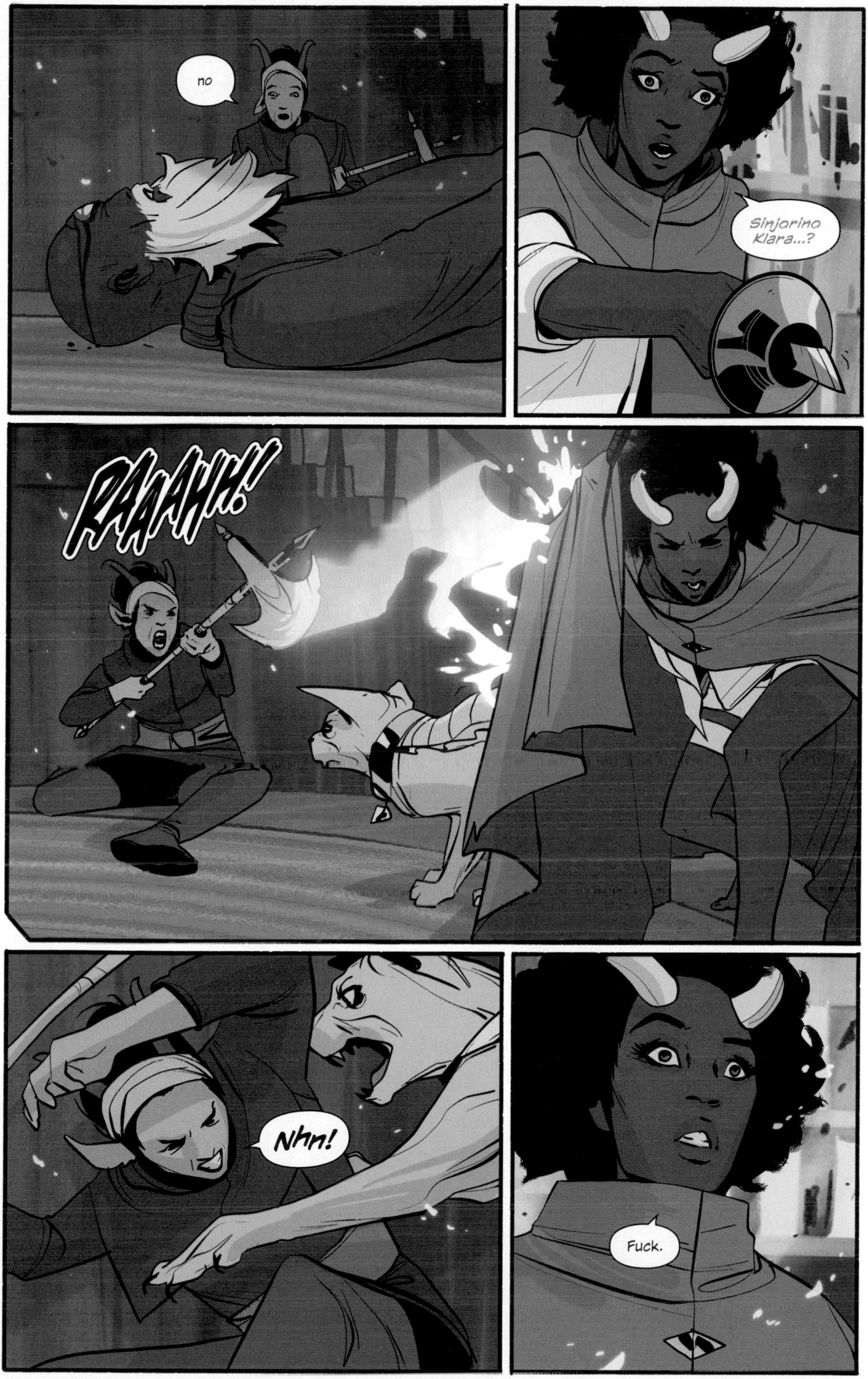
no
Sinjorino Klara...?
RAAAHH!
Nhn!
Fuck.

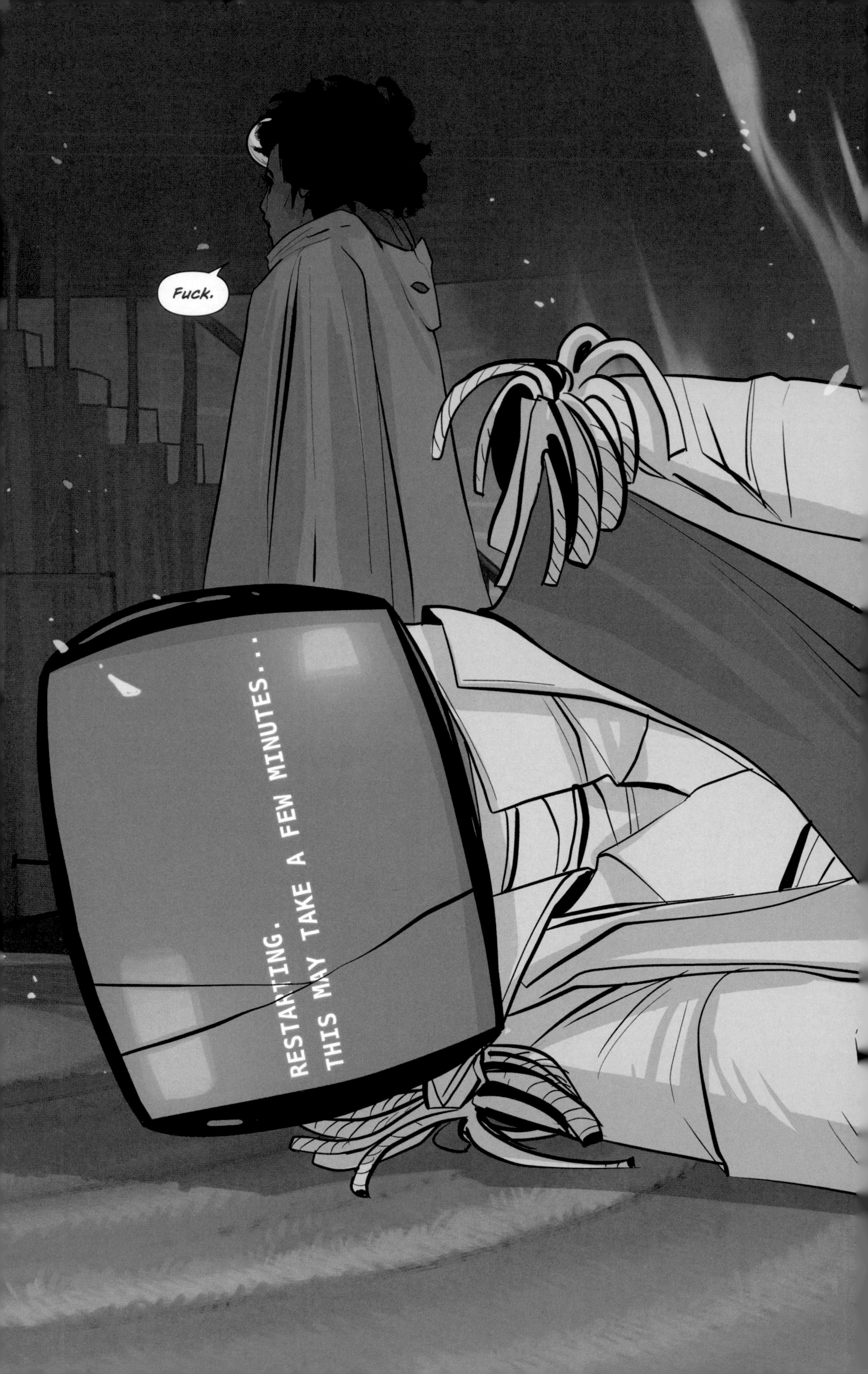
Fuck.
RESTARTING.
THIS MAY TAKE A FEW MINUTES...

end chapter seventeen

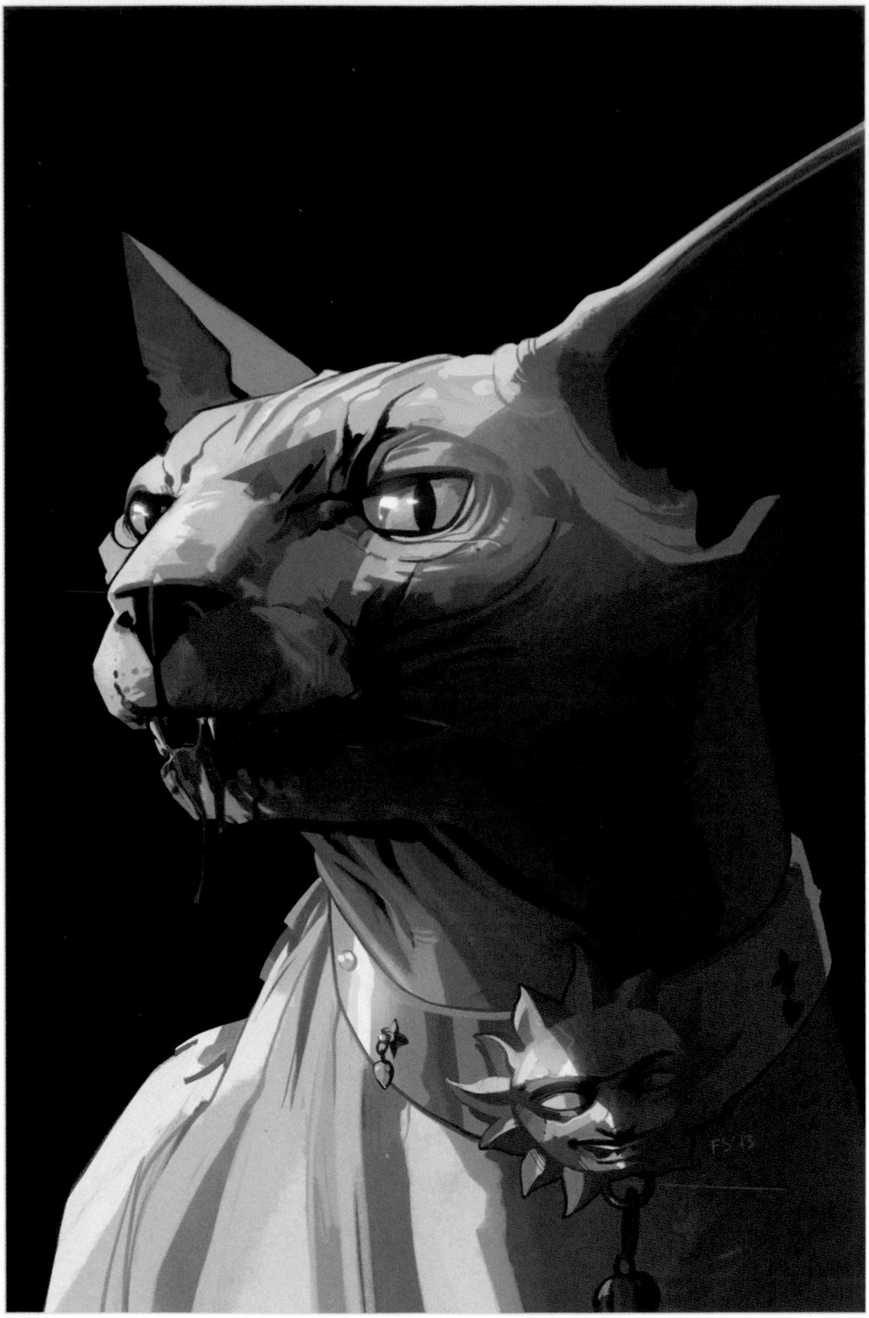
FS'13

CHAPTER
EIGHTEEN

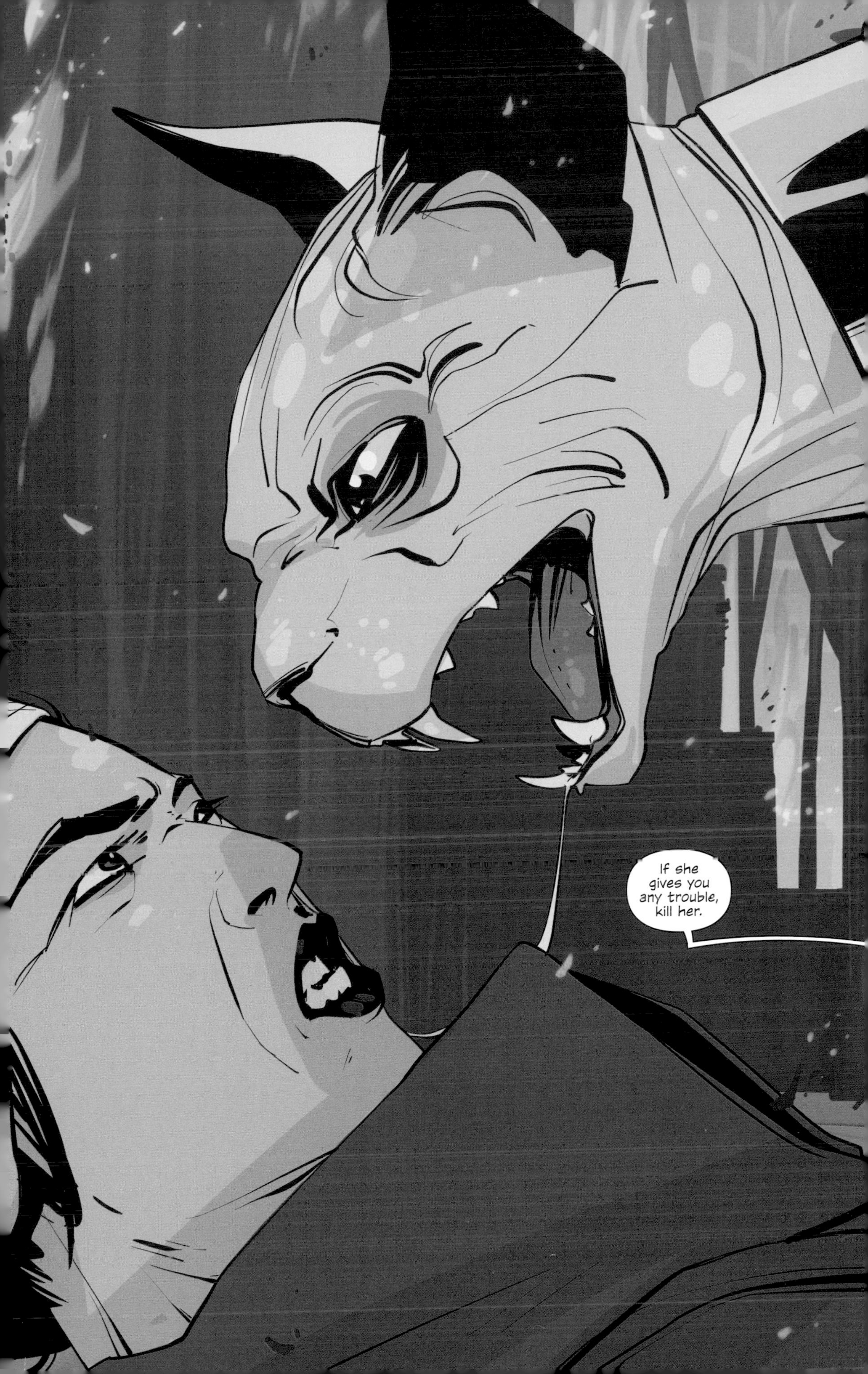
If she gives you any trouble, kill her.

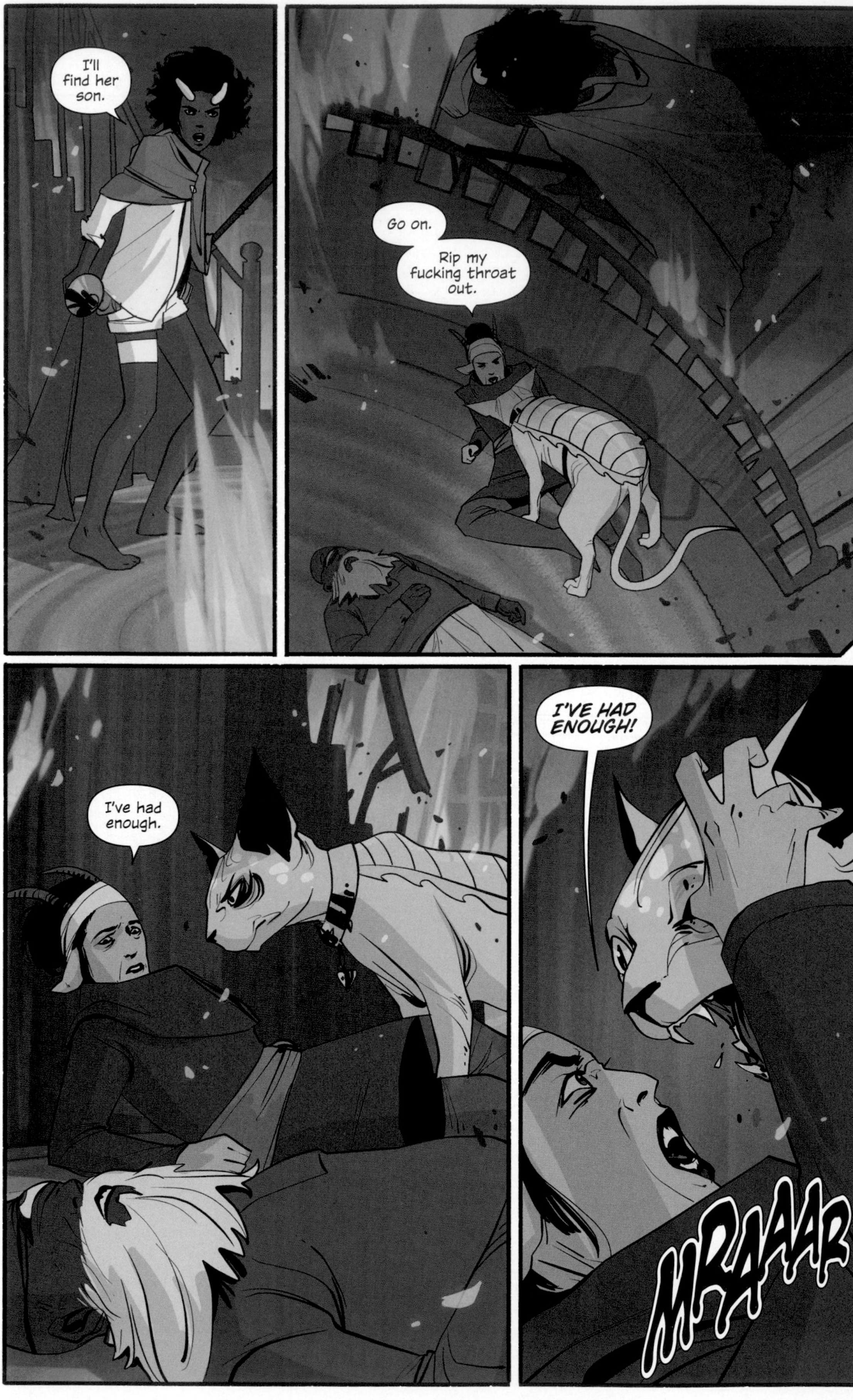
I'll find her son.
Go on.
Rip my fucking throat out.
I've had enough.
I'VE HAD ENOUGH!
MRAAAR

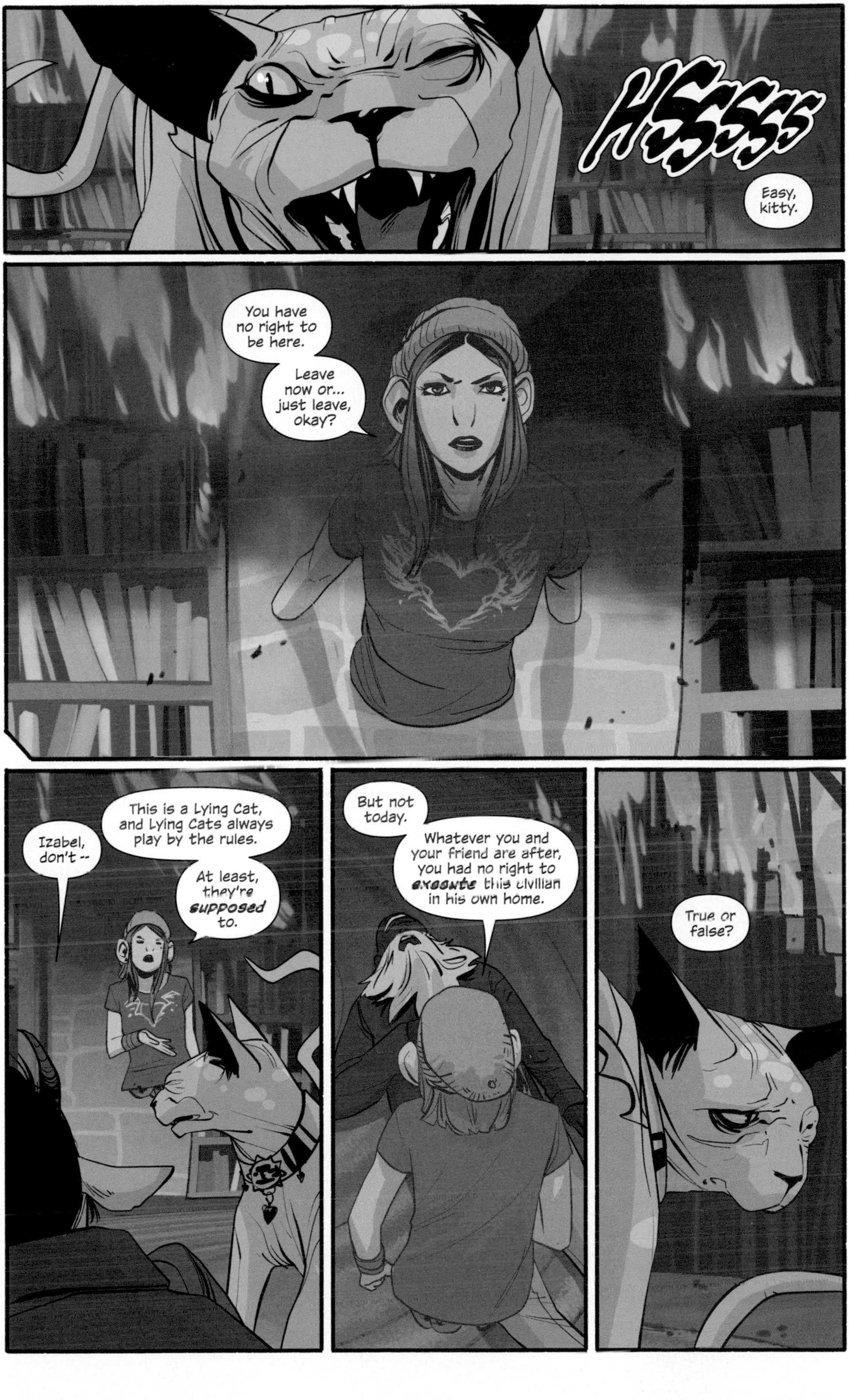
HSSSSS
Easy, kitty.
You have no right to be here.
Leave now or... just leave, okay?
Izabel, don't --
This is a Lying Cat, and Lying Cats always play by the rules.
At least, they're *supposed* to.
But not today.
Whatever you and your friend are after, you had no right to *execute* this civilian in his own home.
True or false?

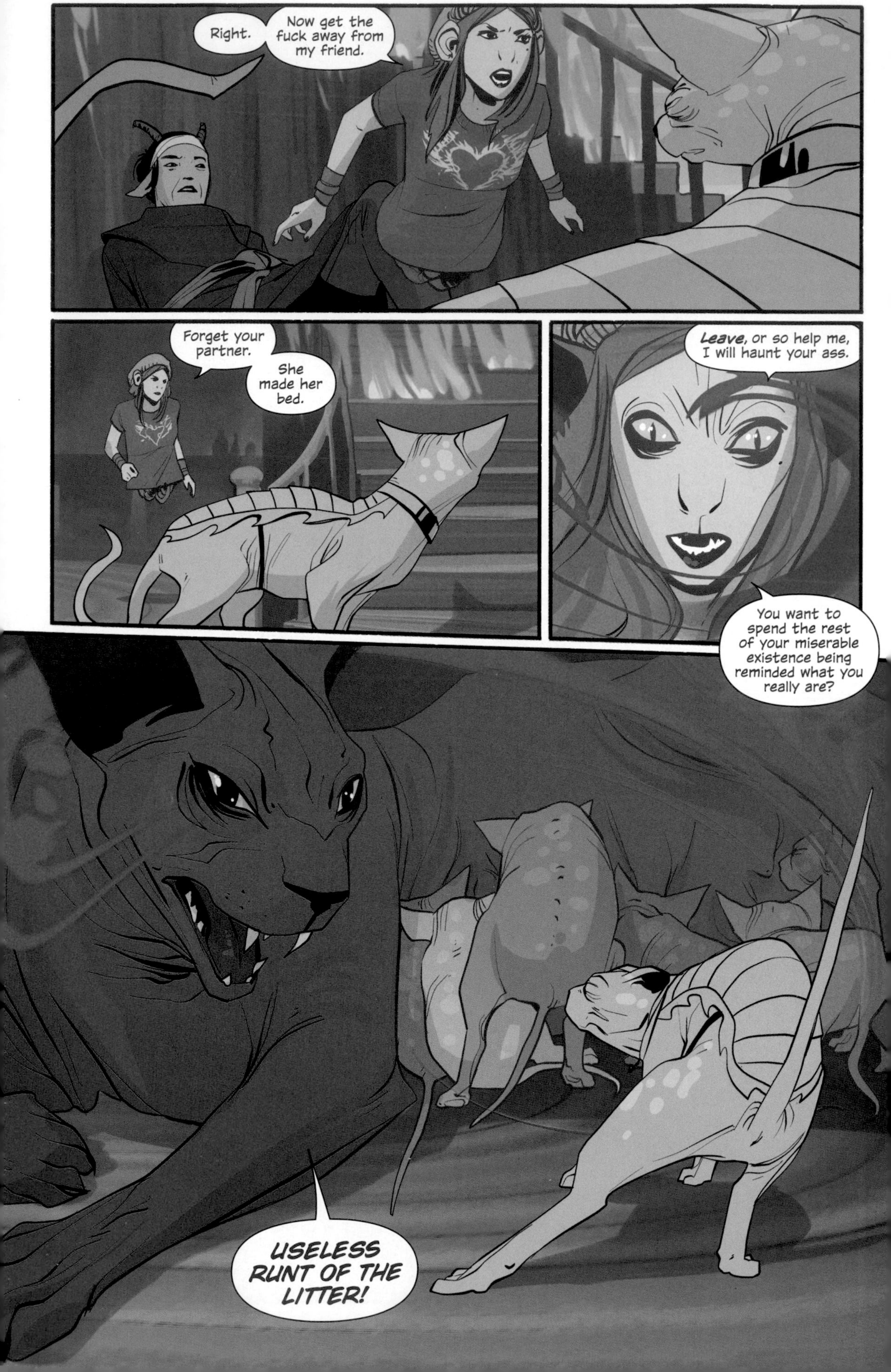
Right.
Now get the fuck away from my friend.
Forget your partner.
She made her bed.
Leave, or so help me, I will haunt your ass.
You want to spend the rest of your miserable existence being reminded what you really are?
USELESS RUNT OF THE LITTER!

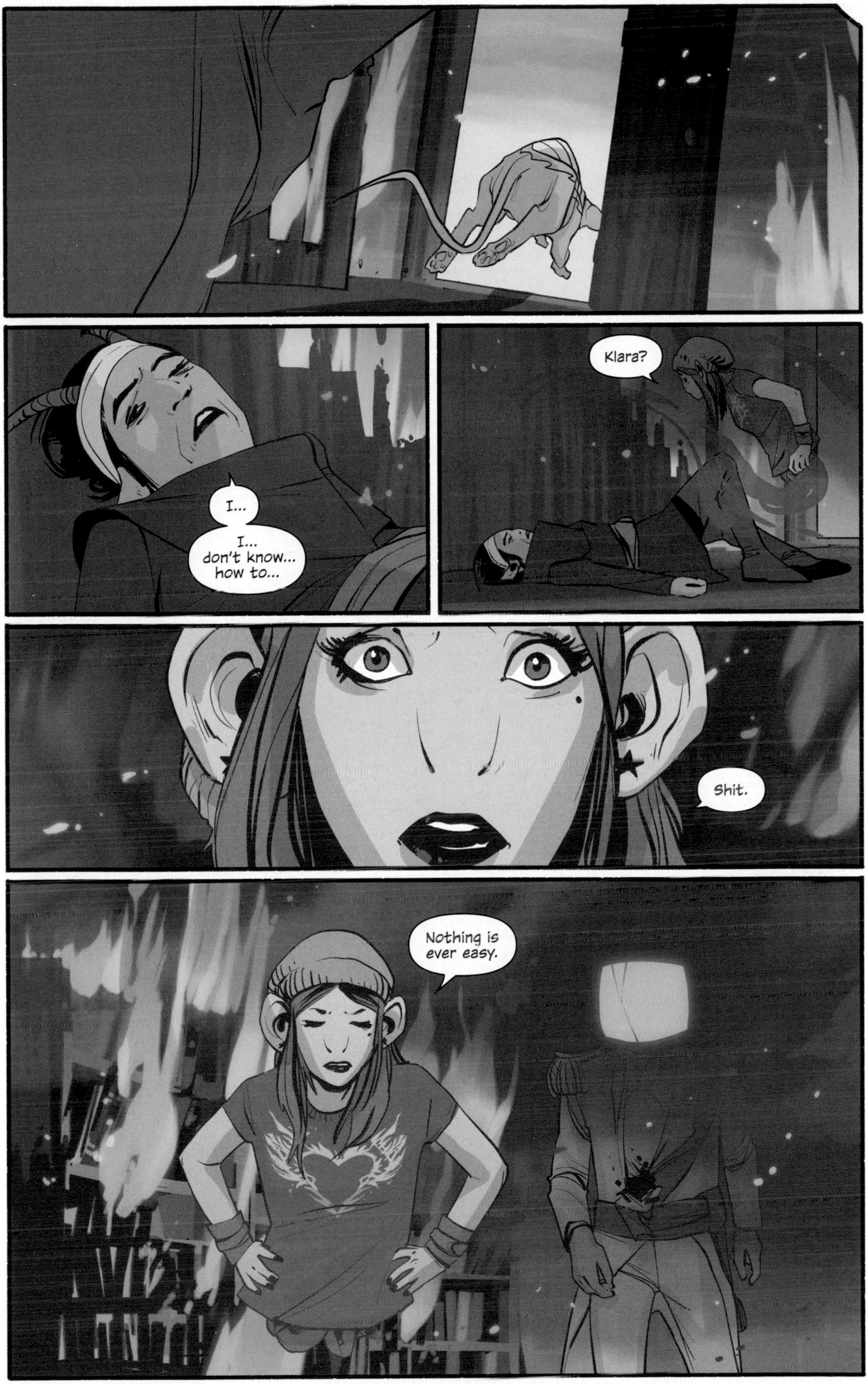
I...
I... don't know... how to...
Klara?
Shit.
Nothing is ever easy.

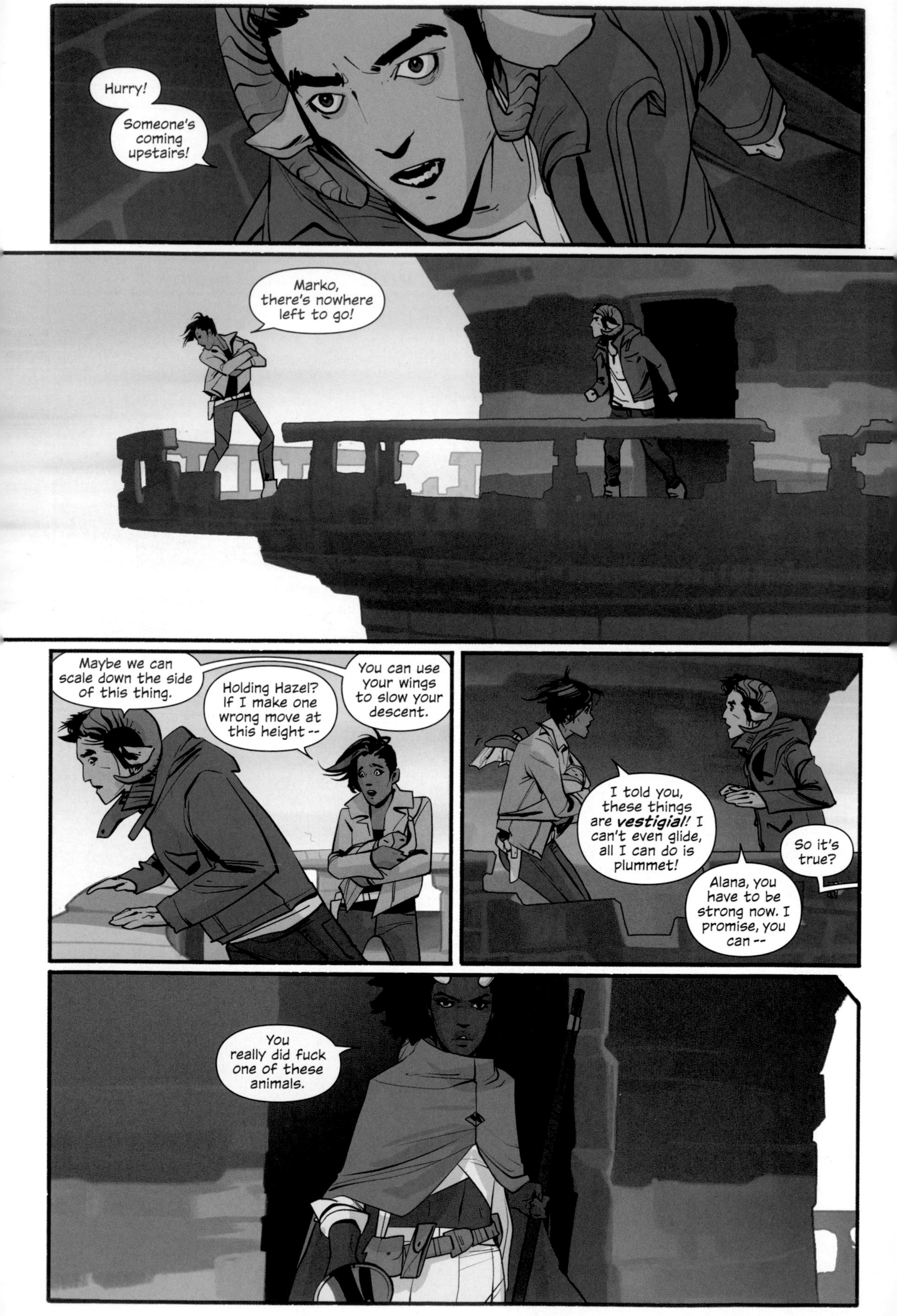
Hurry!
Someone's coming upstairs!
Marko, there's nowhere left to go!
Maybe we can scale down the side of this thing.
Holding Hazel? If I make one wrong move at this height --
You can use your wings to slow your descent.
I told you, these things are ***vestigial!*** I can't even glide, all I can do is plummet!
Alana, you have to be strong now. I promise, you can --
So it's true?
You really did fuck one of these animals.

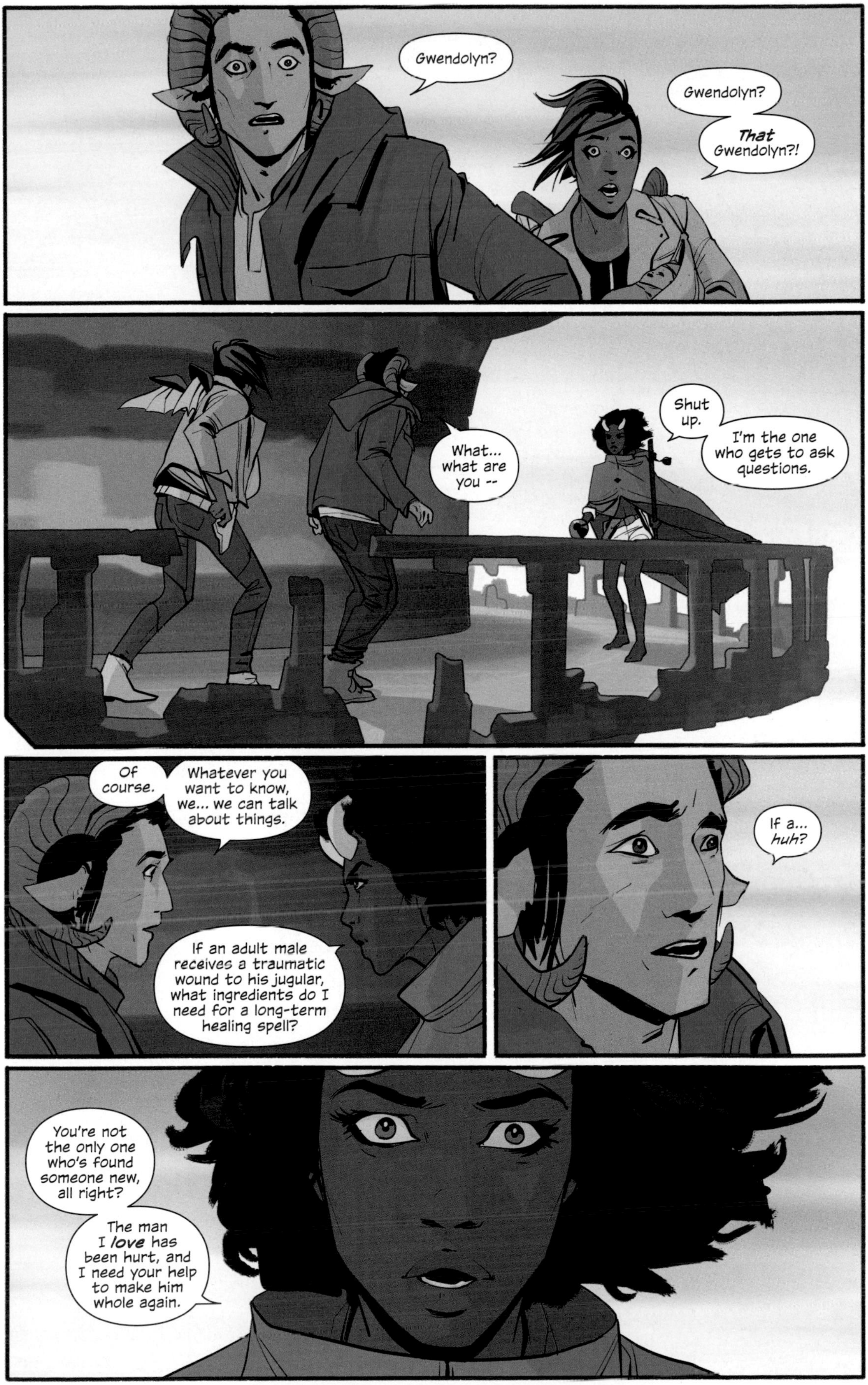
Gwendolyn?
Gwendolyn?
That Gwendolyn?!
What... what are you --
Shut up.
I'm the one who gets to ask questions.
Of course.
Whatever you want to know, we... we can talk about things.
If an adult male receives a traumatic wound to his jugular, what ingredients do I need for a long-term healing spell?
If a... *huh?*
You're not the only one who's found someone new, all right?
The man I *love* has been hurt, and I need your help to make him whole again.

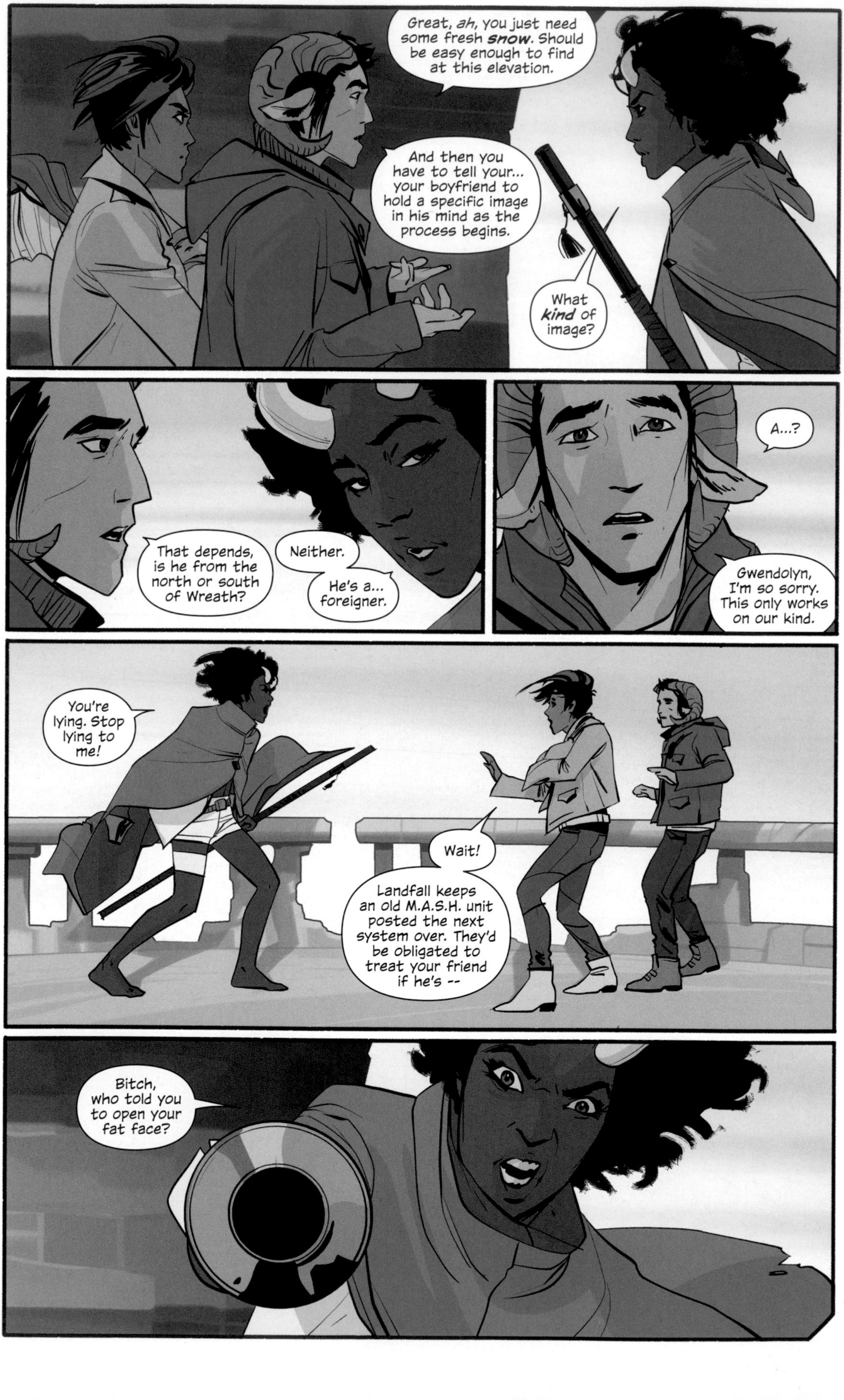
Great, *ah*, you just need some fresh **snow**. Should be easy enough to find at this elevation.
And then you have to tell your... your boyfriend to hold a specific image in his mind as the process begins.
What *kind* of image?
That depends, is he from the north or south of Wreath?
Neither.
He's a... foreigner.
A...?
Gwendolyn, I'm so sorry. This only works on our kind.
You're lying. Stop lying to me!
Wait!
Landfall keeps an old M.A.S.H. unit posted the next system over. They'd be obligated to treat your friend if he's --
Bitch, who told you to open your fat face?

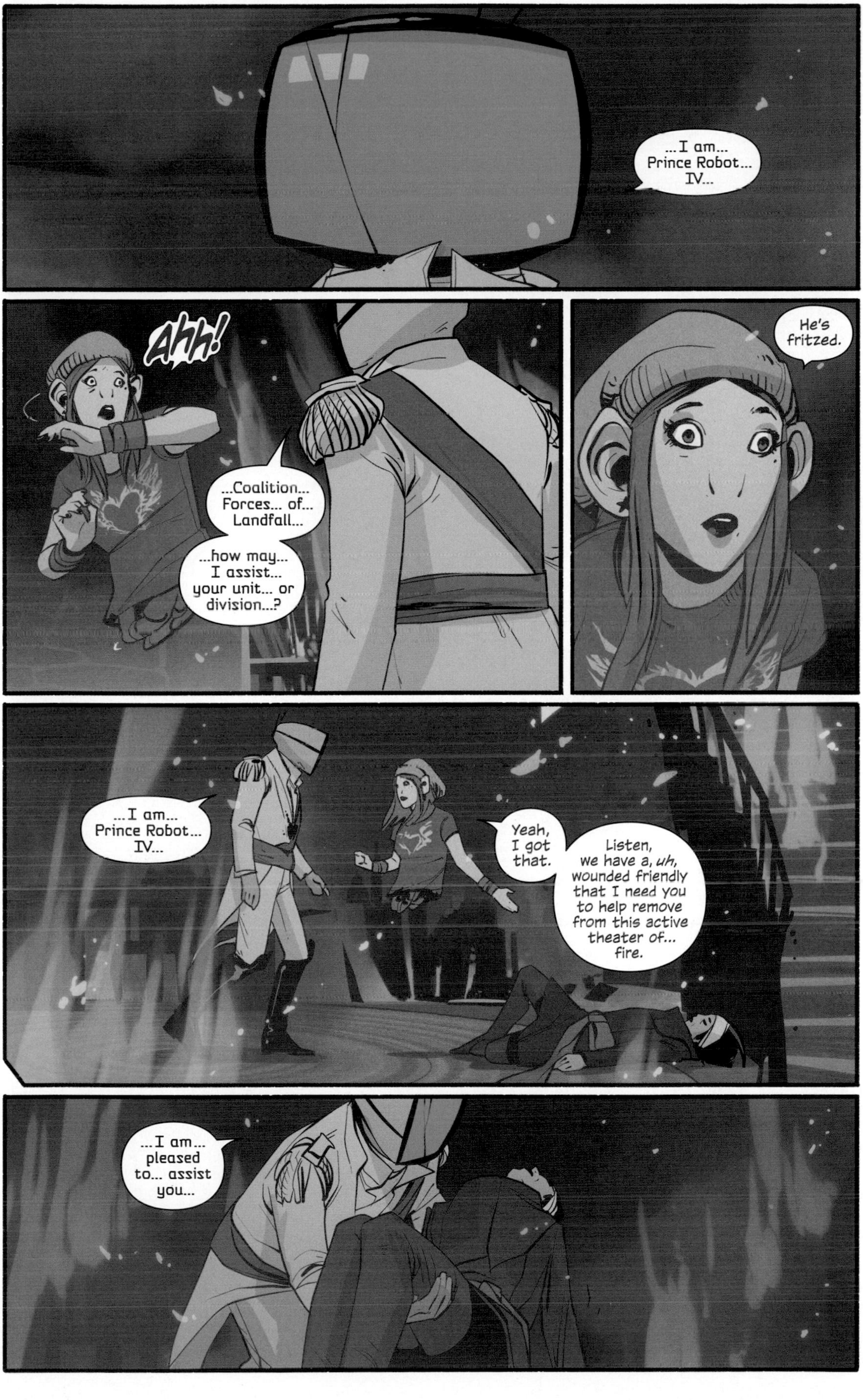
...I am... Prince Robot... IV...
Ahh!
...Coalition... Forces... of... Landfall...
...how may... I assist... your unit... or division...?
He's fritzed.
...I am... Prince Robot... IV...
Yeah, I got that.
Listen, we have a, *uh*, wounded friendly that I need you to help remove from this active theater of... fire.
...I am... pleased to... assist you...

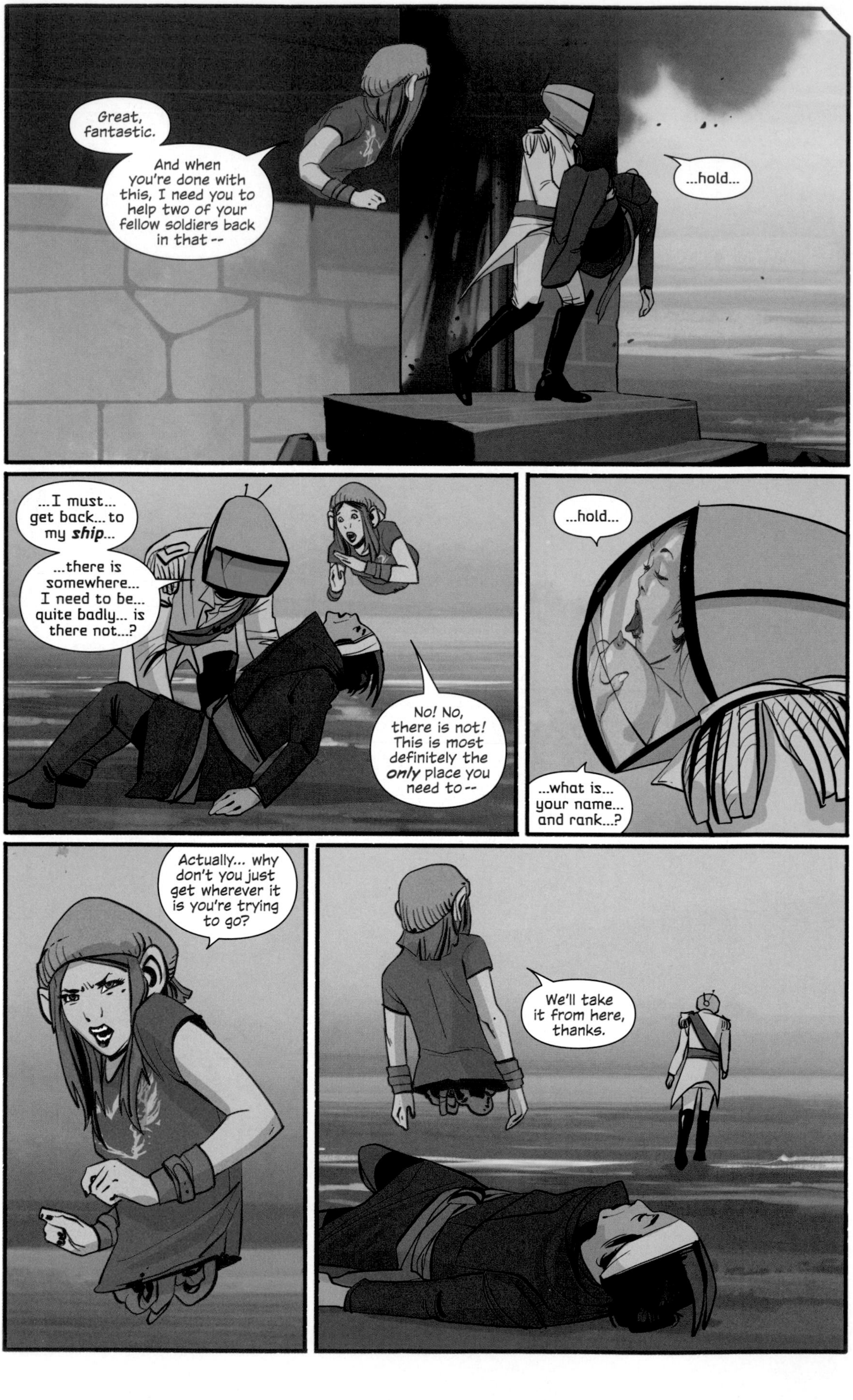
Great, fantastic.
And when you're done with this, I need you to help two of your fellow soldiers back in that --
...hold...
...I must... get back... to my *ship*...
...there is somewhere... I need to be... quite badly... is there not...?
No! No, there is not! This is most definitely the *only* place you need to --
...hold...
...what is... your name... and rank...?
Actually... why don't you just get wherever it is you're trying to go?
We'll take it from here, thanks.

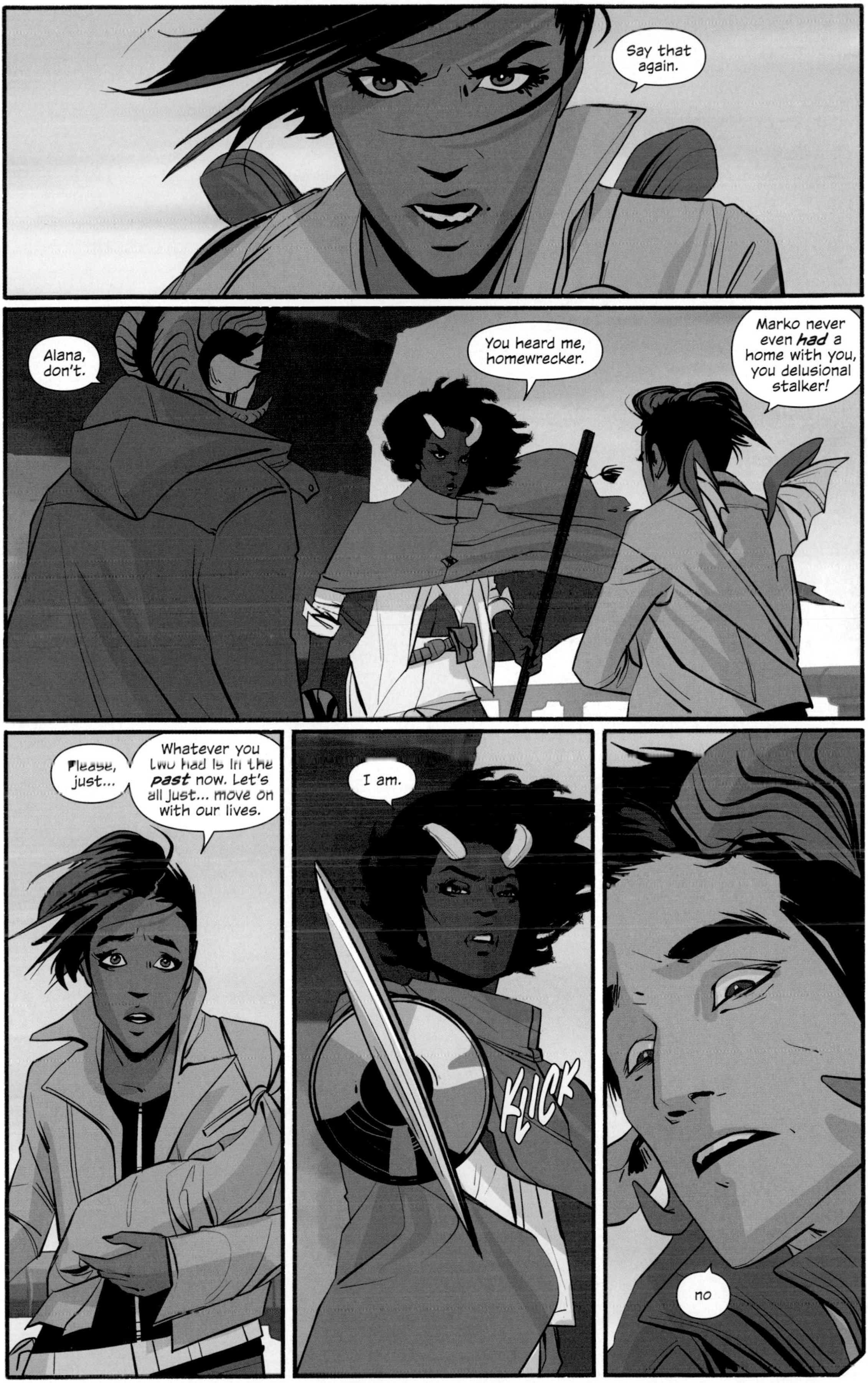
Say that again.
Alana, don't.
You heard me, homewrecker.
Marko never even had a home with you, you delusional stalker!
Please, just...
Whatever you two had is in the past now. Let's all just... move on with our lives.
I am.
KLICK
no

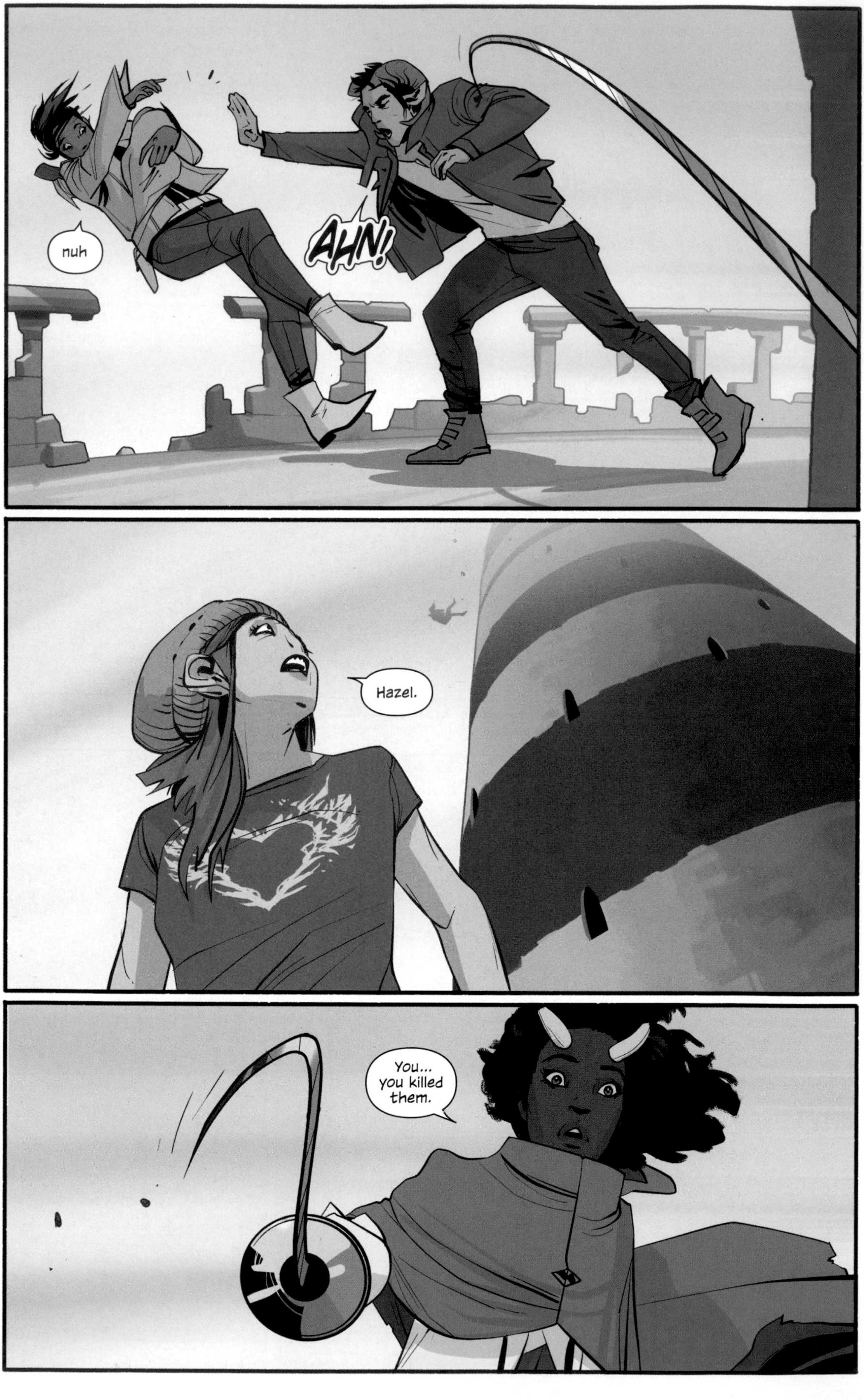
nuh
AHN!
Hazel.
You...
you killed
them.

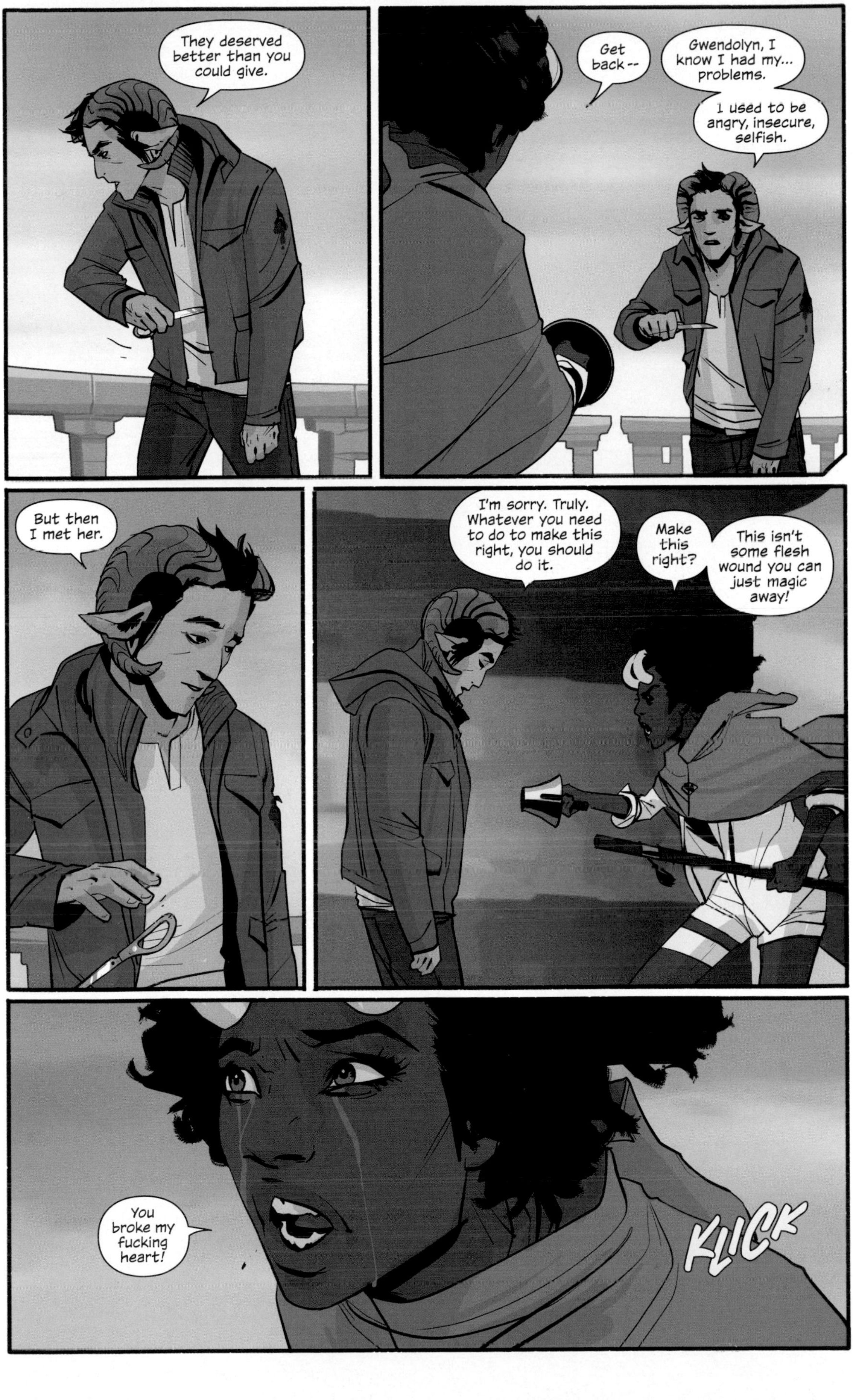
They deserved better than you could give.
Get back --
Gwendolyn, I know I had my... problems.
I used to be angry, insecure, selfish.
But then I met her.
I'm sorry. Truly. Whatever you need to do to make this right, you should do it.
Make this right?
This isn't some flesh wound you can just magic away!
You broke my fucking heart!
KLICK

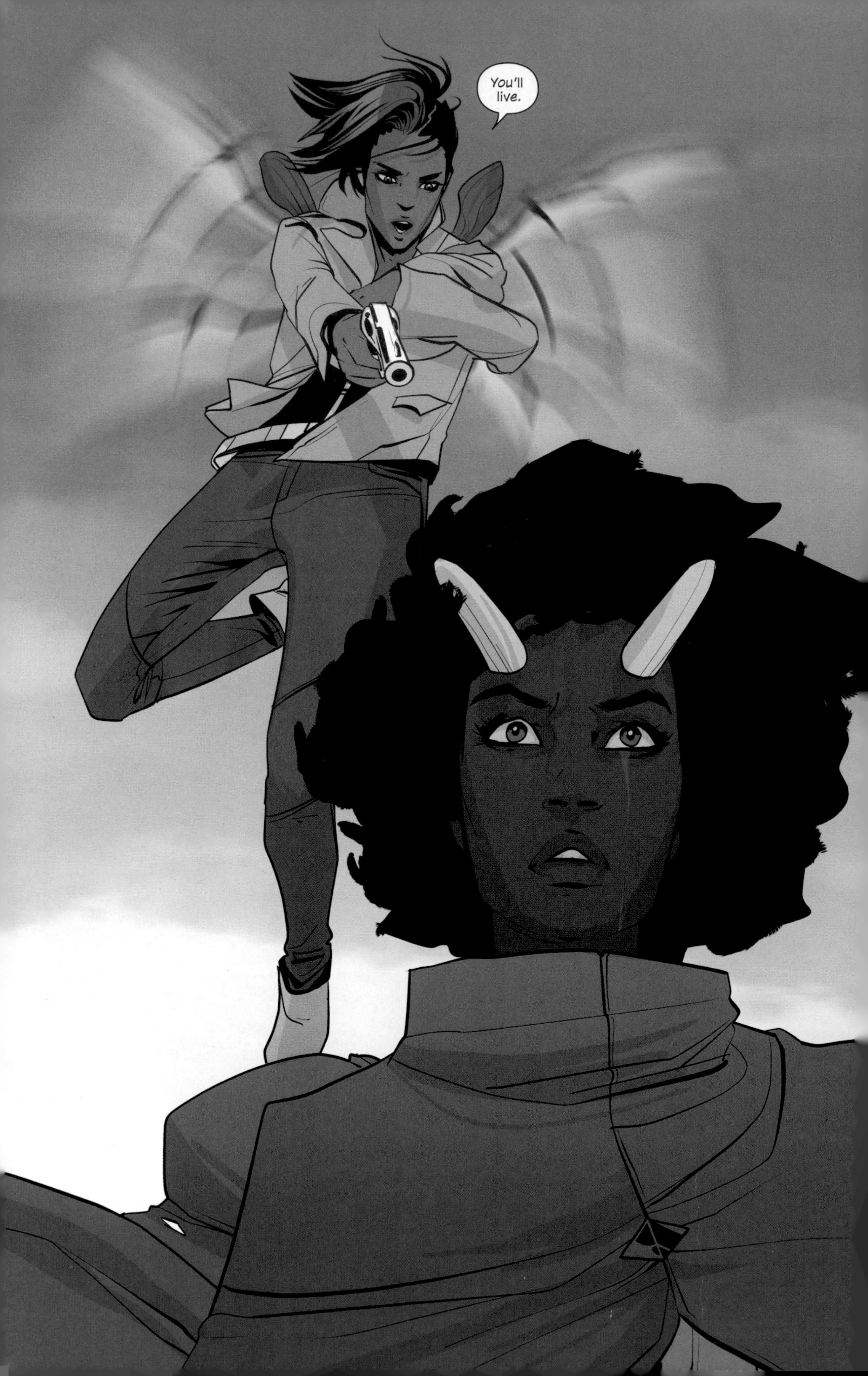
You'll live.

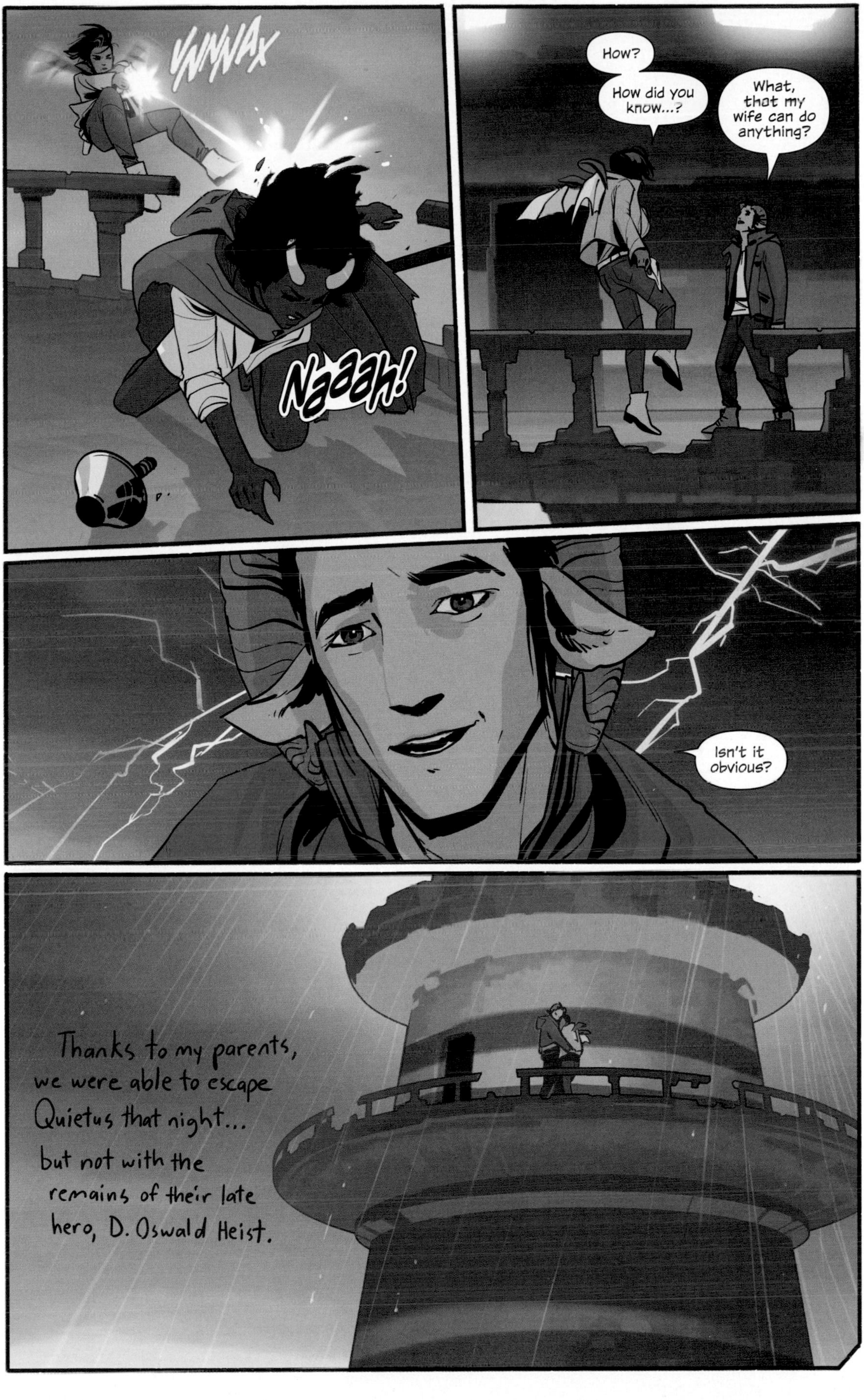
VNNNAX
Naaah!
How?
How did you know...?
What, that my wife can do anything?
Isn't it obvious?
Thanks to my parents, we were able to escape Quietus that night...
but not with the remains of their late hero, D. Oswald Heist.

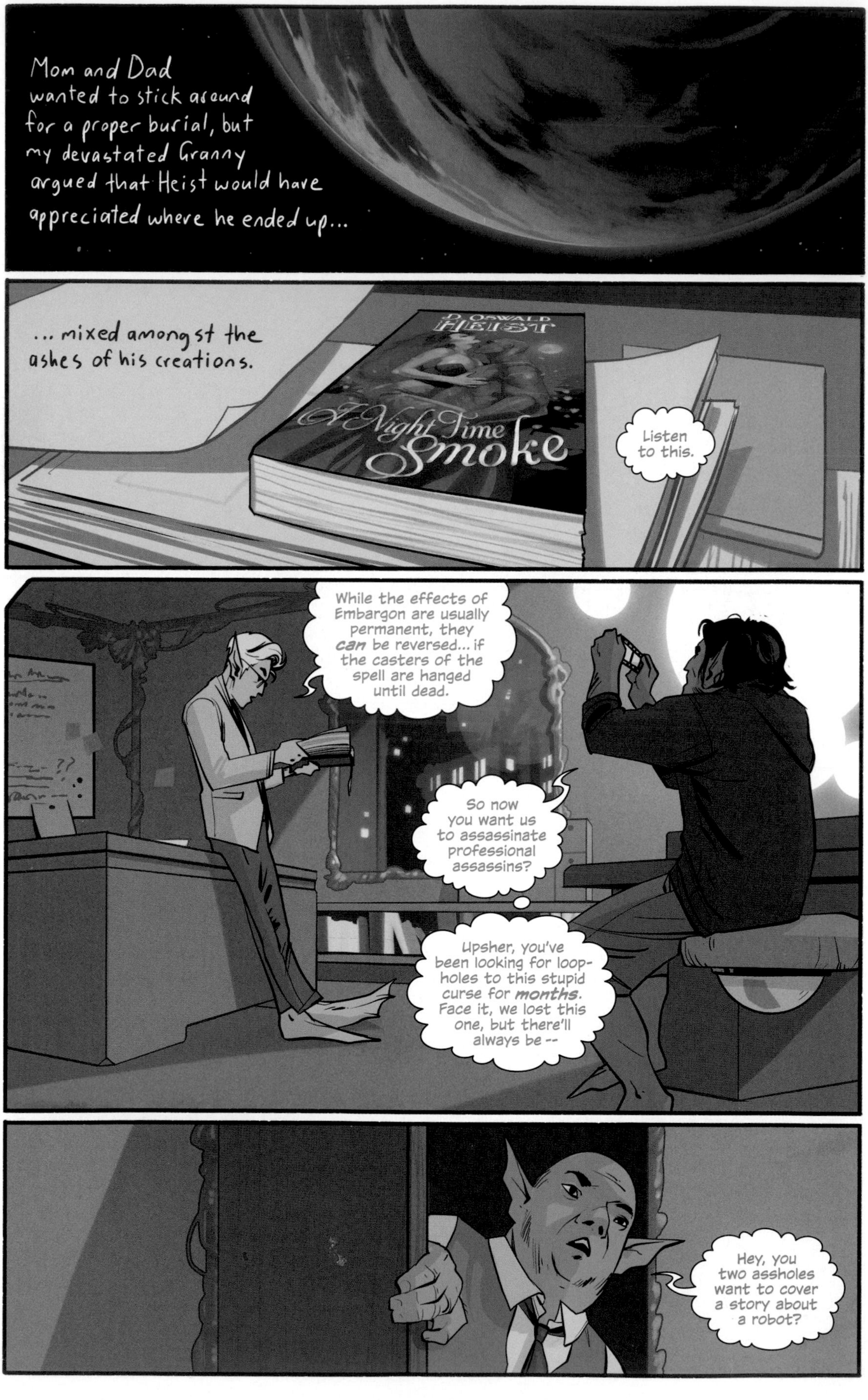
Mom and Dad wanted to stick around for a proper burial, but my devastated Granny argued that Heist would have appreciated where he ended up...
...mixed amongst the ashes of his creations.
D. OSWALD HEIST
A Night Time Smoke
Listen to this.
While the effects of Embargon are usually permanent, they *can* be reversed... if the casters of the spell are hanged until dead.
So now you want us to assassinate professional assassins?
Upsher, you've been looking for loop-holes to this stupid curse for *months*. Face it, we lost this one, but there'll always be --
Hey, you two assholes want to cover a story about a robot?

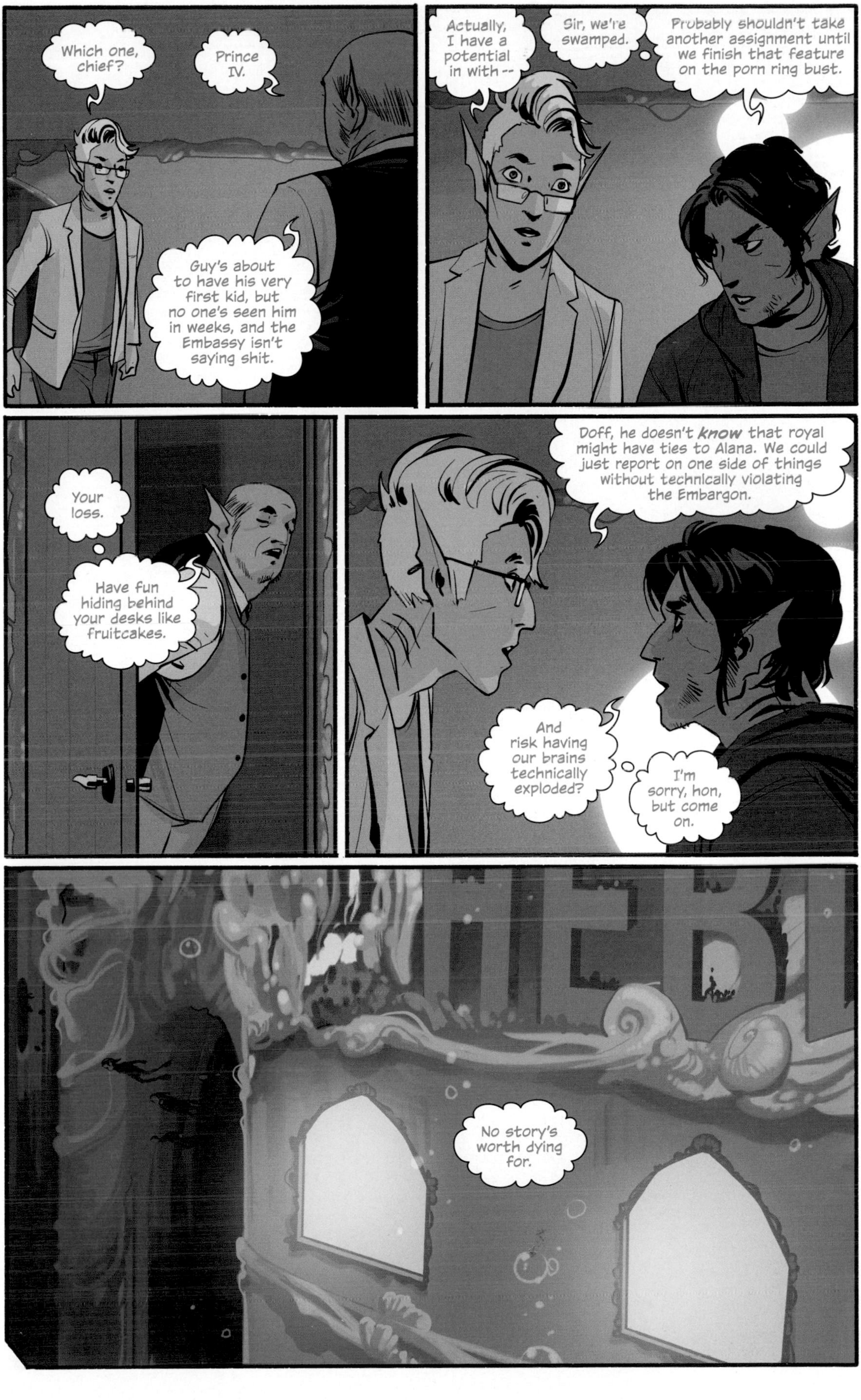
Which one, chief?
Prince IV.
Guy's about to have his very first kid, but no one's seen him in weeks, and the Embassy isn't saying shit.
Actually, I have a potential in with--
Sir, we're swamped.
Probably shouldn't take another assignment until we finish that feature on the porn ring bust.
Your loss.
Have fun hiding behind your desks like fruitcakes.
Doff, he doesn't know that royal might have ties to Alana. We could just report on one side of things without technically violating the Embargon.
And risk having our brains technically exploded?
I'm sorry, hon, but come on.
No story's worth dying for.

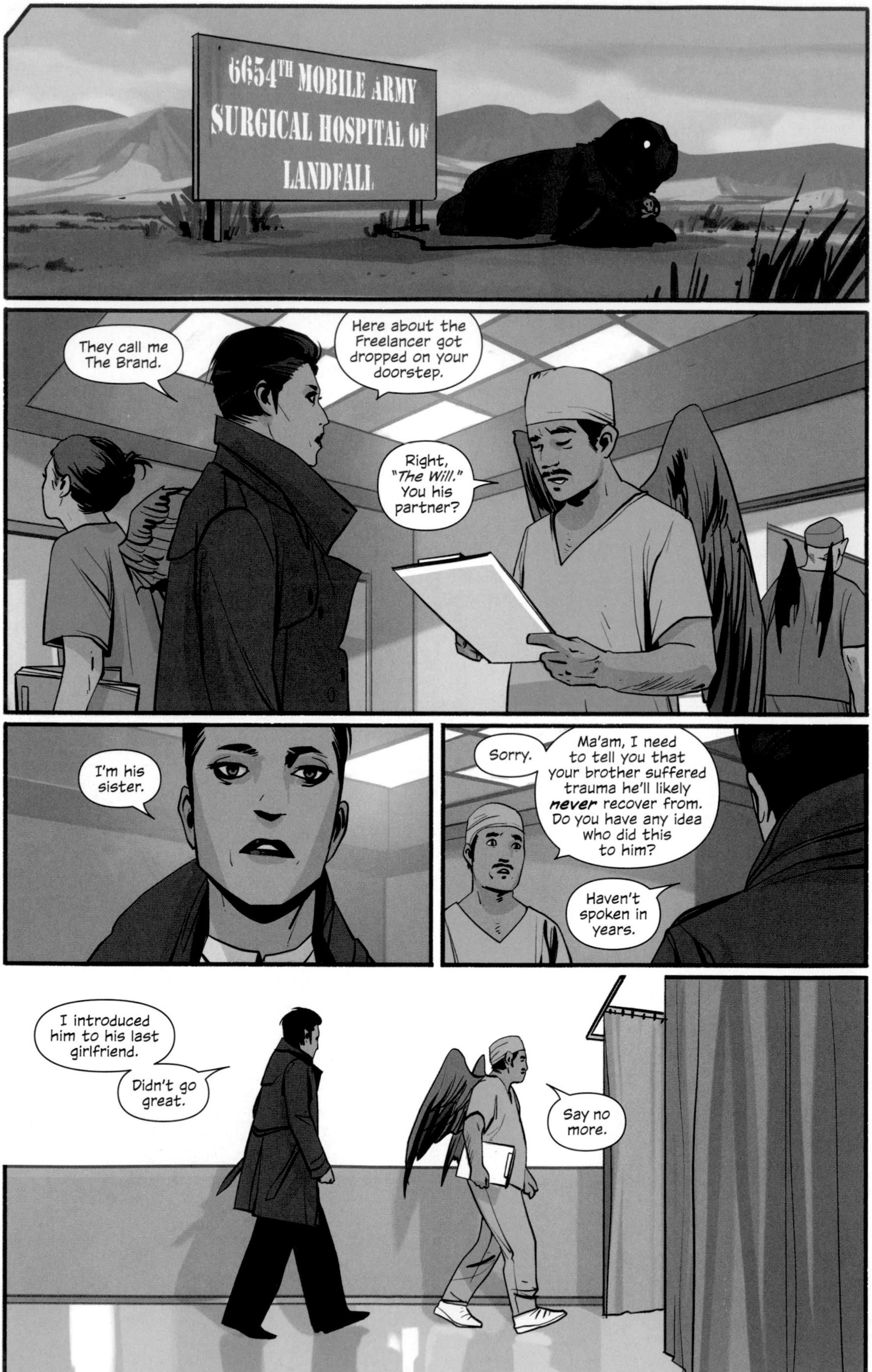
6654TH MOBILE ARMY SURGICAL HOSPITAL OF LANDFALL
They call me The Brand.
Here about the Freelancer got dropped on your doorstep.
Right, "The Will." You his partner?
I'm his sister.
Sorry.
Ma'am, I need to tell you that your brother suffered trauma he'll likely **never** recover from. Do you have any idea who did this to him?
Haven't spoken in years.
I introduced him to his last girlfriend.
Didn't go great.
Say no more.

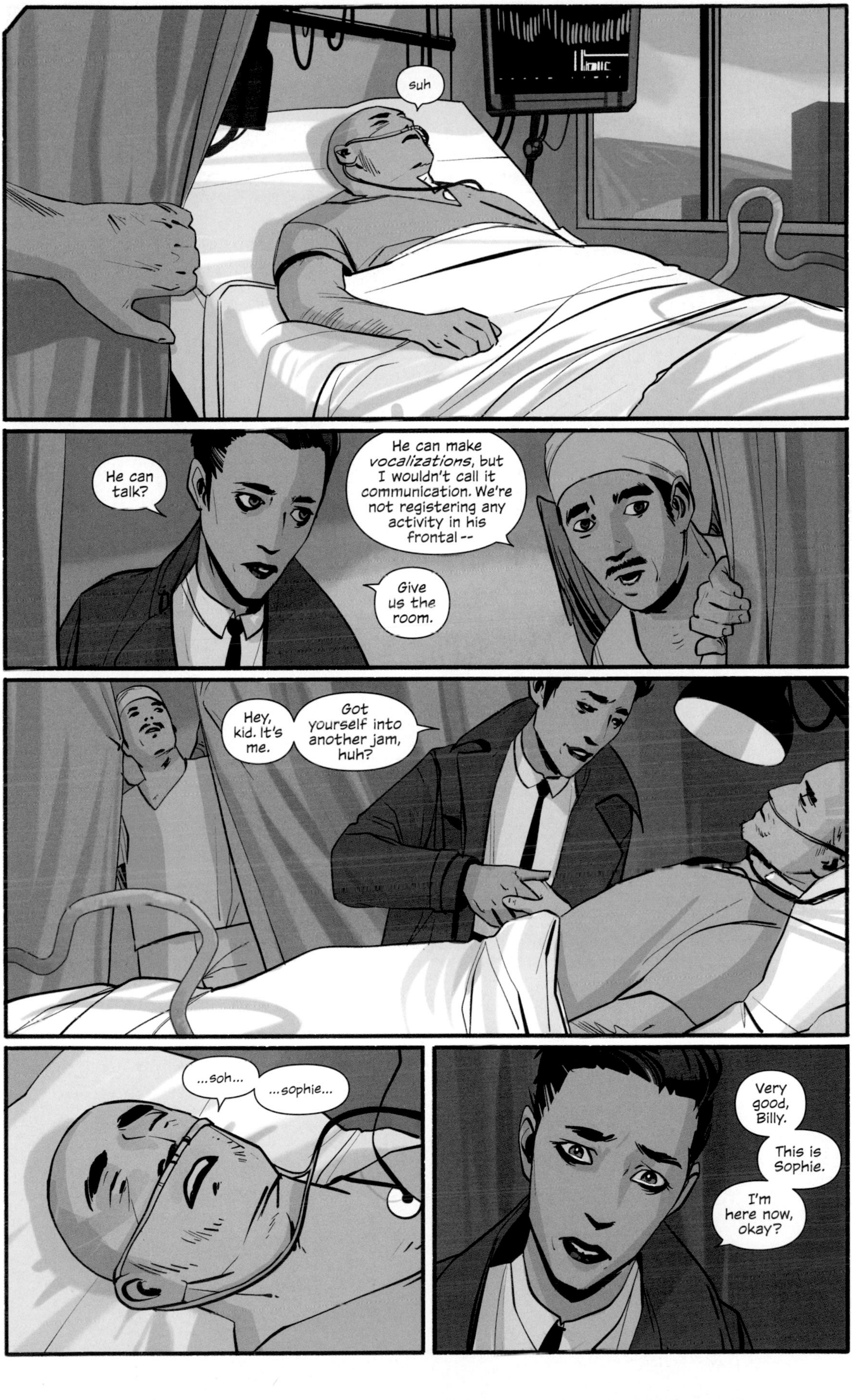
suh
He can talk?
He can make *vocalizations*, but I wouldn't call it communication. We're not registering any activity in his frontal --
Give us the room.
Hey, kid. It's me.
Got yourself into another jam, huh?
...soh...
...sophie...
Very good, Billy.
This is Sophie.
I'm here now, okay?

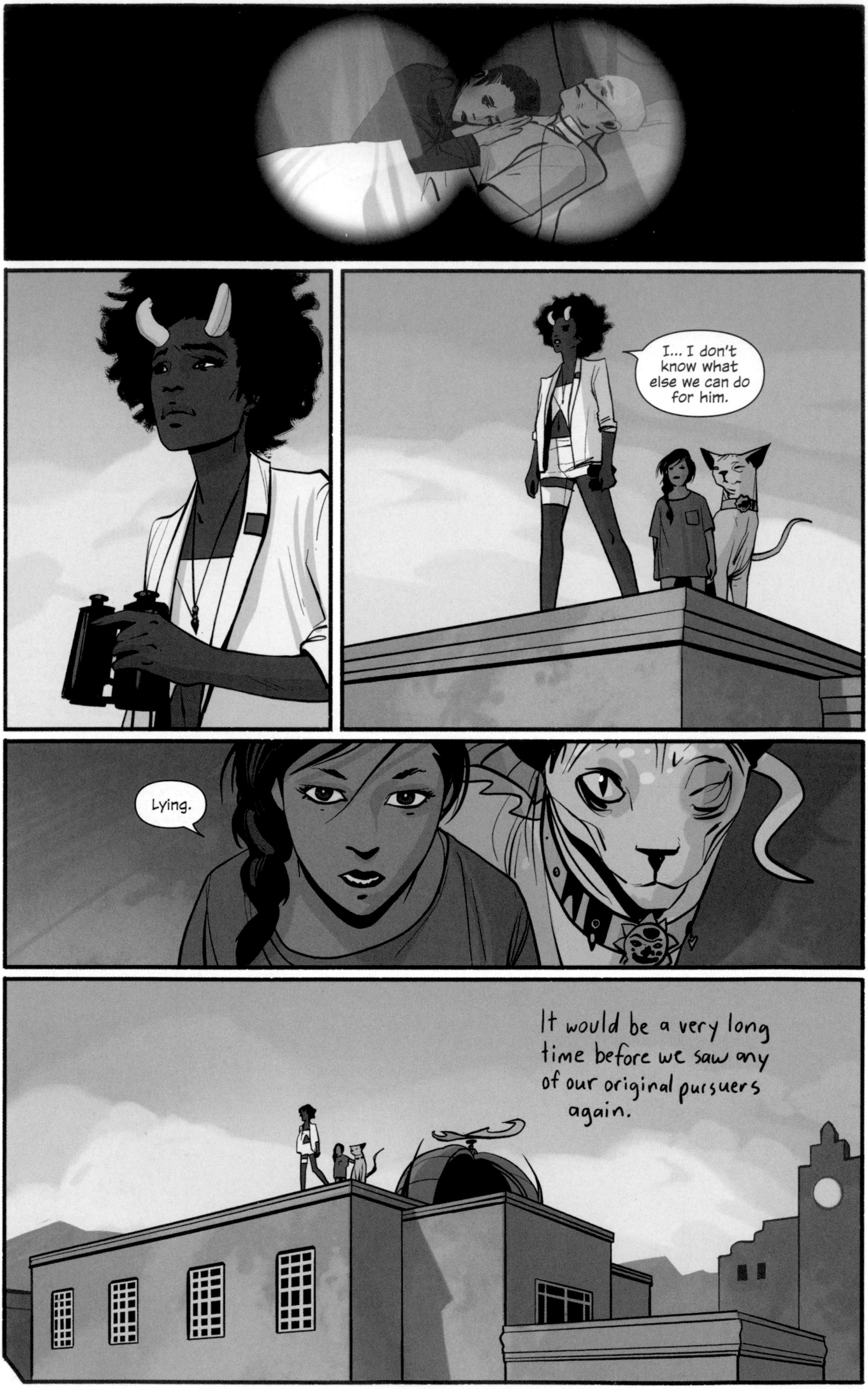
I... I don't know what else we can do for him.
Lying.
It would be a very long time before we saw any of our original pursuers again.

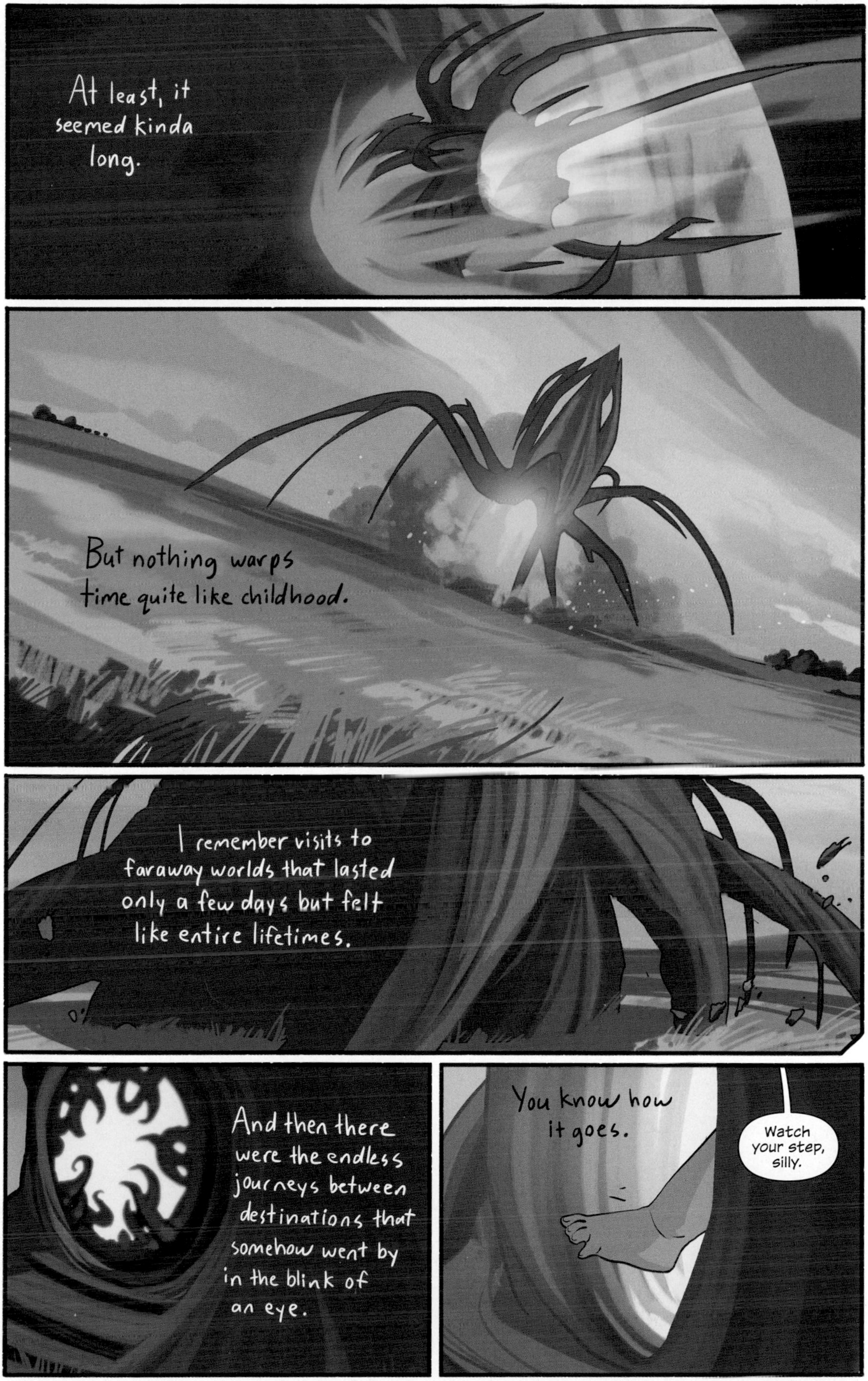
At least, it seemed kinda long.
But nothing warps time quite like childhood.
I remember visits to faraway worlds that lasted only a few days but felt like entire lifetimes.
And then there were the endless journeys between destinations that somehow went by in the blink of an eye.
You know how it goes.
Watch your step, silly.

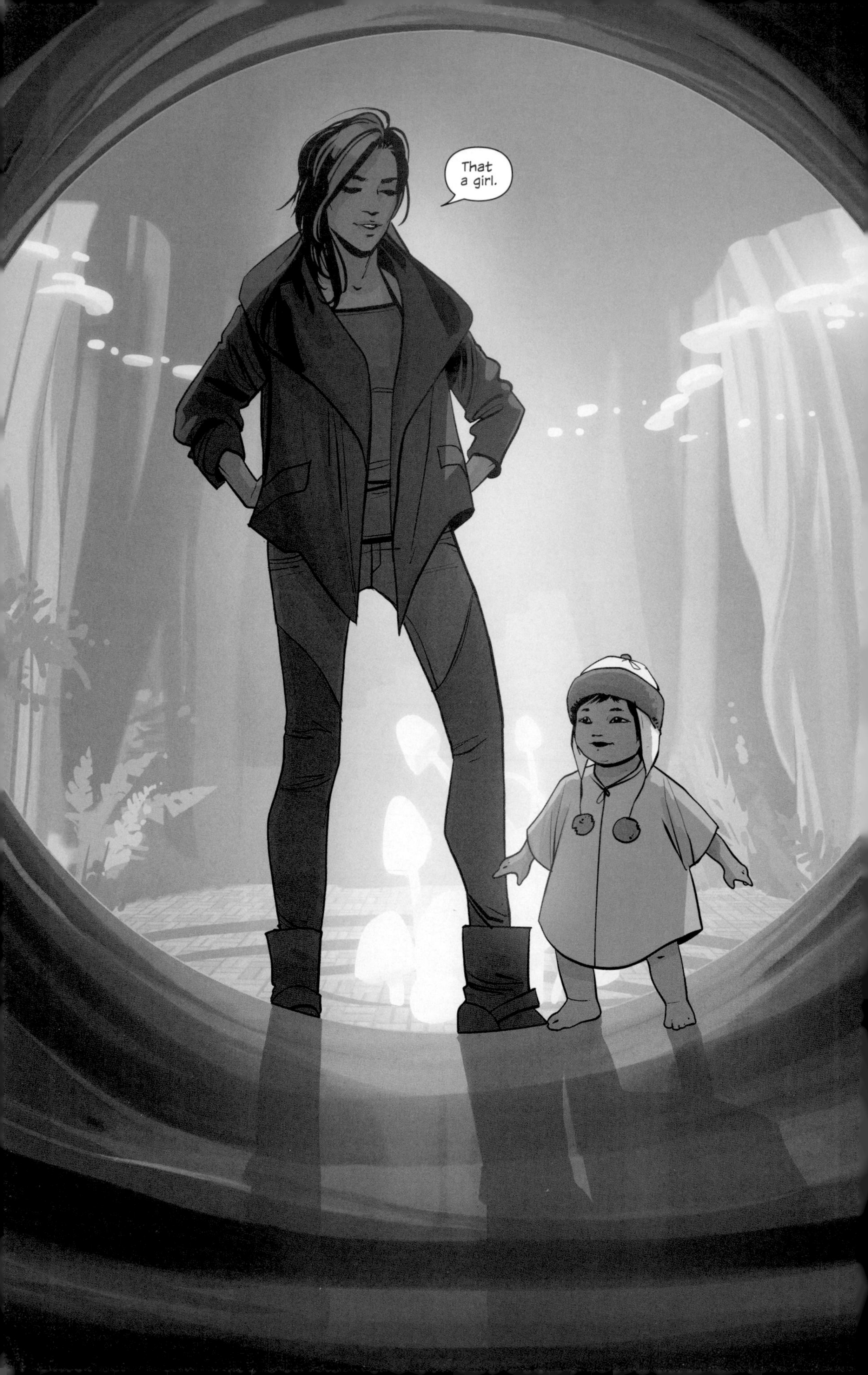
That a girl.

to be continued

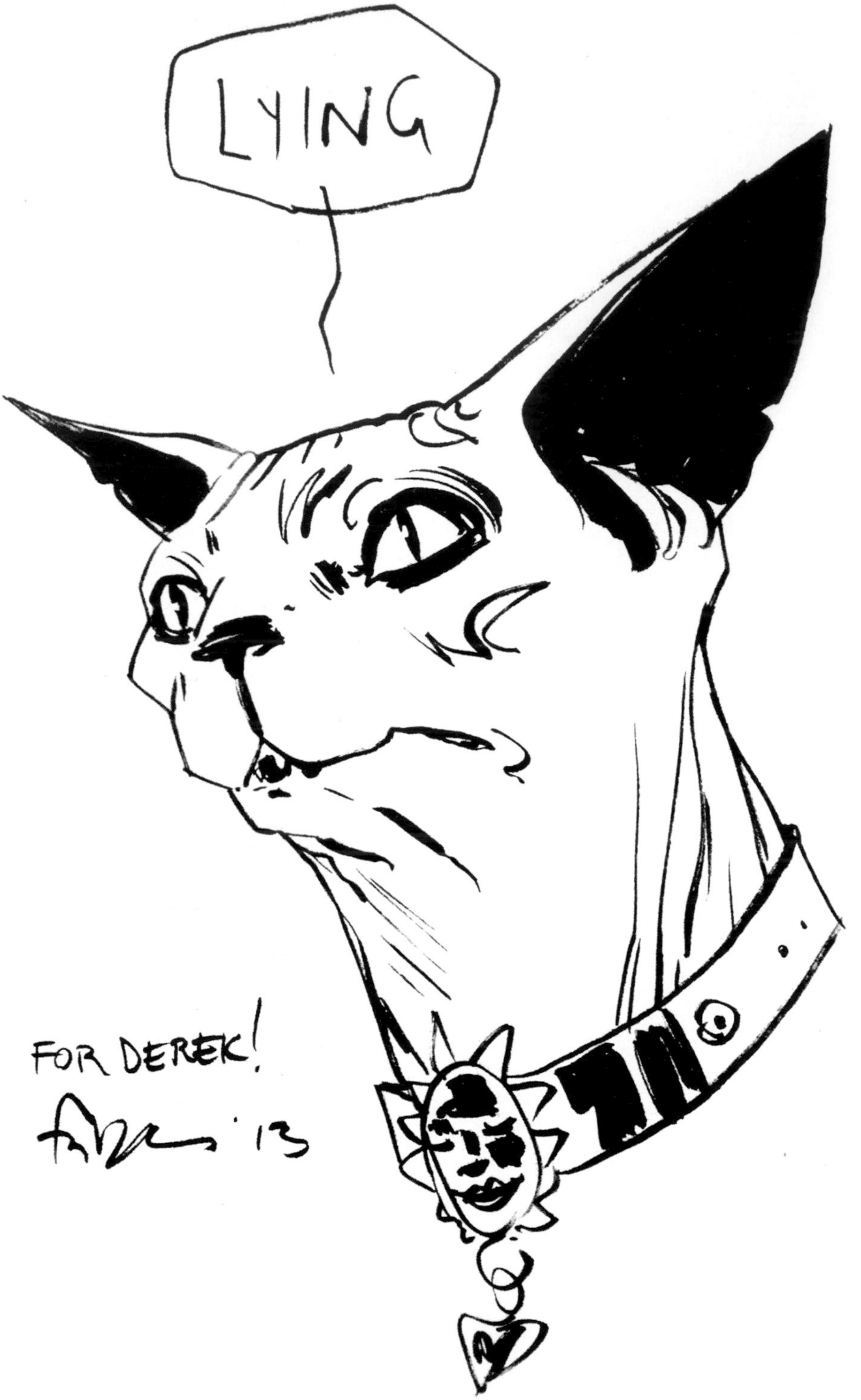
LYING
FOR DEREK!
'13

Lying Cat convention sketch

Ghüs convention sketch

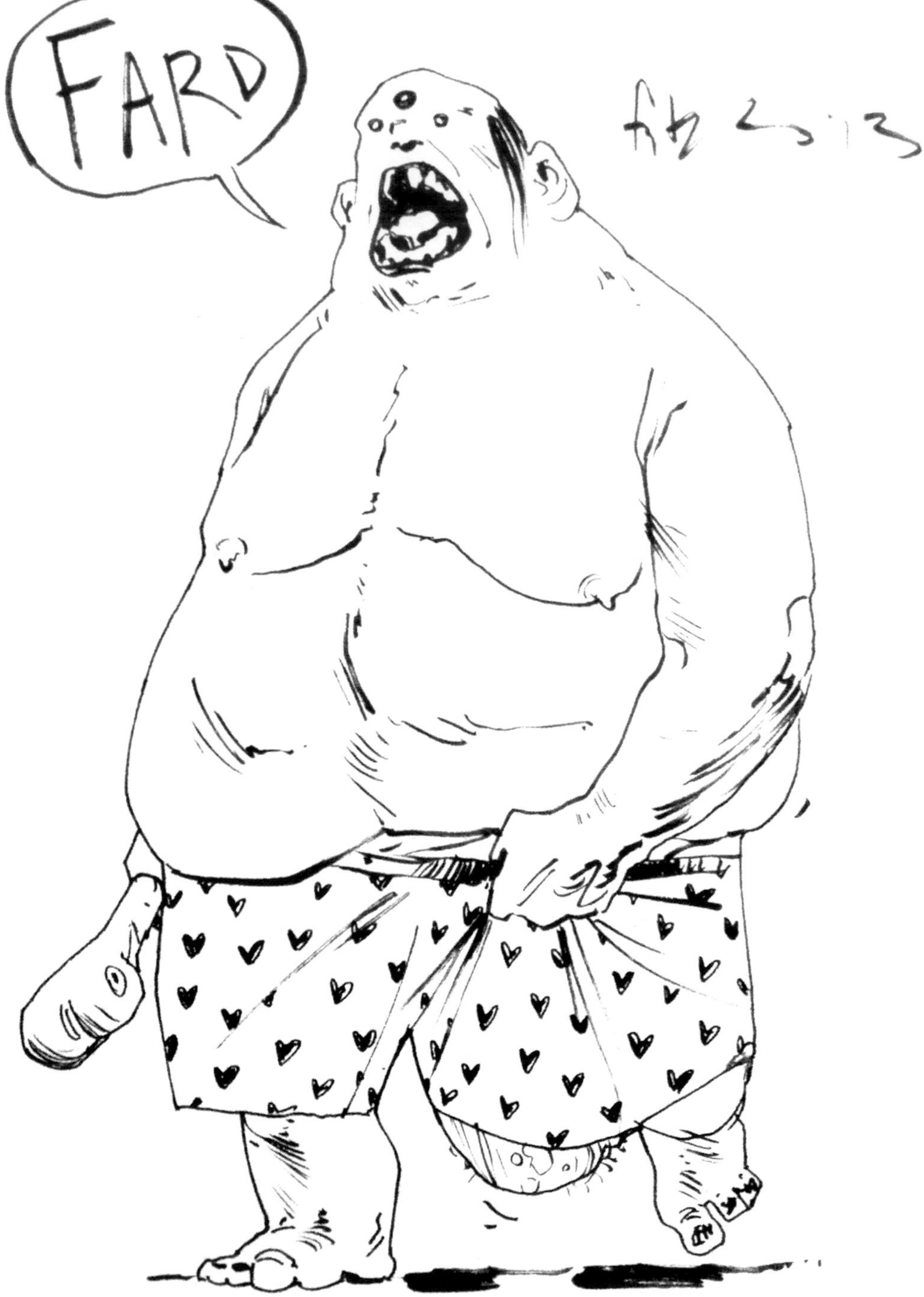
FARD

Fard convention sketch

RUMFER

FOR J.V.!

Rumfer convention sketch

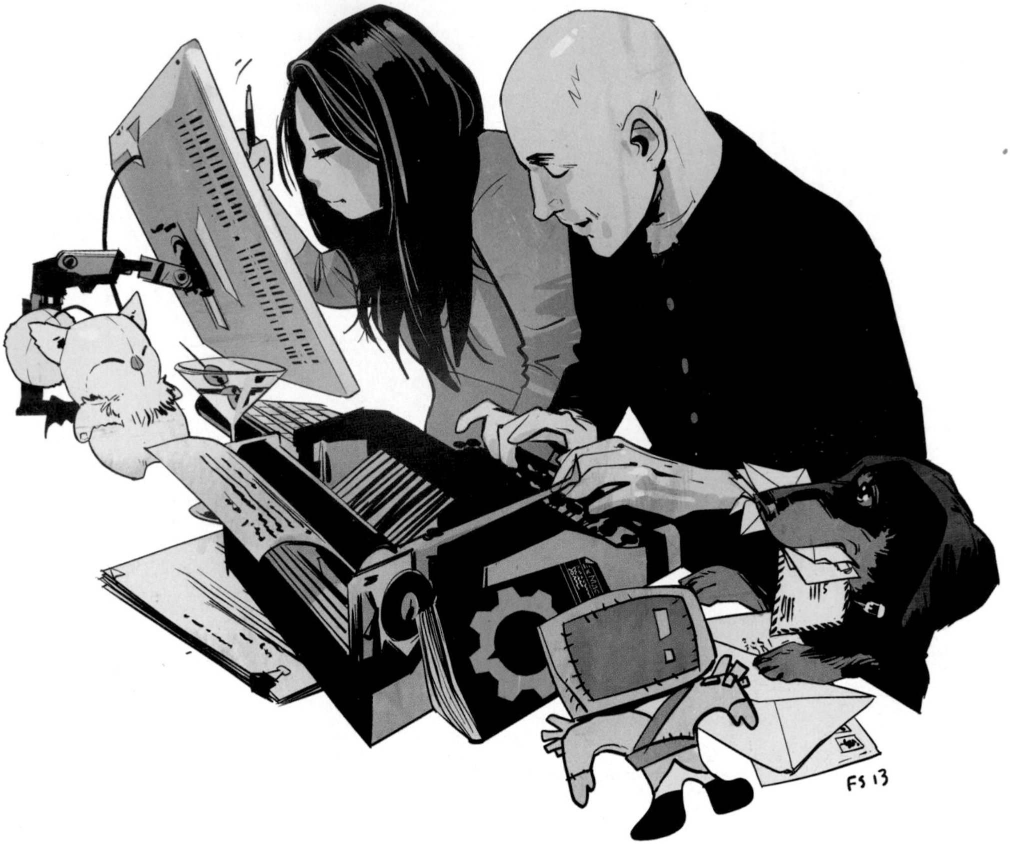
FS 13

Illustration for *TIME* magazine article on *Saga*